SPLINTERED ICON

"It's hard not to get sucked into Bill Napier's incredible vortex. Truly an extraordinary tale, and one that throws the perfect bridge from England to the Americas . . . Sir Walter Raleigh's da Vinci Code. More, it's smart as hell. It reads like an exploding brush fire . . . what a ride! *Splintered Icon* is a really terrific novel, head and shoulders above the genre."

—Jeff Long,
New York Times bestselling author of *The Descent*

"Napier nimbly twists two separate tales into a thrilling novel of exploration, discovery, and, ultimately, survival. Fans of Dan Brown take note, this is a one-sitting book."

—Jack DuBrul,
USA Today bestselling author of *The Medusa Stone*

"Intriguing and imaginative. An inventive piece of storytelling."

—Steve Berry,
national bestselling author of *The Amber Room*

"Deftly mixing history, science, and fiction, Napier keeps the action escalating toward a satisfying climax."

—*Publishers Weekly*

NEMESIS

BILL NAPIER

St. Martin's Paperbacks

This is a work of fiction. All of the characters, organizations and events portrayed in this novel are either products of the author's imagination or are used fictitiously.

NEMESIS

Copyright © 1998 by Bill Napier.

Cover photo © Art Archive / Devizes Museum / Eileen Tweedy.

ISBN: 0-312-93680-X
EAN: 9780312-93680-8

Printed in the United States of America

HEADLINE BOOK PUBLISHING edition first published in 1998
HEADLINE BOOK PUBLISHING paperback edition published in 1999
St. Martin's Paperbacks edition / September 2006

St. Martin's Paperbacks are published by St. Martin's Press, 175 Fifth Avenue, New York, NY 10010.

10 9 8 7 6 5 4 3 2 1

For paterfamilias

NEMESIS

I AMERICAN SHINDIG

II ITALIAN MASQUE

III MEXICAN CARNIVAL

Part One
AMERICAN SHINDIG

shindig [?] 1. a dance, party or other affair. 2. shindy, a noisy disturbance; commotion.

THE FIRST DAY

$E = 10^7$ Mt, $I = 45°$, Target = Tertiary Andesite

The meteor comes in high over the Gulf of Mexico, in a blaze of light which darkens the noon sun from the Florida Keys to Jamaica.

Two thousand miles to the north, and four minutes before he dies, Colonel Peter "Foggy" Wallis is in his office watching television. The office itself is dark and comfortable, a restful place. It is made of steel. It sits on springs whose coils are made from steel rods three inches in diameter. Steel walkways connect the office to another fourteen similar, self-contained rooms. The entire office complex is contained within a giant cavern hollowed out from a granite mountain. Steel pins up to thirty feet long are driven into the cavern walls, and steel mesh is suspended below the ceiling high overhead, to protect him from dislodged boulders should a hostile giant ever strike the mountain. Access is through steel doors, each weighing twenty-five tons, and along a tunnel fourteen hundred feet long.

The television picture comes from a camera twenty-five thousand miles above the surface of the Earth. It is beamed down into a huge antenna near Alice Springs, relayed across two oceans, cabled a thousand feet into the bowels of the Rock and then up into the colonel's television set for his personal perusal.

The colonel pulls open a Seven-Up and sips at the fizzy

lemonade. An oil well is burning in Iran. Its long smoky trail, bright in the infrared, has been longer at every shift for days, and now it has at last reached the northern Himalayas. Otherwise nothing much has changed. He flicks a button and the black night-time Pacific now appears, ringed by lights. To the left, the Sea of Japan glows softly, illuminated from within by the lights of the Japanese shrimp fishermen. Hawaii appears as a central dot. Idly, he flicks a switch and the dot resolves itself into a string of coastal lights dominated by Honolulu on Oahu and Hilo on Big Island.

Suddenly the lights fail; the VDUs dissolve into snow and die. A chorus of surprised profanity begins to emerge from the dark, but almost immediately the lights flicker and come back on, and the screens return to life.

"Now what was that?" Wallis asks nobody in particular. Rapidly, he scans the screens, flicking through the signals from sensors on land, sea, air and space. They reveal nothing: no anomalies, no intrusions. On the other hand, power cuts have never happened before.

"David, check it out."

While the young major sitting to the left of Wallis speaks into a telephone, Wallis himself taps out a command on the console in front of him. A mass of coloured symbols obscures his god's eye view of the world. He types again, and all but a handful of the symbols vanish.

Over the Barents Sea, just north of Novaya Zemlya, a patrol of ageing Tupolev Blackjack bombers is high over the pack ice and the seals; another three hours on that bearing and they would invade Canadian air space, heading south for the Kansas silos. A flock of MiG 23s is heading out over the sea of Japan: six hours, if only they had the range, and they would reach Hawaii.

Only ten minutes ago a big KH-11 satellite passed over Kirovsk on the Kola peninsula, recording the Badgers, Backfires and MiGs which swarm like bees in and out of the four military air bases surrounding the city; elsewhere inside the mountain, careful men watched their movements; they collated and analysed, using massive computers: alert for the unusual, paranoid towards the unexpected. But the computers detected no strangeness in the patterns, and the careful men relaxed.

For twenty years following the collapse of the Empire, Kirov has been a ghost city. The bees flew to distant Eastern bases, or were executed by order of disarmament treaties. Some of the careful men were reassigned to tinpot dictatorships; most left to take up lucrative jobs with McDonnell Douglas or IBM. They no longer collated and analysed. But then came the food riots; and the Black Sea mutiny, which spread like a plague first to the Pacific Fleet and then to the elite Tamanshaia and Kanterimov divisions; and the chaotic elections in which Vladimir Zhirinovsky, heavily supported by the Red Army, swept to victory. The man who had publicly threatened to nuke Japan and the United Kingdom, and whose declared intention was to expand the Russian Empire by force, was in the Kremlin.

And now the Badgers are back in Kola, and the careful men have returned to the mountain.

Stuff like that doesn't bother Wallis in the slightest. It just makes his job more interesting.

He types again. Thirty assorted ships in formation. Slava and nuclear-powered Kirov cruisers, skirting Norway and heading for Scapa Flow.

So what?

A handful of dots appears on the screen, obtained at vast expense from hydrophone arrays sprinkling the seabed along the GIUK Gap, the choke-point bridging Greenland, Iceland and the Orkneys. A couple of ancient Yankees and a Foxtrot are heading out into the North Atlantic. Yesterday, the combat team followed a Typhoon heading north, twenty-four thousand tons of displacement whose signals were soon lost in the clicking of shrimps and the cry of whales.

The hell with it. There are no abnormal movements; the

computers are seeing no suspicious patterns. It has been a long shift, and the colonel, three minutes and twenty seconds before he dies, leans back in his chair, stretches and yawns.

It strikes ground in the Valley of Morelos, a hundred miles south of Mexico City. It is sparse, hard land, a countryside of dry, stony tracks, overloaded burros, maize fields and giant cacti.

In the time it takes Wallis to yawn the asteroid has vaporised, ploughed to a halt ten miles under the ground and generated a ball of fire five miles wide and a hundred thousand degrees hot. Shock waves carrying four million atmospheres of pressure race outwards from the fireball, ancient granites flow like water.

"Sir, the generator people say it was some sort of ground surge. It seems the national grid got it too."

"Any reason for it?"

"They're checking it out. There's a big storm complex around Boulder."

"Okay. You're looking bushed, boy."

The major grins. "It's the new baby, sir. She never sleeps."

"The first sixteen years are the worst," Wallis says.

In the time it takes to discuss the major's baby the fireball scours out a hole fifty miles wide from the Mexican countryside. The hole is ten miles deep and a sea of white hot lava pours upwards through the cracked and fissured mantle. Around the rim of the big hole, a ring of mountains builds up from the torrent of rock. Molten mountains are hurtling into the stratosphere, leaving white-hot wakes of expanding air. The blast moves out over the map. Mexico City vanishes, an irrelevant puff of smoke.

The ground waves too race outwards from the hole, leaving a wake of fluidized rubble. The rubble is forming into ripples and the ripples, tumbling rocky breakers reaching five miles into the disturbed sky, roar towards Panama, Guatemala and the United States.

All the way up the Pacific seaboard the morning mists are

rolling in. Foghorns wail round Vancouver island like primeval monsters, a thick white shroud blankets San Francisco and the traffic is snarling up in downtown LA. But now electric currents surge overhead as the fireball pierces the stratosphere, rising back through the hole punched out by the asteroid, and electrons spiral back and forth between the Earth's magnetic poles. Spears and curtains burst into the black Arctic sky and dance a silent, frenzied reel, while the frozen wastelands below reflect the shimmering red and green. Counterflowing currents surge over the Americas; cables melt, telephones die, radios give out with a bang, traffic stops in the streets.

Just over the border from Mexico, early morning shoppers in Tucson, Yuma and San Diego see long black fingers crawling up from the horizon to the south. The fingers reach out for the zenith. And as the shoppers stop to watch, the blue-white fireball too rises over the horizon like a bloated sun, and with it comes the heat. Everything combustible along the line of sight burns; and all living things along the line of sight crisp and shrivel.

And in Wallis's office, apocalypse stirs.

"Sir, we have a system interrupt on OTH," says the major. "We're losing Chesapeake and Rockbank."

"Roger."

"Hey Colonel, I'm not getting a signal from the DSPs." This from Lieutenant Winton, the solitary woman on the team.

"Sir, Ace has just bombed out."

"What the . . . ?" Wallis says as the images in front of him dissolve once again into snow.

"Sir. We've lost Alaska, Thule and Fylingdales. Colonel . . . we've lost all coverage on the Northern Approaches." Wallis goes cold; he feels as if a coffin lid has suddenly opened.

"Okay, soldier, keep calm. Get the general down here. Major, would you get me Offutt? Pino, interrogate REX, get a decision tree on screen Five." Wallis issues the orders in a level voice.

"Sir, are we under attack?" The nervous question comes from Fanciulli, a tough, grey-haired sergeant to Wallis's right.

"Pino, where are the warheads?"

"Yeah but we got some sort of EMP . . ."

"Nuts; all we got is cable trouble."

"Negative, sir." It is Lieutenant Winton again, her small round face unusually pale. "We have tropospheric forward scattering modes up top, and we've lost on VHF. There's some sort of massive ionospheric disturbance."

"Sunspots?"

"No way, sir."

"Colonel we have reduced bandwidth on all—"

An alarm cuts into the chamber and a light flashes red. Somebody wails. And Pino, his face wax-like, mutters a string of profanities as he types rapidly on a keyboard.

"Colonel, Screen Three."

Covering the walls of the office are enormous screens. Mostly these show arcane lists of data—coded refuelling points, the tracks of satellites in orbit, numbers of aircraft aloft—but one of them is instantly comprehensible. It is a map of the USA. And on the map, red lights are beginning to wink.

"The General, sir." Wallis looks up at the glass-fronted observation room. General Cannon has appeared, flanked by a civilian and a second general: Hooper, Chairman of the Joint Chiefs of Staff. Wallis snatches up a telephone, but Cannon, impassive as an Indian chief, ignores the urgent ringing.

One of the screens has changed. There is a blurred, jerky picture. Somebody is pointing a camera from an airplane cockpit. They are flying high over a city and the plane is tilted so that the camera can look down. There are skyscrapers, and long straight roads with cars, and parks. The camera pans and there is an ocean wave. It is almost level with the aircraft, and it covers half the city. Here and there, on the lower slopes of the wave, the tops of the skyscrapers protrude, some of them already slowly tilting over. Wallis stares in utter disbelief. The wave towers high over the remaining buildings; it looks frozen, but white specks are falling off the top and tiny cars are dotted here and there in the broad rising sheet of water. Someone shouts, in a voice edging on panic, *That's San Diego!* Wallis kills the alarm.

The camera points backwards. It is unsteady, like an amateur movie. The ocean stretches into the distance and the wave with it. There is a long smoky contrail and a glimpse of wing, and racing up from behind is a churning black wall as tall as the sky, and then the camera shakes and there is a helmet in close-up, and inside a young black face, eyes staring in fright, is shouting silently, and then the screen goes blank.

The major gabbles into the phone. Fanciulli, tears streaming down his cheeks, points to one of the big screens. New red lights are winking on virtually every second. Winton is saying Sir, why doesn't the General answer. Then:

"Offutt, sir." Wallis snatches up another telephone, the blue one. But already new messages are flashing; lists of names are tumbling down the screens faster than they can be read. Wallis, his ear still to the telephone, stares at the map of the USA. The red lights, each one a Strategic Air Command base scattered to the winds, have formed a broad front, slowly creeping up from the south.

The decision tree is up. REX is requesting more data.

A voice on the telephone. It speaks in harsh, staccato tones. Wallis forces his attention from the advancing wave and listens. He replies, hearing in astonishment that his own voice is shaking and frightened: "Sir, I agree a threat assessment conference . . . no sir, we lack dual phenomenology . . . negative, negative . . . not if we go by the book . . . we have no evidence of hostile warheads or hostile intent . . . agreed . . . agreed . . . sir, how the fuck would I know? Some sort of blast coming from Mexico . . . I urgently advise we do not get Eagle into Kneecap . . . repeat do not get the Chief aloft . . . no sir, keep the B-2s on the tarmac, their wings would just tear off . . . sir?"

The line has gone dead.

There is a stench of fresh vomit. Wallis feels a tug on his sleeve. The major has apparently lost the power of speech; he is staring ahead, as if looking at his own death. Wallis follows the young man's line of vision. The wave of red lights is now passing in a long arc from California through Kansas to Virginia. Its progress is slow but steady over the map. It has almost reached the Rock.

"Sir, we're buttoned up. Hatches closed and filtration on. Sir?"

But Wallis is looking helplessly up at the observation room. The civilian and the generals look stonily down.

Then it reaches them.

Abduction

Buachaille Etive Mor, Glencoe, Scotland. 0630 GMT

Something.

The young man opened his eyes with a start, some dream fading from memory, and stared into the dark. Unaccountably, his heart was thumping in his chest.

At first he could make out only the flap-flap of the canvas inches from his head, and the *Whee!* of the wind around the guy ropes. And then it came again, a distant roar, deep and powerful, coming and going over the noises of the storm. Puzzled, he strained his ears.

Then it dawned.

Avalanche!

He shot out of his sleeping bag and tugged frantically at the rope lacing up the front of the hurricane tent. The knot was an impenetrable tangle and the noise was growing in intensity. Desperately he scrabbled in the dark for a bread-knife, found it, cut the rope, hauled back the canvas and pitched head-first into the dark night.

The blizzard hit him with a force which made him gasp.

For a panicky moment he thought to run into the dark but then remembered where he was: on a mountain ridge next to a precipitous drop. And the roar was coming from the gully below.

He dived back to the tent, and felt for the paraffin lamp and a box of matches. The wind blew the match out; and the

next and the next. The fourth match worked, and he hooked
the glowing lamp up to an aluminium pole. He looked around.
Snowflakes like luminous insects were hurtling from the void
into a circle of light about ten yards in radius around the tent;
he could just make out the edge of the ridge, about twenty
yards away.

A cone of bluish-white light rose out of the gully, passing left to right before disappearing from the man's line of
vision.

Avalanches don't come with blue lights.

The man's legs were shaking, whether with cold or relief
he didn't know. The light cone was drifting up and down in
a sweeping pattern, snow hurtling through the beam.

It occurred to him that a man in a Glencoe blizzard,
dressed only in boxer shorts, probably had a life expectancy
of minutes. Already his back was a mass of sharp, freezing
pain. Hastily, he reached in for corduroy trousers and sweater,
pulled them on and slipped into climbing boots. He tripped
over untied laces, picked himself up and ploughed through
deep snow to the edge of the ridge overlooking the Lost Valley. The sweater, he realized, bought him at most another
five minutes: the wind was going through it like a chainsaw
through butter.

The light cone rose and approached. It was scanning the
mountain slopes. Suddenly light flooded the ground around
him. An intense spotlight rose into space and approached; the
roar became overwhelming; the ground vibrated. Dazzled,
the man caught a glimpse of a whirling rotor passing straight
overhead. A giant insect, a yellow flying monster of a thing,
circled him and then sank towards a sloping patch of snow
about thirty yards away. It almost vanished in the blizzard
kicked up by its rotors. It tried to settle down, backed off, tried
again, but its undercarriage slithered over the snow and the
machine slid perilously sideways towards the edge of a precipitous drop. The pilot gave up and rose over the man's head.

A spider emerged in silhouette from the side of the machine, and began to sink down on a swaying thread. It settled on to the knee-deep snow within arm's length of him, resolving itself into a young airman in a khaki-coloured flying suit. "Flt Lt A.W.L. Manley" was stencilled on his helmet. "Doctor Webb?"

Webb stared in astonishment, and nodded.

"You're coming upstairs. Quickly, please."

St-Pierre de Montrouge, Paris. 0730 Central European Time

Five hundred miles to the southeast, in Paris, the Atlantic storm had softened from the harsh reality of a potentially lethal blizzard to a bitter, wet, gusty wind.

As was his custom, the professor left his apartment at 7:30 a.m. precisely. Dark clouds swirled just above the rooftops, a newspaper streaked along the road and a solitary pigeon was attempting a speed record; but he was well clad in trenchcoat and beret, and as usual he walked the two hundred yards to the Café Pigalle. There he took off his sodden trenchcoat and sat at the marble bar. Without waiting to be asked, Monique served him two strong espresso coffees and a croissant with butter and strawberry jam, which he consumed while watching the early morning Parisians scurrying past.

At eight fifty, as he always did, he set out along the Rue d'Alesia, jumping over the flowing gutters and avoiding the bow waves from passing trucks. He turned off at the church of St-Pierre de Montrouge and headed briskly towards the Sorbonne. He had no reason even to notice the man purchasing cigarettes at the kiosk. The man was squat and bulky, with grey hair close-cropped almost to the scalp. His bull neck was protected from the rain by the pulled-up collar of his sodden jerkin. A policeman stood on the edge of the pavement next to the kiosk, his back to the professor, watching the flow of traffic through the little waterfall pouring from the brim of his sodden cap.

As the professor drew level with the kiosk, the squat man suddenly turned. "Professor Leclerc?"

Startled, Leclerc looked into the man's eyes, but they showed no expression. "Who are you?"

From the corner of his eye the professor saw a big Citroën pull up, the rear door open and another man step out: thin, tight-lipped, with eyes set back in his head. Suddenly, and instinctively, the professor was afraid.

"Please come with us, Professor."

"Why? What is this?"

"I do not know. A matter of national security. Get into the car."

Thinking assassination, Leclerc turned to run; but powerful arms seized him, held him in a painful neck lock. He wriggled furiously, his beret falling to the ground, but another pair of hands twisted an arm behind his back. Half-choked, he tried to shout but he was pushed into the back seat of the car, one man on either side of him. Leclerc forced his arm free and hammered on the rear window. The policeman turned away a little more, his back squarely to the professor. The driver took off swiftly, cutting into the path of a taxi. The man at the kiosk tidied his newspapers, the Parisians scurried by, and the policeman, water streaming down his shiny cape, tossed the beret into a litter bin while keeping his eye firmly on the glistening rush-hour traffic.

Baltimore, Maryland. Midnight

The warm ocean which powered the Atlantic storm was also dumping its energy into the far north of the planet; here the air, turned away from the sun, was exposed to interplanetary cold; here, it responded to the Earth's ancient rotation, and circulated anticlockwise around the Arctic Ocean: a huge blizzard howled out over the pack ice and the seals, the killer whales and the sunless wastelands.

The blizzard rampaged over the pole, down through Alaska and the North West Territories, passed over a thousand miles of Baffin Island, and howled through a few Inuit hunting groups who knew it as the Chinook, a hostile force which drove itself up nostrils and winkled out tiny gaps in snow goggles. The blizzard was still a blizzard over Quebec Province and New York State but, far from the oceanic heat engine, it was beginning to die. Even so, swirling along Broadway and Times Square, the dying snowstorm could still send late evening theatre crowds scurrying into warm bars, and traffic cops into a state of sullen paranoia.

Passing over the Great Lakes, the wind went into a rapid decline until, in Baltimore, Maryland and Washington, it finally died, leaving only snowflakes drifting down on sleeping houses: a traditional Christmas, all Bing Crosby, Silent Night, and Christmas trees glittering from a million dark windows.

In at least one Maryland suburban home, however, the night was neither still nor silent, and the owner barely heard the chime of the doorbell above the party hilarity and the raucous dance music. Reluctantly, Hilary Sacheverell detached herself from her white-haired, tall dancing partner, and weaved a path through the party. In the hallway she stepped over a young couple sitting together on the floor, backs to the wall. She opened the door, a smile half-formed on her face in expectation of late arrivals. A gust of freezing night air wafted around her exposed shoulders and she shivered.

Two men, in their thirties, one white, one black. Strangers. Snow sprinkled their heads and dark coats like tinsel decoration. A black Buick convertible had somehow snaked its way through the Mercs and Dodges which cluttered the driveway. A third man, in the Buick, just discernible through its dark windscreen. The woman was suddenly alert.

"Mrs. Sacheverell?" the black man asked.

She nodded uneasily.

"Is your son here?"

"Which one?"

"We're looking for Doctor Herbert Sacheverell, ma'am."

"Herby is here," she said. "Is there a problem?"

"If we could just have a word with him."

A hardness about the eyes; a professional alertness. Some instinct prevented her from inviting them in from the bitter cold. "Wait a moment, please."

It was a full minute before she found a skeletally thin, middle-aged man with thick spectacles and red, spiky hair seated at the kitchen table with the Ellis woman. A near-empty bottle of Jim Beam stood between them. The girl had her elbows on the table and was resting her head in cupped hands, staring into Sacheverell's blue eyes with open admiration. Sacheverell, thus encouraged, was extolling the merits of legalizing cannabis, itemizing the points with the aid of his bony fingers.

"Herby, two men for you," Mrs. Sacheverell said, looking through the Ellis female. "They look sort of official. Have you been naughty?"

Herby shook his head in bewilderment. He stood up carefully, oriented himself towards the open kitchen door and navigated towards it with exaggerated steadiness.

"Enjoying the party?" Mrs. Sacheverell asked.

"Oh yes, Mrs. S. Herby is really good to me."

"Tell me, have you tried anything for that big spot on your chin?" Mrs. Sacheverell asked, curling her lips into a smile.

The smile was returned. "I'm using a cream. It's supposed to be good for wrinkles too—I'll hand it in to you some time."

"That would be lovely, dear. Do keep drinking."

A minute later, the doorbell rang again. Herb Sacheverell stood between the two men. He was tight-lipped, and his face was white and strained. "I'll be gone a few days. Urgent business."

She glanced in alarm at the men on either side of her son. "There's something going on here. Who are these people?"

"Mom, it's okay. But one thing. It's important that you tell nobody about this. If anyone asks, friends have turned up and I'm taking a few days' holiday."

Hilary Sacheverell's suspicion was overlaid by her sense of the practical. "Let me pack a suitcase for you."

"There's no time. They'll look after me. Now I have to go."

Hilary Sacheverell watched the dark Buick snake through the driveway and then, on the road, accelerate swiftly away. She wended a path back to the living room, a smile firmly fixed on her face.

North Atlantic, 0650 GMT

"You've got the wrong man. I'm not a medical doctor."

"This isn't a rescue mission. If you're Webb, you're wanted on board."

"Who are you people?"

"We don't have a lot of time, sir!" the airman shouted.

"The hell with you!" Webb shouted back.

"Sir, I am authorized to use force."

"Don't try it. On whose authority?"

"We don't have a lot of time, sir." The airman took a step forward. Webb instinctively turned to run but, looking into the whirling blizzard and the blackness beyond, immediately saw that such an action would be a lethal folly. He raised his hands in an angry gesture of surrender and furrowed his way through the snow back to his tent. The downdraught from the big rotor was threatening to flatten it and the guy ropes were straining at the pegs. Inside, the noise of the flapping canvas was deafening and the paraffin lamp was swaying dangerously. Papers were fluttering around the tent. He gathered them up, grabbed a laptop computer, turned off the lamp and ploughed back towards the lieutenant, tightly gripping papers and computer. The airman pointed towards

the white blizzard and the man ran forwards into it; under
the big rotor, the downdraught was fierce, and he felt as if
he was being freeze-dried. The airman shouted "Hold on!"
and slipped a harness around him. Then Webb's feet were
off the ground and he was gripping the papers fiercely as
the winch swung and spun them upwards through the gusting wind.

A Christmas tree, tied tightly, and with baubles attached,
lay along the length of the machine. Half a dozen sacks with
"Santa" in red letters lay on the floor. Two civilians, men in
their fifties, were at the back of the helicopter. They were
identically dressed in headphones, grey parkas and bright
yellow lifejackets. Webb recognized one of them but couldn't
believe his eyes.

The airman pointed and he tottered to the front, flopping
down on the chair behind the pilot. The wet sweater felt horrible against his skin.

The pilot turned. He had a red, farm-boy face and seemed
even younger than his navigator. His helmet identified him
as W.J. Tolman, and "Bill T." was printed on the back of his
flying suit.

Manley said, "It's force eight out there, mister; we're not
supposed to fly in this. Put on the lifejacket!"

Webb looked out. Daylight was trying to penetrate the
gloom. Across the glen, he could just make out sheets of
snow marching horizontally against the backdrop of granite
mountains. The top of the ridge opposite was hidden in dark,
sweeping cloud. He began to feel faint.

The pilot pulled on the collective and the big machine
rose sharply upwards. Webb's stomach churned. Tolman
looked over his shoulder. "What gives with this trip? Are
you some sort of James Bond?"

The helicopter began to buck violently. Webb looked down
and glimpsed his hurricane tent, a tiny black dot against the
massive, white top of the Big Herdsman. Then the machine
was roaring over the Lost Valley and they were rising bumpily

towards the Three Sisters. As it reached the summit it was hit by the unshielded force of the blizzard. It lurched and tilted on its side, throwing Webb against the fuselage. "Jesus Holy Mary Mother of Christ!" the pilot yelled. Then the helicopter had righted and was thrusting roughly into the wind, its wipers clicking in vain against a wall of white, while another wall, made of granite, skimmed past.

Webb stared out. His faintness had given way to terror. Below, white Highland peaks came and went through dark scudding clouds; and then they were passing along Loch Linnhe and the Sound of Mull; and then they were heading out over an ocean made of white churning milk; and the waves on the milk moved in slow stately progression; and they were bigger than houses.

The pilot turned again. "I was supposed to meet a nurse tonight," he said accusingly. "Knockers like melons and game for anything. James bloody Bond on a secret mission I do not need. By the way, your pals from SMERSH are waiting."

The young man made his way unsteadily to the back of the machine. "You don't mind if I smoke, Webb?" asked the Astronomer Royal, lighting up a Sherlock Holmes pipe. He was buckled into a seat at a small circular table screwed into the metal floor. There was no telling what lay behind his blue eyes and Webb judged that the man on the chair next to him wasn't an artless rustic either. He collapsed into a seat opposite, buckled in and put on the headphones in front of him.

"This is the fellow," said the AR.

"Walkinshaw," the stranger said. He looked like a headmaster, half-moon spectacles mounted on a grey skull-like head. It was a civil servant's handshake: prudent, cautious, economical. The helicopter was into its stride, moving briskly if roughly about five hundred feet above the big waves. The civil servant glanced forward at the airmen; they too were wearing earphones.

"I expect you're wondering what's going on, Webb," said the Astronomer Royal, unscrewing the lid of a flask.

"The question did flicker across my mind, Sir Bertrand," said Webb angrily. "I have, after all, just been kidnapped."

"Don't exaggerate. The Sea King is transporting us to Skye."

"Skye?"

"Skye. Where Walkinshaw and I will be dropped off. You, however, will continue on to Iceland."

"Iceland?"

"Webb, try not to sound like a parrot. I am informed that we have only twenty minutes to brief you. Six of these have already gone." A match flared and Webb waited while the King's Astronomer got up more smoke. "Father smoked an ounce a day, lived to be ninety. Walkinshaw here is from some God Knows What department of the Foreign Office. Webb, we have a problem."

"Just a moment, Sir Bertrand. Sorry to interrupt your Christmas vacation, Doctor Webb." Walkinshaw nodded at the sheets of A4 paper, covered with handwritten mathematical equations, which the man was still unconsciously clutching. "Although you seem to be on a working holiday."

"Will someone tell me what is going on here?" Webb said. He was trembling, through a compound of shock, fear, anger and cold. He folded the papers up and slipped them into his back pocket.

"First there are a couple of formalities. Number One." Walkinshaw leaned forward and passed over a little plastic card. Webb held it towards the nearest window. There was a Polaroid photograph of the civil servant, looking like a funeral undertaker, over an illegible signature. Next to the photo was a statement that

W.M. Walkinshaw, Grade Six, whose photograph and signature are adjacent hereto, is employed by His Britannic Majesty's Government in the Foreign and Commonwealth Office, Department of Information Research.

Webb nodded warily and returned the card.

"And Number Two." The civil servant reached into his briefcase again and handed over a sheet of paper. "An E.24, quite routine. If you would just sign there."

The Astronomer Royal unzipped his parka. "It's hot in here," he said, holding out a pen. Webb ignored it and read

OFFICIAL SECRETS ACT

To be signed by members of Government Departments on appointment and, where desirable, by non-civil servants on first being given access to Government information.

My attention has been drawn to the provisions of the Official Secrets Act set out on the back of this document and I am fully aware of the serious consequences which may follow any breach of these provisions.

Webb felt the hairs prickling on the back of his head. On the back, he read that if any person having in his possession or control any secret official code word, password, sketch, plan, model, article, note, document, or information which relates to or is used in a prohibited place or any thing in such a place, or which has been made or obtained in contravention of this Act, or which has been entrusted in confidence to him by any person holding office under His Majesty or which he obtained or to which he has had access owing to his position as a person who holds or has held a contract made on behalf of His Majesty, or as a person who is or has been employed under a person who holds or has held such an office or contract, communicates . . . or uses . . . or retains . . . or fails to take reasonable care of, or so conducts himself as to endanger the safety of, the sketch, plan, model, article, note, document, secret official code or password or information, then that person shall be guilty of misdemeanour.

He handed it back unsigned.

The Astronomer Royal made no attempt to hide his annoyance; his teeth audibly tightened on his pipe. He returned the pen to an inside pocket, and glanced quickly at Walkinshaw. The latter nodded briefly.

Tolman's voice cut sharply into the intercom: "Do not smoke. Put that pipe out immediately."

Sir Bertrand continued to puff. Bleak Atlantic light from a window had turned his wrinkled face into a mountainous terrain. The helicopter was filling with blue smoke. He said, speaking carefully: "The Americans suspect that an asteroid has been clandestinely diverted on to a collision course with their country."

Webb stared at him, aware of a sudden light-headedness as he struggled to take it in. "*What?* You could be talking a million megatons."

"Webb, I'm aware that you think I'm just an establishment hack. However even I can multiply a mass by the square of its velocity." Sir Bertrand pushed a little metal stubber into his pipe. "The Americans informed their NATO allies late last night—the Eastern bloc partners excepted of course—and the Foreign Office requested my assistance at four o'clock this morning. But as you know asteroids are not my field."

"An asteroid like that would devastate half the planet. This has to be wrong."

"If only."

"Which asteroid?"

"You're missing the point," said the AR. "The idea is that you tell us."

Webb tried to grasp what he had just been told. The AR and the civil servant watched him closely. "Okay, you've scared me. What you're asking is insane. It would be easier to find a needle in a haystack."

"Nevertheless it must be done and done quickly. The Americans will need to find some way of diverting it."

"You must have some information about it."

The AR shook his head. "None whatsoever. All we can say is that at some unknown future time it will manifest itself over American skies as a meteor of ferocious intensity."

"An asteroid impact on North America could leave two hundred million dead. Suppose I fail, or make a wrong identification? I can't take responsibility for that."

"There is nobody else. And I would prefer a more respectful tone."

Webb felt his mouth beginning to dry up. "I'm sorry, Sir Bertrand, but the moment I say yes, I'm swallowed up in God knows what. Get someone else."

The Astronomer Royal's voice dripped with acid. "I know this will sound absurdly quaint in this day and age, Webb, but there is the small matter of one's obligations to humanity."

"Hold on a minute. I went to Glen Etive for a reason." He tapped his back pocket with the papers. "Listen. I'm on the verge of something. I think I can put some meat into general relativity. You know GR is just a phenomenology, it lacks a basis in physical theory, and that Sakharov conjectured . . ."

The Astronomer Royal's tone was icy. "You were instructed not to spend time on speculative theoretical exercises."

"I happen to be on leave, trying to do some real science for a change. You have a problem with an asteroid? Get someone else to look into it."

The Astronomer Royal took the pipe from his mouth, his face wrinkling with angry disbelief. He made to speak but Walkinshaw quickly raised his hand. "Please, Bertrand." The civil servant lowered his head, as if in thought. Then he leaned forward, to be heard above the engine. "Doctor Webb, I apologize for the melodramatic descent from the skies, but the fact is that we are engaged in a race, with an asteroid, which we must not lose." The helicopter was tilting and Webb gripped the table. He sensed that his face was grey. "The

Americans are trying to put together a small team to look
into this. They have specifically requested a British contri-
bution. We do not know when impact will occur but it must
be clear that time is vital. We must get you to New York instantly. As Sir Bertrand says, there is nobody else in this
country."

The AR, at last, poured a black liquid into the plastic lid
of the flask. Webb took it and sipped at the warm tea. His
stomach was churning and he was beginning to feel nauseous. "Who diverted the asteroid?"

The civil servant remained silent.

"There's some risk attached to this, right?" Webb peered
closely at Walkinshaw, but the man had the eyes of a poker
player.

The AR turned to Walkinshaw. "A wasted journey," he
said contemptuously. "Turn the Sea King back. I'll get
Phippson at UCL."

"Phippson? That idiot?" Webb said in astonishment.

The AR waited.

"But the man's a total incompetent."

The AR cleared his throat.

"He couldn't find the full moon on a dark night!"

The AR stubbed the tobacco in his pipe, a smirk playing
around his lips.

"Damn you, Sir Bertrand," Webb said.

Sir Bertrand removed his pipe, exposed his teeth and
emitted a series of loud staccato grunts, his shoulders heaving in rhythm. Webb was enveloped by a wave of nicotine-
impregnated breath. He gulped the tea and handed the flask
lid back to the Astronomer Royal, who was grinning triumphantly.

Walkinshaw's eyes half-closed with relief. "Very well.
The country is grateful etcetera. Now the quickest route
from here is the polar one. After this briefing—" Walkinshaw
glanced at his watch "—which must end in four minutes, we
will be dropped off on a quiet beach near the Cuillins. You

will carry straight on to Reykjavik Airport. There you will board a British Airways flight to New York. It's the quickest route we could devise from this Godforsaken land."

He pulled out a buff envelope from a briefcase. "Your ticket, some dollars, an American Express number on which you can draw, and a passport."

"How did you get my photograph?"

"You would be amazed, and at four o'clock this morning. You are Mister Larry Fish, a goldsmith. A precaution in case unfriendly eyes are watching the movements of asteroid people. What do you know about gold, Webb?"

The Sea King was sinking fast, and Webb's stomach rose in his diaphragm.

"Atomic number seventy-nine, isn't it? The least reactive metal but alloys with mercury."

Walkinshaw assimilated this answer. Then he said in a toneless voice, "In no circumstances hold any sort of conversation with anyone en route."

"Unfriendly eyes," Webb said. He felt almost paralysed with fear. "So there is some risk attached to this?"

"My goodness no," said Walkinshaw blandly.

"If there is trouble nevertheless?"

"Never heard of you. You're a crackpot."

"A popular opinion in some circles anyway," Webb replied, giving the Astronomer Royal a look. The AR stared unflinchingly back.

The long backbone of the Cuillins was hidden by low, fast cloud sweeping in from the Atlantic. They stepped out into low, fast sleet sweeping in from the Atlantic. Fifty yards away on the black sand, a dark insect was poised to jump. It was bigger than a house. It had mysterious protrusions, and a row of windows along its dark side, and huge twin rotors throwing spirals of water into the wind. The sand under the Sikorsky was rippling and the Sea King was suddenly a child's toy.

Webb stared in alarm at the monstrous thing.

Walkinshaw shouted, "The Air Force will make sure you catch the plane at Reykjavik. Sign the credit card as Larry Fish. Any expenditures must be accounted for but you shouldn't need it."

"Then why give me it?"

"A precaution," was the enigmatic response. "I am informed that you know the Goddard Institute at Broadway. You are expected there around now. Still, they tell me you can beat the Sun at polar latitudes. Something to do with the Earth turning, but we pay you people to know about things like that, don't we, Bertrand?"

"What about my tent?"

"Webb," the AR replied with a show of infinite patience, "Have you quite grasped the situation? The issue here is not your scientific research, nor your evident fear of flying nor the fate of your blasted tent. The issue is the survival of the West. His Majesty's Air Force have laid on travel gear in the Chinook, and His Majesty's Astronomer will personally dismantle your tent and return it to your office."

"I'll be missed at the Institute," Webb pleaded.

"The hell you will!" the Astronomer Royal roared. "Nobody knows what you do in that damned basement all day. Anyway, you sent a note saying you've extended your leave. My secretary does signatures."

"I'm not getting into that contraption!" Webb finally shouted, but he knew he would.

"Just find the asteroid, Webb," the Astronomer Royal shouted back. "And quickly! And keep your mouth shut!"

The freezing rain drove into the Astronomer Royal's wrinkled face, and he screwed up his eyes as the massive helicopter rose and tilted over the sea. He watched as it dwindled upwards and vanished into the clouds. He puffed reflectively on his pipe, the wind blowing a thin stream of smoke across the beach.

Walkinshaw looked worried. "Bertrand, are you sure about this? What sort of man spends Christmas alone on a mountain, in a blizzard, calculating?"

"A hermit, of course. Speaking as his Director, he's a nightmare."

"In what way?"

"He's restless, the very devil to control. Needs a woman if you ask me. He keeps diverting from well-established lines of research into cosmological speculation. There's no funding for stuff like that these days, and anyway nobody quite understands what he's about. However he pursues his ideas with great exuberance and determination."

"Family?"

"I know little of it except that he comes from a large, poor one with no sort of academic background."

"Then I understand him," Walkinshaw declared. "A large family with little privacy will make him invent his own private space, a world in which he can daydream. Hence the cosmological speculation. And the need to compete with siblings will make him pursue his own ends with determination. Throw in an exceptional intelligence and there you have him."

A deeply sceptical expression came over the AR's face. "Very neat, Walkinshaw, wonderfully glib. I don't suppose you're into palmistry as well as amateur psychology?"

"His evident unworldliness has the same source. There is no great ingenuity without an admixture of dementedness. Seneca said that, not me. Still, Bertrand, I'm worried. We need a team player for this one, not some go-it-alone eccentric."

The Astronomer Royal smiled a thin, sour smile. "That, I fear, is a problem for our American cousins. After all, they wanted him. Indeed, they were very insistent."

The Goddard Institute, New York

Outside the warm Kennedy terminal, a gust of icy air hurt Webb's ears, watered his eyes and froze his ankles, and he found that the Royal Air Force had given him a suit transparent to wind. A man with a Cossack hat rode a strange, shaking machine which sucked up dark-streaked snow from the road and sprayed it at him. The morning sky was a menacing, dull grey. He headed for the airport bus but two men, warmly wrapped against the cold, emerged from the background and intercepted him. "Mister Fish? I am Agent Doyle of the FBI, and this is my colleague Agent O'Halloran. Forgive us if we don't show our badges in a public place. Would you come this way, please?"

Webb settled into the back seat of a nondescript Buick with darkened windows. The car was deliciously warm. Agent O'Halloran took it silently over Brooklyn Bridge towards Central. Patches of crystal blue sky were beginning to show through the cloud. On Broadway, they continued north to the edge of Black Harlem. Good smells drifted from delicatessens and coffee shops. The snow was deep at the side of the road, and the breaths of pedestrians steamed in the bitter cold.

They stopped at the entrance to the Goddard Institute, an anonymous doorway with neither sign nor symbol to proclaim its NASA affiliation. Webb stepped out of the car. Across the street, rap music was blasting out of a stereo from a first-floor window. A phalanx of black children swooped down threateningly, but at the last second split and reconverged past him with marvellous precision. The stereo went off with a swipe, and the skateboarders swept off round the corner, ghettoblasters screeching. The limousine drove off.

"Mister Fish, good morning, we've been expecting you," the stout, black guard at the desk said cheerfully. "First floor, elevator's over there."

On the first floor was a door with a sheet of paper saying "Do Not Enter" pinned on it. Webb knocked and a key turned. The room was bleak and almost unfurnished, apart from a green baize table strewn with notepads and water carafes. Four people sat around the table. The man who had opened the door, slimly built with close-cropped hair and light blue eyes, shook Webb's hand. "Welcome to New York, Doctor Webb," he said. "Have a seat and we'll get on with it."

Webb sat down and looked round the table. The smell of cigar smoke hung lightly in the air. Through it Webb thought he detected a sour odour which he could not place. Three of the faces he knew; the others were strangers.

Noordhof's tone was informal but decisive. "First, gentlemen, a small organizational matter. This is a USAF project and as of now you are under my direction. The Europeans included, by consent of your respective governments. Does anyone object to this?" He looked round the table.

"Okay. Now we're all here, let me make the introductions. Proceeding from my right, we have Herbert Sacheverell, from the Sorel Institute at Harvard." A man of about forty, his red hair standing vertically on his scalp, thin, greasy-skinned and wearing a dirty black headband, nodded at the assembled group. "Doctor Sacheverell is our top asteroid man." Jesus, Webb thought, America's answer to Phippson: who put that loud-mouthed clown on the team? Sacheverell's expression returned the compliment.

"Next to him we have Jim McNally, Director of NASA." McNally, a slim, balding man of about fifty, dressed in a business suit with a slight, up-market shimmer to it, smiled and said Hi.

"The American contingent is completed by Wilhelm Shafer. What can you say about a hippie with one and a half Nobel Prizes?"

There was no need; a huge intelligence clearly lay behind Shafer's restless grey eyes. He was, like McNally, about fifty; he wore a copper-coloured T-shirt decorated with a Buddha, and an elastic band held his long grey hair back in a ponytail. He grinned and nodded towards Leclerc and Webb. For Webb, the presence of the awesome Willy Shafer on the team underlined the gravity of the emergency as much as any lecture by the Astronomer Royal.

"On my left, let me introduce our two European partners. Oliver Webb, still catching his breath, is the British asteroid man. Next to him we have André Leclerc. André knows as much as anyone in the West about the space capabilities of the former Soviet bloc." A tall, gaunt man, with a red bow tie and a black and white goatee beard, smiled and bowed to the centre of the table.

"And I'm Colonel Mark Noordhof. I know a thing or two about missile defence technology."

"Who needs the Brits?" Sacheverell asked, staring at Webb with open hostility. "We have all the know-how we need in the States."

"In part this is politics," said Noordhof. "An attack on America is also an attack on NATO. If we get zapped on Monday the Russians could roll over Europe on Tuesday. But the essence is we need the best for this one."

Sacheverell continued to glare, his eyes tiny through his thick spectacles. "Webb is a bad choice."

Noordhof added: "And security. Sure, we're up to our ears in civilian experts but what if they started dropping out of sight wholesale? We can't treat this like the Manhattan Project. So, we're using minimum numbers, drawn from a widely dispersed net. Small is beautiful is what the President wants. Kay, now let's get down to it."

Noordhof produced a cigar and played with the cellophane wrapping. He continued: "My brief comes from the President. I have to lead a team which will find the asteroid, estimate where and when it will impact if it does, estimate the impact damage, and determine whether it can be destroyed or diverted. I report directly to the SecDef, Nathan Bellarmine. He in turn informs the President, the DCI and the Joint Chiefs of our progress. The resources of these people are available to us and that's some awesome resources. If you want the Sixth Fleet in Lake Michigan, ask and it shall be given unto thee."

"Seek and we shall find," said Shafer. "I hope."

"Understand this," said Noordhof. "This is not some cosy academic conference. This is a race, and the prize is survival. We have no precedent for this situation, no experience we can call on. We have to make up the rules as we go. Comments, anyone?"

"I'm not long out of bed," Webb said. "How do we know that an asteroid has been diverted towards the States?"

"I'll pass on that for now."

"What are the political implications? Does it connect to the Red Army takeover?" Leclerc asked, speaking good Parisian English.

"That we don't know."

"We need a handle on the time element," Sacheverell said. "It could be hours, weeks, months, years before the asteroid hits."

A smoke ring emerged from Noordhof's puckered lips. "We've been given five days to identify the asteroid and formulate an effective deflection strategy. This is Monday morning. Deadline is Friday midnight."

Sacheverell laughed incredulously. "In the name of God . . ."

Noordhof continued. "And I'm authorized to say this. If at the end of five days we have failed to identify the asteroid, the White House will then formulate policy on the assumption that it will never be found before impact. I think it's safe to assume that aforesaid policy will be highly aggressive."

Shafer said quietly, "I think the Colonel is telling us that either we find the asteroid by midnight on Friday or the White House will retaliate with a nuclear strike."

The room went still. Sacheverell paled, McNally flushed purple and Leclerc puffed out his cheeks. Noordhof leaned back and took a leisurely puff, whirls of blue smoke curling upwards. Webb felt suddenly nauseous.

"So we split the effort. Item One. Our masters want to know what will happen if the asteroid hits. Which one of you eggheads wants to take that one?" Noordhof looked round the table.

"I guess I'll look into that," said Sacheverell. "Sounds like a big computing job and we have the hardware at the Sorel."

"Agreed?" Noordhof asked Webb, who nodded. The issue had already been raked over by experts; Sacheverell couldn't do much harm channelled into that one.

"Item Two. Say we detect the asteroid on the way in. What can we do about it?"

"That's a solved problem," said McNally. "NASA looked into this on instructions from Congress some years back, when it was all a theoretical exercise. Anything we do will involve getting up there and zapping it."

"Now hold on, zap it how?" Shafer asked sharply.

"With nukes, of course." McNally looked bewildered.

"I've seen that stuff, and the Livermore Planet Defense Workshop, and the Air Force 2025 study. Theoretical's the word. What do you think you'll be zapping, Dr. McNally, shaving foam or a giant nickel-iron crystal? Hit it with nukes and you might wipe us out with a spray of boulders. We have to divert the thing without busting it up. How do you propose to do that without knowing its internal constitution?"

"It was only a suggestion," McNally complained.

"Willy, Jim, liaise on the problem of how to handle the

asteroid if we do find it. I'll fix access to classified Lawrence Livermore reports as well as the public domain one. That leaves Item Three: where is this thing? Opinions, anyone?"

"I can draw up a list of candidates," Webb said, still feeling queasy, "and get them checked out. We'll need to use wide-angle telescopes."

"Like the UK Schmidt?" suggested Sacheverell.

"They've mothballed it. We need Spaceguard and supernova patrol telescopes, say fast Hewitt cameras with CCDs. The Australians have one at Coona."

"Colonel, this is an example of the security you can expect from these guys," said Sacheverell. "Time on these machines is more precious than gold. You can't just break into established observing programmes, not without people shouting like hell."

"Ever heard of service time?"

"Cool it, gentlemen," said Noordhof. "Wait until you see what we've laid on."

Sacheverell said, "Whatever you've laid on, Colonel, our chances of identifying this rock in five days are practically zero. Especially with Webb guiding the search."

"Jesus frigging Christ, don't say things like that." Noordhof stubbed out his cigar agitatedly.

Webb said, "What especially worries me is that these things are invisible most of the time. It could come at us from sunwards, in which case the first we'll know about it is when it hits."

Noordhof poured water from a carafe into a tumbler and took a sip, wetting his dry lips. Tense little wrinkles lined his face as he assimilated Webb's information. He said, "Let's name this beast."

"I suggest Nemesis," Sacheverell said. "After the Greek Goddess of Destruction." There were nods of assent.

Noordhof said, "Nemesis. Good name. I have to tell you there is no chance of identifying it by conventional intelligence-gathering techniques. It's down to us."

"Many orbits will be unreachable by the Russian Federation even with their Energia boosters," said Leclerc. "Perhaps Doctor Webb and I can co-operate."

"I have programmes at Oxford which might help," Webb said.

Noordhof nodded curtly. "You'll have facilities to FTP them over. Now, gentlemen, we're heading for Arizona. We have a Gulfstream waiting for us at LaGuardia. And from now on you free spirits are firmly corralled. No wandering the streets, no phone calls, no e-mails to colleagues. Lest you think this is paranoid, consider this. If the Russian leadership learn that we know about Nemesis, they can anticipate getting nuked in retaliation. So they'll get their strike in first, to minimize damage to themselves."

Shafer completed the logic: "Except that, since we know they'll be thinking that way, we'll have to get in first."

Noordhof nodded again. "A careless word from anyone here could trigger a nuclear war."

They stared at each other in fright. At last Webb recognized the sour odour. It was the smell of sweat, induced not by exertion but by fear. The chairs scuffled on the wooden floor as they stood up. "Strictly," Webb said, "Nemesis is the Goddess of Righteous Anger. Have you people upset somebody?"

Southern Arizona

The desert air was cold, the sun was setting, and a bright red Pontiac Firebird, straight out of the nineteen-seventies, was waiting for them. It had fat tyres and a front grille like twin nostrils, and flames extended from the air intakes back along the bonnet and down the sides in a wonderful expression of psychedelic art from the period. The woman leaning on the car was about thirty, small, with shoulder-length, curly, natural blonde hair. She was wearing a slightly old-fashioned dress which didn't disguise the fact of elegant bodywork underneath. She waved cheerfully at them.

Noordhof took the driving seat, Shafer sitting next to him. Webb added his holdall to a pile of luggage in the boot and squeezed into the back beside the blonde. She was diminutive against his strong six foot one frame. Leclerc sat on the other side of her and immediately delved into a sheaf of papers.

"Judy Whaler," she said, shaking hands. "So you're our European astronomer."

"What's your field, Doctor Whaler?"

"I'm a Sandian."

"Is that a religious cult?"

She smiled tolerantly. "Sandia National Laboratories. The Advanced Concepts Group. We're supposed to identify threats to national security and propose countermeasures."

Noordhof said, over his shoulder, "The rest of the team's on site." He eased the car on to the road. Once on Speedway he opened the throttle and they moved throatily north on the broad street, past Mexican restaurants and cheap motels. It took about twenty minutes to cross the city and then they were clear, still heading north, and the grey Catalina Mountains were getting bigger. Paloverde cactus and little creosote bushes started at the roadside and stretched into the far distance. The sky was blue, but streaky clouds were beginning to form around the peaks, and above them was high cirrus. A four-engined jet was drawing a contrail.

In the confined space it soon became clear that Judy enjoyed bathing in cheap perfume. Her thigh was warm against Webb's but he tried not to notice that—after all, she was a colleague. The road began to climb and twist and they passed over narrow bridges straddling deep canyons. Webb's scrotum contracted, as it always did when he faced great heights or imminent danger. It would do a lot of contracting over the next few days.

Half an hour north of the city Shafer fell in impatiently behind a big, gleaming American truck with a vertical exhaust. The corrugated door at the back portrayed a leering, gluttonous child, with a frost-covered head, eating a Monster Headfreeze Bar. The road went steeply up the mountainside and the truck dropped gear noisily with a surge of exhaust smoke, labouring heavily. A second truck appeared on the skyline like a hostile Indian and bore down on them at alarming speed. Noordhof put his foot flat down and they sailed past with ease.

"Six point six litre V8," Judy said, "delivering three three five bhp. The suspension's too simple to cope with it." The truck drivers blasted their air horns but the big Pontiac was already long past. At the top of the hill Noordhof slowed, and turned sharply off on to a stony, unpaved track. In seconds they had lost the highway and were heading steeply upwards, towards high mountains. Something momentarily glinted silver, on the summit of a high distant peak. The cactus gave way to a scattering of scrub oak and piñon pine.

After some minutes a cluster of timber houses appeared, straight out of the Wild West. A notice said *Piñon Mesa, alt. 5500 ft.* There were no signs of life.

"Survivalist community," said Noordhof. "They're armed to the teeth and they don't like us. But you won't be down here."

The track ended at a wooden barred gate, and Noordhof kept the engine running as Webb fumbled with a padlock, feeling exposed. The buzz of a chainsaw came from the woods beyond, but he saw nothing through the trees. Then the real climb got under way, and the engine started to labour in earnest, and the air got colder, and Judy's thigh got warmer, and the scrub oak gave way to juniper pine, and then the juniper gave way to big, heavy ponderosa. Through the trees Webb caught glimpses of the setting sun to the left, and tiny bugs crawling along a ribbon cutting through the desert. The Firebird's suspension coped well with the potholes, but the heating didn't seem to work.

Higher still, and the branches were covered with thin, freshly fallen snow, and they were following the tracks of some vehicle which had gone before.

They ran into cloud from below, and for the next fifteen minutes were enveloped in a light freezing mist, visibility about fifty yards, as the car continued to toil upwards. Finally the road began to level, the tops of buildings appeared over the trees and then the car was round a last hairpin bend and driving past the buildings into a paved car park at the side. Noordhof turned to them. "Eagle Peak. I'm told nobody ever comes here in the winter apart from astronomers and the odd black bear. But I still want you people sticking close to the Observatory. No wandering the hills."

"Why haven't you fenced it off, Colonel?" Shafer asked.

"Just in case some stray backpacker comes by. Guards and fences going up round a civilian building might draw attention. Our best protection is the semblance of normality."

They climbed out, stiff, breaths misting. The air was fresh

and pine-scented. Judy flapped her arms against her sides. To Webb, the combination of hairstyle and dress made her look like a resistance heroine from a World War Two movie. He stretched and walked round to the front, curious to explore his new surroundings. The snow was powdery underfoot and Shafer was having problems assembling a snowball. Noordhof piled their luggage out on to the tarmac.

A small, wiry man, with a neat grey beard, appeared at the front door. "Doctor Webb," he said, stretching his hand. "Heard you in Versailles last year. Delighted to meet you at last. And I've read a fair number of your papers, of course. I feel as if I know you." So this was Kenneth Kowalski. His Polish origins were obvious in his polite manner and his slightly clipped accent: second-generation American. Webb knew Kowalski's reputation. Amongst observers, he was highly regarded, a careful stargazer who had transformed Eagle Peak from a dilapidated museum piece into a respected scientific tool. It didn't have the world-class clout of Gemini at Cerro Pachon or the huge Keck ten-metre on Hawaii; but for rapid sky coverage, which is what the problem called for, it had these monsters licked. "We must talk about your work on the revised steady state theory after this is over. Of course you're wrong. It's an observed fact that the Universe is different at high redshift."

Webb returned the grin and bowed. "All right-thinking people agree with you. So, this is the famous Eagle Peak Observatory?"

"You're just at Base Camp," Kowalski said. "The telescopes are much higher up." He pointed to a squat grey building fifty yards away, and just visible in the mist. Through its windows Webb could see a small silver cable car. A thin cable stretched up from the roof of the building like a giant metal beanstalk, disappearing into the grey mist overhead. He looked at the tinny death trap apprehensively before realizing that, as a theoretician, he would have no reason to go up in it.

He smiled in relief and said, "Eagle Peak is a private bene-faction?"

"Yes, it was a gift to the nation from the Preston dynasty in the thirties. It was modernized a few years ago with NSF funding. We were swarming with Air Force personnel yesterday, putting in extras for our visitors."

Leclerc and Whaler joined them, and they made for the building. Sculpted in red sandstone over the outer door was a circularly coiled snake swallowing its own tail: the Pythagorean symbol of perfection and eternity. Inside, separating the atrium from the inner sanctum, was a double swing door made of glass framed in mahogany; each partition had the zodiacal signs engraved on it, six on each, in two columns. Through these doors and into the building proper, the warm air enveloped Webb like a hot bath towel. Kowalski led the way along a corridor lined with framed NASA photographs. Two doors led off to the left, and both were open.

The first of these revealed a large square kitchen with a long, cluttered farmhouse table. Then there was the common room, airy and spacious, with a panoramic window and a view of fog. In this room was a snooker table, and armchairs, and a bookcase full of paperbacks, and a coffee table with magazines and bowls of fresh fruit and sweets. Sacheverell and McNally were head to head in an animated discussion. As Judy passed the open door Sacheverell stopped in mid-conversation, adopted an angelic smile and said, "Well hi there," and Webb hoped Nemesis would smash through the roof and turn Sacheverell into a red pulp.

The end of the corridor led into an open, glass-fronted area from which further doors led off. One led back into the common room. Kowalski pointed to a red door opposite it. "The nerve centre," he said. "Later."

Straight ahead of them was a flight of stairs, covered with a deep-piled blue carpet, so as not to disturb night observers sleeping by day. They went up these and found themselves in a long corridor. "The four rooms at the end are taken. If you like a desert view, take One or Two. If you like to look at mountains, take Seven or Eight." The nearest door handle to Webb was attached to Number One and he took it. Leclerc took Number Two, while Judy Whaler presumably liked mountains and headed for Room Eight, directly opposite Webb's.

The room had a log cabin feel to it and smelled of new pinewood although, again, a thick pile carpet covered the floor. A red, bloated sun was beginning to penetrate the fog.

Alone at last, Webb flopped on to the bed and tried to take stock:

(a)   He'd been whisked off a remote Scottish mountain,
(b)   told a tale of imminent Armageddon,
(c)   transported to Iceland in a giant helicopter, in a blizzard,
(d)   been flown over the roof of the world thence down almost to Mexico, and
(e)   he was now on a remote mountain site surrounded by backwoodsmen.
(f) And he thought,
      I don't need this.

Money, Webb had learned soon after he joined the Institute, drove everything. Science was something you snatched in precious moments in between writing grant applications and publicity handouts. And in between meetings: the management loved meetings. The science, he had also learned, had to be Approved. The streetwise might aspire to soft carpets and executive desks, but the iconoclast stayed in an icy basement. The point of Buachaille Etive Mor had been to escape, get to work on real science. Webb wondered how they had found him, in that remote mountain setting.

What I do need is deep, dreamless, eight hours of sleep. He had a shower, washing away the camping and travel, and wrapped himself in a large white towel. The beautiful, climactic moment came when he approached the bed, weary muscles tingling in anticipation of flopping down on it. He savoured the moment, he flopped, and there was a sharp knock on the door.

Noordhof was in Command Mode. "The cable car. Five minutes. Observing suits in the dormitory cupboard."

You're in the army now, Webb thought.

The tiny silver cable car barely took four people and had the feel of something cobbled together by an enthusiast with a Meccano set. Noordhof, Sacheverell and Webb squeezed in, dressed like Eskimos, with Sacheverell taking up three quarters of Webb's bench. A notice said

> On no account stand up, change seats, shake the car or lean out of the window. Keep clear of the door handle in transit.

Kowalski marched over to a control panel, pressed a red button and pulled a lever. On the panel, a row of lights flashed on. There was a clash of engaging gears, a loud whining, and a large metal wheel started to turn. He trotted swiftly to the car and climbed in next to Webb, pulling the door shut just as the cable took up the slack and the car started to move. "It's quite safe," he said. "If you work it by yourself just remember to get in quickly."

From about fifty yards up, the ground faded into the mist and they lost nearly all sense of motion; they were sitting in a gently swaying cable car, immersed in a co-moving grey bubble. After some minutes they cleared the mist. Far above, almost over their heads, was a pinnacle of rock, still in sunlight. On its summit Webb could barely make out a building. Near-vertical rock faces fell away from it in every direction; lines of ice filled the ridges and angles. Webb looked up at the dizzying height and thought *Why not? What more can they throw at me?* Below them, the receding cloud turned out to be fairly localized, and they could see the track they had taken in the Firebird, twisting through the forest. Beyond it, the desert was now dark.

Webb assumed that his hypothetical Meccano enthusiast had known all about wind-pumped resonances, and metal fatigue, and the tensile strength of tired old steel. He was delighted to see that Sacheverell was even more terrified than him. There was sweat on the man's brow and his eyes were staring. He produced a handkerchief and wiped his face with it. Mischievously, Webb turned the screw a little. Trying to sound casual, he asked Kowalski: "Ever been an accident with this?"

Kowalski looked at him curiously and glanced quickly at Sacheverell. Then he nodded solemnly. "Once."

The car began to sway, a long, slow oscillation as the cable vibrated like a bowstring. After some minutes the vibration died and the car's upward climb slowed; the machinery seemed to be struggling. Only a few yards away was an icy, vertical rock face; the car was being hauled almost vertically up its cable. Sacheverell giggled, but it was a bit high-pitched. The car edged up and slotted into a gap in a concrete platform projecting into space. They piled out. There was a gap of nine inches between car and platform, and about three thousand feet of air below the gap.

Eagle Peak was a spacious natural platform, about a hundred yards by eighty. Its perimeter was marked out by a stone wall about four feet high. There were two observatory domes, copper-coloured in the light of the sinking desert sun. One small, no more than fifteen feet in diameter; it was dwarfed by its companion, about a hundred feet across. The air was wonderfully clear, and bitterly cold.

Kowalski took them into the little dome. He picked up a metal handset from mobile steps and pressed a button. The dome was filled with the noise of machinery as the shutter opened. Temporarily Webb had the illusion, familiar to an astronomer, of standing on a rotating platform underneath a static dome. Kowalski rotated the dome until the sinking sun streamed into the open slot. In the centre of the circular building stood a circular metal platform about three feet tall and six wide. The top of the platform was clearly built to rotate, and two stanchions rose from it, supporting between them what looked like a big dustbin about three feet in diameter and six feet long.

"The supernova patrol telescope," Kowalski said with, Webb thought, a touch of pride. "With an altazimuth mounting," he added, mentioning the obvious, "to save weight. This is a fast survey instrument and it needs to travel light. For supernova searches we're just measuring the apparent magnitudes of galaxies, looking for any change which might indicate a stellar explosion. Speed is the priority and we don't need long exposures."

Webb asked, "How faint do you go?"

"Magnitude twenty-one in ten seconds, over a one-degree field. The instrument has a pointing accuracy of one arc second. We no longer need equatorial mountings now that we can use computers to update the altitude and azimuth of the target star. The slew rate, galaxy to galaxy, is less than a second. It is probably the best supernova hunter in the business."

It was an impressive instrument.

Sacheverell tittered. "Forgive me, Doctor Kowalski, but it has as much chance of finding Nemesis in six days as I have of winning the lottery."

"Will you cut out talk like that," Noordhof said.

Kowalski smiled politely and said, "Now let me show you the other telescope."

They made for the monster dome. By now the sun was down and Kowalski switched on the light to reveal a telescope about sixty feet tall, on a classical equatorial mounting. He led them up metal stairs to a circular balcony. They spread themselves around the balcony and looked across at the giant, battleship-grey instrument. A metal plaque said "Grubb Parsons 1928"; it had been shipped over from the UK or Ireland at some stage. Mounted piggy-back on the main frame was a secondary telescope, and next to it a mobile platform, with a guard rail, which would raise and lower the observer depending on where the big telescope was pointing in the sky. Attached to the bottom of the telescope, at the location of the eyepiece, was a metal box about four feet on each side, from which cables trailed across the metal floor to a bank of monitors clear of the instrument. At the prime focus of the telescope, far above their heads, was a cylindrical cage. The cage contained the secondary mirror. It also came with a chair and harness; the observer had to supply the steel nerves.

It was twenties technology, a masterpiece of precision and power, updated for the new millennium with cutting edge instrumentation. As a tool for discovering Nemesis, Webb would without hesitation have gone for a pair of binoculars.

"This is of course the ninety-four-inch reflector," Kowalski said. "As you see we have set up a spectrograph at the prime focus. The atmospheric seeing at this site is excellent. In good conditions it can be sub-arcsecond, and I've even seen it diffraction-limited."

"I hope you don't expect to find Nemesis with this," Sacheverell said in a tone of incredulity.

Webb said, "The Grubb Parsons will be very useful if we do find Nemesis. We can use it for astrometric backup to get a high-precision orbit, and we'll need it to get a spectrum."

"What do you want a spectrum for?" Noordhof asked.

"Nickel iron or shaving foam, Colonel? We'd be able to work out the surface mineralogy which might be vital in formulating a deflection strategy. However, first catch your hare."

Noordhof gave Webb a look. "That's what you're here for, Mister."

Kowalski said, "The Grubb can only be operated from up here. If you want broadband spectrophotometry you have to change the optical filters, which means you have to go into the cage. But we can control the supernova patrol telescope from down below. It can sweep the whole sky to magnitude twenty-one in a month."

Sacheverell's head shook inside his fur cape. "It's not nearly good enough. Nemesis is a moving target."

By now the desert was black; the sky was dark blue and stars were beginning to appear, unwinking in the steady air. Far below, Base Camp was a tiny oasis of light in the dark. The little car swayed in space as Sacheverell, Webb and Noordhof squeezed in. The cable car lurched and Kowalski ran out of the wheelhouse, jumping in just as the car launched itself into space. He pulled the door shut with a tinny *Clang!* and in a second they were sinking fast.

Sacheverell was looking at the dark cliff drifting past a few yards away. His breath misted in the freezing air. In a tone of exaggerated casualness, he asked: "About this accident. What happened?"

"It was a lightning strike. The car stopped half-way down with one of our technicians in it, and it was three days before anyone noticed. This was last winter."

"He survived?"

"Heavens no. We had to thaw the corpse out on a kitchen chair before we could get it in a body bag. You should have heard him cracking."

A look of pure horror came over Sacheverell's face, and Kowalski grinned. He'd had his revenge.

Eagle Peak, 24^{h}00, Monday

The red door was solid and heavy—or maybe, Webb thought, he was just feeling fragile. It had a small brass label marked "Conference Room."

The conference room was brightly lit, like a stage, and measured about twenty feet by twenty. There was a heavy dark blue curtain on the left, a long blackboard on the right, and an old-fashioned circular clock, looking like railway station surplus, on the wall straight ahead. Its hands showed three minutes past midnight. Otherwise every foot of wall in the nerve centre was taken up with desks, computer terminals, printers, scanners and deep bookshelves stuffed with scientific journals, books and gleaming brass instruments from an earlier era.

The centre of the room was taken up with a long pine table, already scattered with papers. There were deep leather armchairs scattered around, their dark blue matching the curtain, and working chairs around the big table, and seven colleagues on these chairs awaiting Webb's dramatic entrance, and vertical, disapproving wrinkles above Noordhof's lips. "Webb, you're three minutes late. I'll say it again: this isn't some cosy academic conference. If Nemesis is coming in at twenty miles a second, you've just cost us three thousand, six hundred miles of trajectory. Half the diameter of the Earth. The difference between a hit and a miss."

Webb flopped down at the end of the table. "I'm feeling a bit fragile." The soldier shot Webb a venomous look and then turned to Sacheverell. "Let's get into this. Herb, what's the state of play in the hazard detection arena?"

Sacheverell leaned back in his chair. "As you'd expect, the big players are the Americans. We have two main civilian programmes, one in New Mexico, and one right here in Arizona. Lowell Observatory have a point six-metre Schmidt at Flagstaff, just a few mountains to the north of us, and the University of Arizona have Spacewatch Two on Kitt Peak, to the south. And the University of Hawaii are just starting a massive programme on Maui, one of the Hawaiian Islands. It's a sixty-million-buck project, financed by the USAF."

"Is that it?" Noordhof asked.

"There are photographic programmes but if you don't have a CCD you're not in the game. Put a charge-coupled device at the eyepiece of your telescope and you'll get as much light in two minutes as you would with a two-hour exposure hour on a Kodak plate. In that two minutes Flagstaff can cover ten square degrees of sky down to magnitude twenty. Spacewatch Two covers only one square degree, but it gets down to twenty-one in half the time."

"Sacheverell has overlooked the rest of the world," Webb pointed out. "For example, the Japanese have a private network of amateurs and they've also started with a pair of one-metre class telescopes. The Italians have a small-scale network centred round their instruments in Campo Imperatore, Asiago and Catania. The French and Germans have a one-metre Schmidt on the Côte d'Azur."

Sacheverell waved his hand dismissively. "I don't want the survival of America to depend on a bunch of Japanese amateurs. As for the Italians, they're penniless. Half the time their telescopes are lying idle. We're detecting three Earth-crossers a night."

Kowalski said, "And we have our upstairs telescopes. We operate our Schmidt remotely, as a robotic telescope, from this room. Normally we feed in a pre-selected list of galaxies over there but we could just as easily scan the sky looking for a moving object."

Noordhof tapped the table. "Like I said in New York, you people have every conceivable facility at your disposal."

"You mean Pan-STARRS?" McNally asked, round-eyed. "The Hawaiian system?"

"Ay-firmative. With immediate effect, it's yours."

"What are their CCD chips in these systems like?" Webb asked.

Sacheverell waved sheets of paper. "While our token Brit is feeling fragile I'm downloading from Albuquerque, with the Colonel's help. They're large format, high quantum efficiency, fast readout. They perform close to the theoretical limit."

Shafer was scribbling furiously on a yellow notepad. He had dispensed with his ponytail and his long grey hair was swept down over his shoulders. "What's the sky coverage with these Pan-STARRS telescopes?"

Sacheverell said, "Nine square degree starfields, reaching mag twenty with twenty-second exposures. They don't go as faint as Spacewatch Two but like I say their CCDs have fast readout. They can carry out a saturation search in half the time of Spacewatch. Spacewatch has depth; Albuquerque has breadth."

Webb said, "I'm impressed. Herb, impress me even more. Tell us what you've got in the southern hemisphere."

Sacheverell hesitated. "Okay, we're weak there."

"What's your point, Oliver?" Noordhof asked.

"We have almost no coverage of the southern sky. Nemesis could sneak up on us from south of the celestial equator when all our telescopes are scanning the sky to the north. Maui can look south to a limited extent, and the ESO Schmidt in Chile might have picked it up serendipitously if they hadn't shut it down."

"The British closed down the UK Schmidt in Coonabarabran," Sacheverell accused Webb, pointing a skinny finger in his direction. "Why did you guys leave yourselves with no asteroid-hunting capability?"

"The giggle factor. Our Minister for Science thought the impact hazard was a joke."

"Are you telling me half the sky is uncovered?" Noordhof asked in dismay.

"It's worse than that. I'm thinking of the Atens."

"Excuse me?"

"I hate to add to our troubles, but there's a blind spot about thirty degrees radius around the sun. Anything could be orbiting inside it. An Aten is an asteroid with an orbit which puts it inside the Earth's orbit, and therefore in the blind spot, most of the time. Only a handful have been discovered but nobody knows how many there really are. Now say the Russians discovered one on a near-Earth orbit."

Noordhof acquired a thoughtful look. Leclerc had been writing in a little red leather Filofax. He looked up and said, "The probability that we would independently discover it is remote. It would hide in sunlight until it pounced. An Aten makes a lot of sense as a weapon."

Webb continued, "Sacheverell's telescopes are all geared up to search the sky around opposition. They're pointing high in the night sky, far from the sun. But if an Aten is coming at us, it won't be there. It will come at us low in the sky, close to the sun. Most of Herb's telescopes can't even reach that low. If Nemesis is an Aten you might see it before dawn, or just after dusk, a few days before impact. Binoculars would do."

Noordhof took a cigar from his top pocket. "I need a consensus on the detection issue. Can you people deliver or not?"

Shafer had finished his scribbling. Now he stood up and moved over to the blackboard. He picked up yellow chalk and started to write in a fast, practised scrawl. "The way these telescopes are operated, sure there's a strong selection effect acting against the discovery of Atens. But I disagree with Ollie about Atens as weapons. For precision work the

Russians would need something they could track for a long time, maybe years, and you can't do that with The Invisible Asteroid. I say Nemesis is reachable with Spacewatch and Pan-STARRS. There are 4π steradians of sky and each steradian is $180/\pi$ degrees on a side. That gives us forty-three thousand square degrees of sky over the whole celestial sphere. How much of that can we cover? For a start these things are faint, which means we have to go deep. But we can only do that in a pitch black sky. Okay, so there's no moon this week. But to avoid twilight the sun has to be at least twelve degrees below the horizon, and to avoid atmospheric absorption the sky we're searching has to be at least thirty degrees above it. I reckon we have maybe only five or six thousand searchable square degrees of sky on any one night."

"Declining to zero if it's cloudy," Judy Whaler pointed out.

"The five-day local forecast is good," Kowalski said. "Except for the last day."

Shafer continued: "Okay, from Herb's figures I reckon the whole of the world's asteroid-hunting telescopes will cover no more than two or three hundred square degrees of sky an hour. That means say a month to cover the whole sky once."

"And we've been given five days," said Whaler. "Six to one against."

"Not even remotely," Shafer disagreed. "Look at square A on Monday, and by Murphy's Law Nemesis is in square B. Look in B on Tuesday and it's moved to A or C. Apart from which, most of the time it will be too faint to be seen, because it will be too far away, or hidden in sunlight like Ollie's Atens, or camouflaged against the Milky Way."

"So how long, Shafer?" Noordhof asked impatiently.

Shafer drew a graph. He measured off tick marks on the axes and labelled the horizontal one "diameter in km," and the vertical one, "p % per decade." Then he drew an S-shaped curve, copying carefully from his paper. Webb saw what the physicist had been calculating and was awestruck at the speed with which he had done it. Shafer tapped at the blackboard. "Assume Nemesis is a kilometre across, with the reflectivity of charcoal. That gives it absolute magnitude eighteen at one AU from Earth and sun." He drew a vertical line up from the 1-km tick mark on the x-axis to its point of intersection with the curve, and then moved horizontally across to the vertical axis, where he read off 0.85. "You want to discover Nemesis with eighty or ninety per cent probability, with all the world's asteroid telescopes going flat out? Assuming it's not an Aten? It will take us ten years."

"We have five days," Noordhof reminded Shafer in a flat tone.

"So consult a psychic," said Shafer, going back to his chair.

The tense silence that followed was broken by the loud crackling of cellophane as Noordhof unwrapped his cigar.

"Willy, I think your calculation is flawed," Webb said, knowing this was a rash thing to say to the mighty Shafer. "If it's coming at us in a straight line out of a dark sky then it's already close and bright. We don't have to spend ten years looking."

The physicist gave Webb a disconcertingly hard look. "Ollie, if it's close and bright and coming at us in a straight line out of a dark sky, we're about to be history."

"It's our only chance to find it."

Sacheverell shook his head sadly. "It must be the jet lag. Willy has just told us that by the time it's close enough to be found it's too late to be stopped."

"We can harden up on this." Webb crossed to an empty bit of blackboard. "Say Nemesis is going to hit us in thirty days. There are 86,400 seconds in one day. If it's coming in at fifteen kilometres a second then it's only $30 \times 86,400 \times 15 = 39$ million kilometres away now, a quarter of an AU, which makes it sixteen times brighter than it was at one AU. Herb, what's the brightness of a one-kilometre asteroid at one AU?"

"Eighteen for a carbonaceous surface. Everybody knows that."

Shafer was tapping at a pocket calculator. He said, "Inverse square brightness, forget phase angles. Yes, if Nemesis is a month from impact it could have magnitude fifteen. We should be able to pick it up now."

Webb said, "Go for sixteen or seventeen visual and we cut the exposure times to seconds. We might even have a continuous scan. We could cover the sky in a week. It's then down to bad luck, like coming at us out of the sun or approaching from the south."

McNally's slim fingers were agitatedly drumming on the table. "Can we inject some realism into this? If we're a month from impact what am I supposed to do about it? Call up Superman? I need a year minimum, preferably two or three, to build some hardware."

"But if Nemesis is a year from impact now, we'll still only detect it in eleven months' time, when it's on the way in. A last-minute deflection is the only scenario you can work on."

"Let me understand this," Noordhof said. "If you guys are right, the chances are hundreds to one against our finding this thing in the next five days. Unless it's so close that it's maybe a month or two from impact. And even then maybe not if it's coming at us out of the sun."

There was a silent consensus around the table.

"Shit," Noordhof added, looking worried. He turned to the Director of NASA. "McNally, you have to come up with a deflection strategy based on the month-from-impact scenario."

"For Christ's sake, that's just off the wall." The NASA director's face was flushed.

Firmly: "You have no choice in the matter." Noordhof was playing nervously with his unlit cigar. Webb had a momentary vision of Captain Queeg rolling little metal balls in his hand.

"Jim," Shafer's tone was conciliatory. "We're the A team. Maybe you and I can come up with something."

McNally shook his head angrily.

Leclerc asked, to break the tension, "What would happen if say somebody in Japan found an asteroid?"

"The whole astronomical community would know it within hours," Sacheverell said. "Civilian discoveries go straight to the Minor Planet Center which has electronic distribution to all the major observatories. But look, forget Japan, Europe and Atens and crap like that. The action is at Lowell, Spacewatch and Hawaii"—Kowalski winced slightly, but said nothing—"and we're linked in to these places here. We'll see the exposures build up in real time."

Webb said, "Detection isn't enough. If we don't follow it up, we lose it. We have to track it long enough to get a reliable orbit."

Sacheverell said, "Follow-up means we come back to it every few hours, using the interval in between to search for other asteroids. An interval of a few hours gives you its drift against the stars enough to pick it up again the following night. To get a believable orbit, you need to track it for at least a week. To get decent precision, say to launch a probe at it, you have to update over months. There are follow-up telescopes in British Columbia, Oak Ridge Massachusetts and the Czech Republic. Also at Maui."

Kowalski nodded. "We're well placed for follow-up here. Our Grubb Parsons has a long focal length and its point spread function is small. On a good night we can do very high-precision astrometry."

"The Grubb Parsons is vital," Webb agreed. "Without it follow-up would double the load on the discovery telescopes."

Leclerc, pen hovering over his Filofax, asked again: "Suppose you find an asteroid and follow it up. What then?"

Webb said, "Nearly every one we find will be harmless. We're looking for a needle in a field of haystacks. Old Spacewatch could pick up six hundred moving objects on a clear winter's night, and overall twenty-five thousand asteroids a year. Out of all that, fewer than twenty-five were Earth-crossers. The rest were main belt. Now with all the new systems combined the detection rates are fifty times higher. But that means we have also fifty times more junk to be sifted through. With the CCD mosaics you people are talking about I reckon we need to interrogate about a billion pixels every ten seconds. We have nothing like enough computing power on site to handle the data."

Noordhof attempted a smile. "We have the Intel Teraflop at Sandia. It makes your hair stand on end. That too is yours, a personal gift from a grateful nation."

Judy said, "That's Wow, but how do we transfer the data over? Ordinary cable transmission can't handle the flow."

"We have satellites that will."

"In that case," she replied, "problem solved. I'll download the CCD processing software from Spacewatch and transfer it over to our magic machine."

"We have orbit calculation packages at the Sorel," Sacheverell said. "I'll pull them over to your computers. I presume it's all Unix-based?"

Noordhof nodded. "All communication between here and Albuquerque must be secure. I'll get a key encryption package installed when I'm fixing access to our computers. Judy, work at it through the night. Let's be operational by dark tomorrow. Herb, when can you give me a damage profile for Nemesis?"

"Two or three days, if I can access the Sorel."

"Have you been listening, Herb? At that rate we might as well wait for the field trial. I want a report over breakfast. O seven hundred sharp, all present, and nobody feeling fragile."

Webb said, "We're doing this all wrong."

Shafer said, "Oliver, I was joking about a psychic."

DAY TWO

Eagle Peak, Tuesday Morning

The smell of scrambled eggs and coffee drifted into Webb's room, and sunlight had found weak spots in the heavy curtains' defences. He reached for his watch with an arm made of lead, focused on the little hands, and knew he was in for another of Noordhof's special looks. He rolled on to his stomach and looked longingly at the laptop computer and the crumpled sheets of paper scattered over the floor, which had shared his journey from Glen Etive. But there was no time. He skipped shaving and made it with minus two minutes to spare.

Breakfast things were laid out on the kitchen table and Shafer was dithering around the microwave oven. Judy was in an easy chair; she was into a severe white blouse and black skirt, a plate on her lap, and she was using her sharp, red-painted nails to carefully peel a hard-boiled egg. Sacheverell sat next to her with a plate on his lap. He was also pouring her a coffee and she flashed him a smile. McNally, Leclerc and Kowalski were at the window, sipping coffee and looking out over an expanse of desert from which the occasional tree-covered mountain protruded like an island in the sea.

Noordhof was busy on a croissant. A row of cigars protruded from a shirt pocket. He made a show of looking at his watch as Webb entered.

Webb poured himself coffee from a big percolator, heaped a plate with sausage and scrambled egg, and settled down at the farmhouse table. "You're giving me a hard stare, Colonel."

"Please God, deliver this man unto my sergeant," Noordhof prayed.

A screen on a tripod had been set up and an overhead projector on the end of the kitchen table was throwing white light at it. The soldier nodded to Sacheverell, who had a stubble and looked a bit ragged.

Sacheverell put fork and plate aside, wiped his fingers with a handkerchief, took a pile of transparent overlays to the projector and moved them on and off the machine as he spoke. The first one showed three teddy bears of different sizes, with bubble text coming from the mouth of each, like a comic. One bear was saying 10^4 Mt, another 10^5 Mt and the third 10^6 Mt. "I examined three scenarios which straddle the likely energy range. I'm calling them Baby Bear, Mummy Bear and Daddy Bear. As you see Baby Bear is ten thousand megatons, Mummy Bear a hundred thousand and Big Daddy is a million.

"First I had a look at Baby Bear, deep ocean impact. I had the idea that maybe the aggressors—the Russians?—might want to take out the UK or Japan while they were about it. Anyway, the Atlantic and the Pacific are big, easy targets. Okay. So half a minute into impact we have a ring of water three or four hundred metres high. Wave amplitude falls as it moves out but you're still looking at a fifteen-metre wave a thousand kilometres from the impact site."

"In the open sea?" Shafer asked.

"In the open sea. Tsunamis are long-range, because the ocean is a surface and specific energy drops linearly with distance rather than inverse square. An earthquake in Chile in 1960 created ocean waves which travelled over ten thousand miles and killed a lot of people in Japan."

"What was its wave height?" McNally asked, coming back from the window.

"In the open sea, twenty centimetres. The wavelength is hundreds of kilometres."

"An eight-inch wave killed people?" McNally asked, bewildered.

Sacheverell winced. "No. When the wave runs into shallow water the same amount of energy is being carried by less and less water. So when it approaches a shoreline it rears up. The twenty-centimetre wave became a metre or two high. Killed a couple of hundred people, if you count the ones that just went missing."

"So what's the run-up factor on your fifteen-metre wave, Herb?" Shafer asked.

"Ten to forty, depending on the shoreline. If we say twenty, the wave is three hundred metres high when it hits land, assuming the impact was a thousand kilometres offshore."

"The height of the Eiffel Tower," Leclerc said. "How far inland would a wave like that travel?"

"Again it depends. Topography, roughness of surface. Flat agricultural land would flood for ten or twenty kilometres inland. When I say flood, I mean the wave is still two hundred metres high maybe five kilometres inshore."

Webb said: "An Atlantic splash of that order would take out nearly all the major cities in Britain." Although he was actually trying to visualize a half-mile tsunami roaring up Glen Etive.

"I don't believe these figures," Shafer said, without bothering to explain why.

"Europe is protected by a steep continental shelf," Sacheverell informed Webb. "It reflects about three quarters of the energy back into the ocean."

"Great," Webb said. "Really great. Now I know that when I turn into Piccadilly the wave coming at me is only a hundred metres high."

Noordhof went to the percolator and came back with a refill. "And if Baby Bear hits land?"

"Blast, heat and earthquake. The blast is a pressure pulse followed by a hot wind. The nuclear weapons people use an overpressure of four psi to define total devastation although there's huge loss of life even at two, mainly from blizzards of flying glass in urban areas. Hit L. A. and you'll blow the roofs off houses in San Diego. A Baby Bear on Philadelphia would rip people up from Baltimore in the south to New York in the north."

"You could take out England from London to Newcastle," Webb interrupted, still doing his patriotic bit.

"Who would want to zap your feeble little island?" Sacheverell asked. "I've taken the threshold for fire ignition to be about a kilowatt applied to a square inch for a second. It turns out you ignite everything in sight—tyres, grass, everything flammable. A hundred miles away, it's like standing four inches from an electric fire for ninety seconds."

"That must depend on whether the asteroid hits the ground or breaks up in the air," said McNally.

"No. The heat comes from the hot wake trailing the fireball. Lastly, earthquake. I've taken Gutenberg-Richter Nine as defining total devastation, and I've assumed five per cent of the kinetic energy goes into shaking the ground. We're looking at Nine over a region about a thousand kilometres across."

Noordhof took a sip at his coffee. "So Baby Bear takes out a few cities or floods one of our seaboards. But it doesn't totally destroy the USA and it leaves our nuclear potential intact. So let's turn the screw a bit. Herb, take us to Mummy."

"Wave height scales as the square root of the impact energy, and the flood plane extends as the four thirds power of the run-up wave. These are approximations. They're beginning to crumble when you get to the really big numbers. Mummy Bear makes an open ocean wave fifty metres high a thousand kilometres away. The run-up factor stays the same so you hit the coast with a wave a kilometre or two high. I guess the Rockies or Appalachians would protect the central USA. For an Atlantic impact, I don't know how much of Europe would be left."

Shafer said: "That's just movie stuff. A wave that big would break up. The tsunami would only take out a few million people."

Noordhof interrupted: "Our Kansas silos stay intact."

Shafer said, "But you're not expected to shoot back. This is just a great natural disaster, right?"

"And a land impact? Blast, heat, earthquake?" Noordhof's voice had an edge to it.

"Ten times the impact energy gives you ten times everything else. And a sixteen-mile crater as a bonus."

"I don't like the sound of that," Noordhof said. "You want to tell us about Big Daddy?"

"Give me an extra power of ten and I'll shower the States with ballistic ejecta. At the impact site, everything as far as the horizon vaporizes. It gets thrown above the atmosphere, recondenses as sub-millimetre particles at a thousand degrees and falls back over an area equal to the USA. Allowing for heat lost to space etcetera I find that the thermal radiation at the surface is about ten kilowatts per square metre for an hour or more after impact. It's like being inside a domestic oven. Try to breathe and your lungs fry. The whole of the United States turns into one big firestorm. I guess nothing would survive."

Sacheverell tidied up his papers to show he was finished. There was a thoughtful silence. Webb broke it by saying, "These computations all have big uncertainties. My reading is you'd have less earthquake and more heat. You'd burn the States even with Mummy Bear. Partly I'm thinking of the Shoemaker-Levy 9 comet fragments which hit Jupiter in 1994. We had a coherent stream of material which gave us twenty impacts on to the planet. The heat flashes from the fallback of ejecta were a hundred times brighter than those from the fireballs themselves."

Shafer stirred his coffee. "Big Daddy is good news." There was an astonished silence. Noordhof's cup stayed poised at his lips.

Webb nodded. "I believe so, Willy. There are maybe a couple of a million cometary asteroids out there, any one of which could give us a hydrogen-bomb sized impact. They probably happen ~~every~~ century or two. This century we had Tunguska in the Central Siberian Plateau on June 30th 1908. It came in low from the sun at about 7:15 a.m. That was ten to thirty megatons. Hundred megatonners come in every few centuries. They've been recorded as celestial myths in Hesiod's *Theogony* and the like. If you go to a few thousand megatons, you're probably into the Bronze Age destructions: the climate downturn, Shaeffer's mysterious earthquakes in the Near East."

"What has this guy been smoking?" Sacheverell asked.

"Do you accept your own impact rates? The ones you keep re-publishing?"

"What of it?"

"With a decent chance of a thousand megatonner in the last five thousand years?"

"Sure," Sacheverell sneered. "Probably at the north pole."

"So we had ten megatons in Siberia in 1908, a megaton in the Amazon in 1930, another few megs in British Guyana in 1935, but the five thousand years of civilisation before that were missile-free? And what about Courty's Syrian excavations showing Bronze Age city destructions caused by blast? And when Revelation talks about a great red dragon in the sky throwing a burning mountain to earth, and the sun and moon darkened by smoke, and the earth ablaze with falling hail and fire, and a smoking abyss, and the same celestial dragon keeps appearing throughout the Near East, in Hesiod in 800 BC, Babylon in 1400 BC and so on, and Zoroaster predicts a comet crashing to Earth and causing huge destruction, this is all poetic invention, drawn from a vacuum, based on no experience? You are aware, Herb, that comets were described as dragons in the past? That a great comet has a red tail? You have actually heard of Encke's Comet and the Taurid Complex?"

Sacheverell's face was a picture of incredulity. "I can't believe I'm hearing this. You are seriously telling us that responsible policymaking should be based on a Velikovskian interpretation of history? You want to throw in the Biblical Flood? Maybe von Däniken and flying saucers?"

"This is breathtaking," Webb said. "We're dealing with a threat to hundreds of millions of lives, and you think you can responsibly ignore evidence of past catastrophe just because you don't have the balls to handle it?"

Sacheverell stabbed a thin finger. His voice was strident and the eyes behind the thick spectacles were angry. "You want to identify gods with comets and combat myths with impacts? What sort of a scientist do you call yourself? I say you're a charlatan."

"That's it, Herb, go with the flow like a good little party hack. I say stuff your cultural hang-ups and your intellectual cowardice."

Judy had frozen, mouth wide open to receive a hard-boiled egg. Shafer was grinning hugely. Noordhof, his face taut with anger, punched a fist on the table. "Enough! Now get this. I could spend hours listening to you guys at each other's throats. Unfortunately we don't have hours to spend. Now simmer down. Ollie, get to the point. Explain to those of us down here on Earth why Big Daddy is good news."

Sacheverell sat down heavily, flushed and rattled. Webb said, "Because we could spend two or three thousand years looking for Herb's Little Bears. Because we have a better chance of detecting Big Daddies further out. And because we can maybe hit a big one harder without breaking it into a swarm."

Shafer brushed his grey hair back from his shoulders with both hands. "And because the actuarial odds are that we've been hit by a few Tunguskas and maybe even a Baby Bear or two in the historical past, but civilization survived. The damage is relatively local. If you want to utterly destroy America, you have to go for bodies between half a kilometre and two kilometres across. Too little, and you leave the surviving States with lots of muscle and fighting mad."

"You guys are wrong," McNally said. "We're only fighting

mad if we know the impact was an act of war. And like Herb said, we're not supposed to know that. Look, even with the Baby Bear scenario you have an America with half its population wiped out, its industrial base gone, no political infrastructure, probably just chaos and anarchy. This is a gun society. We'd destroy ourselves, finish the job the Russians started. Zhirinovsky could do what he liked, where he liked and we'd be too busy to care."

Shafer said, "Jim, you just want a Baby Bear because it's easy to shift."

Noordhof lowered his head pensively. Then he said, "I go with McNally. The uncertainties are too large for confident statements about the political intentions of the enemy, whether to incapacitate us or utterly destroy us. We conduct the scope of our search to encompass the full range from Baby Bear to Big Daddy."

"Forgive me, but that is utterly impractical," said Kowalski. "If you want to go down to ten thousand megatons you have to reach extremely faint limiting magnitudes. Which means very long exposures even with quantum-limited CCDs. You could wait a hundred years, as Oliver says. Upstairs, in zero moonlight, we can only go to magnitude twenty-two visual at solar elongations more than seventy-five degrees."

Shafer said, "If you're drunk and you lose your keys you look under the street lamp. Not because they're necessarily there, but because that's where you have the best chance of finding them. Meaning, we go for what's practical. Extremely faint magnitudes take too long."

Webb piled on the pressure. "You're wrong on this one, Mark. The important thing is to cover the whole sky as fast as possible, and keep covering it until Nemesis swims into the field of view. Let's just hope Nemesis is a big one. That way we have a chance of finding it while it's still far out. And we get maybe months of warning. I say we aim for full sky coverage in a week. We should go for ten-second exposures on Kenneth's supernova hunter, limiting magnitude seventeen."

Noordhof looked at Sacheverell, who nodded reluctant agreement. The soldier said, "Okay I guess I've been flamed. Forget the Baby Bears. For now."

Shafer asked, "Can you fix Pan-STARRS for us, Colonel? Give instructions for a magnitude seventeen search?"

"I'll do better. We'll control the telescopes remotely from here. We'll use encryption in both directions."

"We can spread it around," Shafer suggested. "Route it through half a dozen sites."

"Flagstaff and Spacewatch Two have preset sky search regions to avoid overlap," said Kowalski. "I'll set up the patrol to do likewise. Christ knows we have plenty of unmapped sky."

Noordhof took a cigar out of a top pocket and started to unwrap the cellophane. "Right. We now have an observing strategy. We know what we're facing if we can't find this thing, and we know we're fighting hellish odds. It's a start." He produced a match, struck it underneath the table, glanced at his watch, lit up and carried on speaking all at once.

"I know we all need a break but time's moving on. So we'll split into teams. Kowalski and I will set up liaison with Pan-STARRS and the other observatories. McNally and Shafer will come up with a deflection strategy. Do it, I don't care how. Webb will tell us why we're going about this the wrong way. Liaise with Leclerc, as he suggests. Sacheverell, you're due to brief the Chiefs of Staff and the President on the impact scenarios later today."

"What?"

Noordhof grinned sadistically. "What's the beef, Herb? You have five hours and maybe you'll even find time to shave. Prepare something non-technical, maybe a movie. This is your schedule: At thirteen hundred, you're collected upstairs by chopper and transferred to a jet at Kirtland Air Force Base. You arrive Cheyenne Peak at fifteen hundred and brief the brass. They're fixing up a little simulation and want your help. At twenty hundred you sit in on a DCI briefing in

Washington and at twenty-one hundred you brief the President."

Sacheverell, looking stunned, appealed to Judy Whaler. He tried another angelic smile. "Can you help me? Maybe with some simulations."

Judy gulped down the last of her boiled egg, gave Noordhof a look of disbelief and said, "Give me an hour, Herb. I need to talk to Ollie." Sacheverell scurried out of the room, shoulders hunched, heading either for the conference room or a toilet.

"Please can I have a helicopter too?" Shafer asked.

"Within the hour. Just keep your mouth firmly shut and that includes chatting to the pilot. And make damn sure you're back here with answers at twenty-one hundred precisely. That applies to all of us." Webb got a heavy stare.

"I've been going through the kitchen cupboards," Webb said. "Kenneth, you're brilliantly stocked with spices."

Kowalski grinned. "Doctor Negi is a regular observer here."

"We have to eat. This evening I'll take an hour and make a curry that will transport us straight to heaven. I didn't mean it that way," Webb added.

McNally said, "I don't seem to be getting through to you, Mark. No hardware exists that will enable me to deflect Nemesis a week or a month from today."

Noordhof blew one of his smoke rings. "I'll tell you why you're wrong, Jim. Because if you're right, we're dead."

Judy brushed eggshell from her well-filled blouse. She looked at Webb with wide eyes and said, "Didn't Herb do well."

Webb displayed his teeth. The oaf hadn't uttered a single original thought. He'd missed out on nuclear reactors scattered to the winds; catastrophic chemical imbalances in the atmosphere; invisible, scalding steam sweeping over doomed seaboards. He'd missed out on the typhoid and the bubonic plague which would surely sweep through surviving populations, deprived of the most basic amenities. He'd missed out on the fact that the big tsunami would hit again and again as the ocean sloshed, maybe half a dozen times or more over a few hours. Most of all he'd missed out on the cosmic winter: the darkened post-impact sky, below which nothing would grow; the freezing gales which would turn what was left of America into a blasted Siberian wasteland in the weeks following the crash; and the terrifying risk of a climatic instability which would close down the Gulf Stream and switch off the monsoon, bringing calamity far beyond American shores.

On the other hand, Webb thought, quite a few of these things had been missed by others; and he had to admit Sacheverell had done a moderately competent Internet search. For an idiot.

And now, Webb thought, everybody knows what to expect and it's simple. There will be little warning. A huge burning mountain will be thrown to earth; it will set the earth ablaze with falling hail and fire; it will darken the sun and moon; and it will plunge us into a smoking abyss.

Vincenzo's Woman

The sky was still dull blue, and a light early morning mist was hugging the Tuscan fields, when the soldiers of Christ came for Vincenzo.

The monk was awakened by a violent shaking of his shoulders. His woman was over him, her grey hair brushing his face and her eyes wide with fear. "Vincenzo! Robbers!"

He threw back the sheets and ran to the window, pulling open the shutters. Horses were clattering into the courtyard below.

There was a heavy thump from below. It shook the house, and came again. The woman screamed, but the thump-thump continued, and then there was the sound of splintering oak, and running footsteps on the marble stairs. A youth of about sixteen ran into the room. He wore a white jerkin, a white cap and striped black and white tights. He was breathing heavily, had an excited gleam in his eyes, and he was carrying a short, broad-bladed sword. It looked new and unused. He stared at Vincenzo and then turned his eyes to the woman. He seemed uncertain what to do next. He was staring excitedly and kept swinging the sword.

An older man, stocky and bearded, followed him into the room. "Get dressed!" he ordered Vincenzo, ignoring the woman. More men ran in. They started to haul open drawers and cupboards, flinging clothes on to the floor and overturning chairs and tables which got in the way. Vincenzo's woman threw on a woollen dress, and then grabbed the young man's arm. Flushing with humiliation, he turned to hit her but stopped as a man, dressed in a long dark cloak embroidered with golden crucifixes, stepped into the bedroom.

The man approached the old monk. "Vincenzo Vincenzi, son of Andrea Vincenzi of Padua, you are under arrest."

"Why? What have I done?"

"You are being taken to Bologna, where you are to be tried for heresy."

The woman screamed in fright, and settled down to a torrent of abuse delivered in an increasingly excited voice. The old monk tried to pacify her and finally persuaded a terrified maidservant, peering round the door, to take her down to the kitchen.

The monk had hardly finished buckling his tunic when they bundled him downstairs. An open carriage was waiting. Early morning dew was beginning to steam off the red pantiled roofs where the sunlight touched them. A cluster of servants, some of them half-dressed, gaped from the shadows of a cloister. As the carriage clattered out of the courtyard, Vincenzo looked back and glimpsed a cart into which his notebooks and instruments were being tossed—including his perspective tube which, they were later to say, had been invented by the heretic Galileo if not by Satan himself. Minutes later the soldiers, clearly in a hurry, mounted up and galloped out of the courtyard, the cart rattling noisily over the cobbles.

Vincenzo's mistress had dashed out of a back door from the kitchen just as the soldiers were leaving the front, fleeing along a broad gravel path through a garden scattered with cypress and myrtle trees, statues and tinkling fountains. She ran the two kilometres to her brother's house and arrived in a state of near collapse. Her brother, a prosperous wool merchant, had a stable with half a dozen horses. A servant saddled one up and she set out for Florence, forty kilometres away, trailed by her brother whose horsemanship was constrained by age and gout. Entering the city through the Gate of the Cross, with the exhausted horse slowed to a trot, she headed for the city centre. She used Brunelleschi's cathedral dome and the tall bell-tower of the Old Palace as landmarks to find her way to the *Ponte Vecchio*. Across it, at the Grand Ducal Palace, she dismounted and tied the horse to an iron ring next to a window.

A soldier with a pikestaff, his tunic bearing the fleur-de-lys of the Medici family, stood at an archway. She approached, almost too breathless to speak. "I must have an audience with His Highness."

The soldier stared with astonishment, and then laughed. "Franco! Come here. Your grandmother wants a word with the Duke. Maybe he didn't settle up last night." A stout man appeared from within, his mouth stuffed and a thick sandwich in his hand. He took in the work-worn hands, the wrinkled face and the cheap woollen dress at a glance. "Try the back entrance. He's helping out in the kitchens."

The woman held her hand to her side in pain. "Deny me access, with what I have to tell him, and he'll have you disembowelled and tossed in the Arno."

The sandwich man's amused expression gave way to an angry glare. "Don't talk to me that way, bitch. Just what do you have to tell him?"

"The words are for His Highness, not his dogs."

The soldier's expression of anger was replaced by one of fear. "Franco, is this a witch?"

"Shut your mouth, Steffie. You, wait there."

"And be quick," the woman said. "If you want to keep your fat belly."

Fifteen minutes passed before a tall, thin man of middle age, dressed in black, appeared at the lodge. She curtsied. He beckoned, without a word, and she followed him into the interior of the building, through a large courtyard and under another archway; a door was opened and Vincenzo's woman followed him into a small anteroom.

"I am the Altezza's secretary. And you will now explain yourself."

"Sir, Vincenzo Vincenzi has been taken by soldiers."

The man sat upright. "The Altezza's mathematician? What soldiers? When did this happen? And who are you?"

"Sir, I am Vincenzo's woman . . ."

"Ah!" Recognition dawned in the man's eyes. "Of course, I have seen you in the Poggia. Proceed please."

"It happened an hour, two hours ago, at dawn. The soldiers came. They took Vincenzo and all his books and charts, and his instruments."

"These soldiers. Describe them."

"What can I say? They all wore white tunics and caps, and—"

"Soldiers? So far you have described strolling players. Their weapons?"

"Pikestaffs, daggers, arquebuses."

"Common bandits. If they think they can demand ransom from His Excellency . . ."

"I thought so at first. But then their leader said that Vincenzo was being taken to Bologna to face trial for heresy."

The man stood up, staring at the woman in astonishment. "Impossible!" he said to himself. Then: "Wait here."

Minutes later Vincenzo's woman was standing outside a door. The secretary turned. "You will curtsy on introduction and dismissal. Address the Grand Duke as Altezza or Serenissimo, and speak only when spoken to. Now, compose yourself."

Through the door, along a high-ceilinged room and on to a broad verandah where a man and woman sat at a breakfast table with milk, bread, and a bowl of apricots and apples. Servants hovered around, one of them holding a baby. The man was about thirty. He had a bulbous nose, a thick, turned-up moustache and bags under his eyes. The woman was fat and double-chinned, and stared at Vincenzo's woman with open disdain. The man waved Vincenzo's woman over. Awestruck but determined, she forgot to curtsy and without invitation launched into the tale of the abduction. The man showed little emotion other than a raising of his heavy eyelids, and waited patiently until she had finished.

"You have done well to inform me so quickly. Enzo, see that she has a ducat or two."

"Highness, I need only the return of my Vincenzo."

"At least you will accept an escort back to the villa. And my household will repair the damage these men have done."

The woman gone, the Grand Duke threw a napkin angrily on to the table. "Barberini?" he asked.

The secretary nodded. "Who else?"

The Grand Duke snapped a finger at a trembling servant. "Get that fat pig Aldo out of his bed."

The fat pig appeared in a minute, his white hair dishevelled, pulling an indigo-dyed cloak over his red tunic.

"Sit down, Aldo. And use that contorted mind of yours to tell me what game His Holiness is playing."

"Your Grace, this is an outrage."

"Do you refer to the abduction of a scholar under my sanctuary, or to the fact that you have been roused from your licentious bed?"

"Sire, the law is clear on this matter. The Holy Office is not free to arrest a heretic outside the papal states without the permission of the secular authorities, who in this case are embodied in the person of Your Grace. This need for permission is particularly so if extradition is involved. This arrest is a gross violation of accepted procedure and an unlawful intrusion on your authority and property. An insult compounded by the fact that this Vincenzo is under Your Grace's patronage and protection."

"I have not yet had an answer to my question: what game is Prince Maffeo Barberini playing?"

Aldo continued. "I can think of only one reason." He paused.

"Well?"

"The one actually given. The Church does not tolerate heresy."

The secretary butted in: "Serenissimo, it is a warning. If I may speak frankly?"

The Duke nodded, but his expression warned against too much frankness.

"I too have warned you," the secretary said. "Your patronage of the arts and music is renowned, and it gives many of us joy to see you continue in the great tradition of your family back to Lorenzo. To praise man is to praise his Creator. But this Vincenzo? He is suspected of magic and worse. And Your Grace—forgive me—I have often suggested that you are too tolerant towards Jews and visiting foreigners. There are more Jews in Livorno than any other city in Italy. And many of the foreigners are suspected of being Lutherans." The secretary hesitated, wondering if he had already gone too far, but the Duke, peeling an apple, encouraged him with a gesture.

"Worst of all, sire, is the clandestine book trade. You allow it to flourish. In the past year, in the streets of Pisa, Lucca and Pistoia, I could have bought prohibited books by arch-heretics like Melanchthon, Bullinger, Brenz and Bucer. I have even seen, with my own eyes, peddlers selling Calvin's *Institutes*, Castellio's *De Haereticis*, and Luther's *Small Catechism* in streets not a stone's throw from the Duomo. These godless men bring them down over the Alps from the Reformationist printing presses in Geneva and Basel. The abduction of Vincenzo is a warning, sire."

The Grand Duke stood up and approached to within a foot of his secretary. He was plainly angry, but his voice was controlled. "My dear Enzo, in promising religious toleration I merely continue the tradition set by my grandfather. Through it Florence has flourished; Livorno is a jewel in the Medici crown. And must I remind you that my own father invited Galileo to Florence where he spent the last years of his life? Am I to be denied the same? And why have they taken Vincenzo's works? To be burned? Will they never be added to the great Library which Gian Carlo, Leopoldo and I have devoted our lives to creating? And are we to stand here discussing my political philosophy while horsemen ride off with a scholar to whom I have offered patronage and sanctuary?"

The secretary bowed. "So, Altezza. Let us intercept Barberini's mercenaries before they reach Bologna, and hang them at the roadside."

The Grand Duke turned to Aldo. "Aldo, you are chewing your lip."

"I expect they are taking him to Rome: why else say Bologna for all to hear? But that is not why I chew my lips. Your Grace, we must be careful here." Aldo paused, as if gathering his thoughts.

"Note our magnificent patience, Aldo, while we await your words of wisdom and the horsemen flee with my scholar."

"The Church sees erosion. Erosion of faith. It is being questioned not only by the northern Lutherans but right here in her midst, by men who look at the sky. She has already pronounced on the Copernican heresy. Only last year, when Galileo died, a heretic patronized by your father, the Church forbade you to erect any monument in his memory."

"Nor did I."

"Indeed. But what did Your Grace do instead? Buried the heretic's remains in the Novice's Chapel at Santa Croce. It is dangerous to provoke a wounded animal."

"The man who discovered the small bodies which orbit Jupiter, and named them the Medicean planets, deserves honour in return. And the Pope is the lawbreaker here," the Grand Duke pointed out. "In any case, what can he do?"

"He could induce his unruly relatives to go to war with you . . ."

"—God preserve me from these Barberinis . . ."

". . . and he could excommunicate you. In that eventuality

the citizens of Florence are also bound to be excommunicated unless they remove you from office. Without pardon for their sins, they risk an eternity of damnation. It could create a dangerous situation for the House of Medici."

The secretary concurred. "Some day this city will sink under the weight of its sin."

"So. I allow Barberini to tweak my nose? My legal authority to be flouted?"

Aldo said, "Better than blood in the streets, Altezza." He added slyly: "And His Holiness will not live forever."

"Aldo, you have the mind of a poisoner. I do not wish to hear more." The Grand Duke paced up and down in thought. Then he turned to his secretary. "Go to Rome. Ask His Holiness to bless me. Wish him a long and happy life. Aldo is right, as always. I do not seek trouble with the Holy Office. But do what you can for Vincenzo. I do not want him to burn."

The secretary bowed and turned to leave. The Grand Duke called after him. "Enzo, I do want the return of Vincenzo's works. Some day they must take their place in the Palatina."

"And if the cost of saving Vincenzo is a quarrel with the Holy Office?"

The Duke sighed. "Do not bring me back a quarrel, Enzo."

Piñon Mesa

Noordhof, sensing an atmosphere, said, "Okay you people, take a short breather. Then break into our agreed teams. Reconvene here at sixteen hundred."

Webb and Whaler noisily transferred dishes to a dishwasher. Sacheverell came back from the toilet. He jacked up a radiant smile. "Hey, Miss Nukey, how about some ping-pong?"

Webb experienced a moment of pure distilled hatred. Judy, however, just shook her head politely. Sacheverell shrugged, and shortly he and McNally were thrashing a ping-pong ball in the common room. Shafer had put some frozen packet into the microwave oven and was watching it intently. Noordhof and Kowalski went into an intense discussion over more coffee.

Webb interrupted them. "Colonel, I have a friend, Scott McDonald, with a robotic Schmidt on Tenerife. I could operate it from here."

Noordhof's eyes showed surprise. "You don't say?"

"I didn't know it was operational," Kowalski said.

"It isn't. It's still being commissioned, which means there's no pressure of time on it. It should be free over Christmas. I can link in to Scott's Oxford terminal, with his permission, and control it from here."

"I'll think about it, Oliver."

It was Webb's turn to show surprise. "What's to think about? We need all the eyes we can get on the sky. With a nine-hour time difference we can seriously extend the night sky coverage."

"There are security considerations."

"Mark, let's not get too paranoid. Operating a telescope remotely is what you're supposed to do with a remote telescope. The control signals will route through Oxford."

"I said I'd think about it."

Webb sighed. "It's your country." He retreated to his room, had a quick shower and then rummaged in the dormitory cupboard. There was a heavy Shetland wool pullover, left by some visiting observer. Red and yellow lightning stripes weren't his fashion statement but it was warm.

"Oliver." Leclerc startled him. The Frenchman was looking worried. He spoke quietly, almost conspiratorially. "Oliver, we have to talk."

"Sure." Webb took him into his room and closed the door firmly.

Leclerc looked at Webb uncertainly. "Oliver, there is something very strange going on here."

My opinion exactly, Webb was tempted to say, but instead waited for him to continue. But Leclerc was judging his man, clearly in an agony of doubt as to how far he could trust Webb.

A brisk knock at the door. "Join me in a run, Oliver? Or are you still feeling fragile?" Judy, bouncing up and down outside Webb's door.

"One minute!" he called out, and there was the sound of retreating footsteps.

"We'll talk later," Webb said quietly.

"We must. But only you and me. Nobody else."

Judy, in a grey tracksuit, jumped up and down outside the building, waiting for her colleagues. Webb emerged. She beckoned him over, taking advantage of their eye contact to assess him with a swift female intuition. His muscular frame and untidy, curly brown hair gave the impression of an outdoor type rather than the quiet academic he clearly was;

subtle lines around his jaw suggested a determined streak, and around his blue eyes an unusual intelligence; but at the same time there was a sort of naivety about him. She sensed that he could be humorous, but that he was also shy, even awkward in company. It made for an interesting and unusual colleague.

Webb trotted over to Judy, stretching in the crisp fresh air and the sunlight.

"This is a working run, right?" Webb said.

"Absolutely!" Judy exclaimed, jumping. "We need it to clear the cobwebs."

Leclerc appeared a minute later, taking no chances: he was wearing last night's Eskimo suit. Parisian elegance peeked defiantly over the fur-lined collar in the form of a spotted red bow tie. Webb had never before seen a jogger in a bow tie; unaccountably, the minor eccentricity put Leclerc up in Webb's estimation.

"*Wagons ho!*" she called out. They took off on a slow trot down the road.

She smiled broadly at Webb. "That was fun. What gives with Sacheverell and you?"

"Herb is a mafia hit man. He's a bully, a megaphone, a weather vane, a party apparatchik of the lowest order . . ."

"But Oliver," Judy laughed, "he's our top man in the field."

"Sure, if you measure scientific excellence by media coverage."

Leclerc was taking it wide at the hairpin bend, puffing. "Why the seething hatred, Oliver? Academic rivalry? Or did he reject some paper?"

Judy was beginning to speed up. Webb let her get ahead. "Not at all, it's because I care about truth. Herb rewrites history in a way that would make Stalin blush. He rigs conferences, stuffs his own people on committees, manipulates opinion . . ."

"Ah, now we're getting to it," suggested Leclerc. "He succeeds where you have failed to communicate your . . ."

". . . but his scientific talent is minimal. He's never had an original thought in his life. He's put the field back a decade."

"Oliver," Judy called over her shoulder, "we don't need stunning new insights for this one. An identification will do."

"Herb will try to take over this show and if he succeeds we'll screw up."

Judy was now loping. In spite of her shorter legs Webb, beginning to pant, was having difficulty keeping up. Leclerc was beginning to trail. "I think you just like a good fight."

"My dear Doctor Whaler, you malign me. I'm a quiet academic taken away under protest from an important piece of research."

"More important than the planet?"

"So, they kidnapped you too, Oliver?" Leclerc asked, catching up with an effort.

"It was more like an offer I couldn't refuse. What about you, Judy? Don't they abduct people in flying saucers in this neck of the woods?"

"No abduction. I just drove here from Albuquerque. The Pontiac is mine."

"Oliver, how many objects are we dealing with out there?" Leclerc was red-faced.

"The known Earth-crossers? About a thousand over a kilometre across. And Spacewatch are finding new ones at the rate of two or three a night."

"I didn't know interplanetary space is so crowded. I'm surprised life on Earth has survived."

"It nearly hasn't. It was almost wiped out at the Permo-Triassic. Big Daddy's a mouse compared with some of the stuff out there. Hephaistos and Sisyphus are ten kilometres across. They'd yield a hundred million megatons. But it's not a simple impact thing."

Judy was now well ahead. The men were gasping. "Bear track!" she called over her shoulder, and the men followed her off the road on to a narrow path through the trees.

"Not a simple impact, Ollie. Meaning?" The ground under

the snow was a soft carpet of pine needles. They had adopted a loping motion and were descending at a fair pace, but it did leave Webb wondering about the return trip.

"Chances are the big ones come in as part of a swarm." Webb was weaving through low, snow-covered branches. "It's more in the nature of a bombardment episode, with supercomets disintegrating to dust and choking off sunlight for thousands of years at a time. We think the planetary system is surrounded by a huge cloud of comets, reaching nearly to the stars. The whole solar system, comet cloud included, orbits the Galaxy in a two-hundred-million-year cycle. But as it goes round and round it also goes up and down like a carousel. So, we go up and down through the plane of the Galaxy. Every thirty-six million years we hit the Galactic disc."

"Which disc we see as the Milky Way," Judy said, scarcely out of breath.

"I saw it last night. From here it's brilliant. Anyway, because the Galactic disc has a concentration of stars and massive nebulae, every thirty-six million years when we go through it we get gravitational tides which perturb the comet cloud. The comets are thrown out of their old orbits, they come flooding into the planetary system, the Earth gets bombarded and we have great mass extinctions. Therefore life goes in thirty-six-million-year cycles. Old life is swept away to make way for the new."

"Not so fast!" Leclerc shouted. They stopped. Leclerc leaned forward, resting his hands on his knees and taking big gulps of breath. Webb looked up. The observatory was out of sight. Their voices were muffled in the snowy woods.

"*Alors!* All those years you mock the astrologers, and now you tell us our fate does lie in the stars. Where are we now, Oliver, in this great cycle?"

"We're slap bang in the disc now, and we're due for another mass extinction."

"This Galactic connection," Judy mused. "Is it relevant to Nemesis?"

"Could be. Some of the Earth-crossers are just strays from the asteroid belt. Herb will tell you they all are, but there are also serious people who think that. However I reckon that, because we're at a peak of the extinction cycle, maybe half are degassed comets. A comet comes sunwards and grows a nice tail so you can see it from a hundred million miles away. But after a time so much dust from its tail has fallen back on to the nucleus that it chokes off. The comet becomes blacker than soot and almost undetectable. It becomes a soft-centred asteroid."

"I see the relevance," said Judy, panting a little. "If it's a main belt stray it's a cannonball. If it's a degassed comet it's a snowball disguised as a cannonball. Get it wrong when you try to deflect it and we have ourselves a nice little mass extinction. If we have no time to drill holes in Nemesis, the big picture becomes part of the equation. Up or down?"

Leclerc pointed downhill, and they set off again, Judy still leading. After five minutes the snow began to thin and the Ponderosa pines were giving way to scrub oak, through which they caught glimpses of sunlit Arizona desert in the far distance.

"Oliver, how should we be short-listing for Nemesis?" Leclerc asked.

"Whatever asteroid the Russians used, it had to be reachable. What could they reach, André?"

"For deep space missions the Russians launch from Earth orbits two hundred kilometres high. Even with Proton boosters, their cosmonauts could not rendezvous with and return from any asteroid with an interception speed of more than"— Judy was leaping over a fallen tree, light as a gazelle "—say six kilometres a second." The men took it together like a couple of Heavy Brigade chargers.

"That means we're looking for asteroids in Earth-like

orbits, that's to say low eccentricities, low inclinations and semi-major axes close to the Earth–Sun distance. There are at least half a dozen Nemesis-class asteroids which inter-weave with the Earth's orbit. They have plenty of launch windows with δV in the range four to six kilometres a second, round trip times three months to a couple of years."

"In energy terms they are surely easier to reach than the Moon," Leclerc suggested.

"Much. We've already soft-landed on a couple. You know, we could check out the orbits of these in short order."

"Maybe the cosmonauts weren't bothered about returning," Judy called back.

That hadn't occurred to Webb. "A suicide mission?"

"Why not? Save on re-entry fuel, put it into reaching a more distant asteroid. Would you die for your country, Ollie?"

"My love of country is undying. André, say Judy is right. What δV will you give me?"

Leclerc exhaled, "For a one-way ticket? We must relax the criteria to twelve kilometres a second."

"That means they could have reached anything in the inner planetary system."

"*Merde!*" They pounded on down, exhaled breaths steaming.

"There's another tack," Webb said. "Very few kilometre-sized asteroids *could* be diverted on to us. It has to be a near-misser, a potentially hazardous asteroid that already passes between us and the Moon."

"So what does that do to your list?" Judy asked. They were now half loping, half scrambling down the steep mountainside at speed; by unspoken consent they had abandoned thought of the return climb.

"Depends how big a punch the Russians could deliver and how long a start they had. If they had summoned up a hundred-megaton punch say five years ago they could have gone for quite a few hazardous objects in the kilometre class. There are plenty of asteroids which pass close by. Too many."

"Like two trains going round intersecting tracks, Oliver," suggested Leclerc, puffing. "You only have a collision when they reach the point of intersection at the same time."

They slowed; Judy went down on her backside, and edged down some scree. Webb said, "What you and I ought to do, André, is match past Russian interplanetary probes to asteroids along their track. The further in the past they deflected it, the bigger the shift they could have achieved by now."

"Good, Oliver. You draw up a hit list of near-missers and I will see whether any of the Phobos and Venera series could have passed close to them, maybe even with a side probe fired off."

Now they were off the scree and running together down lightly wooded hillside. Inside his Eskimo suit, Leclerc was sweating, red-faced.

"Even a fast flyby," Judy suggested. "Our kamikaze cosmonauts could have—" she raised her hand and they stopped, almost cannoning into each other. "Did you hear that?"

Webb strained his ears.

"Gunfire," Leclerc said, and sure enough there was a crackle of shooting down and to their right. It seemed as if several weapons were being fired.

"Hunters?" Leclerc wondered, gasping for breath.

"The survivalists," Webb suggested. "How far have we come?"

"We must have dropped a couple of thousand feet." Suddenly, even after their exertions, the woods seemed chilly.

"Maybe we should cut off to the left and find the road," Judy proposed.

"Let's take five minutes," Webb said, glancing in alarm at Leclerc's beetroot face. They sat down on the pine needle carpet and, joy of joys, Judy produced a large bar of chocolate. The gunfire had stopped. They munched quietly for a while, a little uneasy. Leclerc got up and strolled in the direction the gunfire had been. He vanished into the gloom of the woods.

A couple of minutes later Whaler and Webb were relieved to see him strolling back.

"See anything?" Webb asked.

Leclerc gave a Gallic shrug before flopping down again. "I am not sure. Perhaps some animal."

"Let's get out of here," Judy suggested.

They stood up. The Frenchman glanced nervously back in the direction he had come. "We are lost, yes?"

"Somebody knows where we are," Judy said looking into the trees on the route they had just come down. A man of about twenty, wearing khaki and green battledress and carrying a long-barrelled rifle with a telescopic sight, emerged from the shadows. A country boy, overweight but with an abnormally thin face smeared with black. The dark eyes in the face were set close together. Webb recognized the eyes as he approached. They were xenophobic eyes, intolerant eyes; they were eyes filled with ignorance and suspicion and the superstition of centuries.

"Mo'nin'. You folks from the Fed'ral Gov'ment?" Spoken through tight, disapproving lips.

"No, we're just visiting," Webb said, slipping into an exaggerated Oxford accent. Leclerc would lay on the Parisian and Judy would keep her mouth shut.

"But y'all from up top, right?"

"The observatory, yes."

The man contemplated that, his close-set eyes flickering from Webb to Judy to Leclerc and then back to Judy. He rested his rifle on his forearm.

"One thang I kin shorely tail is y'all ferners." He paused, his face expressionless. "Y'ain't bin spyin' on us, have you now?"

The Barringer Crater, Northern Arizona

The man stood in shadow, on the floor of the giant bowl, shivering in the cold desert air. Six hundred feet above him, sunlight was illuminating a thin strip of clifftop and creeping down the rock face. He willed it to go faster, but the laws of celestial mechanics remained unmoved. A green lizard looked at him from an eye at the side of its head, and then scurried along an abandoned girder where men long dead had once tried to reach down to the nickel-iron meteorite they thought was buried far under the ground. The chopping sound of the helicopter high above faded as the small, bright blue machine disappeared over the rim of mountain.

The man turned to his companion. "Are there snakes here, Willy? I hate snakes."

"Welcome to the Barringer crater, Jim," said Shafer. "Ever been here?"

McNally looked around at the bowl surrounding them. "Seen pictures of it. Please say there are no snakes here."

"Snakes are not an issue here, Jim. Not like they are in New York, where they smoke crack and carry guns."

McNally looked relieved. "I believe you, my feel-good index has just gone up."

"Now the scorpions, that's another matter."

"Thanks a million. Why are we here, Willy?"

"I thought a big hole in the ground might lend a little spice to our deliberations. Anyway, genius makes its own rules. We're a small club, the rest of you can only look on and wonder. Let's do the tour."

McNally turned slowly like a lighthouse, gazing at the circular wall of rock which rose six hundred feet above him on all sides. Then he set out after the physicist, making for the base of the wall a few hundred yards away.

"Some impact," McNally said.

"A penny firecracker," said Shafer. "A few megatons about forty thousand years ago. There may have been people around."

"So where are we at, Willy? Do we smash it to rubble with H-bombs?" McNally asked.

"Where did you get that from, Jim, your Los Alamos Workshop or a bad movie? Say you tried that and you ended up with a thousand fragments. Each one maybe a hundred yards across and coming in at maybe seventy or eighty thousand miles an hour. The bits would drift apart slowly but they'd keep close to the old trajectory. By the time they reach us they'd come in as a spray, countrywide. Instead of a rifle bullet you get buckshot, coming in over a few hours. So you don't get a million megaton shot, you get a thousand impacts instead, each one with fifty thousand times the energy of the Hiroshima bomb. Ungood."

"I'm still trying to get a handle on this," McNally admitted.

"Think of America on the receiving end of a nuclear attack. Then multiply by fifty."

"So let's take it a stage further, literally pulverize it. Could it be done?"

Shafer started to scramble up the steeply sloping inner wall. "Depends who you listen to," he called down. "One school of thought says the Earth-crossers are just dried-out comets, maybe even just dust balls. In that case, maybe you could. That's the Webb line. Sacheverell thinks otherwise. He says they're strays from the main belt asteroids between Mars and Jupiter. In that case they could be rock or iron and no way could we deliver the energy to smash one up into dust."

"What's your view?" McNally asked.

"There was this Crusader," said Shafer, sitting down. "He wants to show off his strength to a Saracen. So he gets this iron bar and swipes it with his two-handed sword, and the iron bar breaks in two, and he says beat that if you can. So the Saracen gets a silk handkerchief and he throws it up in the air. He holds the blade of his scimitar upwards, and when the handkerchief floats down over the blade it splits in two."

"That is very poetic, Willy. I like poetic stuff, I didn't know you were a poet as well as a genius. Maybe if I had a Nobel prize too and a head full of parables I would get your drift, but you see just being an ordinary Joe with an ordinary-sized hat who's frantically trying to save his country, the significance of this poetic story passes me by."

Shafer grinned and threw a fist-sized stone playfully down at the NASA administrator. "That comes from running big bureaucracies. Loosen up, Jim, think lateral. So if the asteroid is rocky, when it comes in it hits us like a two-handed sword and we're blasted to hell. If it's a dust ball, and we turn it into a powder with bombs, the dust floats gently down like a Saracen's handkerchief and cuts off our sunlight. We could end up with a few billion tons of dust dumped into the stratosphere. If it's sub-micron, like condensation from vaporized rock, it blocks out sunlight and we go around in deep gloom. It takes a year for dust to settle out and meantime we've killed off commercial agriculture. So our food chain collapses. Experience shows that people without food eventually die. That's your Saracen option, Jim."

"If I could corner the market in canned beans . . . is that lateral enough?"

Shafer clambered down and the two men began a circuit of the Barringer crater. "Forget about pulverizing Nemesis," said the physicist. "The only way we can handle this is to

knock Nemesis off course the same way it was knocked on.
We need a controlled explosion."

"You mean use the debris from the explosion like a
rocket exhaust?"

"You got it."

"How much would we need?"

Shafer glanced at his watch. "I'll be showing some calculations. If we had ten years' advance warning, we'd only need
to shift Nemesis by a centimetre a second, about the speed of
a fast snail. The long-term orbital drift does the rest."

"Snail's pace," repeated McNally. "I like snails, right
from the time I was a boy I liked them. My feel-good index
has just jumped again. Tell me what you need from NASA.
Maybe we could just smash a heavy spaceship into it."

"Depends how big Nemesis is. I think we have to assume
a one-kilometre asteroid, enough to take out the States com-
fortably. In that case you could do it with a three hundred ton
spaceship. It would be a kamikaze mission, crashing into the
asteroid at twenty kilometres a second."

"Three hundred tons!" McNally exclaimed. "NASA
doesn't run to the Starship *Enterprise*, Willy. And we don't
have ten years, right? Say we reach Nemesis a couple of
months before it's due to hit us."

"Then you have to shift it at a brisk walking speed."

"What would that take?" McNally asked.

"Forget kamikaze. Hitting it with the Starship *Enterprise*
fails by a large margin. We'd need to eject billions of tons of
asteroid. For medium-strength rock or hard ice, we'd need
maybe ten million tons of high explosive."

"Or its nuclear equivalent. Ten megaton bombs surely exist. So we bury one at some optimum depth . . ."

"There you go again, Jim, getting your ideas from old
movies. Truckloads of mining gear, diesel engines running
on oxygen, engineers holding on to a spinning asteroid like
the Keystone Kops. No, on any timescale likely to be available to us, burial is not a practical option. We'll have to be

guided by Judy on what a surface burst can achieve. And we still need to know what the asteroid is made of. Say it had the strength of cigarette ash? You're back to the Saracen option."

"So test it on the hoof. Zap it with a laser as we approach and get the composition from the spectrum of the vapour, like the Russians did with the Martian satellites. Then use an on-board computer to work out your bomb-placing strategy as you close."

The physicist shook his head doubtfully. "Even with a nanosecond-pulse laser you'd be lucky to vaporize anything at over a hundred kilometres' range. That gives your spacecraft maybe three seconds to analyse the spectrum of the vapour, work out the size and composition of the asteroid, calculate the optimal position for the bomb and then actually get itself into a corrected position which might be miles away. Forget it."

Sunlight was now halfway down the crater wall and a light dew was steaming off, but down at the floor, the bowl was still in shadow and the desert air was freezing. McNally was beginning to feel a sense of oppression, as if the walls were closing in on him.

"How can we?" asked the NASA Director. "You're telling me Nemesis might be approaching at twenty kilometres a second. We have no launch vehicles which could get out there fast and then slow down to match an approach speed like that."

"In which case America is about to be exterminated."

"Damn you, Willy, I have six grandchildren."

"I'm just as fond of my dog."

They paced on in silence. After some minutes Shafer said: "What about your big heavyweight, the Saturn Five? As I recall it could just about match the Soviets in booster power. I know you phased it out when the Shuttle came on line, but you must still have the blueprints and the launch infrastructure."

McNally pulled the collar of his jacket up around his neck. "Sure. The blueprints are on microfilm at Marshall, and Federal Archives in East Point hold three thousand cubic feet of old Saturn documents. And sure, the old launch pads were converted for Shuttle use, but we might convert one back again with a little help from Superman. But Willy, where do we find firms to supply sixties vintage hardware? It would take so long to redesign for modern hardware and modify a pad, we'd be as well starting from scratch with a clean sheet design. You're talking years."

Shafer kicked thoughtfully at a stone. "By which time we're dead."

"Willy, there are two ways we can approach this. With an unmanned module, or a manned one." Shafer nodded encouragement, and the NASA Chief continued: "We could build fast from an existing manned module design, or even revamp one from the Smithsonian Aerospace, and get it aloft on a Saturn/Centaur combination."

"How long?"

McNally pondered. "The moon landings were a child's game by comparison. The Phase A study alone would take nine months in normal circumstances. I might cut that to three or four. Acquisition planning a month, systems engineering and testing another year. Life support systems are a lot of sweat. Absolute minimum a year to launch."

"By which time we're dead," Shafer repeated. They walked on. The silence in the big bowl was becoming tomblike.

"A shuttle carries people," said Shafer. "Stuff its cargo bay with fuel. Once the astronauts are in low Earth orbit they could blast themselves into interplanetary space."

McNally shook his head. "The Mark Three can lift eighty tons of payload into a low orbit. Even if that was pure fuel it still wouldn't be enough. Look, Willy, ideas for boosting the lift capability of the baseline shuttle are coming out of NASA's ears. Liquid boosters, carrier pods under the external tank, carrier pods above it, extra side-mounts etcetera. They all need more time than we've got."

Shafer persisted; his voice was beginning to acquire an anxious edge: "Half a dozen shuttle launches, each time with a booster tank in the cargo hold. Fix it so the crews can take the boosters and join them on to a single shuttle like Lego. Skip the test phase"—McNally's eyes widened with disbelief—"that way you use off-the-shelf systems all the way and all you need is a plumber."

They were halfway round the circumference. Another lizard scurried away from them, its reptilian legs a blur of speed. McNally threw a stone after it and missed. "I'm sorry, Willy, but you're now into fantasy."

The familiar egg-beater sound began to echo off the crater walls as the helicopter appeared, and sank down towards them. McNally waved it away with a grand sweep of the arm, and it tilted alarmingly before veering out of sight. The sunlight had almost reached the floor of the crater.

Suddenly McNally froze. He raised a hand to silence Shafer, an unformulated thought just out of reach. Then he nodded his head, and he said, "I have a very bad idea."

"Let's hear it," Shafer encouraged him.

"The Europeans have a comet soft lander. It's called the Vesta. It could reach the asteroid."

Shafer stopped. "That's a bad idea?"

"The project's well along and we're lending them our telemetry systems. Trouble is, their Ariane Five isn't powerful enough for a soft land."

"Oh no," said Shafer.

"Oh yeah. ESA are shipping Vesta to Byurkan. The Russians are launching it for them with a Proton booster." McNally narrowed his eyes. "They're building Vesta at Matra Astrium in Toulouse. If we could somehow get our hands on it, without arousing suspicion, we might lift it with a Saturn–Centaur combination."

"I agree," said Shafer excitedly. "It's a terrible idea. A new procurement policy for NASA. Theft."

"My career would be ruined. I might have to commit suicide," said McNally happily, his eyes gleaming.

Shafer stopped and let McNally walk on. The NASA Chief Administrator paced slowly up and down for some minutes, muttering eccentrically to himself. He came back, his eyes narrowed. "Willy, we could bring a bomb up on a Shuttle to save payload on the Saturn. The crew would rendezvous with Vesta two hundred miles up and transfer the bomb over before the spacecraft goes hyperbolic. Goddard and JPL could handle the trajectory planning if we ever find Nemesis. Lawrence Livermore have experience with mission sensors and the bomb. I could get the Naval Research Lab to look at the overall mission design. We have our Deep Space Network . . ."

"Don't use it," Shafer said sharply. "The Russians would pick up the ionospheric backscatter. Once this thing leaves the ground it's on its own."

"Where am dat chopper?" McNally started to perform a sort of war dance, whooping and staring up at the crater rim. "If it gets me to Phoenix I could connect with New York this afternoon and then a Concorde to Paris . . ."

"Hey, Jim, calm down. Even if you reached Nemesis you wouldn't know what to do with it. And something else. Try to acquire Vesta from the Europeans and the Russians will realize we're on to them. If you're seen within five hundred miles of Toulouse you'll trigger a nuclear strike. I'm sorry, Jim, and I'm sorry about your grandchildren, but we've screwed up before we start."

Eagle Peak, Tuesday,
Late Afternoon

"Let me get this straight," Noordhof said. "First, the West's finest brains have so far failed to come up with a strategy to find Nemesis in any reasonable timeframe. Second, even if you do find Nemesis, you have come up with no practical means of delivering a punch to it."

"Be reasonable, Mark, we're barely in the door," said McNally. There was a collective murmur of agreement round the conference table.

Noordhof sighed. "But you only have until Friday night. Where are Kowalski and Leclerc?"

"Kenneth's gone to bed," Webb said. "He'll be observing all night."

"We left André taking a walk round the grounds," said Judy. "He said he was meditating."

"Gone to bed; taking a walk; meditating. Jesus wept, do you people understand the situation?"

"Maybe you should shoot one or two of us, to encourage the others," Shafer suggested.

"You probably meant that as a joke," said Noordhof grimly.

"I'm here," Webb said happily. The backwoodsman from *Deliverance*, the one with the Fenimore Cooper rifle and the intolerant, ignorant eyes full of medieval superstition, had turned out to be a philosophy student from the University of

Arizona in Tucson, in his final year of an MS and writing a thesis on the Influence of the Platonic School on Aristotelian Cosmological Doctrine, a fact which had reminded Webb that you can't always go by appearances. The astronomer's backside was still sore from the metal floor of the student's suspension-free Dodge.

Noordhof stared angrily at the astronomer. "That was an unbelievable breach of security. What right do you people have to endanger this operation by wandering off over the mountain?"

"Nobody ever comes here in the winter, Mark. You said so."

"Has it occurred to you that the Russians might have feelers out? That a place like this might be under surveillance?"

"Astronomers visit observatories, Mark. It can be Hawaii one week, Tenerife the next, Chile after that. No security breach was involved."

"Allow me to judge that. As of this moment nobody steps more than one hundred metres from this building without my permission, except to go up to the telescopes." The soldier turned to Shafer. "Okay. You don't know where it is. You don't know how far away it is. You guess it's a kilometre across and closing at maybe twenty kilometres a second. But now the good fairy comes along and she waves her fucking wand and you find Nemesis some time in the next few days. Then she waves it again and McNally rustles up a launcher and gets a probe out to it. Okay Willy, now it's up to you. Your mission, should you decide to accept it, which of course you do, is to find some way to stop this frigging thing."

Shafer rubbed a day-old stubble. "Say it's coming in on a bullseye geocentric orbit. To miss the Earth, we have to deflect it so that by the time it gets here its orbit has shifted by at least one Earth radius. Six thousand kilometres." He moved to the blackboard and picked up chalk. A blackboard was the logical way for everyone to follow his logic, but

Webb suspected it was also the way he liked to work. "Say we intercept it a week from impact."

"A week!" McNally gasped incredulously.

"If $R_{\oplus}$ is the radius of the Earth and t is the time before deflection, you need a velocity increment $\delta V = R_{\oplus}/t$ if you want to punch it sideways. A transverse movement of say seven thousand kilometres in seven days comes to one thousand kilometres a day, or forty kilometres an hour."

"But Nemesis won't be going in a straight line. The Earth's gravity will curve it in," objected Sacheverell.

Webb joined Shafer at the blackboard and they both started to scribble. Webb got there first. "Hey, Herb finally got something right. Gravitational focusing will add to the Earth's target area. The gravitational target area exceeds the geometric one by $1 + (V_E/V)^2$ where V_E is the escape velocity from the Earth and V is the Nemesis approach speed."

"But we don't know V," McNally complained. "We don't know how fast Nemesis will come in."

"We guess. V_E is about eleven kilometres a second and a typical Earth-crosser might hit us at twice that speed. That adds twenty-five per cent to Willy's estimate. Intercept Nemesis a week out and you need to deflect at over fifty kilometres an hour."

"Okay," Noordhof said. "So what does Nemesis weigh?"

Webb and Shafer scribbled, and this time Shafer got there first: "Pretend it's a rocky sphere a kilometre across, say with density 2.5 grammes per cc. Okay, that means we're dealing with about—yes, 10^{15} grammes. A billion tons."

"To be knocked sideways at 30 mph," said Noordhof.

"Without breaking it up," Webb added. "We can't shower the Earth with fragments."

Noordhof said, "Nuke it."

McNally was looking worried. "That's what I said. But I've been wondering about the legalities of that. As I recall Article Four of the Outer Space Treaty forbids the placing or use of nuclear weapons in space."

"So how do you think the Russians deflected Nemesis? With a pea-shooter?"

"But the ABM Treaty of 1972 . . ."

"Jim, hear this. Screw all treaties. I include in the screwing thereof the Outer Space Treaty of 1967, the Nuclear Non-Proliferation Treaty of 1968, the Convention on Registration of Objects Launched into Outer Space of 1978 and any other protocols and codicils I haven't thought of or don't know about. Let's just find Nemesis and nuke it."

Judy Whaler said, "That's the kind of talk I've been waiting to hear. We can blow a big hole in its side, and use the recoil from the ejecta to deflect it. A rocket effect."

Noordhof said, "You people tell me how big a hole we need."

McNally said, "With a week's notice, nobody outside a Bruce Willis movie is drilling holes in it."

Noordhof said, "In that case you have a surface burst. We surely have empirical data from the Nevada H-bomb tests."

The NASA Director asked, "With a one megaton bomb, what weight are you asking me to launch?"

"A ton," Judy replied without hesitation, moving over to a terminal. McNally nodded his satisfaction. They waited as she tapped her way into a web site. "My home page. It's full of goodies." She moved the cursor to an icon and clicked the mouse. A table of numbers appeared.

"Here we are. The Nevada tests."

"But these are tiny explosions," Leclerc said, looking over her shoulder.

Judy nodded. "Schooner was 35 kilotons, Sedan a tenth of a megaton. But I agree, mostly like Jangle or Teapot they were just a kiloton or two. You don't want the neighbours screaming when you set off your A-bombs."

"Can you do a least squares fit?" McNally asked.

"It's been done." She clicked again, and a graph appeared on the screen. Shafer got there first: "So, if we believe the fit, a one-megaton surface bomb excavates a crater six or seven

Bomb	yield (kilotons)	depth of burst (metres)	size of crater (metres)	depth of crater (metres)
Jangle S	1.2	1.1	14	6.4
Jangle U	1.2	5.2	40	16
Schooner	35	108	130	63
Teapot	1.2	20.0	45	27
Danny Boy	0.4	34.0	33	19
Johnnie Boy	0.5	0.5	18	9
Sedan	100	194	184	98
Palanquin	4.3	85	36	24
Buggy	1.1	41	76	21
1004	125	180	200	100

hundred metres across. The crater could be as big as Nemesis. We'd shatter it."

"Maybe, maybe not," Sacheverell said.

"Let's run with a megaton for a while," Webb proposed.

"It is not enough to know the size of the crater," Leclerc pointed out. "We need also to know its depth before we know the volume excavated."

Back to the table. A red-painted fingernail traced along a row. "Jangle S was a surface burst. It had a depth about half its diameter."

Sacheverell said, "These bomb craters were made in terrestrial gravity. How can we trust these results on Nemesis?"

Leclerc was scribbling on the back of an envelope. "Shall we ignore details like gravity? If we extrapolate Judy's figures we find we could excavate maybe fifty million tons of Nemesis with a megaton bomb."

"We can also get at it from the crushing strength of rock," Webb said, "Assuming Nemesis is made of rock. If it takes

5×10^8 ergs to crush a gramme of medium-strength rock, and a megaton is 4×10^{22} ergs, Willy's bomb has the energy to excavate eighty million tons."

Shafer frowned. "Once again making a hole as big as the asteroid. Meaning we probably break it into thousands of fragments, and shower America with super-Hiroshimas."

"Now hold on," said Sacheverell. He sat down next to Judy and rapidly typed in an instruction. A coal-dark, pitted surface filled his screen. "I'm into JPL and this is Mathilde, a near-Earth asteroid. It has a crater practically its own size and it held."

"Okay, say for now that we blast a hole in its side and Nemesis stays in one piece. Would it hit or miss?" Noordhof wanted to know.

"We still need to know the speed of the ejecta," McNally said.

"So let's work it out. How fast do your nuclear explosions take place, Judy?" Shafer asked.

"The energy release is over in about a hundredth of a microsecond. It comes out as an X-ray pulse. Ground heating is complete in less than a microsecond. The trouble is, it gets so hot in that microsecond that the ground just reradiates most of the energy back. Only about five per cent goes into making a crater."

Shafer said, "We hit Nemesis with a one-megaton bomb. It stays intact. A twentieth of the energy goes kinetic. So use $1/2mv^2$ and believe André's fifty million tons of ejecta to get at v." He scribbled rapidly and Webb let him get on with it. The physicist turned back from the board. "The debris recoils at a hundred metres a second."

"In all directions," Webb reminded him.

Shafer nodded his agreement. "The horizontal components of motion just cancel. The actual orbit shifting is done by the vertical velocity component, which will be fifty metres a second. Are you still with us, Jim lad?"

NASA's Chief Administrator said, "You're telling me that

if I deliver a one-megaton bomb I can blast about five per cent of the asteroid's mass into space at 50 m/s. Times 3,600 gives me 180 kilometres an hour. So how fast does Nemesis recoil?"

Sacheverell said, "That's high school stuff. From momentum conversation Nemesis itself is deflected at five per cent of fifty metres a second. Two metres a second."

"Now hold on," McNally said. "You've just told me we need thirty metres a second."

Noordhof said, "Hit Nemesis a week before impact and you fail by a factor of fifteen to deflect it with a bomb. It looks like we need to catch this asteroid at least six months or a year out, Willy."

Leclerc raised his hands in a Gallic gesture. "But for all we know it is only weeks out, maybe even days."

Sacheverell said, "The Colonel's right. We need an early warning."

Shafer shook his head in disagreement. "We need ten or twenty years to map out the near-Earth environment down to the Baby Bears."

Noordhof's voice was beginning to border on desperation. "Are you listening? You have to find Nemesis a year out. Your own figures say so."

"Mark, how do we know it won't come in next week or next month?"

Noordhof rubbed a hand over his face. "This is bad news."

Webb rubbed off the equations and scribbled some more on the blackboard. He came back and sat down heavily at the conference table, puffing out his cheeks. "It gets worse."

Inquisition: the Witnesses

"Are you comfortable, Fra Vincenzo?" the secretary asked.

Vincenzo encompassed the room with a wave of the arm. "I have rarely seen greater luxury outside the Palace of His Serenissimo."

The secretary smiled. "Better than the cells of the Sant' Angelo. I suspect they are showing deference to your age."

"I suspect your own hand in the matter, sir. Not only do I have this fine apartment in the Holy Office itself, I am allowed access to a wonderful library downstairs. If I need to, I may call on the wisdom of St. Thomas Aquinas, Scotus and other great scholars in preparing my *Apologia*."

The secretary lounged back on a sofa. "So. They tell me you had a rough journey."

"I contracted a fever. We had to put up for three weeks in Orvieto. They say I almost died, but I remember little of it."

"The Altezza is of course concerned for you. He is also anxious that your works should not be lost."

Unexpectedly, the old monk burst into laughter. "And faced with a choice between my life and my works, which is it to be? No, do not answer, my son. Ferdinand's love of his library is known to all. And he is right. Human life is ephemeral, but my work—it may be of little consequence, but it will surely outlast these bones by many centuries. To be read and studied by men yet unborn. Can there be a closer approach to immortality on this Earth?"

"I fear they may end up on the Index."

"I have another fear. Something I fear more than death."
Vincenzo poured a glass of red wine for his distinguished
guest, and one for himself. His hand was unsteady. "And that
is the torture. I do not believe I could withstand the strappado."

There was a moment's silence. The Medici secretary
sipped the wine, and changed the subject. "All Florence is
talking about your forthcoming trial. The students of Pisa set
fire to the Inquisitor General's carriage with the Inquisitor
still inside. There was fighting at the University of Bologna
between supporters and detractors of the new cosmology.
The authorities called in the mercenaries."

"That is bad news for freedom of thought."

"And worse news for you, Vincenzo. The Church may
feel that it has to make an example."

"Is there no place in Europe where a thinking man can be
safe? They say that Calvin even set aside Geneva's laws to
have Servetus burned alive. Bruno met the same fate in this
city forty years ago."

"And you repeat not only the Copernican heresies, but also
those of Bruno. What a foolish old man you are, Vincenzo
Vincenzi." The secretary stood up. "I will be at the Villa
Medici in the Pincio for a few weeks. I have asked His Holiness to bring you to trial within days if possible. You have the
right to an *advocatus*, which the Duke will pay for. I have
made enquiries. You will be defended by a man of good family. He is young, but already well spoken of amongst the business community of Rome." He turned at the door. "If you fear
the torture, Vincenzo, put yourself in his hands."

On the second day of his nominal imprisonment an earnest,
round-faced young man, wearing lenses in a wire framework
perched on his nose and curled behind his ears, knocked and
entered Vincenzo's apartment carrying a pile of papers.

Keenly aware of his rising reputation, Marcello Rossi

regarded the defence of Vincenzo as both an honour and a hazard. The honour lay in the fact that the great Medici family had chosen him. The hazard lay in the fact that the defence of an obviously guilty heretic, if pursued too vigorously, could lead to his own arrest on suspicion of holding the same forbidden beliefs. Between Medici and Pope he would have to exercise extreme care, or be crushed like a fly between two colliding rocks.

Vincenzo's new advocate came with bad news: the Grand Inquisitor for the trial was to be Cardinal Terremoto. A massive, heavy-jowled man with small piercing eyes and tight, thin lips, his face was so fierce that its appearance was said to have struck terror into a visiting Spanish conquistador. Terremoto was an arch-conservative, a distinguished Jesuit theologian who had studied at Louvain in Belgium in order to familiarize himself with the heresies which prevailed in the North. A man of formidable intellect, he had shown himself zealous in rooting out the heresies which increasingly threatened the Mother Church.

The facts, Marcello Rossi quickly established, could not be disputed. Vincenzo openly declared his belief in the Copernican system whereby the Earth orbited the Sun and was not at the centre of the Universe. The charge against Vincenzo, that he held these opinions, was therefore no more than a plain description of the truth. And since the Holy Inquisition had, in the trial of Galileo some years before, established that the aforesaid beliefs were heresy, denial of the charge would be futile. Vincenzo's only hope was to abjure the heresy, believe all that the Holy Catholic Church told him, and throw himself on the mercy of the Inquisitor. This the young man strongly advised the old one to do.

His reasoning was sound; but he had reckoned without the stubbornness of his client.

Succinctly, Marcello explained the procedures of the Inquisition to Vincenzo. The trial will be held in secret. Evidence will be presented through prosecution witnesses. You will not be permitted to question these witnesses. You will then be interrogated. If by the end of the interrogation you have not confessed, or disproved the charges, you will be given time to prepare your defence. At that stage, you may call witnesses. But if at that stage you still persist in denial, the young advocate told Vincenzo, nobody will dare enter the courtroom to defend your heresies. The only witnesses who might be persuaded to appear will be those attesting to your upright character and piety. Do you have such? Vincenzo requested Fracastoro of Pisa, an old friend who had known Foscarini of Calabria, the supporter of Galileo. The advocate wrote the name down, and said he would submit it to the Grand Inquisitor.

In what circumstances would the trial proceed to torture? Vincenzo asked, in a voice tinged with fear.

You will be tortured if the evidence indicates guilt which you continue to deny, or if it is thought that your confession is not wholly sincere. Since your guilt is transparent, Marcello said, your only recourse is to purge your soul of the false doctrines and embrace the true beliefs as laid down by the Fathers.

But, said Vincenzo, I believe that the Earth orbits the Sun.

But can you then withstand the torture? Countless thousands of witches, under torture, have confessed to casting spells and curses, to night-flying on broomsticks, to attendance at witches' sabbaths; and amongst these thousands of confessions, at least a few must have been false and made only to escape further suffering.

Vincenzo stayed silent, and Marcello left him to his thoughts.

That evening, Marcello returned and pleaded with Vincenzo for an hour to confess heresy and throw himself on the mercy of the Holy Congregation. Vincenzo said simply that the Earth is one of the planets, and it orbits the Sun. At the

end of the day, with the room darkening and an evening
chill drifting in the windows, the young man marched out in
despair.

The Pope's mercenaries came for him an hour after sunrise,
when the city was already alive with the clattering of cart-
wheels on cobbles and the cries of bakers selling their mer-
chandise. They conducted him down broad marble stairs and
along corridors to a small chapel, where he received the
sacrament from a cardinal who would shortly become one
of his judges.

At the very first sight of the assembled cardinals, Vincenzo's heart sank. There were five of them, five red-robed
cardinals, with facial expressions ranging from solemn to
grim, seated at a long table made of polished oak.

After the opening prayer, and ceremonies which had no
meaning to Vincenzo, he was instructed to sit on a low bench
facing the table. The monk was shaking with nerves, and had
difficulty drawing his eyes away from Cardinal Terremoto's
face. A notary sat at the end of the table: everything would be
recorded, even Vincenzo's cries of agony should the trial proceed to torture. The courtroom itself was a tall, airy room, its
high, embellished ceiling supported by pillars. On the wall
behind the notary was a life-sized representation of Christ on
the Cross, and next to it a window which, each afternoon,
would send sunlight slanting into the great room. Through
the window Vincenzo could see the tree-covered hill of
Monte Mario, framed on a light blue sky. Sheep were scattered over the hillside; a couple of shepherd boys were playing some game. It was a tranquil picture, far removed from
the dark clash between world systems being played out in his
own small world.

The first witness of the trial wore the pill-box hat and
long cloak of a professor. He had a neat white beard, and he
carried himself with the appropriate air of authority. He an-

nounced himself as Andrea Paolicci, Professor of Natural Philosophy and Theology at Padua University.

Terremoto opened the questioning. The Cardinal had a deep bass, resonating voice, as if it came from the depths of a crypt. He hunched forward slightly as he spoke, his small dark eyes glittering intensely. "Doctor, do you accept that the use of eye and mind is a legitimate route to the interpretation of Nature?"

"We may approach the Mind of God through all His Works. That is, not only the Sacred Book, but also through His Architecture."

"And that there cannot be a contradiction between the two, the Book of Scripture and the Book of Nature?"

"Clearly not."

"You have studied the Copernican beliefs?" Terremoto asked.

"I have, from the perspectives both of natural philosophy and of faith."

"It is your philosophical perspective which we seek. Doctor, do you find it tenable that the Earth is a spinning ball, a planet like Jupiter and Saturn, orbiting the Sun, with the Sun at the centre of the Universe?"

The Doctor smiled slightly. "I do not. The Copernican system is impossible. The world is fashioned as described in the Bible and as it was understood even before the days of Our Lord, by men of the greatest wisdom and enlightenment. I refer in particular to the teachings of Aristotle."

"But you reach this opinion on the evidence of natural philosophy, and not simply of faith, or from the opinion of scholars from antiquity?"

The Doctor bowed affirmatively.

"Perhaps we can begin with the hypothesis of a rotating Earth," said Terremoto. "What is your objection to this?"

The Doctor explained, glancing at Vincenzo from time to time as if justifying his position to the old monk. "If the Earth truly rotated, what would happen to the air? There

would be a violent, endless wind. All bodies not in contact
with the ground would rush off in one direction. A falling
stone would shoot off to the side as it left the hand. And yet,
to the greatest precision which the eye can detect, and from
the highest towers which we have, a stone falls straight
down. There is no perceptible deviation from the vertical.
The Earth must therefore, of necessity, be stationary, in ac-
cordance with the evidence of our own senses."

"And the Sun as the centre of all things? With the Earth
orbiting it?"

"If the Earth truly orbited the Sun, as Copernicus
claimed, then the stars above would reflect this motion. Over
the course of a year, each one would seem to move in a small
path in the sky. A star at right angles to the zodiac would
trace out a circle. One in the zodiacal plane would be seen to
move backwards and forwards in a straight line. At intermediate celestial latitudes the stars would trace out ellipses. No
such motion can be seen. Therefore the Earth cannot possibly be orbiting the Sun."

"What of the hypothesis that the stars are like the Sun?
That they are not confined to a sphere but scattered through
infinite space?"

"If this were so, the stars would be at different distances
from us. In that case the parallax effect which I have described would result in the constellations changing shape
over the course of a year. They clearly do not. The Bear,
Cassiopeia and Orion are unchanging in the sky. The eye
and the mind are thus in harmony with the sacred teachings.
The outermost limits of the World are set by the crystalline
sphere in which the stars are embedded."

"What then is your opinion of the structure of the World?"

"The structure of the Universe reaches its most perfect
description in the *Summa Theologica* of Thomas Aquinas.
The greatest imperfection exists here on Earth. But when we
die, the souls of the blessed travel upwards through the heavenly spheres, each sphere of heaven being more perfect than

the one before. Heaven, and God, with Christ at His right hand, lies beyond the sphere of fixed stars described by Aristotle. Three orders of angels exist here on Earth, three in the intermediate region, and three in the outermost heaven."

Another cardinal, Mattucci, asked: "But are the complicated wanderings of the planets over the sky not best explained by the heliocentric doctrine? Do they not account for the retrograde motion of Mars as an optical illusion caused by an overtaking Earth? And is the system of Ptolemy not inferior in this respect?"

The professor said, "I cannot deny that in calculating the positions of the planets the Ptolemaic system is complicated. But even as a mathematical contrivance, the Copernican system works poorly. Copernicus created it on the basis of only a handful of observations. Further, my studies reveal that those observations are not reliable. Many of them have been corrupted by frequent copying from Ptolemy. The latter's records are a mighty river to Copernicus's trickling stream. The worst aspect of the Copernican hypothesis is the introduction of a moving centre for the Earth's orbit, a completely arbitrary device whose sole purpose is to save the hypothesis."

Mattucci persisted: "But the system is improved, is it not, by the invention of Johann Kepler that the planets move in ovals?"

"Have I a friend in court?" Vincenzo whispered.

Marcello wrinkled his nose sceptically.

The professor said, "That postulate can be made, but only as a computational device, not as a description of reality. Ellipses lack the appeal of circular symmetry. They destroy the harmony of the spheres. And for the planets to pursue these shapes, Kepler postulates the existence of occult forces proceeding from the Sun whereas, of course, the stars and planets are moved by angels."

The Cardinal Mattucci leaned back to show that he was finished with the questioning. Terremoto took it up. "Doctor

Paolicci, apart from the deficiencies of the heliocentric doctrine, which you have so clearly described, do your eyes and mind give you positive reasons for adhering to the Ptolemaic system?"

Paolicci allowed himself a brief, sly glance at Vincenzo. "It follows logically from the rational nature of the Creator. It cannot be denied that a rational, omnipotent Creator will build a perfect Universe. Of course the Prince of Darkness then induced the Fall from Grace, which is an imperfection, but that exploits the weakness of Man and does not affect the structure of the Universe. Only one object has perfect symmetry, in the three dimensions of length, breadth and height which we inhabit. That is a sphere. A perfect Universe built by a rational Creator must therefore be spherical. And only one type of motion is natural in a spherical universe, and that is circular motion. Otherwise the symmetry would be broken. That is why, of logical necessity, planetary motion must comprise circles, and circles upon circles."

"You do not, then, accept the Bruno hypothesis that the Universe is infinite?"

"An infinite Universe is unthinkable."

"And the plurality of worlds? Men on Bruno's planets?"

"Such could not have been descended from Adam, nor could they obtain Christ's redemption."

Cardinal Borghese took up the questioning. He looked at the prisoner and his lawyer with open hostility before turning to the professor. "Doctor, you have told us that no contradiction is possible between science and faith."

"No Christian can believe otherwise."

"And if a contradiction were to arise?"

"Eminence, with respect, since no such contradiction is possible, your question is without meaning."

"An apparent contradiction, then?"

"Since actual contradiction is impossible, the appearance of it can only arise in the mind of the Turk, or the Jew, or the heretic."

Borghese turned to the notary. "Let it be recorded that Vincenzo is neither a Turk nor a Jew."

A succession of witnesses from universities in Bologna, Pisa, Naples and Venice was then summoned, all saying much the same thing. By midday the room was becoming hot and stifling, and the court was adjourned for four hours.

In the apartment, the young advocate flopped on to the same settee which the Grand Duke's secretary had occupied the previous week. "You have an impressive list of enemies," he said.

Vincenzo gestured with open palms. "Academics are prone to jealousies. And much is at stake. But I also have many supporters."

"Unfortunately, Father, your supporters dare not support you in court, while your enemies appear to have gained the ear of Boniface. Why else would you be on trial?" Marcello reached for an apple in a bowl and started to toss it playfully in the air. "Your old friend Fracastoro—the acquaintance of Foscarini."

"Yes?"

"He is refusing to testify on your behalf, even on the matter of your piety and character. My courier tells me the man is terrified."

"Have I no friends?" Vincenzo asked in despair.

"Perhaps one. The Cardinal Terremoto was told of your predicament with regard to witnesses. At once he instituted a diligent search and has at last found someone willing to testify to your character. I did not find your friend's name."

"Thank God for a small blessing. But it seems I will have to make the scientific case myself."

The advocate took a bite at the apple. "A case which has already been rejected by this same Congregation when Galileo tried to make it a few years ago. Confess to error, Vincenzo. The alternatives are too horrible even to mention."

"Can I retract the truth, my son?" Vincenzo headed for a small bedroom off the apartment. The advocate put the apple core in the fruit bowl, loosened the belt around his stomach and stretched out on the couch.

The court convened again in the late afternoon. A clerk awakened them and led the old astronomer and his lawyer down the stairs and along the corridors.

There was only one witness. A small, stooped man in priest's habit, with a hooked nose and dark, blotchy skin, hurried into the room. Vincenzo turned to Marcello Rossi in alarm. "Grandami!" he whispered. "What is that man doing here?"

"He is your character witness."

"What? But this man is my sworn enemy. He hates me. Who has done this to me?"

"Terremoto."

At that moment, Vincenzo knew he was doomed.

The Martians

Then it reached them.

The two generals and the civilian watched from the comfort of their brown leather armchairs as the combat crew frantically checked through their systems, mag tapes spinning and a babble of messages flooding in. The winking red lights had vanished from the map. The lists of refuelling points and aircraft aloft reappeared. The Blackjacks were almost home. The MiGs were far out over the Sea of Japan. The Kola peninsula was deserted. Winton was cool, Pino was grey and sweaty. Hooper, the Chairman of the Joint Chiefs of Staff, noted with disapproval that someone was hyperventilating.

A telephone rang, the pink one. Wallis observed his own hand trembling as he picked it up.

General Cannon was looking down, telephone to his ear. "Put me on loudspeaker." Wallis pressed a button and the general's voice boomed round the room. "April Fool," it said.

"Sir?" said Wallis, looking up at his commanding officer. Mortified, Wallis found that his voice was as shaky as his hand.

"Somebody just stamped on the mountain. Roof sheared clean off and fell on you. You're dead, son."

"General Cannon, what was that?"

"Martians," the voice boomed.

"Men from Mars?" Incredulously. The combat crew, to a man, stared up at the general.

"Affirmative."

"Sir, Martians aren't allowed. They're not in SIOP."

"Foggy, how do you know there are no little green men out there? We wanted to test how the system reacted to something crazy and the only way was to spring it on you. Operation Martian Scenario. Y'all did just fine. We have you on home movies and it's a whole lot of use to us upstairs. You and your crew'll have a full debriefing at the end of this shift. Then maybe you'll want to get drunk."

Wallis was aware of the eyes of his combat crew on him. In the confines of the steel office, the rage, fear and bewilderment were tangible. He took a deep breath and a chance with his career. "General Cannon, sir, with respect. Damn you to hell."

There was an electric silence. Then a deep, genie laugh echoed round the office. "Son, I'm already there."

"Doctor Sacheverell, your assessment?" Cannon asked.

"I'll need to run a few Monte Carlo simulations. But at a first guess I'd say prompt casualties two hundred million. Dead that is," said the civilian. "Two sugars, please."

"Nice one," said Cannon, pouring coffee. "You've solved the population explosion."

"We'd be looking for a few survivors in freak conditions," Sacheverell continued. "People down mines, stuff like that. Material devastation with this scenario is quite severe though. Maybe cities reduced to dust or rubble over fifty per cent of mainland USA."

Hooper and Sacheverell might have come from different planets. Whereas Sacheverell was thin and stooped, Hooper, the Chairman of the Joint Chiefs, was almost as wide as he was tall. Where Sacheverell had a greasy complexion, Hooper had a deeply wrinkled, tanned face. Where the astronomer had a shock of vertical red hair and a headband, the soldier's hair was short, white and fine. Where Sacheverell dressed like a basic slob, with an untidy grey suit and garish red tie on a turquoise shirt, the soldier was immaculate. And where Sacheverell was stirring coffee, Hooper banged a fist angrily. Coffee spilled into the saucers. "Almighty Christ, am I supposed to believe this? Rubble? *Dust?*"

"And there's no question of any industrial or political infrastructure surviving," Sacheverell added, hastily picking up cup and saucer.

"Cool it, Sam. Doctor, talk about the C-cubed systems," Cannon said.

"With this particular scenario, they collapse. But it is a bit way out and in general I can't be sure. I'd have to get into some heavy analysis on ionospheric plasmas and I don't have time for that." Nor the competence, Sacheverell added to himself. "I guess you have to expect a big electromagnetic pulse over most of the country."

"This is pure crap," Hooper said, flipping through the pages of Sacheverell's hastily constructed scenario. "Our command systems are nuclear hard." In a flash of inspiration, Judy Whaler had laid the report out like a film script, fictitious descriptions of fireball impacts linked together with phrases of the "Meanwhile in San Diego" type. Appended to the Hollywood scenario, and bearing as much resemblance to it as Dr. Jekyll to Mr. Hyde, was a spartan appendix written in the measured language of science, liberally sprinkled with equations, tables, ifs and buts. The CJCS, Sacheverell noticed, was sticking to the film script.

"Not hard enough," Sacheverell said. "A successful Russian first strike only delivers five thousand megatons, most of that near the ground. For all we know there's a million megatons on the way in. Even at one per cent efficiency, that's like a million amps under a potential of a million volts flowing overhead for ten seconds."

Cannon stirred his coffee thoughtfully. "That would melt your fillings, Sam."

Hooper shook his head angrily, as if rejecting the whole

concept. "PARCS and PAVE PAWS would have picked your asteroid up on the way in."

Sacheverell shook his head too. "Your radar software filters out signals with long delay times, so you only pick up stuff very near the Earth. It wouldn't have shown up on the radars until the last minute."

"So? We'll re-programme."

"You could, at the risk of swamping the computers with small space junk. Even so military radars have a limited range. By the time they detected the asteroid it would be a couple of hours from impact, far too late to stop it. Anyway, you have practically nothing covering the southern sky."

Cannon said, "Look, Sam, anything we got into the air would get its wings ripped off even if we were C-cubed operational. This applies to TACAMO as much as Bomber Command. I can't even guarantee we could contact Mitchell's Trident fleet in time."

"Let me get this right," said Hooper, bewildered. "Are you seriously telling me that if this thing hits we're wiped out and we can't hit back?"

"Mitchell's fleet would mostly survive," said Cannon, "but so what? The point is, the thing would just be a great natural disaster. You heard Wallis on the phoney NORAD circuit: there was no attack, no enemy, nobody to hit back at."

The Chairman, JCS, stood up. He walked over to the window and looked out through the Venetian blinds. The rasp of a Prowler penetrated the triple glazing and the room trembled, very slightly. He turned, his back to the window.

"Realistically, how much warning do we get?"

Sacheverell put down his coffee. "If it approaches the night hemisphere you might see it in binoculars an hour before impact. Assuming you knew exactly where to look. It would be visible to the naked eye maybe fifteen minutes from impact."

"Mister, what I want to know is, when do the phones start ringing?"

"When you see it as a bright moving star. Say twenty seconds from impact."

Hooper sat down again, and stared into the middle distance for some moments. "Well it sure beats the hell out of Star Wars," he said at last.

"Sam, it's beautiful," said Cannon. "The thing is undetectable, practically into our air space before we know what's hitting us. When it does hit us, we're obliterated. There's no point in hitting back even if we could because, like you say, it's just a freak natural disaster. Sam, you know I'm due to meet some senators from the Appropriations Committee in a couple of hours. I'm trying to get final approval for Batstrike."

"Which we're selling on Middle East scenarios."

"Fifty billion bucks down the tube, along with the new Grand Forks, our Navy, SAC, brilliant pebbles, C-cubed, all our surveillance systems, the whole BMDO. Everything we have, this thing beats it. And they don't even have to worry about retaliation."

"I don't believe it," repeated Hooper, grey-faced. "This is fantasy stuff."

"And we reckon they set the whole thing up for a day's defence budget."

"What's the timescale for this?" Hooper asked harshly.

"Heilbron thinks the Russians have pulled it off already," said Cannon. "It's somewhere out there now, on the way in."

Downstairs, the shift was nearly over. The normally ebullient Pino had been unusually quiet, wrestling with some inner problem. Finally he said: "Colonel, do you know anything about astronomy?"

"Not much, Pino. What do you want to know?"

"Well, are we sure there are no men from Mars?"

"Relax, Pino, there are no Martians. Vince Spearman said it on TV."

Pino seemed to be examining the arcane names on the screen in front of him. Then: "This guy Spearman—he's okay?"

"AOK. He's been checked out real good."

The sergeant relaxed.

Eagle Peak, Tuesday Evening

Webb said, "If Nemesis is more fragile than a rock . . ."

Sacheverell groaned. "You're not still on that comet crap. Ever heard of the asteroid belt?"

"Which fails to give us the periodicity in the extinction and cratering records."

"What periodicity?" Sacheverell sneered. "There is none. And how come Toutatis, Mathilde, Eros and Gaspra are rock?"

"Mathilde has the density of water. It's a friable sponge." Webb turned to Noordhof. "Colonel, Herb will tell you to plan on diverting a solid rock. But if it's a degassed comet and McNally fires an H-bomb at it, we'll end up with a dust ball heading for us. When the ball comes in it will incinerate the upper atmosphere as it slows from cosmic speed to zero. It'll remove all the ozone. Then it'll take a year to sink through the stratosphere and during that year the Earth will be wrapped in a highly reflective dust blanket. Down here we'll be in twilight. We'll have a major climatic upset. Freezing gales will blow from sea to land. The continents will end up looking like Siberia. We might cut the thermohaline circulation in the Atlantic and switch off the Gulf Stream. If we do, that will feed through to a permanent snowfall in Eurasia. That will switch off the monsoon. Nobody in Asia will eat for a year or so. You'll shift masses of water to the poles as ice and change the spin rate of the Earth. Maybe you'll flip the geomagnetic field, and set off seismic faults and vulcanisms worldwide. Then when the dust clears you'll be exposed to the full unshielded UV of the Sun, and you'll have a global catastrophe on top of a global catastrophe. Herb's certainties could do us in."

"Maybe we want to get it right before we launch a bomb at it," suggested Shafer.

Leclerc was looking puzzled. "I always thought comets had tails."

"Not when they've degassed, André. They may crumble to dust but there are plenty of well-authenticated cases showing that they sometimes turn into asteroids."

Leclerc said, "If we find Nemesis, could we tell its internal constitution by looking at it? Using Kenneth's monster telescope? What do we actually know about the reflectivities of the Earth-crossing bodies?"

Sacheverell said, "We don't. But the museums are stuffed with meteorites. They're fragments of asteroids and they're rocks." He shot Webb a venomous look.

Webb said, "You don't have comet debris in the museums because it breaks up in the atmosphere. Nemesis could be like Halley, with a crusty exterior and a fluffy inside."

"Fluffy snowballs, right?" Shafer asked, narrowing his eyes. "Dust and ice in equal proportions?"

Webb nodded. "Give or take. Try to nuke it and you end up with a billion tons of dust. Look, if we get this wrong we could reduce the species to foraging bands."

McNally's face was a caricature of dismay. He said, "I go for Sacheverell's theory."

Noordhof spoke, in a thoughtful tone. "Ollie. Do you realize what you've just said? That if Nemesis is a comet, the interests of the world at large are best served by letting the USA take it? Are you saying we're on opposite sides, Ollie?" Noordhof asked softly, playing with another cigar. Suddenly the air was electrically charged. Judy, at a terminal, stopped typing and swivelled on her chair to face them.

McNally broke the stunned silence. He gulped, "Hey, if

the Russians changed its course without turning it to dust, so can we."

Webb shook his head tensely, his eyes locked with Noordhof's. "They probably had years of a start, letting them push it a few centimetres a second, without setting up big internal stresses."

Judy Whaler turned back to the terminal. "A standoff burst! With neutron bombs!" she sang out over her shoulder, and carried on typing.

Webb blew out his cheeks with relief. "Thank you, Judy. Colonel, we just handle Nemesis with the utmost care. We use a standoff burst. Ablate a skin with neutrons."

The relief was palpable. Shafer was scribbling. "Maybe yes, maybe no. Even a neutron bomb emits X-rays and they get to the asteroid first. If they create a sheath of plasma the neutrons might not get through. I don't know that neutron bombs would help."

She swivelled on her chair. "We do bombs at Sandia, Willy. We can handle the computational side. Neutron bombs are the ultimate capitalist weapon, remember? They're designed to irradiate people, not destroy structures. Suppose instead of positioning a bomb on the surface of Nemesis we detonate it during a flyby, say a few hundred metres up. Instead of forming a crater, the top few centimetres are vaporized and blown off. The stresses are spread over a hemisphere instead of concentrating around a crater."

Shafer said, "So we bathe the asteroid with neutrons and X-rays. And if it turns out to be a comet, we might still do it gently enough to preserve its structure."

Noordhof asked, "Can we do it? Can we do it?"

Webb suggested, "Try a one-megaton burst at five hundred metres' altitude and suppose the bomb energy is all in neutrons."

Judy unconsciously swept her blonde hair back over her shoulder and said enthusiastically, "Neutrons get absorbed within twenty centimetres. If they just passed through you they wouldn't do damage. It's because they get absorbed within your body that they make such brilliant weapons. The energy will be deposited in a top layer of Nemesis around the thickness of a human body." She turned back to her terminal.

You're a bundle of fun, lady, Webb found himself thinking.

Shafer drew a circle and a point some way off, and tangent lines from point to circle. Webb saw what was coming and tried to keep up on a sheet of paper. Shafer said, "Give Nemesis a radius R and put the bomb a distance d from its centre. We need to know how much of the bomb's energy is intercepted by Nemesis." He scribbled rapidly and said, "Seen from the bomb Nemesis fills $\pi R^2/4\pi d^2$ or $1/4(R/d)^2$ of the sky."

McNally said, "If we explode the bomb five hundred metres up, like Ollie says . . ."

Shafer continued, "Then we have $d = R$ and a quarter of the bomb energy is dumped on the facing hemisphere of Nemesis. That's good. Now let's skip the detailed trig and suppose the irradiation goes to a mean depth of five centimetres."

Webb took up the story. "So we're imagining that over the hemisphere facing the bomb, a surface skin maybe five centimetres thick takes twenty-five per cent of the blast. The concentration of energy will be prodigious."

Shafer rapidly substituted numbers for symbols in a formula. "Okay so about half a million tons of surface regolith is exposed to a quarter of a megaton of neutron energy, coming in at a third the speed of light."

Sacheverell asked, "Can we turn that into a speed?"

"Easy. Each exposed gramme gets a few times 10^{10} ergs, about the same energy as dynamite. So the surface goes off like dynamite. It turns into a vapour expanding at five kilometres a second."

"Now you're talking," said Noordhof. He was leaning forward intently, trying to follow the rapid exchanges between the scientists.

"It's as if you've spread a three-inch sandwich of dynamite

over a hemisphere," McNally repeated, his eyes gleaming. "A puff of vapour expanding at five kilometres a second from one side of Nemesis. It's Christmas after all."

Webb said, "Hey, imagine exploding like dynamite when one of Judy's bombs goes off." Noordhof shot him a cold glance.

McNally returned to an earlier formula. "On the week-before-impact scenario, that would shift Nemesis at two metres a second. We're still well short."

"But we've gained a power of ten," Shafer said. "Maybe we could even use a bigger bomb."

"No," said Webb. "You'd bust it up."

"I agree with Ollie," said Judy, turning back again from the terminal. "Hit the asteroid and it rings like a bell. If you hit it so hard that its velocity change is more than its escape velocity then you'll break it up."

"Now you've lost me," said Noordhof.

"Imagine the asteroid as a fragile bell, made of glass or something. The Russians tapped it with a pencil years ago and made it ring. But now it's rushing at us and we're having to shift it with a hammer."

Shafer said, "You're forgetting that it might have internal strength. Jim, if you can rendezvous with Nemesis a hundred days before impact we might be able to deflect it in principle, maybe even if it's one of Ollie's degassed comets. Fifty days, maybe. Ten days or less and we're in trouble whatever it's made of."

McNally sounded as if he was in pain. "A hundred days? Willy, can we get back to the real world here?"

Sacheverell said, "Cracks and fissures in rock could change the whole story."

Judy turned to them, a satisfied smile on her face. "We're in."

"Where?" Webb asked, startled.

"Welcome to the wonderful world of teraflops, Ollie. While you people are handwaving I log on to God. I fix up a simulation algorithm using Sandia's own shock physics hydrocode, and they run it for me." McNally pulled the curtains half shut to cut down on stray light, and they clustered round her tèrminal. She logged in through a series of gateways, each one with a different password. "I'm using fifty million finite elements and all nine thousand processors. Give me the internal constitution of your comet or asteroid, cracks, fissures and warts, and I'll tell you what happens when you neutron it. Look on my works, ye Mighty, and despair!" She paused, a finger over the keyboard.

"Hey, you read Chaucer?" McNally asked.

Judy raised her eyes to heaven and then pressed the carriage return button with a flourish. "Even the Teraflop will take some minutes."

Noordhof, looking at the blank screen, said, "It seems to me, people, that the critical thing is the internal constitution of this asteroid. Is it rock, iron, ice or what?"

"That's the sharp end of the debate," Webb agreed.

Noordhof said, "I get the impression you guys don't know a lot about what's out there."

Webb agreed. "Here be dragons. But it's vital."

The screen came to life. Judy said, "I want to show you three simulations. Here's number one. I'm exploding a megaton four hundred metres above a one-kilometre rock with the tensile strength of a carbonaceous chondrite." On the little screen, a potato-shaped, black mass appeared. It rotated slowly for a few seconds, as if being viewed from an exploring spacecraft, and then froze in position. A brief flash filled the screen. The rock shuddered. Black fingers spread out in a cone. When the debris had left the screen, a sizeable hole had appeared in the side of the rock, which was drifting slowly off to the left. "This is very satisfactory. The nuclear deflection has worked."

A second potato appeared on the screen, identical to the first. "Okay, this one is stony, silicon oxide. I've made it a fragment of a large asteroid which has been pounded over geological timescales: it's been weakened. It has internal fissures. It's just a rubble pile." This time, when the debris had cleared, the rock had fragmented. Half a dozen large fragments, and dozens of smaller ones, were drifting slowly apart.

Noordhof said, "That looks like trouble."

Judy nodded. "Deep trouble. It depends how early we could deflect Nemesis."

"If we ever find it," said Leclerc.

A third potato materialized. "Now the last one, this is a comet with the tensile strength of the Kreutz sun-grazer. Let's see what happens." The bomb flashed briefly. Instantaneously, the potato disintegrated. But there were no fragments to fly apart. Instead, a white amorphous mass gradually filled the screen, apparently growing white hairs as it approached. "All we've done is generate a dust ball." The simulation ended. McNally opened the curtains and bright daylight streamed into the room.

Shafer moved over to the window and looked out. "I seem to remember the Sandia people carried out Tunguska fireball simulations some years ago," he said over his shoulder. "And the 1908 data were best fit by a rocky asteroid."

"But there were counterarguments," Webb reminded him. "For example the lack of rocks spalling off along the trajectory, and the coincidence with the Beta Taurid comet swarm. And with a small change in the assumed trajectory they could accommodate a comet."

Shafer asked, "What do the spectra say about the Earth-crossers?"

"There are hardly any available. They're too faint."

"Okay," said Noordhof, resuming his place at the head of the conference table. "From what you people are saying it seems to me that I can come to an immediate decision. There's too much at stake here to take chances. We have to invent something that will work whatever Nemesis is made of."

"We could play with all sorts of deflection scenarios,"

Judy said. "Solar sails, laser propulsion, kinetic energy impactors and so on. Either they take far too long to develop or they can't deflect in the time available. Only nuclear weapons stand a chance, but as you've seen they could give us a cluster of debris or maybe even—if Nemesis turns out to be an old comet—a blanket of dust and a cosmic winter."

"Hell," said Sacheverell, "even a pure rock asteroid would give us that after it fried us."

Noordhof put his hands on top of his head. "Am I going mad here? You are telling me the following: One, you will have to deflect Nemesis at less than a metre a second or it will break up and shower us with fragments. Two, you will have to deflect it at more than ten metres a second or it will hit us."

"Depending on how far out it is," Shafer said.

"And you can't even guess that?" the Colonel asked.

"How can we?" Judy raised her hands. "We need to discover the thing."

"Which brings me to Three. You have no hope of finding it on any timescale likely to be useful."

"Pending discovery, we could adopt a hundred-day guideline for interception," suggested Judy.

McNally was in pain again. "This hundred days you keep bugging me with . . ."

Noordhof reminded them: "It's not the hundred days. The White House, in their infinite wisdom, have given us until Friday night. And this is Tuesday night, and so far you people have come up with zilch."

Wisconsin Avenue, 20^{h}00 Eastern Standard Time

The *Salem Witch* screamed as she hurtled along the runway, her headlights picking up only snow rushing out from a point in the dark, and her wheels throwing arcs of slush high in the air. The screaming faded as the little executive jet slowed to a crawl. The pilot taxied bumpily along to a slipway and turned, slipping the Gulfstream in between the parked jumbos and 707s; an inconspicuous dwarf amongst the giants flying the flags of all the world.

They were in a dark corner of Dulles International Airport.

Human forms flickered in silhouette beyond more dazzling headlights. Three men stepped down from the aircraft. Two were in uniform; the third man, a civilian, was clutching a shiny new briefcase to his chest. A sudden gust caught the leading officer's hat and he cursed briefly as he snatched it back from the bitter wind.

Traffic was light and the black Lincoln Continental took them fast and skilfully into town. The driver wore a naval uniform. There was no conversation. Along Wisconsin Avenue the car slowed, turned and halted, its headlights illuminating a wrought iron double gate straddled by a metal spider eight feet wide. The spider's legs were white with snow. A second car, which had followed them discreetly from the airport, drove on. They waited while a camera appraised them from atop a gatepost. Then there was a metallic click, the spider split quietly into two halves and the car sighed on to the inner approach road. They drove through a grove of white-laden trees, lit up by red, white and blue spotlights, and effectively shielding the CIA Director's home from curious eyes and laser microphones.

The avenue curved round to the back of a large, dark house and stopped at the door of a conservatory, lit up from within and throwing an orange glow into the surrounding woods. The three men climbed wearily out of the car, which drove off, its tyres scrunching over the snow. The leading officer opened a glass door and they were met with a surge of hot, foetid air. They walked, single file, along a narrow paved path taking them through dense jungle foliage, past a tinkling fountain and over a small bridge. Colourful fish with long diaphanous fins swam in the pond below. There was a strong smell of narcissus. A slice of Guatemala, preserved in the Washington winter.

There was a sandy, cactus-strewn clearing in the jungle and an elderly man, wearing an oversized grey pullover, was sitting at a circular table, smoking a pipe. He waved them towards white garden chairs around the table. A moth was throwing a giant frantic shadow on the table as it circled to its doom around the light overhead.

The Director's wife came out with a tray of iced tea and biscuits. She had long blonde hair and the slim, elegant frame mandatory for the Washington hostess. The civilian, Sacheverell, guessed she was about fifteen years younger than her husband. She could have been on the cover of *Vogue*, he thought, about twenty years ago.

A breast brushed lightly over his shoulder as she leaned over him with the tray; the light physical contact tingled his nerves. She said, "Don't forget your tablets, honeypie." The Director growled and Sacheverell watched her slim form disappear through the French windows. The moth sizzled briefly overhead.

Sacheverell took stock of the evening's company. There

was Honeypie, alias Richard Heilbron, the Director of the CIA, tapping out his pipe on an ashtray and looking like a professor in some provincial university. There was Samuel B. Hooper, Chairman of the Joint Chiefs of Staff, a small, burly, white-haired man who looked as if he had been born radiating authority. And his companion, the gaunt, self-effacing Colonel Wallis who, with his combat crew a few hours earlier, had been tossed in a fire and grilled like the moth.

"Gentlemen, welcome," said Heilbron. "How was your Martian Scenario, Sam?"

"A catastrophe. Foggy here manages a threat assessment conference with NMCC and Offutt, they deduce that there's a blast coming from Mexico, and then they're dead. There was no counterstrike, no nothing."

"You got nothing away? Not even a Trident?"

"Not even a frigging rowing boat. If the Russians have pulled this off . . ."

"As you know we're due to brief the President at twenty-one hundred. I understand we'll be in the East Wing theatre and I've had your movie set up there, Doctor Sacheverell. What I want to do is go over the CIA evidence with you in advance."

"Rich," said Hooper, "I still think this is the most crack-brained tale I ever heard. I hope I'm about to hear some damned hard evidence."

"What you're about to hear, Sam, is guesswork. Open the folders in front of you, gentlemen. Look at the top two pages. Now this is a translation of a conversation in Russian intercepted by Menwith Hill a couple of weeks ago. It's an exchange between the cosmonauts aboard Phobos Five and their mission control in Tyuratam."

"Phobos Five?"

"Is a deep space probe which the Russian Republic launched six months ago with three men aboard. Their declared intention is to head for Mars, get into a low parking orbit, launch a couple of probes and come back in one piece. It's a two-year round trip. Ever since the days when there was a Soviet Union we've known they would try for a manned landing on Mars early in the millennium and this looks like a prelude. It all fits nicely."

The declaration of a nice fit, Sacheverell thought, came with a hint of world-weary scepticism.

Heilbron nodded towards a small cassette tape recorder on the table. "In this tape the cosmonauts are one week out. Three point three million kilometres away. Speed of light is three hundred thousand kilometres a second. Listen, and try to follow the transcript."

There was a lot of static. Every few seconds a metallic bleep cut through the sound. Then a voice, speaking in Russian. Putting their weariness aside, Sacheverell and the officers followed the script intently:

00.17.27 GROUND CONTROL. Phobos, this is ground control at 173 hours Ground Elapsed Time. We have readings that the charge in cell 7 is fluctuating. Will you check this please? (Long pause.)

00.18.01 COSMONAUT. Phobos. We're all asleep here. (Background noise.) Control, this is Stepanov. I can report that cell 7 has no malfunction that we know of. All our readings are, ah, normal.

00.18.12 GC. We may have a telemetry malfunction. As a precaution will you go through the check routine on page 71 of the manual? (Long pause).

00.18.48 COSMONAUT. (Expletive.) If you insist. Ah—a moment—(garbled conversation)—Vyssotsky tells me he checked the fuel cells this morning, while I was asleep. He says there were no problems.

00.19.00 GC. Thank you, Toivo Stepanov. I have a (garbled) display now. It says we have a minor telemetry problem here on the ground. You can go back into hibernation. What is that horrible noise? (Long pause.)

00.19.30 COSMONAUT. Vyssotsky is singing.
00.19.36 GC. Glad to hear you're all happy. We await your systems report at 175 hours GET. Ground control out.

Heilbron rewound the tape. Hooper picked a winged insect out of his tea and flicked it into the shadows. He said: "It's a bit late for quiz games, Rich."

Wallis said: "The guy on board answered pretty damn smart."

Sacheverell, who had also noticed the fact, looked at the colonel with respect. He said: "Distance is 3.3 million kilometres. With a speed of light of three hundred thousand kilometres a second, that gives a round trip, from the question asked at Tyuratam to the answer intercepted at Menwith Hill, of twenty-two seconds. It fits with all the pauses except the last one."

"I can see we're in smart company tonight," Heilbron said. "Excellent. We can use all the brains we can get on this one. Yes Sacheverell, all the pauses except the last one. What is that horrible noise? Then there's a *nineteen*-second delay and the reply, 'Vyssotsky is singing.' "

"Meaning?" Wallis asked.

"Now hold on, Heilbron," General Hooper interrupted. "Are you trying to tell me the cosmonaut answered the question before he got it?"

"Precisely."

"Christ, Sam, maybe Menwith just screwed up their tapes."

"Negative. We've checked out the technical side."

"What's your conclusion, Mister Heilbron?"

"Patience, Colonel Wallis, there's more, much more. We hadn't paid a lot of attention to the Phobos launch until then, you understand. Plenty of stuff on tape etcetera but processing it wasn't a high priority. The timing hiatus had been picked up by one of my bright young geniuses, a guy by the name of Pal. So I put him in charge of a small team, a sort of

Operation Phobos. They found this—listen. This is from a conversation three days later. I haven't bothered with a transcript. Listen to the timing pulses." They listened to the high-pitched, frightened bat, coming between the deep Slavic tones of the man in the spaceship. Heilbron replayed it several times. The military men shook their heads. Sacheverell frowned.

"It's impure," he said. "Structured." He was beginning to feel light-headed, whether from tiredness or the narcotic effect of the scented narcissus he couldn't tell.

Heilbron nodded encouragingly. "Another Brownie point for our young friend. Now here's the same timing pulse slowed down ten thousand times." He wound the tape on, missed the start, wound it back again and then played it. Sacheverell felt the hair on the back of his neck prickling as the clandestine message came over, a clear, Morse-like, intelligent signal spreading out from the circle of light, through the Guatemalan jungle, over the big lawn and into the dark woods beyond. Heilbron let it run a minute and then stopped it. He said:

"They've slipped in a burst transmission. It goes on for hours. I've had my best people on it for a week, fifth-generation machines trying to talk to it. It even beat the NSA's Cray T3D at Fort Meade." Sacheverell recalled that more mathematicians were employed at the National Security Association's Maryland headquarters than anywhere else on Earth. Heilbron went on: "The consensus now is that it's some sort of one-way encryption system, unbreakable unless you have the key. And the conversation is phoney—the voice people tell me the acoustics aren't quite right or something. What's up there on Phobos Five is a tape recorder. They're playing some sort of charade, ground control asking questions in anticipation of the answers on the tape. Only the tape carries messages and the guy on the ground mistimed, just once."

"What are you telling us? That the Soyuz is unmanned?" Hooper asked.

"Three cosmonauts climbed on board. We took pictures."

"Jesus, Rich," said the Chairman, JCS, in exasperation. "First you tell us some machine on the spacecraft is answering pre-set questions, then you say there are people on board. Why don't they just do their own talking instead of playing an answering machine?"

"Because they're not there any more."

Hooper gave the CIA chief a sceptical stare. "They jumped out?"

Heilbron said, "Take a look at Exhibit B." There was a rustle as envelopes, about a foot square, were opened. Sacheverell, baffled, helped himself to more iced tea. The CIA Director produced a small red pill from a packet and swallowed it with his tea.

"Like I said," Heilbron continued, "nobody was paying much attention to Phobos at the time and the pictures you're going to see were just filed away at first. Look at the first one. This came from the French. It's an unclassified Spot picture. What you're looking at is the Baikonur cosmodrome. The scale's about a hundred miles. Aral Sea's off the picture to the left. The river"—a thin blue ribbon wandered left to right across the picture, passing through a city—"is the Sar-Daya."

"What's the town?" Wallis asked.

"The former Leninsk. It's a hundred miles east of the Aral Sea. Following the Red Army takeover, the whole region has been closed again to Westerners. Leninsk is one of the new science cities: cinemas, culture palaces, sports stadiums and so on. They've built it on to Tyuratam old town— that's the darker colouring on the left."

"What are the arrows?" Wallis again.

"The one in the middle is the Cosmonaut Hotel. We've a first class source there, a lady who's been with us since the old days." Heilbron's pipe gurgled and he poked at it. "Now look at the next few pictures, Sam, and despair."

There was a rustle and Sacheverell found himself looking

at a large black and white photograph with a "classified" stamp on its border. Heilbron continued: "You can just see the railway line and the highway next to it coming in from the bottom. It's a busy line, all the way up from Leninsk. The big grey squares you see in the middle are the Soyuz assembly buildings. We think the ones on the left are for type G and Energia assembly—the brute force boosters. Now the tracks go further north and the railway line carries on. The next photo"—more rustle—"shows the launch complex. The little arrows show what used to be their ICBM silos before Salt Two. Mostly the old SS-X series. Forget them. It's the Energia facility that's got me running to the john. You see it in the next picture. We'd taken routine high-level reconnaissance pictures of the launch, and this was taken by a big Bird on a perigee passage. The thing that's circled"—there was something like a full stop with a white circle round it—"is a military transport. You see the launch vehicle just to the right. On the next photo you see them putting up netting over everything. They've got something to hide."

A cluster of tiny dots, each one a man, was scattered around between the vehicles. They seemed to be pulling something over the ground. "The netting's up in the next picture. Perspective has changed a bit; we're using a different satellite." The same pattern of buildings was there, but now they were throwing long evening shadows. Cloud had edged in and some of the ground was obscured. A solitary dot threw a long shadow on the ground, arms and legs clearly visible. Sacheverell thought he could detect a moustache.

"They screwed up. Look at the next one." The next one showed the netting in place, hiding truck, rocket and launch pad from prying satellite eyes. The sun had almost set.

"What am I supposed to see?" asked Hooper.

"Look at the shadows," said Heilbron. "The sun was shining under the netting. My geniuses used the outline of the shadows and the angle of the sun and they got the next picture." They stared uncomprehendingly at a large Rorschach ink blot; Sacheverell thought he saw a squid with a huge quill pen.

"Now to me this looks like an ink blot," said Heilbron, to Hooper's evident relief. "But my genuises tell me these are the shadows of four men, the rocket, launch gantry, and a lifting crane. Use the computer to deproject and subtract out everything but the thing they're lifting and *Voila!*"

"A carrot!" exclaimed Hooper, staring in bewilderment at the final, blurred computer picture.

"That's right, Sam, it's a carrot," said Heilbron triumphantly. "It's two metres long; they're loading it under netting and they're taking it to Mars."

Wallis said, "I have it." He pushed back his chair, stood up and paced up and down, staring into the middle distance. Then he came back, staring at Heilbron, and nodding his head in agreement.

"Well?" Hooper snapped.

"Some carrot, sir," said Wallis.

Heilbron half-smiled. "Got it in one. Let me tell you about the carrot, Sam. Look at the last picture. It's a nice present from our lady in the Cosmonaut Hotel."

It was a black and white photograph. It had been taken through a door slightly ajar, the camera had been held about two feet back from the crack. Three men, dressed for a Russian winter, their fur hats and coats fringed with snow, stood at the reception desk.

"The little guy with specs is local, just reception for the other two. The guy with the Astrakhan hat we haven't yet identified. But the other guy we do recognize. His name is Boris Voroshilov, former lecturer in physics from Tbilisi, now employed at Chelyabinsk-7. He designs nukes."

"Richard . . ."

Heilbron raised his hand and continued. "Phobos Five is a cover. Somewhere out there the cosmonauts have sent an automated probe with a tape recorder on to Mars on the old orbit. Meanwhile our heroes have slipped their moorings and set out into the blue yonder on a new orbit, complete with carrot. Only it isn't a carrot, Sam, it's a ten megaton hydrogen bomb."

Sacheverell said, "I know of only one application for a hydrogen bomb in deep space. Deflecting an asteroid."

Heilbron pointed the end of his pipe at the JCJS. "Tell me something. Why would Zhirinovsky want to do a thing like that?"

Hooper's face was like an executioner's.

The CIA chief hammered it home: "Sam, we're going to get it right in the Kansas breadbasket."

Inquisition: the Interrogation

The priest settled into the witness's chair. The notary said: "Identify yourself to this Congregation."

"I am Jacques Grandami, of the Jesuit Order. I teach theology and natural philosophy at a number of colleges in France."

Terremoto began the questioning: "You are acquainted with Vincenzo Vincenzi?"

Reptilian eyes flickered briefly in Vincenzo's direction. "I know him from the school of theology in Paris, and later in Bologna."

"What is your opinion of the man?"

"He claims to be devout."

"Claims to be?"

"I cannot say that he is not. He has the outward appearance of piety. In Bologna he took part in the choral recitation of the divine office, and in the daily recitation of faults."

"Why then do you seem to hesitate over his piety?"

"He is extremely disputatious, lacking the spirit of humility. He scorns reasoned argument which does not fit his opinion. He thus shows manifest contempt for the arguments of Scheiner, Ciermans, Malapert and other Jesuits against the Copernican system, which he advocates even though, as this Congregation knows, it has been condemned as false. Komensky of Prague, in his *Refutatio Astronomiae Copernicianae*, has written a brilliant refutation of the heliocentric doctrine. But Vincenzo refuses to acknowledge its intellectual force. Instead he has spoken to me, with approval, of the Bruno heresy that the Universe is infinite and that the stars are suns, with planets and living creatures on them. In addition to his false advocacy, he is not, I regret to say, true to his order. He belongs to the Order of Preachers but does not preach. He has taken a vow of poverty and yet lives in a villa provided by the Duke of Tuscany. He has taken a vow of celibacy but shares a bed with a woman."

Terremoto made to dismiss Grandami but one of the cardinals, a man with a light freckled skin and an accent which seemed to place him in the far north of the country, stopped him. "One moment! You have said that you are a theologian."

"I am, Your Eminence."

"Then perhaps you can answer this question. What is the basis, in the Holy Scriptures, for belief in a stationary Earth?"

Grandami smiled unpleasantly. "How could Joshua have commanded the Sun to be still if it was not moving in the first place? Does the Psalmist not describe the Sun as going forth in a circuit to the ends of heaven? Does Job not write of the pillars of the Earth trembling?"

The cardinal bowed. "Thank you, Jacques Grandami. The Peace of Our Lord go with you."

The interrogation began on the second day, without preliminaries. A row of grim faces met Vincenzo as he was guided to his bench. Cardinal Terremoto opened the proceedings. His piercing eyes were fixed on Vincenzo, and the corners of his mouth were turned down in an unconcealed scowl. Vincenzo felt his legs shaking and his stomach in queasy knots.

Terremoto looked right and left. "This Holy Congregation is now prepared to question the prisoner. Before we proceed, does the advocate have anything to say on the prisoner's behalf?"

Marcello turned to his client. He whispered, "Recant, Vincenzo."

The monk shook his head.

"Recant and throw yourself on the mercy of the court. All these people want is a public abjuration."

Vincenzo's head was lowered. Almost imperceptibly, he shook it again.

Marcello stood up. Terremoto's small eyes were glaring into his own; the hostility was undisguised, bearing down on the young man like a physical force. The lawyer, fear gnawing at his heart, took an instant decision which he knew would affect his future career and forever change the life of his client. "Your Eminences, I regard the guilt of my client as sufficiently well established by these proceedings. As he persists in denying his guilt, and shows no sign of contrition for his erroneous beliefs, I must ask to be relieved of the duty to defend him."

The cardinals murmured between themselves. There was some nodding of heads. Then Terremoto said, "Your duty to the prisoner is discharged. Leave us with good conscience."

"Marcello!" Vincenzo cried out in shock. But the lawyer avoided the astronomer's gaze, and Vincenzo could only watch as his former advocate picked up a sheaf of papers and scurried out of the courtroom, eyes to the ground and bent almost double. He momentarily buried his face in his hands.

The lawyer had hardly left the room when Terremoto began the questioning. "On whose authority do you state that the Earth rotates?"

"My lawyer has sold his soul."

"Answer the question."

"Authority? That of my eyes and brain, Eminence." Vincenzo's voice was shaking.

"I ask of written authority."

"Your Eminence, the English monk Bede stated that the Earth is a ball floating in space a thousand years ago. Nicolas Oresme, over three hundred years ago, stated that the Earth is round and rotates about an axis. And the same was said by Cardinal Nicholas Cusanus over two centuries ago. They even say that Aristarchus and Eratosthenes . . ."

"Do you read Greek?"

"No, Eminence."

"You therefore rely on hearsay, do you not?"

"I rely on generations of scholars produced by the Mother Church, from Reginbald of Cologne to the Jesuit writers of today and even such as Fra Paolo Foscarini of the Carmelites."

"But amongst the heathen scholars of ancient times, does Aristotle not stand head and shoulders above the rest?"

"Eminence, you know that is so."

"And have you studied his *Physics and Metaphysics*?"

"I have, in translation, and there he commits himself to a belief in an Earth around which the universe rotates. But I believe that view to be in error."

"But did not Thomas Aquinas, four centuries ago, show that Aristotle's system is compatible with the Christian doctrine? And is not Aristotle the foundation of natural science throughout the Christian domain? Is it not then possible that the error is yours?"

"Aristotle did not have the benefit of the telescope. Nor the record of centuries of planetary motions which we have."

The Inquisitor looked down at some notes. The room was silent. The sound of a chirping cricket drifted in from the garden. And then Terremoto suddenly sprang a trap: "Do you deny that the Bible is the supreme authority in the affairs of philosophy?"

"I believe that the Bible is intended to teach men to go to heaven, not how the heavens go."

"*Ebbene!* What presumptions are hidden in that neat phrase! Are you also qualified as a theologian?"

"I did not say that, Eminence."

"You have, however, just seen fit to make a theological pronouncement. The Council of Trent, in its Fourth Session, was explicit about where authority lies: the Word of God is to be interpreted strictly according to the unanimous consent of the Fathers. I repeat my question." Terremoto looked across at the notary, who read out in a high-pitched voice: "Do you deny that the Bible is the supreme authority in the affairs of philosophy?"

Vincenzo, colour drained from his face, said, "Eminence, I do."

There was an audible gasp from one of the younger cardinals. Terremoto continued: "Is it also your opinion that the Holy Spirit has allowed the Holy Mother Church to be misled for the nineteen hundred years since Aristotle?"

Another trap, this one with steel teeth.

If Vincenzo replied yes, that the Church had received no guidance from above, then this was akin to denying the Virgin Birth or even the existence of God. If he said no, that the Holy Spirit could not have allowed such an error, then he was admitting to a wilful disregard of the teachings of the Church. Either answer would surely lead to the same fiery end. The notary leaned forward, his face screwed up in anticipation of recording the reply. The cardinals waited. The cricket outside the window chirruped on.

Vincenzo's voice was little more than a murmur: "Your Grace, that is a theological question. I am incompetent to answer."

Terremoto was relentless. "And yet you claim to be a devout Catholic. Did you not consider it your pious duty, even before meddling in hypotheses which attempt to revise the received wisdom of the Church, to ask such a question?"

"I believe with Doctor Paolicci of Padua that the mind of the Creator can be read in His Creation."

"Do you accept that man was created in God's image?"

There was an expectant silence. After the heresies they had heard, the cardinals did not know what to expect of the wretched old man who faced them. But Vincenzo simply said, quietly, "Of course, your Eminence."

"Then how can he be otherwise than at the centre of the Universe?"

Vincenzo murmured something, wringing his hands as he did. The notary asked him to speak up, but the monk remained silent.

"The alternative diminishes mankind, does it not? And opens the door to unthinkable heresies?"

"God has two books, that of Nature and that of Scripture. They cannot contradict each other. I read the book of Nature. It says what it says."

The remainder of the morning was taken up with a close interrogation on technical matters, on the precision of the Alfonsine Tables, the precession of the equinoxes, the motion of the eighth sphere, the angular sizes of the fixed stars, their lack of parallax and the fantastic stellar distances then implied in the Copernican system, and on the meaning of Christ's sacrifice to creatures on the supposed other worlds of Giordano Bruno. Terremoto dominated the questioning throughout, his deep-chested voice booming through the courtroom. He showed himself to have a remarkable grasp of the scientific issues. Only the cricket outside the window seemed uncowed: unimpressed by the Cardinal's powerful voice, it chirruped incessantly. By the time the court recessed, it was early afternoon and Vincenzo was drenched with sweat.

That evening, Vincenzo was offered the chance either to confess and recant or take five days to prepare his defence. To the Grand Inquisitor's astonishment, Vincenzo refused both options. Instead, he made a simple statement. It was brief and to the point. He hesitated briefly, feeling the weight of the Inquisition's hostility crushing down on him like a collapsing house, but then began to speak, his voice quavering but determined.

"I deny the *simplicitas* of Aristotle's universe, whereby the Sun, Moon and planets orbit in epicycles upon epicycles about a stationary Earth. Through the Galilean tube, we see that the Moon is imperfect. It is pitted with craters. With our own eyes we see mountains and valleys like those on Earth. If the Moon is like the Earth, then the Earth is like the Moon. It is therefore just one of the heavenly bodies. The four Medicean planets, revolving around Jupiter, are the clearest proof that not everything revolves around the Earth. We see too, with the tube, that Venus goes through all the phases of the Moon, with the illuminated crescent always turned towards the Sun, and so clearly orbits the Sun and not the Earth. If our Earth is a heavenly body like the Moon, and also a planet like Venus, then we too must orbit the Sun.

"This Holy Congregation has referred to Aristotle, Ptolemy and the Holy Scripture as witnesses for the central position of the Earth. Aristotle also stated that the heavens are immutable. But did we not see a new star in 1572, one which was born, rose in brightness and then died? And if he was wrong in one astronomical matter why can he not be wrong in others? As for Ptolemy, have the new discoveries of the great navigators not made his geography obsolete? Why then should his chart of the heavens not be equally so? Many wise philosophers throughout history have believed that the Earth moves and the Sun stands still.

"As to the Scriptures, we should heed the warning of Saint Augustine, who tells us not to be concerned when the astronomers seem to contradict the scriptures. It implies only that another interpretation must be sought for the Sacred Texts. Pererius, of the Collegio Romano, tells us that *non potest Sacrarum Literarum veris rationibus et experimentis humanarum doctrinarum esse contraria*. In any case, what are we to make of the words of Job: 'Who moves the earth from its place?' Your Eminences are not trained in natural philosophy and are not competent to make judgements in that realm. In the interpretation of the world, it is the book of Nature which we must read, not that of the Holy Scripture."

A tangible ripple came from the cardinals' table. Vincenzo, his die cast, carried on. "I believe that the stars are made of fire. There are many more stars in existence than those we see. The perspective tube of Galileo resolves the light of the

Milky Way into myriads of stars. These must be suns like
our own, at immense distances. That is why the constellations do not change and the stars do not trace out ellipses in
the sky as the seasons progress: the stars are at such immense distances that the parallax is too small to be seen. You
declare that the Earth is stationary as a matter of faith, and
that I am therefore a heretic to hold otherwise. But suppose
that, in years or centuries to come, the astronomers prove
beyond doubt that it is the Sun which is stationary and that
the Earth moves around it? Then you who try me, the cardinals of this congregation, will be seen as the heretics. The
Mother Church will be exposed to scandal, and forced to reverse Her doctrine, and Her enemies will delight in exposing
Her to ridicule. Eminences, you commit a grave error in
making matters of faith out of astronomical questions."

The old man flopped down, drained. The cardinals, virtually accused of heresy, sat stunned. Terremoto's expression
had gone through all the stages of amazement, horror and finally outrage as Vincenzo's audacious statement had pro-
ceeded. Their Eminences filed out without a word.

That night, Vincenzo slept not in the luxurious apartment
of a Holy Office official, but in a damp cell in the Castel
Sant' Angelo. And while he slept, his judges discussed his
case by candlelight, and decided on their next step: the *territio realis*.

The White House, East Wing Theatre, 21ʰ00

Sacheverell sat, his stomach churning, in the front row of the little theatre. The door opened and a tall, elderly man peered in. His shirt sleeves were rolled up and he was wearing an outrageously multi-coloured waistcoat.

"Coffee, son?" the old man asked.

"Thank you, sir. Two sugars." The man shuffled out. Minutes passed, while Sacheverell's mouth dried up. Then the door was opened with the push of a foot and the man reappeared, a paper cup in each hand. He sat down beside Sacheverell and passed a cup over. The astronomer noticed that the old man had one sock black, one blue.

"Two sugars. Now before we get started. We're farmers; we're bankers; we're lawyers. Me, I'm just a country boy from Wyoming. So keep it simple."

"Will do, Mister President."

"Okay. This will be new to most of the people here. I've had a preliminary briefing from the Secretary of Defense and he tells me this asteroid thing will devastate us when it hits. But what does he know? You're the horse's mouth, son, and that's where I want to hear it from."

"I'll do my best, sir," Sacheverell gulped.

The President grinned. "What is an asteroid anyway?"

"An asteroid is a lump of rock, sir, going around the Sun just like the planets. They're a few miles across and blacker

than soot, very hard to find. Maybe there are a thousand or
two big ones in orbit between the planets. It could be half a
million years before one of them hits the Earth but when it
does you get a giant explosion."

"How giant?"

"Say a big one hit Mexico City. The blast wave would hit
us here at three hundred miles an hour. Now with an ordinary
explosion, say from a bomb, the blast is just a sudden wind,
over in a fraction of a second. But with this one, a wind following the blast would go on for hours. Air temperature while
it's blowing would be four or five hundred degrees Centigrade, more or less like the inside of a pizza oven."

"That was quite a speech, son. But I thought you said
these things are only a few miles across." The President's
country-boy grin had faded as Sacheverell had talked.

"It's their speed, sir. You have to think of it as a big mountain covering twenty miles every second. When it hits the
ground it vaporizes in about a tenth of a second. You could
get half a million megatons easy. I've prepared a movie
which should give an idea what to expect."

The door opened and half a dozen men wandered in and
spread themselves around the little theatre. Sacheverell had
spoken to two of them, Heilbron and Hooper, only a few
hours previously. Heilbron caught Sacheverell's eye and nodded. The Secretary of Defense sauntered over and sat down
beside Sacheverell. He was about fifty. Away from the television cameras, Sacheverell noticed, Bellarmine had a slightly
jaundiced complexion and a receding hairline. "Hail!" he
said. The Chief nodded amiably. Sacheverell, wedged between the President of the United States of America and the
Secretary of Defense, felt his skin tingling.

Heilbron walked over. "Mister President, I've got a
movie."

"Okay let's get into this," said President Grant. He finished the coffee and crumpled the paper cup, letting it fall to
the floor. "Seems we're in for a matinée performance."

Heilbron stepped up on to the dais and picked up a short pointer. The lights went down. Maps and photographs appeared in succession on the screen. Heavy-jowled Slavic faces appeared under fur hats. Heilbron kept waving the pointer flamboyantly. A shaky amateur movie showed a military transporter leaving some camp surrounded by a tall barbed-wire fence; another showed tarpaulin-covered train wagons being hauled across an icy, blasted landscape. When the dark conical shape of the hydrogen bomb appeared the President said "Stop!" and the movie froze, the black shape filling the screen in blurred close-up.

Grant stood up, the picture of the bomb illuminating his face and chest. "Jesus, is that it?"

"Just about, Mister President. We've intercepted a coded message from Phobos but it's got us beat."

"Rich, this strikes me as paper thin."

"Sir, we've often had to act on less. I believe the balance of probability is strongly tipped towards a hostile act against us."

"By whom?" The Russians alone? Khazakhstan? The whole damned Federation?"

Heilbron shrugged.

"Just what is the significance of this?" the President asked, turning grimly to Sacheverell.

Sacheverell put down his cup and walked nervously to the dais. Heilbron sat down wearily in Sacheverell's chair, and the President sat on the edge of the little platform, his knees crossed. Suddenly, in the half-light, the astronomer found himself facing men who had shed their homely television faces, men with calculating eyes, and ice in their veins, and powers beyond those of the gods. He fought back a surge of near panic.

"Sir, it is technologically possible to divert a near-Earth asteroid on to a collision course with any given country." Sacheverell realized with horror that his mouth had dried up, he was almost croaking. "It would take state of the art

technology and extreme precision. The technique would be
to blast some material off the asteroid at an exact place and
time, diverting its orbit. The problem would be controlling
the devastation, which could spill over into neighbouring
countries. My movie illustrates a range of possibilities.
Movie, please."

The projector whirred quietly at the back of the room.
Mysterious numbers and crosses appeared on the screen. A
black and white title read

Impact: 10^7 Mt, vertical incidence.
Assailant: Nickel iron, tensile strength 400 MPa, $H_2O = 0.00$
    by mass.
Target: Bearpaw shale, tensile strength 0.2 MPa, $H_2O = 0.14$
    by mass.

The title disappeared, replaced by a grid of lines covering
the bottom half of the screen. The only movement was a
tumbling of numbers on the top right of the screen, next to a
label saying *Lapsed time =*. The audience waited.

A green spot came in rapidly from the top. It struck the
grid. The lines buckled, and formed a hole with a raised rim.
Green splodges hurried off the edge of the screen. Away
from the hole the grid of lines was vibrating at high speed,
like a violently shaken jelly. The lines vanished and there
was an old movie taken at the Nevada test site. There was a
timber-framed, Middle America house. At first, nothing was
happening. But then the paintwork started to smoke, and curtains were burning. And suddenly the house was splintered
wood and smoke streaking into the distance and Sacheverell
was saying this is what to expect a thousand kilometres away.

Now there was a coloured map of the USA, with cities
marked in bold font. Circles were radiating out from a spot in
the middle of Kansas, like ripples on a pond, as if the map
were under water. The numbers were loping along in minutes now, rather than seconds, and Sacheverell was saying

you expect Richter Nine up here on the Canadian border and down here in Chicago. The map disappeared and more old footage followed; this time the camera was panning over horribly flat rubble. A few dazed individuals in Arab dress stared at the camera. Others were crawling over a mound of debris, like ants over a hill. Sacheverell was saying of course these are stone houses and we can't be sure this applies exactly to New York or Chicago but you would surely cause massive destruction coast to coast. He was aware that he was beginning to gabble but he couldn't help himself. His voice was now a croak.

Then of course there's the fire, he said, rising to the tension he sensed in his audience. About thirty per cent of the land area of the States is combustible in the summer and twenty per cent in the winter. You would expect thousands of fires over an area the size of France. They could merge into one giant conflagration so you would take out the whole of central USA with flames from the exposure to the rising fireball and this is Hamburg during a firestorm only with red hot ash thrown over the whole country you might set the whole country alight and then of course there's the biomass the biomass yes especially as fat melts at forty-five Centigrade I mean Celsius but they're the same really you expect living people to fry in their own fat over most of the States your skin will bubble and peel off in a few seconds and then your blood and water will boil and then your fat will combust and you will just carbonize while the blast is sweeping you along at the speed of a jet.

The audience sat riveted.

Now the movie was showing something that looked like one of the more lurid products of a Hollywood studio. An ocean was boiling. Now the boiling green lines formed into a pattern; they reared up into a wave, a tumbling, foaming breaker which washed over little cartoon skyscrapers like a wave over pebbles, and Sacheverell was saying we're not sure about the stability of waves that big but we're working on it with the Sandia teraflop but a splash like this off the Eastern seaboard would wash over the Eastern States but the Appalachians would stop it and you would be okay in Bozeman, Montana. Then there were more flashing symbols, the projector stopped whirring and the lights went up. Sacheverell swallowed nervously, blinking in the light.

His audience remained frozen.

"You got casualty estimates for this, son?" The President finally asked, quietly.

"Hard to judge, sir. Most of the USA is less than two thousand kilometres from Kansas. A million-megaton bang on Kansas I reckon would leave two hundred million casualties from the prompt effects."

"You mean injured?"

"No sir, dead."

"What about survivors?" the Vice-President asked.

"With this scenario one to ten per cent of North America would survive the initial impact. But they would have big problems. Mainly lack of food, medical care and sanitation. I reckon most of them would be taken out with starvation, typhus, cholera, bubonic plague, stuff like that."

"Comment, anyone?" the President asked, turning round.

"What you're saying," said the Secretary of Defense, his features drawn tensely, "Is that the technology is available to create a weapon a million times more powerful than a hydrogen bomb?"

Sacheverell nodded.

"You're some sort of nut," the Secretary of Defense said.

"It only takes a gentle push, sir. There are plenty of these asteroids around. The trick is to find one that passes close to the Earth. Then you soft land a small atom bomb on it. If you explode the bomb on the right place at the right time, you nudge the asteroid into an Earth-crossing orbit. It doesn't need much. With a mid-course correction—a second explosion with a small atom bomb or even conventional explosives—you could target the asteroid to within a couple of hundred miles."

Grant turned to Heilbron. "You say they've pulled it off already?"

"In my opinion it's on the way in now."

A slim, hawk-nosed man in his late fifties, wearing an expensive, dark three-piece suit, was standing at the back door of the theatre. He spoke angrily. "In the name of God, Rich, you're telling us we're at war."

Grant raised his hand quickly. "Not here, Billy." He turned to the DCI. "How many people know about this?"

"The seven of us in this room, two of my staff, and one of General Hooper's aides. On the European side, about an equal number. About twenty people in all. And a team of eight trying to find the thing. They're hidden away in a mountaintop observatory in Arizona."

"Doctor Sacheverell, we know where to reach you?"

"Yes, sir. I'm one of the team, in Eagle Peak Observatory."

"Don't even discuss this with your dog. Gentlemen, that applies to us all. I want no apocalyptic statements, no veiled hints, no unusual moves. Nathan, Sam, the Green Room at 3 a.m."

"With respect, sir . . ."

"Nathan, I'm about to entertain guests. Like I said, no unusual moves. What do you want me to do? Send him out for a pizza?"

DAY THREE

The Green Room, Wednesday, 03h00

Grant and his wife, accompanying King Charles, Camilla Parker-Bowles and His Britannic Majesty's Ambassador, walked along the long Entrance Hall, the sound of Liszt's *Hungarian Rhapsodies* coming from a dozen violins still entertaining a hundred guests in the State Dining Room. The President's head was fuzzy from Chateau Latour and his cheeks ached from hours of enforced smiling. By protocol, he led them to the elevator taking them up to the residence for a private talk.

An hour later Charles and Camilla, looking exhausted, were being escorted by Secret Service men to Blair House, across the road from No. 1651. Grant gave it another hour and then came back down by the stairs to the Entrance Hall. He turned through the colonnade into the Cross Hall. Adam-style chandeliers and bronze standard lamps threw a warm glow on to the marble walls. Images of past presidents looked down at him. The violins were now silent. Somewhere three chimes of a clock cut into the stillness.

A door was ajar and he turned into the Green Room. Logs crackled in the fireplace, and a whiff of woodsmoke unexpectedly evoked a distant memory: a camp fire, sausages sizzling on a stick, smoke stinging his eyes, young men and women laughing. But before he could place the image in time, it had gone forever.

The Secretary of Defense, Nathan Bellarmine, was sprawled in a Federal-period chintz armchair at the fire. He had smooth, black hair, was slightly balding, and wore a dark three-piece suit. The dark waistcoat and Brylcreemed hair made him look slightly like a snooker player.

Occupying the chair at the other side of the fireplace was a small, hook-nosed, middle-aged man with white hair and eyes like dark pebbles: this was Arnold Cresak, the President's National Security Adviser and a long-standing confidant.

The third man in the room was Hooper, sitting upright on a hard-backed chair, underneath Durrie's nostalgic *Farmyard in Winter*. There were dark shadows under the soldier's eyes. Grant waved them down as they began to rise, tossed his dinner jacket on to the carpeted floor and himself sank with a sigh into deep upholstery.

"Is the room clean?"

Cresak nodded. "It's been swept."

The President loosened his black tie. "I don't like this early hours stuff, but what can we do? What are we doing?"

Bellarmine said: "I informed the British Prime Minister, and the Presidents of France and Germany, as you instructed. They sent us a couple of specialists Monday morning. I now have a team of seven trying to locate the asteroid. They're being run by a Colonel Noordhof, who's with USAF Space Command. I assigned him to 50 Wing, Falcon Colorado. Special Projects, which covers no end of sin."

"Look, one whisper and we're fried. Who are these seven samurai?"

"We have McNally, the NASA Administrator. The rest are top scientists, for example Shafer, the CalTech genius."

"Shafer. The hippie scientist?"

Bellarmine said: "With two Nobel Prizes. He was on the cover of *Time* last month."

"I don't trust these superbrains: you don't know what they're really thinking. And what are we doing with Europeans on the team? That sounds to me like a couple of loose cannon."

"We want the top people whoever they are. We're in a life-or-death situation here."

"They know the timescale we're working to?"

Bellarmine nodded. "Consensus is the chances of success are very slim."

The President held the palms of his hands towards the fire. "Sam, where in your opinion will the Russians hit us?"

"Kansas. First, they maximize their chance of hitting land. Second, they get Omaha, Cheyenne Peak and the re-vamped silos. If you believe this Sacheverell they'll roast the States in less time than it takes to roast a chicken."

"Kansas is a reasonable guess," said Cresak. "But so is California. Maybe they're going for our economic base. They don't even care if they miss because a Pacific splash would submerge the West Coast."

"And an Atlantic one would decapitate us," said Hooper. "But who cares? We're dead wherever it hits."

"Okay." Grant took a deep breath and visibly tensed. He looked like a man about to jump off a cliff. "Now say we don't find Nemesis in time."

Hooper said, "Sir, in that case the parameters define a very narrow envelope."

"Sam, I'm a tired old man. If you mean we have limited options just say so."

"We have to assume the worst-case situation."

"Which is?"

"A blue sky impact. The asteroid comes in from day-light. The first we know about it is when it hits the upper at-mosphere at sixty thousand miles an hour and we get a two-second warning."

"Excuse me, but did you say a *two-second* warning?"

"Yes sir. Two seconds."

"As His Royal Majesty expressed it to me, in his very British way, it would freeze the balls off a brass monkey in here." The President poked at the fire and threw in a couple of logs. "Anyone want a hot chocolate?" Cresak leaned over to a work table next to the fireplace, pulled a telephone from a drawer and muttered an order.

"Now in those two seconds," Hooper continued, "while it's punching our air away, it seems it will also generate a massive electric current overhead. So it screws up our C-cubed systems."

"I thought we had fibre-optic cables from here to Omaha," the President said.

"A few, not a complete network. The real trouble is, the optical links still need electronic relays to boost the signal every so many miles. If the EMP zaps the relays, then the optical links go dead. Of course our satellite links collapse and we get cut off, isolated from everything at the critical moment."

"Well now that's just dandy. A few thousand engineers spend a few gigabucks of public money trying to fix it so we maintain integrity of command while the nukes are falling, only when it comes to the crunch you tell me what we really need are smoke signals."

Hooper remained impassive. "The links might survive through a nuclear war, Chief, but the asteroid, now that's a new ballgame."

Bellarmine said, "So we lose contact with our counterstrike forces at the moment of atmospheric entry, and impact takes place two seconds later?" The Chairman of the Joint Chiefs of Staff nodded.

"I like your technique, Nathan," Grant said, turning his palms once again towards the rising flames. "I like the casual way you slipped the word *counterstrike* into the conversation."

An elderly man, wearing a dark blazer with the presidential seal on the breast pocket, came in, followed by a young maid. A table was set up with four steaming mugs. They left without a word.

Bellarmine turned to Hooper. "*Could* we counterstrike?"

The soldier shook his head. "Not effectively, Mister

Secretary. When Nemesis cuts loose we'll turn into a snake without a head. Even at Defcon One we couldn't contact our silos, and our bombers would be torn to bits even if we got them aloft."

"We still have our submarines," Bellarmine said.

"How do we contact them? VLF, blue-green lasers and ELF. Very Low Frequency needs a wire a kilometre long trailed behind a TACAMO bomber. But all our command posts would be overwhelmed even before we contacted the bomber. The blue-green lasers beam down from the ORICS satellites. But"—Hooper checked off the points with his fingers—"One: the subs and satellites have to be in the right positions. Two: you have Kansas up there in the stratosphere giving us an umbrella of red-hot ash over the States. Three: you have an ionosphere gone crazy. So the signals don't get up to our satellites in the first place."

"And ELF?"

"We use a forty-mile antenna buried under Wisconsin. The radio pulses vibrate the whole Laurentian Shield. The vibration can be picked up from anywhere on Earth."

Grant grunted. "So? That's Nemesis-proof."

"We still have to be alive to send messages."

Bellarmine said, "Not necessarily. If we keep broadcasting Condition Red with the ELF, and other communications channels break down, standing orders are for submarine commanders to launch their nuclear weapons."

The soldier leaned forward intently and said, "There's a problem with that."

"You may as well lay it on, Sam," said the President.

"If we launch missiles they'll run into Kansas on the way up and disintegrate. It's like Brilliant Pebbles in reverse, a sort of natural Star Wars destroying our own counterstrike. Anyway, our submarine fleet carries only a small fraction of our megatonnage. Even if we get off a few Tridents the new ABM rings round Moscow, Kiev, Leningrad and so on could handle them. Mister President, it's simple. If they get Nemesis in first our capacity to respond is smashed. Russia will incur acceptable losses, but we'll be dead and gone."

The President sighed. "Okay Nathan, get it off your chest. What are our options?"

"They're stark. We can accept the annihilation of America and do nothing about it. We can wait for the impact and then try to hit back with our offensive capability smashed. Or we can beat them to the punch. Launch a nuclear strike now."

"Uhuh."

The President closed his eyes. Hooper wondered what thoughts were running through the old man's head. The soldier said, "Only the third option has military credibility."

A surge of fear suddenly went through Cresak's nervous system like an electric shock. It was more than the fact that the unimaginable prospect of a nuclear war had entered the discussion; it was the fact that it had slipped in, by stealth, almost without conscious reasoning. "Crap," he said, his voice unsteady. "The Russians would hit back. Then Nemesis would come in and finish off whatever was left of us."

"The time for the Major Attack Option has never been better," Bellarmine said. "They don't expect it, their political system's in chaos, and we have a dozen Alpha lasers in orbit to handle any Russian missiles that do get launched."

"You're insane," said Cresak. "What about Carter's PD-59? They could survive a strike long enough to obliterate us."

"Nuclear war is winnable," said Hooper emphatically. The situation has moved on since McNamara and Carter; we have the Alpha shields now. The winner is the one who hits first. Central Command computers show that a first strike will be decisive and that's why our command and control systems are geared for a first-strike capability. We've always known that a second strike, one under attack, would fail utterly. Sir, we'll never get another chance like this."

"This is lunacy," said the National Security Adviser. His voice was shaky but determined. He ticked the points off with his fingers, one by one. "The Russians kept their C3 system intact through all the political upheavals. Even with SALT and START they still have seven thousand ICBMs and a thousand submarine-launched missiles. They have two thousand bomb-proof bunkers to protect their top leadership. The situation has changed in Russia too. They've now got a streamlined chain of command, straight from their General Staff to their missile units. The new leadership have thrown away the old safeguards. They've obtained the unlock codes from the old KGB. The political officers have long gone from the system. They've taken away the electro-mechanical switches for sealing bomb doors."

"Get to the point, Arnold. What are you driving at?" asked the President.

"Sir, they could respond in seconds. And if even a handful of their Sawflies got through, America would be finished."

"Hell, Arnold, we can handle it," Hooper said. "The Alpha lasers. And the leadership would be fried before they even reached their bunkers."

The President sipped at his chocolate. It was too sweet. "What's the modern view on nuclear winter?" he asked.

Hooper pulled a thin blue document from a battered briefcase at the side of his chair. "Our climate modellers have looked at all sorts of smoke injection scenarios. Mostly they darken the sun for about three months and could wipe out agriculture in the growing season. That's another reason for an early strike, to let the sky clear by July."

Grant said, "Sam, let's not get too excited. There may not even be an asteroid. All we have is a string of circumstantial evidence that Heilbron has woven into a pattern. We can't go levelling the planet just because the DCI has an overactive imagination."

"With respect, sir," Bellarmine insisted, "if there is an asteroid, chances are the first we know of it is when it hits, by which time we're too late for an effective counterstrike. The only realistic option is Number Three."

"I believe we're seeing a sort of collective insanity here," Cresak said, his fear betraying itself in his voice.

"Okay, let's get down to basics," said Grant. "What's the strategic purpose of your third option, Sam?"

Hooper put down his mug of chocolate. His face showed real bafflement. "I must be missing something, sir."

"What purpose is served by destroying Russia?"

"Retaliation," said Hooper, the bafflement giving way to incredulity.

Bellarmine sensed something. He said, "Mister President. It's been the official policy of every administration since World War Two that a Russian attack on mainland America will be met with the Major Attack Option."

"Public policy, yes," Grant replied. "And you know damn well our true policy is that if the diplomatic game ever gets hot we hit first. Hooper's right. It's the only chance of winning a nuclear exchange."

"So!" Bellarmine raised his hands in an Italian-like gesture. "For fifty years mutual assured destruction has kept the West safe. What's the difference between this asteroid thing and a big missile attack? The logic's identical. We play it out."

"Why?"

Bellarmine stayed silent. His expression was an exercise in suppressed bewilderment and outrage.

Cresak drove the point home. "I guess maybe the Chief thinks it's pointless. Two big dust bowls instead of one."

Bellarmine said, "Arnold, your jaw has got disengaged from your brain. Responsibility for the Russian people lies with their leadership, not with us. Our policy has been spelled out, clear as crystal, ever since World War Two. We serve future generations better by following through than by just backing off when the chips are down. The lesson will be remembered for a thousand years."

"No doubt the cave dwellers for the next thousand years will be grateful for the lesson," Cresak replied, his voice heavy with sarcasm. "And the two hundred million innocent people you burn will see the point too. We don't seem to have progressed since the Salem witches."

"Sure!" Bellarmine snarled. "Our ancestors thought they were doing right and they got it wrong. And if we get entangled in moral problems now we'll get it just as wrong as they did. This is the White House, not a department of moral philosophy. Our business is to respond, according to publicly laid-down policy, to circumstances imposed on us by the Russians."

"It's getting hot in here," said the President.

Hooper said, "Look. We're under attack, so we defend. Period. Like any country, man or creature since time began. The only live issues are targeting policy and battle management."

"What targets do you have in mind, Sam?"

"I've arranged a murder session with JSTPS in Offutt at twelve hundred hours. You'll have our prepared options within forty-eight hours. The target sets will depend on whether we launch under attack or go for pre-emption. Mister President, I'm pushing for pre-emption. We have to finish this East–West thing once and for all. The prime target will be Russia but we should also take out Armenia, Belorussia, Moldavia, Kazakhstan, Georgia, Uzbekistan, Tajikistan and Estonia. We may also want to think about Cuba, Vietnam and China while we're about it. I'm thinking of updating the old SIOP-5D list."

Grant peered into Hooper's eyes. The soldier stared unflinchingly back. "Some shopping list," the President said. "What, specifically, do you mean by take out?"

"I mean destroy all nuclear and conventional military forces, the military and political leadership, the major economic and industrial centres, and all cities with more than 25,000 population."

"LeMay would have been proud of you, Sam. Why China?"

"We'll be so weak after Nemesis that we can't afford to leave potential enemies around. Mister President, I want your unconditional assurance on this matter. That in the event of an asteroid strike on America becoming a proven eventuality, you will order a retaliatory counterstrike."

A log collapsed in the fire, sending a little shower of sparks up the chimney. Grant lowered his head, strumming his fingers lightly on his knee. The others stared at him, frozen like models from a tableau in a wax museum. Thirty seconds passed, each one a century long.

"At this moment of time I will give no such assurance."

"I don't believe I'm hearing this," said Bellarmine. His tone was aggressive. "Massive retaliation has been the backbone of our defence posture for generations, endorsed by successive administrations. It can't be capriciously set aside by one individual. Not even a President. Your first duty is the defence of America. If you fail in that, you fail in your duty as President of these United States."

"Why thank you, Nathan, a homily on my duty as President is just what I need at this time of night." President Grant stretched and yawned. "Well, I've enjoyed our little fireside chat. Could this thing hit tonight?"

"Unlikely. Of course we don't know for sure." Bellarmine was trembling with anger.

"What's the warning time for a night impact?"

"We think ten to forty minutes, sir," said the Chief of Staffs.

"Better than two seconds. Nathan, Arnold, I want you guys to come up with a joint memorandum on the policy options facing us on the assumption that Nathan's team fails to identify Nemesis or can't find any way to stop it. I want it in time for the extraordinary NSC meeting on Friday midnight."

The President stared into the fire for some moments. Then he seemed to come to a decision. "We must keep our options open. I'm prepared to go some way with you, Sam. Increase our state of alert. Let's go to Orange."

Bellarmine nodded his agreement. "Sam, upgrade to Defcon 3 worldwide."

The President stood up, and the men followed him into

the hallway. "Oh by the way, gentlemen. Merry Christmas." He made his way towards the secret stairway at the East Hall which would take him to the third floor and the Family Quarters, an old man longing for rest. Cresak went back into the Green Room and sat down, staring into the leaping flames. Hooper went off, heading for the back exit. Bellarmine paced up and down the long corridor for ten minutes, feeling stunned. Then he too went towards the rear of the building.

The air was sharp and cold, and there was a bitter breeze. The grounds were white with a foot of freshly fallen snow. A pine tree, its coloured lights swaying in the breeze, stood on the central lawn. Hooper, wearing a long army coat and a white scarf, was standing on the steps of the North Portico, flapping his arms against his sides. A few Secret Service men hovered in the background; they looked frozen stiff.

"Was I hearing right in there, Mister Secretary?" asked Hooper, his breath misty in the freezing air.

"Give me a lift," said Bellarmine grimly. "We have to talk."

"Too damn right. Where you heading?"

"Virginia."

"Big place. Defcon Three can wait awhile."

Hooper pressed a button and a glass partition slid up, cutting them off from the army driver. The general lit up a small cigar and its tip glowed red in the dark.

"You have to smoke these disgusting things?" Bellarmine asked.

"Privilege of rank," Hooper replied, exhaling a dense smoke cloud. "Anyway, these disgusting things just happen to be fine Havana cheroots. Heilbron gets his field people to bring them in from Cuba."

They passed on to the Ellipse. A group of youths stood shivering, scarves round their necks and woollen hats pulled down almost to their eyes. Bellarmine just caught the words "Say No To Torture" on a placard as the beam of light from the car swept across it.

"A pacifist for a president, at a time like this," said Hooper. Now the headlights were picking up the broad swathe of Constitution Avenue.

"What do you want—Rambo?"

"Rambo we could handle." Hooper inhaled the cigar smoke. "Nathan, we can't let it happen."

"Meaning?"

"You know what I mean."

The car was driving past the Vietnam War Memorial. Beyond it the rotunda of the Lincoln Memorial was lit up with a ghostly glow. Bellarmine began to feel his lungs outlined by cigar smoke. "Grant's mother was a Quaker," he said. "Can it be relevant?"

Hooper took another big draw. "No pacifist should hold the office of President."

"Sam, talk like that is highly dangerous."

"Uhuh."

The car crossed the Woodrow Wilson Memorial bridge; little ice floes on the Potomac reflected orange in the street lights. Snow, compacted by earlier traffic, covered the Beltway. The driver pulled out to pass a truck and grit pattered briefly on the windscreen.

After twenty minutes, marked by a stunned silence and a rapidly increasing smoke density, a sign said Langley and the car turned off the highway. They drove along a tunnel of light. The CIA Headquarters was lit up by yellow spotlights. It reminded Bellarmine of a Soviet housing complex, all massive concrete blocks and narrow windows. The driver stopped near the main entrance.

Hooper repeated, grimly, "No pacifist has the right to hold the office of President."

"So you said." The driver opened the door and Bellarmine

stepped out into the icy air. After Hooper's smoke-filled car, the fragrance of the night was delicious. While the driver held the door, the Secretary of Defense turned back and leaned in to the car. "The question is: *what are we going to do about it?*"

Eagle Peak, Wednesday

Webb rummaged in a cardboard box in the dormitory cupboard, and found a woollen hat to match the multi-coloured jumper. He pulled the hat on and headed for the kitchen, intending to make a hot chocolate before facing the chilly outside air once more. Shafer was staggering into the kitchen with a rabbit-sized boulder, coated with snow. Noordhof opened the door of the microwave cooker, and Shafer heaved the boulder in, setting the timer for five minutes.

Webb rattled a saucepan on to the cooker and added milk. "It won't work," he said, looking for a tin of hot chocolate in a cupboard stuffed with the detritus of past visiting observers.

"Mark's idea," said Shafer. "He's just shown me a *Newsweek* article by Broadbent from some months back. Mark can't confirm without clearance, which would take time, but listen to what this guy says." He picked up the opened magazine from a kitchen work surface:

> "In the euphoria of the First Cold War thaw, and with the easing of security in government laboratories around the States, previously tight-lipped administrators appeared to confirm what many academic scientists outside the system had long claimed: that Star Wars was a spectacular, and highly expensive, failure. A year of investigative reporting by our team, however, has turned up a different story.

"Blah blah blah. The guy goes on to say there was an element of disinformation in the 'Star Wars Failed' stuff. He says the Army have an array of antennae not too far from Albuquerque. They call it the Beta maser, and it's arguably in contravention of the ABM Treaty. You'll note that Mark isn't contradicting me. Broadbent even says that on one experimental run the Beta maser destroyed a warhead they'd launched from Mid-Pacific, the moment it appeared over the horizon. So if the Beta exists maybe it could do something to the asteroid, but Mark has the right to remain silent, which right you'll notice he's exercising."

Noordhof said nothing, but he was looking pleased with himself.

"That is one impressive zap," said Kowalski, looking up from a sheaf of papers. "Assuming there's truth in the story, maybe it's the answer to our prayers. Colonel, you must cut through the tape. Get us clearance for this stuff right away."

"No need," said Shafer. "We can work out what we need from the article. If these guys can really vaporize a warhead at say five thousand miles' range, it means they penetrate the ablation shield and raise the missile's internal temperature to a thousand degrees within two or three seconds. So let's see how hot this rock gets in five minutes with a miserable kilowatt and use it to get its thermal conductivity."

The milk was coming to the boil. Webb pummelled hard-caked chocolate powder in a tin. "It won't work," he repeated, stirring in the chocolate. Noordhof scowled.

The microwave oven pinged and Shafer put his hand on the rock. "Warm to the touch. It went in at zero Centigrade so it's gone through thirty degrees in five minutes, say five or six degrees a minute."

Webb took a sip at the hot chocolate and sighed happily. "I expect your rock is still cold inside."

Shafer nodded. "So is Nemesis. And if it's rock the maser heat will get conducted down quickly. Okay, say a kilowatt gives us half a degree a second on this little stone, and the

Beta maser heats a target at five hundred degrees a second."
The Nobel man counted fingers. "Hey, these guys must be
beaming one megawatt per square metre at five thousand
miles' range, can you believe that?"

Noordhof radiated happiness. "Nothing could withstand
it. And laser beams don't spread out with distance. We'll ablate Nemesis clean out of the solar system, punch boulders
off it. Hey, who needs the eggheads? I thought of this all by
myself."

Shafer shook his head sorrowfully. "No dice, Mark. Laser
beams do spread out. Imagine two mirrors at the ends of a
tube, reflecting light back and forth, one of the mirrors with a
pinhole. You generate fluorescence inside the tube, and the
light reflects and gets pumped up to huge intensity. The only
light that makes it out through the hole has travelled the full
length of the beam, but there's still an angular spread. It's the
wavelength of the light divided by the diameter of the gun."

"Maybe it's a very big gun," Noordhof interrupted, "Giving a very small dispersion."

"You have the Alpha lasers in orbit. They're hydrogen-
fluoride, emitting at 2.7 microns. I guess their peak power
can reach ten or twenty megawatts, but they can't be more
than a few metres across."

Noordhof waved the magazine at Shafer. His tone was a
mixture of triumph and desperation. "But this guy is talking
about masers, not lasers. Everything is much bigger at radio
wavelengths."

Shafer shook his head again. "No way can you guys be
hiding an array more than ten kilometres across, not even in
the New Mexico desert. *Ergo*, if you're beaming centimetre
waves the angular spread is at least one part in a million."

Noordhof spread his hands. "So? Nothing!"

"Nothing at five thousand miles. But if you catch Nemesis
a million kilometres away the centimetre wave beam is
spread out over one kilometre, the whole size of the asteroid.
With attenuation like that you couldn't boil an egg. Uncer-

tainties in thermal conductivity or internal temperature will make no difference. I'm sorry Mark, but your top secret, Darth Vader, gigabuck, Space Dominance, missile-zapping Star Wars supermaser is as useful as a peashooter. We're back to nukes."

Webb couldn't resist it: "I told you it wouldn't work."

"Where the hell do you think you're going, Webb? Are you looking for Nemesis in the woods?"

"I'm looking for inspiration, Colonel. From the performance I've seen here, I'm more likely to find it with the squirrels."

Noordhof opened the microwave door angrily. "Well, you might take the friggin' rock out with you."

Shafer was still laughing when Webb left the building.

At the far end of the little car park there was a gap in the trees which, on closer examination, turned out to be the beginning of a natural path. It was close to a cluster of garbage bins and Webb suspected that it might be a raiding route for some animals. He took off along it, and found that the path skirted the foot of Eagle Peak, rising gently as it went, with the cliff easily visible to the left through the heavy ponderosa trees. After about twenty minutes, far beyond Noordhof's hundred-metre limit, he turned off to the base of the cliff, brushed the powdery snow off a broad boulder and sat down on it. There was the merest hint of cable rising above the trees about a mile back; otherwise there were no signs of human artefact. For the first time since he had been snatched from another snow-covered mountain, halfway round the planet, Webb had time to stop and think.

A last-minute asteroid deflection was a crass thing, a hefty punch with a barely controllable outcome. A punch on the nose, slowing Nemesis down long enough for the Earth to slip past, was more effective than a sideways swipe. But as the warning time dwindled so the punch became increasingly desperate, to the point where either you risked breaking the asteroid into a lethal swarm or you could do nothing to ward it off. Just which side of the threshold they were on they wouldn't know until they had identified Nemesis.

The Russians, however, had had a different problem: that of precision. Probably, Webb thought, they had used a stand-off explosion of a few megatons to give a crude impulse of a metre a second or thereabouts. The bigger the bomb the more potential asteroid weapons were available, and the Russians had hundred-megatonners in their arsenal. For every asteroid liable to hit the Earth they would have a hundred or more potential weapons in the form of near-missers.

But after that they would have had to finesse. A hit within a few hundred miles—or even a thousand miles—of Kansas would be adequate to obliterate the States. But a thousand miles is *precision*! After the initial big explosion, possibly years in the past, they would have required a series of small shepherding explosions, maybe little more than Hiroshimas, to guide the asteroid in.

All of which implied a fair amount of clandestine space activity, maybe using the Phobos or Venera series as a cover. Leclerc's knowledge of past Russian space trips was the key.

There was a movement in the woods. A couple of crows were cautiously dropping from branch to branch about fifty yards away. And something small was scurrying through the trees. A white fox popped its head up and looked at Webb curiously. In a flash of inspiration, Webb suddenly realized that there was another key. He jumped up and the fox and crows disappeared.

In passing he looked in the kitchen and the common room, and knocked on Leclerc's door. He threw off the hat and jumper. Back down to the conference room. "Where's André?" he asked. Judy looked up briefly from a terminal and shrugged.

Webb picked up a pile of blank paper and made his way to the common room. It was empty. Warm afternoon sunlight was streaming in through the panoramic window. A green leather chair had a worn, comfortable look about it.

He settled in. The sun was warm on his thighs and a light scented breeze was coming in through the window.

In some anonymous galaxy near the boundaries of space and time, two neutron stars had collided. With collision velocities close to the speed of light, the stars had annihilated their own matter, transforming it into a flash of radiation of incomprehensible intensity. Before even the Sun and Earth had formed, the radiation was spreading out through the Universe as a thin, expanding spherical shell. And then came the Sun and planets, and life evolved in the oceans, and then the reptiles had crawled on to land and the big archosaurs had ruled the Earth until the solar system entered a spiral arm, whence they had died in a massive bombardment of dust and impacts. It was an episode which had left the mammals and the insects, in their turn, to inherit the Earth. By the time the first primates had appeared the gamma rays were invading the Local Supercluster of galaxies; when *homo sapiens* was learning to carve on rocks the radiation was sweeping through the cave man's own galaxy; and finally, at the very instant the apes had learned how to throw little metal machines around the Earth, the shell had momentarily rushed through the solar system, on its endless voyage to other stars and other galaxies.

But as the energetic photons swept past, a tiny handful had been picked up by the satellites which the apes had just developed; a millisecond gamma ray burst was duly recorded; theoreticians speculated; papers were written and debated; and arriving from cataclysms scattered through the cosmic wilderness, other gamma ray bursts were being picked up, recorded, discussed and debated, and catalogued.

And this was Webb's problem. The Universe snaps and crackles across the whole electromagnetic spectrum. Neutron stars collide; massive stars run out of thermonuclear fuel, collapse and then destroy themselves in a gigantic thermonuclear explosion; red dwarfs dump their atmospheres on to white dwarf companions; relativistic jets squirt from the nuclei of galaxies and stars. Somewhere in this tremendous background of noise was a local event. A sprinkling of X-rays, perhaps, from an illegal nuclear explosion; or a brief flash of light in the sky. An explosion on Nemesis would throw hundreds of thousands of tons of debris into space. Maybe ice, maybe boulders, but surely dust. A cone of dust, fanning out into space and sparkling in the sunlight; a beacon in the dark interplanetary void.

Amongst the thousands of X-ray flashes picked up by CHANDRA, there might just be a signature of a different sort. Or maybe even the wide-angle camera on SPITZER had picked up a fading infrared glow as the debris from the crater dispersed into the zodiacal dust cloud. Or the Hubble had picked up something.

The first thing was to calculate the signatures that would discriminate between natural astrophysical processes and the effects of a bomb. He would have to investigate a wide range of physical processes. Maybe the hefty thump of 14 MeV neutrons from the thermonuclear fireball yielded a characteristic signature; or the timescale for dispersal of the dust yielded a light curve unlike that from any eclipsing binary. Webb sighed and pulled over a coffee table with a dish of Liquorice Allsorts and jelly babies. It was going to be a long session.

Lunch came and went unnoticed. Colleagues came and went through the common room; Webb was not disturbed. The level of the sweets in the dish next to Webb slowly declined. Around six in the evening Judy went into the kitchen and the smell of curry soon wafted around the common room. Kowalski appeared shortly afterwards, dressed in his Eskimo suit, and then Shafer and Noordhof emerged from the conference room, arguing about something; their voices changed to a low murmur but Webb appeared not to notice. Someone handed Webb a coffee and switched on a lamp. The sun set. Papers scrawled with formulae piled up on the coffee table. The sweets disappeared.

Around midnight Webb completed his calculations: he had his electromagnetic signatures. The best bet had turned out to be the simplest: an unexplained flash of light, seen in the telescope of some amateur comet hunter somewhere on the planet. It might just have been recorded in the IAU Circulars, the electronic clearing house for transient and unexpected astronomical phenomena.

He looked at his watch in surprise, and realized that he hadn't eaten. There was a plate of chicken curry, boiled rice and a Nan bread in the microwave oven. He fired it up, was tempted by the can of Red Stripe on the kitchen table but decided against it. He gulped the food down and then went straight through to the conference room along the now darkened corridor. The room too was dark apart from the light from the terminals. Judy and Sacheverell were sitting at terminals. Starfields were drifting across their vision.

"How did the briefing go, Herb?" Webb asked.

"No sweat," Sacheverell said without looking up.

"We're filtering out the main belters automatically," Shafer said, "otherwise we'd snarl up."

"And between Spacewatch, Flagstaff and ourselves we've found thirty Earth-crossers already," Judy said. "Thirty-one," she added as the terminal beeped.

"How are you handling them?" Webb asked.

"No sweat." Sacheverell again. "The Teraflop is coping with everything we throw at it. We come back to the new ones after an hour or two. Look." He pressed a terminal key and the single picture was replaced with a dozen small squares, each centred on a bright spot. The little pictures, like frames from a movie, showed clearly that the spot was drifting against the stellar background. "Usually they've moved several pixels, sometimes dozens. We might not get an orbit but if it has a strong tangential drift we know it's not an immediate hazard."

"Where are you searching?" Webb asked Shafer.

"Where you expect to find them," Sacheverell interrupted.

"In and around the ecliptic plane. I hope you're not going to start on crap about high inclination dark Halleys."

"They're not practical weapons, Herb. Anyway it doesn't matter where you look, you haven't a hope."

Sacheverell looked up from the screen. "Hey, we finally agree on something."

"But don't tell the Colonel what we're agreed on. He's already had a bad day." Webb sat down at a spare terminal and quickly typed into the Internet. Once into the IAU Circulars, he began to read every one, starting from the most recent and going back through time. Each unexplained flash of light, each gamma ray burst, each surge of X-rays reported in the sky, had to be matched against the theoretical expectations he now carried in his head. It was a slow, painstaking, tedious grind.

Around 3 a.m. Judy disappeared, and half an hour thereafter Webb too felt he had to take a break. He wandered across the darkened hallway to the dimly lit common room and flopped down in an armchair. The urge to sleep was almost irresistible. There was a smell of perfume. "Hey, Mister!" Judy said in a soft voice. "Not even Superman could keep that up." Startled, he saw that Judy was in the armchair opposite. In the dim light he could just make out that she was wearing a long green dressing gown; her hair was tousled and her blue eyes were strained with tiredness.

Without thinking, he said, "What's a nice girl like you doing in nuclear weapons? You should be having babies."

She bristled, but then burst out laughing when she detected Webb's sly grin. "Webb the sexist! I'm sure. I'm in nukes for the same reason you're in astrophysics, Oliver. I love the subject."

He felt unable to think. When he spoke, the words were slurred with exhaustion. "So the lady loves nukes. I still can't think why."

In spite of her exhaustion, enthusiasm came through in her voice. "Think of a nuclear fireball in the first microsecond of its formation. The power to devastate a small country in something the size of a beachball. There's a wonderful purity about a nuke, Ollie. It sweeps away everything; even elements are transmuted. It's as near as we can get on Earth to the Creation."

"You make getting nuked sound like a religious experience," Webb replied, hardly caring what he said. "But you want to destroy things, and I want to understand them. I happen to think we were created from something like your fireball."

"The Big Bang?" she asked.

Webb shook his head. "The nucleus of the Galaxy. This is something that nobody in their right mind believes. But I still say women are for childbearing. They're supposed to create, not destroy."

"All females defend their young. Having had our babies we need to protect them. I do create, Oliver, I create peace. Is that not a noble pursuit in a barbaric world? You have the nerve to sit there and bask in the purity of your subject, with Nemesis on the way in? We can only manage miserable ten-megaton firecrackers, but you? You go cosmic."

"I also love dogs," said Webb.

"I prefer cats. And cars. I can strip a Pontiac to its gudgeon pins and reassemble it in a day."

Webb said, "You can strip me to my gudgeon pins any day. I'm a fair cook, and I climb mountains." He thought, This conversation is getting surreal.

She shook her head. "I'd rather fly over them in my Piper. But maybe you can cook me a dinner some time."

Webb's skin tingled at the invitation and he thought, hell I must still be alive. "Which brings me to boyfriends. Got any?"

"Lots of them, all strictly platonic. So far I find nukes more interesting."

"Are all nuclear physicists as beautiful as you?"

"Only the females." She stretched her slim legs out on the coffee table between them, nudging papers aside with her bare feet. "What about you?"

"The ladies? I have an effect on them. But haven't had time to explore the subject. I notice you paint your toenails, ma'am."

"I hope you paint yours, Oliver. Otherwise we have nothing in common."

Noordhof marched in and switched on a light. He took one look at the exhausted scientists, blinking in the light, and said, "You two. Get to bed before you collapse, and that's an order. You're no damn use in that state."

Judy waved and more or less staggered towards the dormitory. Webb felt his way along the pitch black corridor and stepped outside. The snowy landscape glowed softly in the light of the Milky Way and the stars. He breathed in the scented air, letting his eyes, strained by hours of terminal-staring, adapt to the dark.

The IAU circulars had revealed nothing.

Mars was high in the south, a bright red, unwinking beacon which, in a couple of hundred years, would hold a teeming human population, a population which would marvel at the havoc their ancestors had wreaked on the beautiful blue planet. A few lights were scattered over the desert far below.

He strolled on to the road which, that morning, he had pounded down with Leclerc and Whaler. Some animal screamed in the distance, a prolonged scream which set Webb's nerves jangling.

The next step would be the SPITZER catalogue and maybe some ultraviolet stuff, maybe even going as far back as the IUE which had closed down in 1997. But he knew it wouldn't wash; these were shots so long they had to be a last resort.

Something.

Something; a new idea trying to climb out from his subconscious. But what?

The animal screamed again, closer; or was it another animal? And what makes an animal scream in the night?

Suddenly cold and nervous, Webb turned back towards the observatory. He was asleep within two minutes of collapsing into bed.

Webb was in the cloister of a monastery, hiding behind a potted palm. In the cobbled central courtyard, hooded monks were building a scaffold. The carpenter, a monk with Noordhof's face, had a row of six-inch nails protruding from his grinning mouth. They were hammering the scaffold together at superhuman speed, only the scaffold turned out to be a big wooden cross and the hammering was overwhelming and it transformed into an urgent tapping at Webb's door, dragging him from his lurid subconscious world into the real one. The dream faded and Webb thought that perhaps Judy had overdone the chillies.

"Oliver!"

Feeling drugged, the astronomer heaved himself out of bed, put on a robe and opened the door, blinking in the subdued light of the hallway. Judy; still in her dressing gown, still with tousled blonde hair and tired, strained eyes. "Kenneth called. They think they've found something. He's gone up in the cable car with Herb."

Webb followed Judy down to the darkened conference room. Noordhof and Shafer were clustered round a terminal, the light from the screen giving a blue tinge to their faces. Shafer was in boxer shorts and singlet, and his hair was drawn back into a ponytail by an elastic band. Noordhof was fully dressed. The colonel moved aside and Webb looked at a hundred thousand stars. A wisp of nebulosity crossed the bottom of the screen, probably a remnant from some past stellar cataclysm. The starfield wasn't drifting: someone had set the telescope for a long exposure.

"You see the little triangle of stars near the middle? The top one has moved." Judy said.

"What's its angular rate?" Webb asked.

"Extremely low," Shafer said. "About a pixel an hour."

"So it's either heading away from us or straight at us."

"It's coming at us," Shafer informed Webb. "It's slowly brightening."

"Have you any orbit at all?"

The physicist pointed to an adjacent terminal. The centre of the screen showed a coin-sized disc. A series of near-parallel lines criss-crossed the screen, the longer ones going from edge to edge; each line passed through the centre of the disc. "This is one of Herb's programmes. We're projecting the two-sigma error ellipses on to the target plane."

"Only you don't have distance information so the ellipses come out like lines."

"That's the problem. You see they've been shrinking as the data accumulate, but they still pass through the Earth. Collision is a definite possibility."

"I agree, Willy, but so is a miss. These are still long lines. We need an accurate orbit and we're not going to get that with a one-hour time base."

"You said it yourself, Ollie. The Earth's gravity pulls things in when they get close. In the last stages these lines will shrink to a point."

"What are the chances, Ollie? Is this Nemesis?" Noordhof asked anxiously.

"At a minimum, it's going to be a very close encounter."

"What does that mean? Do I wake the President or not?"

Another elongated ellipse suddenly appeared on the screen, shorter than its predecessors. Its centre still passed firmly through the coin-sized Earth.

"This is it, right?"

Webb lowered his head in thought. "Mark, we're not going to answer your question with the orbital dynamics to hand."

"But we can't wait. Not if this is the big one."

Webb asked, "Do we have brightness information?"

Shafer nodded. "Herb says its magnitude has gone from twenty-one point five to twenty-one point two in the last hour."

"I thought we weren't looking fainter than seventeen?"

Shafer shrugged. "Mark ordered it. He's still fixated with Baby Bears."

Noordhof said, "Screw you, Willy. I made the right call and there's the living proof."

"Kenneth and Herb are trying to get its spectrum with the ninety-four-inch," Judy volunteered.

Webb said, "At m equals 21? Full marks for effort. Look, the orbital accuracy is horrendous but we might be able to use δm. Anyone got a calculator?" Shafer thrust one into Webb's hand. "Point three magnitude change translates into a roughly thirty per cent brightening in the last hour."

"Maybe it's just a rotating brick," Shafer suggested.

"Too much light change in too short a time. Chances are the bulk of it is due to its approach. With inverse square its distance from us has decreased by fifteen per cent in the last hour. A spectrum is pointless. It'll be on us in seven or eight hours."

Shafer said: "Jesus." The tone sounded more like a sudden conversion to Christianity than an oath.

Noordhof had an unlit cigar between his fingers. "If this is Nemesis we're dead. Is it Nemesis?"

"Willy's point about rotation is partly right. We just don't know the approach rate precisely enough to be sure."

"Wonderful!" Noordhof snarled. He crushed the cigar and threw it to the floor.

"Let's guess it's approaching at twenty kilometres a second. In six hours that puts it"—Webb tapped buttons on the calculator—"Crikey. Less than half a million kilometres away. What's the time?"

Noordhof looked at the big railway clock. "Four fifteen."

"From the way you guys have been operating I guess Kenneth's supernova telescope has picked this thing up near the meridian. We're probably looking at an eighty per cent sunlit face rather than a night-time crescent."

"Make this quick, Webb," said Noordhof. "The White House are going to need every second we can give them."

Webb crossed to the blackboard and used his sleeve to wipe a clear space. There was just enough light to scribble. "A one-kilometre carbonaceous asteroid has magnitude 18 at one AU. This thing is 0.003 AU away which with inverse square luminosity would make it a hundred thousand times brighter than that, size for size. Use the magnitude/brightness formula

$$m_2 = m_1 + 2.5 \log (L_1/L_2)$$

Put $m_2 = 18$ and $L_1/L_2 = 100,000$. At that distance, a one-kilometre asteroid would have magnitude 5.5. You could see it with the naked eye." Webb stabbed the air with a piece of chalk. "But this one is 20.5, fifteen magnitudes fainter. For every five mags you go down, you lose a factor of a hundred in brightness. Ten mags down gives it only one ten thousandth of the intrinsic luminosity of a one-kilometre asteroid, ditto the surface area. This beast is less than a hundredth of a kilometre in diameter. Hey, we can relax. It's only ten metres across."

Shafer laughed. "A glorified beachball!"

"Are you sure?" Noordhof wanted to know.

Webb nodded. "At the ninety-nine per cent level. Even if it hits it'll just be a brilliant fireball in the sky. We get these all the time. Colonel, you're a fool. You've thrown away priceless hours of observing time. Forget the Baby Bears."

An expression close to terror crossed Noordhof's face. "I was about to waken the President." A collective outburst of laughter relieved the tension. Judy headed for the kitchen and started to fill the coffee percolator.

"By the way," Webb asked, "Where's André?"

"He's not in his room," Judy called through.

"And he's not up top," Noordhof said.

Shafer put his hand to his mouth. "Ollie, I haven't seen Leclerc since lunchtime."

Webb looked at Noordhof. "Mark, it's been a bad day. First a blind alley with your laser. Then a false alarm with this beachball. And now it seems that one of your team has gone missing."

The Tenerife Robot

Judy pulled her dressing gown lapels round her neck and made for the dormitory. Webb, swaying with tiredness, headed in the same direction.

"Where do you think you're going, Webb?"

"I'd have thought that was obvious, boss." Webb saluted ironically.

"I've given thought to your friend's automated telescope. The one in Tenerife. You say you can work it from here?"

"I can work it from here. The instructions go to Scott's Oxford terminal and get routed through. Anyone sniffing cables at Tenerife would believe the operator was in Oxford."

"With an external phone line? And an open modem?"

"Yes, for direct access. But it's password protected and I have the password."

"And your friend?"

"Scott's in Patras. His wife is Greek and they're with her family over Christmas. I have an open invitation to use the robotic telescope until it's properly commissioned."

"So, with half a million megatons coming in, and a telescope sitting idle, your action plan is to fall asleep."

"I was waiting for your authorization, remember? Are you telling me you're getting over your paranoia?"

"I have to balance risks here. Go ahead with it."

"The sun's up over Tenerife by now, Mark, but I'll check that I can access it from here. Meantime, Herb and Kenneth must be turning into icemen, trying to get the spectrum of your beachball. Why don't you call them back down?"

Webb sat heavily down at the terminal Judy had been at. The chair was still warm. Another small ellipse had appeared on the screen, the disc representing the Earth still firmly inside it. By the time the bolide arrived the Pacific would be in darkness, and a brilliant shooting star would light up the night sky, to be seen only by the uncomprehending eyes of flying fish. He routed the picture over to an empty terminal, and typed in a file transfer protocol. Immediately, the terminal asked for his user-name and password. He gave these and a fresh window appeared on screen: he was now in effect sitting at his own computer in Wadham College. He asked for a second FTP to be opened up, the one linking him to the robotic telescope. Webb was asked for a PIN number. He supplied it and found himself in effect in Tenerife, at the console of Scott's telescope, in little more time than it took to say Beam me up Scottie. The whole procedure had taken less than thirty seconds.

Webb could now use the mouse to control the movement of the telescope, little numbers at the top right hand of the screen giving the celestial co-ordinates at the centre of the starfield. The shutters of the telescope dome were closed in daylight hours, but he had confirmed that he could contact the telescope from here.

Then he switched to the external camera, mounted on a pillar about fifty yards from the main instrument.

The picture came through immediately. The camera was looking back at the telescope, whose silver dome was gleaming in the morning sunlight. He rotated the telescope dome and saw it swivel immediately. He scanned slowly, and the camera panned over the rocky foreground. A cluster of telescopes came into view, the massive William Herschel conspicuous amongst them. Someone was walking outside the big dome. He carried on scanning, and the camera picked up the tops of clouds further down the mountain; they were above the inversion layer, and the atmosphere was likely very dry. He pressed another button and temperature, pressure, humidity and prevailing wind at the site were displayed. Then he swung the camera over the Tenerife sky; it was cloudless. Everything was operating smoothly. Tonight he would use the robot to search for Atens. As the signal came in to Eagle Peak it would automatically be reproduced a few hundred miles away, at Albuquerque, and the Teraflop would interrogate each picture element on the screen, comparing it with a digitized star chart and the co-ordinates of known asteroids. Any discrepancy would be recorded as a flashing point on the terminal VDU.

The thing would be to get as close as he could to the horizon, close to the sun but before the dawn light flooded the CCDs. Experimentally, he typed in an altitude and azimuth. Again the telescope's response was swift.

In fact, remarkably swift: there was something odd.

Webb felt his scalp prickling.

His exhaustion suddenly lifted. He typed in another celestial co-ordinate. He tried a third and a fourth, each one with the same amazingly fast response.

He took a surreptitious look around. Shafer was at a terminal, leaning back in his chair, arms flopped at his side. With his eyes half shut and mouth half open, and with his stubble and ponytail, he looked more like a moron in a gangster movie than one of the sharpest scientists on the planet. Noordhof was at the conference table reading some report. Both men seemed past the point of exhaustion. Quietly, Webb logged on to the Internet and navigated his way to an infrared satellite image of Europe and North Africa. The image was less than ten minutes old. Tenerife and La Palma were covered with cloud. No mountain tops protruded above them. And yet the Tenerife camera was showing a clear, sunny sky.

Slowly, a fact almost beyond comprehension sank into Webb's mind.

The observations from the robot telescope were a fake.

Lake Pepsi

Wallis rolled one of the general's Havana cheroots from one end of his mouth to the other, spat, and heaved again on the oars. Little whirlpools spun away from the boat and it lurched erratically forwards.

Wallis thought he might as well be rowing a corpse. The CJCS lay back, motionless, a hand trailing in the water. His small mouth gaped open and a strip of hairy stomach lay exposed between his Hawaiian tunic and the top of his trousers.

The corpse was calculating. From time to time Wallis thought he saw the fat man's eyes briefly studying him from behind the reflecting sunglasses. They were about half a mile out from the shore, the general's jeep a little splodge of fawn next to the jetty.

The lake, set in a ring of wooded hills, was like the caldera of some ancient volcano. A flock of snow geese flew in formation, honking high overhead, preferring the winter in Baja California to the one in Siberia: voting with their wings.

He needs an opening, Wallis decided. He said: "Quite a place you've got here, as they say in old movies."

The corpse stirred. "Margaret's," said Hooper. The comment was unnecessary: his marriage into one of the wealthiest families in America, with both showbiz and dubious New York family connections, had long been a staple of tabloid gossip. "This particular land was bought on some killing with Pepsi futures. You're practically rowing on the stuff. Foggy, feather your oars and stow your barnacles or whatever it is matelots do. Now we're going to drink a little beer, catch a coupla fish and have ourselves a friendly little talk."

The Chairman of the Joint Chiefs of Staff sat up and opened the lid of the wicker picnic basket. He moved aside a six-pack of Red Stripe and the small black briefcase which never left his side. He struggled with some fishing tackle; it looked new and the general gave the impression of a man who couldn't tell a fly from a spinnaker. A little white worm wriggled in silent agony as a hook was thrust through it, and then it was whipped through the air into the water. The geese vanished behind Jacob's Mountain and the honking faded away.

"Margaret likes her barbecues, good chance to meet people. Probably Teddy, the Clinton people and a few of her showbiz friends, maybe the Newmans. Oh, and some Mexican band. You may not want to come after you've heard me out."

"General, I've long since deduced that I'm not here for the fishing."

"Son, what you are here for will blow your mind apart. First I want to ask you a few questions. All on a hypothetical level, none of it's for real, if you get my drift."

"I get your drift."

Hooper gave a half-smile. "Sure you do, you're a bright boy. How come they call you Foggy?"

"It goes back to Parrot Island, sir. I guess I go around in a kind of haze."

"Which haze doesn't fool me. You're bright enough to know that if you report this conversation I will deny that it ever took place. Talking about boys, how's your one getting on? He's on some sort of camping trip in Allegheny, ain't he?"

Wallis's heart gave a jump. It was a distinct thump in the chest. "Didn't know you knew about it, sir," he said casually. His son had arranged it with a teenage friend only the week before. *Nobody* outside the family circle had known about it.

"Real mountain man country up there. Straight out of *Deliverance*. You got balls letting your boy go out there. Still,

I reckon they've got to find their own feet some time." Below the sunglasses, Hooper's mouth had formed into a prim smile, and the incredible fact dawned on Wallis that his commanding officer had issued a threat.

"General, why are we here?" Wallis threw his half-smoked cigar in the water with a nervous gesture. The atmosphere was suddenly tense.

"Nemesis."

"The Martian scenario."

"A tiny handful of people in America know about it. You're one of them."

"No doubt for good reason, sir." Wallis waited, an unformed sense of dread washing over him.

"Colonel, in what circumstances would you commit treason?"

Wallis stared, aghast, but all he got was his own distorted image, bulbous in the fly's eyes of his commanding officer's sunglasses.

"Sir, the question is an insult. I don't want this conversation to continue."

"The honour of your country is at stake."

"If you put it that way." Wallis retreated into his shell, slipping into a formal, military-style tone. "As you well know, sir, my oath of allegiance calls on me to serve my country, and to obey the orders of my superior officers to the limits of my conscience. If there's something in the book about treason I guess I missed it."

Hooper's eyes showed approval. "Sinews of an army, son. Without loyalty and discipline and obedience, sometimes even blind obedience, you don't have an army, you have a rampaging horde. Trouble is, obedience is morally neutral—it serves all sorts of masters. But this man's army is based on values. Cripes, the lettuce Margaret puts on my sandwiches. 'Kay, let's start easy. Suppose your superior officer was under some incredible strain, to the point where he was cracking up, couldn't think straight? If he gives some wacky order, or even worse, if he fails to act when he should, what would you do about it?"

"It's in the book, sir. I'd go over his head."

"Uhuh. And if said superior officer was right at the top?" Hooper opened a Red Stripe; he tossed the ring into the water, and it glinted as it spiralled down to oblivion. He held out a sandwich to Wallis but the colonel shook his head.

"Excuse me, but the man at the top is the President."

Hooper didn't reply. He sipped froth off the top of the can. Wallis said, quietly, "I advise you to proceed with extreme caution, General. You're on a minefield."

"Who isn't these days? I repeat my question."

"I get the drift, General, but we serve a democracy, not some banana republic. If the man at the top gets it wrong the people throw him out, not the Army."

"Sure." The general re-cast the line. It whipped through the air, and fresh ripples spread over the smooth lake surface. "A hypothetical, like I said. Suppose Eagle One has cracked under the strain. Gone pacifist, can't fulfil his duties, whatever. So he has to be removed. But say the act of removing him leads to a nuclear strike against America?"

"How could that situation arise?"

"Simple. What do you impeach the President with? Failing to counterstrike against the Russians? Do we go public with Nemesis? And what would our Kremlin friends do then? Wait for us to zap them? Fact is, they would—"

"Now hold it there, sir. The only thing you go public with is that the President is unfit for office because he's ill."

"Get real, Wallis, there are intelligent men in the Kremlin. They would read the signs. They would have to pre-empt our strike. You want to gamble America on the Russians being dumb? That's some chip to put on the table."

"The fact remains that the National Command Authority rests with the President, not with traitors."

"Colonel, your head is stuffed with mush. Remember your school history? Remember how the good guys always won, eventually? How can this be? It's not God, it happens by definition. The winners shape what later generations believe to be good. *By definition*, retrospective definition, the patriots are the guys who win and the traitors are the guys who lose. Maybe it's okay for Eagle One to let our country be attacked and do nothing. Maybe he can waive his Oath of Office. Maybe our Peacemakers and our B52s and our entire defence posture, they were always a big bluff, we never intended to retaliate when the nukes were pouring down on our frigging cities. Is that your line, Colonel? Who's the patriot—the guy who supports his country or the one who brings it down by supporting faulty constitutional structures?"

"General, I would like for us to go back now."

"They'll bite, Foggy, give them time. Deal with the facts. Fact One, Nemesis is coming in: we're under attack now. Fact Two, the Chief is psychologically paralysed: he's unable to discharge his duty to defend America. Fact Three, any appeal to the people by way of Senate or Supreme Court or any constitutional mechanism alerts the Russians and exposes us to nuclear annihilation. That's why you're here, that's the problem, and I still haven't heard your solution."

"Are you asking me to join a conspiracy?"

Hooper paused, then he grinned slyly and said: "Hell no, Foggy, this is a purely hypothetical discussion, remember? You're being asked to think. For the first time in your life, to judge by your performance so far."

"Sure. Hypothetical like the man from Mars."

Hooper forced the point relentlessly. "What we have here is a flaw built into the Constitution. Say your Commander in Chief is abandoning his responsibilities, betraying his Oath of Office. Now say that public impeachment of said Chief would alert the enemy and bring forth the Day of Judgement. What I need from you is an answer: what would you do about it?"

"Not my problem."

"On the contrary, Foggy, for reasons which will emerge this evening, you're the key. Answer my question."

Wallis felt as if doors were closing all around him. He said, "I'll have that beer now."

Hooper tried another tack. He wedged the fishing rod between his knees and reached for a can, tossing it to the soldier; water lapped against the underside of the boat with the slight movement. He opened his briefcase and pulled out a sheet of paper. "Typed it out this morning. Listen:

> "A strict observance of the written laws is doubtless one of the high duties of a good citizen, but it is not the highest. The laws of necessity, of self-preservation, of saving our country when in danger, are of a higher obligation.

"Okay so far? Now listen to this:

> "To lose our country by a scrupulous adherence to written law would be to lose the law itself, with life, liberty, property and all those who are enjoying them with us; thus absurdly sacrificing the end to the means.

"Straight from the horse's mouth, boy, from Thomas Jefferson. The guy who *wrote* the frigging Constitution. You know, reading this, Jefferson practically anticipated Nemesis."

"I know what you're asking me. I need time."

"Time, laddie, is the one commodity we do not have. Hey!" The line went taut. Hooper began to pull at the rod, reeling it in. "Hell, Foggy," the CJCS went on in a more conciliatory tone, "we've all been programmed with particular values and these work for us nearly all the time, but democracy is only a tool. It has limits like any other tool and sometimes you have to do things for the public good that the public would lynch you for if . . . damn you, I'm trying to talk to this guy . . . look, this is a new game and you need new rules . . . stop wriggling . . ." Hooper stood up and the boat rocked dangerously as he reached out for a writhing fish.

"Steelhead, General, it's a beauty."

"Time's running out, Colonel, and we need to know where you stand."

"We?"

"Party starts about eight o'clock. We'll be looking for answers." Hooper, grimacing horribly, held up the squirming fish. "Now what the hell's bells do I do with this?"

The Party

[Extract from testimony before the Defense Appropriations Sub-Committee of the House of Representatives in relation to USAF budget. John Chalfont, Utah Democrat, presiding.]

Chalfont: Well, what I'm asking is, say the President has a heart attack or something and he doesn't relinquish authority, who then can make the decision to launch if the situation requires it?

Hooper: Sir, that is not an area we like to talk about much.

Chalfont: But the word has to come from someone, is what I'm getting at. We can't just be a headless chicken.

Hooper: No sir, it has to come from the Vice-President. We are at all times available to respond.

Chalfont: Well, say SecDef walks into your office and tells you to launch your missiles, you don't need codes or stuff like that and he has the authority because the President is sick. Do you do it?

Hooper: The policy is that the President makes that decision.

Chalfont: But he's sick.

Hooper: I don't believe I can answer that.

Hamilton: What my colleague is getting at is, with the new Russian threat, we can't afford another Haig fiasco, we have to get the right finger on the button. Who has the authority to press the button if the Commander-in-Chief is out of it? Say the national interest suddenly required a launch.

Hooper: The Vice-President has the authority.

Chalfont: General, I don't want to sound as if I disagree with that, but is it not still the case that the CJCS needs to be consulted?

Hooper: He's subordinate but yes, he has, that hasn't changed from the First Cold War days.

Hamilton: He holds the appropriate codes?

Hooper: A lot of us hold the codes, down to the Brigadier-General on the Cover All plane.

Hamilton: A hypothetical, General. Say the President and the Vice-President are killed in a plane crash and Zhirinovsky sees his chance . . .

Hooper: We could respond.

Hamilton: Are you then telling us that a military authority exists for launching nukes separate from the civilian one?

Hooper: I did not say that, sir.

Hamilton: What does that mean? Is that a denial?

Hooper: Well, there's no actual military authority as such but look, the Situation Room is soft and Raven Rock is hard. Say Washington is wiped out and nukes are pouring down on our country. What would you expect military commanders to do in that situation?

Hamilton: So authority to launch passes from the President to the Vice-President, with CJCS in consultation, and what we're trying to get at is, what does the decision handbook say if they're both incapacitated? What is the civilian authority?

Hooper: It has to be the Secretary of Defense, in consultation with the Joint Chiefs.

Chalfont: And if SecDef was in that plane crash?

Hooper: Well, that's a pretty hypothetical scenario, if I may say so, sir.

Chalfont: But what if?

Hooper: You're into a massive decapitation there, but there are still procedures. [Remainder of reply deleted.]

*There's a conspiracy to overthrow the President, maybe
kill him. They want me to join it, and I'm thinking about it.*

The gorilla leaned precariously backwards, mouth agape,
scratching its armpits and making what it imagined were
gorilla-like noises. A French whore, her slim legs straddling
the neck of her onion-selling companion, stretched her arm
over the gorilla, unsteadily trying to pour a glass of red Martini down its throat. The onion seller staggered, the whore
screamed, Martini arced through the air and a little crowd
cheered as they collapsed on to the grass and the gorilla
jumped up and down shouting *Ooh! Ooh! Ooh!*

God, I hate these people.

Wallis had another problem. She was a dusky, blonde,
man-eating southern belle, full of pouting coyness; she was
dressed in a red crinoline dress of alarming cleavage; and
she was also, Wallis had learned with increasing desperation, persistent to the point of obtuseness. Ten minutes of
guttural snarling in response to her subtle probing had failed
to dislodge her.

"What exactly do you do, honey?" she finally asked outright, in an Alabama drawl.

"I'm a sanitary engineer," he said in a sudden inspiration.

"You mean you're not in movies?" she asked in dismay,
the demure pout vanishing and the accent becoming pure
Bronx.

"Hell no, I'm in excrement, Miss. You know the Chinese
have been spreading sewage on their fields for thousands of
years? Well a bunch of us thought, why can't we do the same
here? So we've got a pilot plant going, trying to turn the
sludge into little pellets for fertilizer. It's working fine except the stuff smells, but we're working on that too. Say, that
guy near the marquee—oh, he's just gone in—wasn't that
Hal Brooker?"

"Hal Brooker the movie producer?" she asked, turning.

"Yeah I think so. They tell me he's casting for some cos-
tume piece about the Civil War. Anyway, the beauty is, we

extract the methane from the crap and use it as a fuel to operate the process. So the plant costs nothing to run, isn't that exciting?"

"Real exciting," she said. "Listen, it's been nice talking to you."

"But there's more. Methane is a greenhouse gas," Wallis called after the retreating figure. "By burning it up we're helping the environment." But Miss Low Cleavage had vanished along the flight path to the marquee.

God, I hate these people, Wallis thought again. He drifted casually across the lawn, drink in hand, judging the ebb and flow of the crowd. Past the pool. Don't catch anybody's eye. Expensive bridgework sparkled at him out of a tanned face; Wallis pretended not to see it. People were dancing. The Tijuana Brass were sending soft, metallic notes over the rich, the beautiful and the Mexican waiters in short red jackets and tight black trousers.

Report the conspiracy and condemn my son to death. A boy of sixteen, somewhere in the Alleghenies.

Down the steps to the patio, where a large pig was covered in banana leaves, with its body cavity stuffed and its alimentary canal replaced by a long metal spit. The pig rotated unhappily about its horizontal axis while flames roasted its flesh and its fellow mammals nibbled at canapés and drank tequila from salt-encrusted glasses. The smell of burning charcoal and flesh hovered over the party. Wallis passed by.

Report it to whom? How deep does the treason go?

About fifty yards out from the lodge, the crowds began to thin. Little clusters of people chattered and laughed under the floodlit magnolia trees and the monkey puzzles. The trees were draped with tinsel and linked by long chains of multicoloured lanterns; but the Christmas lights were more for effect than illumination, and here the shadows were dark. An overheated Santa Claus, his face flushed, was into a serious discussion with a Barbary pirate. Wallis nodded to them but he passed by unnoticed. Then he was at the edge of the

lawn, marked out by bougainvillaea. He glanced behind,
and casually strolled through them, into the shadows and
the fir trees.

He went steadily on, the carpet of pine crackling under his
feet. A couple of hundred yards in he stopped. There were
shafts of light through the branches, but no human silhouettes:
he was alone. Latin American rhythm was still in the air, but
the night sounds of the forest were beginning to compete.

*But what if the President is the traitor, and the conspira-
tors are the loyal Americans? Are the patriots really the guys
who win, by definition?*

He came across a track, just visible in the darkness.
Whether made by humans or large animals he could not say,
but he followed it. It climbed steeply up. About half a mile
from the lodge, panting with exertion, he cut away from the
path and wandered randomly, still climbing. He came to a
clearing about twenty yards wide, and sat down. The ground
was bone dry and covered with moss. Pinewood scented the
air. There was a gust of laughter and a woman's scream from
far below. Someone had fallen or jumped into the pool.

*I don't need to think about stuff like that. The President is
my commanding officer. I obey his orders. Period.*

A half moon had risen over the mountains to the right,
and it was reflecting off the snowy peaks, and the roofs of
the Mercs and Porsches parked behind the lodge. The Pacific
was a huge black hole over to the left.

The classic Nuremberg Defence. I vass only obeying orders.

Wallis had a brief, fantastic urge to get out of it, find a
freeway, hitch a lift to anywhere. But not at night, in flowing
Arab robes. Not even in California.

There was a metallic glint from far along the approach
road to the lodge. Wallis could just make out a shadowy figure, standing. The man might have been speaking into a
walkie-talkie.

I'm not cut out for this frigging moral dilemma stuff.

The soldier lay back, his eyes by now dark-adapted. The

broad swathe of the Milky Way was overhead, dazzling, amazing. The filmy ribbon was divided by a great black rift; it swirled across the sky, a highway for gods and ghosts and creatures of the mind.

Was Jefferson right? Country before obedience? But who sets the acceptable limits on obedience? The guys giving the orders?

Something came into his vision, approaching from the Pacific. It was a moving star. It grew brighter and Wallis sat up. A faint chopping sound came over "Stranger on the Shore" and the shrilling cicadas. A helicopter. Two miles out from the lodge, its lights were extinguished. It was just visible in the moonlight. It flew low over the trees, descending. The soldier lost it behind a hill but it reappeared, sinking towards the lodge. It touched down about three hundred yards back from the car park. A solitary figure came out, bent double, and moved briskly towards the back of the lodge. The chopper revved up, rose and soared away, following the line of the approach road and disappearing from Wallis's sight.

Wallis wondered about that. He was startled to find himself wondering about the beliefs, quietly held and strongly cherished, which had guided his life.

Maybe everything I've ever believed is junk. Maybe patriotism and loyalty and morality are just brain implants, devices put in my head from the age of five for purposes of control. Maybe it's all just a game and there's no right and wrong beyond my own sense of right and wrong. So follow my private conscience and screw the rules?

He lit up a small Jamaica cheroot, his match throwing a brief circle of light around him. He was still thinking in confused circles, a cigar later, when the hairs on the back of his head began to prickle. There was the faintest crackle of breaking pine needles, somewhere behind him. Casually, he stood up and turned. A young man, standing in the shadows. Twenty yards away. Smart, dark suit, close-cropped hair. Motionless as a statue.

"Sorry to startle you, sir. General Hooper's compliments. He requests that you rejoin the party."

"Evening, fella. Now how the hell did you find me way up here?" With a gut-wrenching start, Wallis realized that he must have been under surveillance from the moment he had left the party.

"If you'll follow me down, sir."

The party was three drinks noisier. The Tijuana Brass were into some frenetic number, but a young couple were dancing, waist-high in the water, to some private music of their own. Wallis followed the young man across the lawn, past the pool and over the patio. The young man nodded farewell and made off in unparty-like, military strides. A fat man in dark glasses and a blue sombrero had a slice of pork wedged between two thick slices of bread in one hand, and a large cigar in the other. He saw Wallis and detached himself from a group. Silver sequins covered the man's sombrero and extended down over his black suit, as if he had been showered with sticky confetti. Wallis recognized him first by the whiff of Macanudo cigar smoke.

"Ah, there you are, Foggy. Great party, huh? Saw you and the Farmington girl. Should've stuck in there, boy, that family owns half of Texas."

"Which half?"

"The one Margaret doesn't own."

"I'm an old married man, sir," said Wallis.

"Sure you are, yes sirree. Son, you can't just hide away like that, the world's too small and we're too smart. You want to mix mix mix. We got a visitor. Follow follow follow."

Hooper, wriggling his fat bottom energetically, rumba'd his way past the now half-eaten pig. He gobbled the last of his sandwich and lifted two red Martinis from a passing silver tray, leaving the smoking cigar. He blew the waiter a kiss, but the man's Aztec features remained frozen. Then the soldiers were through the open French windows of the lodge.

A log fire crackled in the downstairs room, throwing its flickering light over a dozen hugging couples.

Wallis followed his leader up the pinewood stairs and along a corridor whose floor was soft with Chinese carpet and whose subdued lighting showed walls lined with paintings signed by de Heem, Marieschi and Laurencin. They passed Wallis's bedroom and turned left into a small study, all red decor and mock colonial furniture. The band had started up on "Rudolf the Red-Nosed Reindeer" and the door shut it off with a pneumatic clunk.

A werewolf, in a dark three-piece suit, was lounging back in a grey swivel chair behind a desk, the hairs of its face bristling. A lamp and a thin, red book were on the desk, which was otherwise bare. Eyes assessed Wallis from behind the mask. The werewolf indicated chairs and the soldiers sat down. Hooper took off his sombrero and dropped it to the floor, and the bonhomie went off with it. The soldiers put their drinks on the desk.

"The Ayrab—is he with us or not?" the werewolf asked.

"We have a definite maybe," Hooper replied.

"What's his hangup?"

"Some crap about his oath of allegiance."

"Look," said Wallis, "what General Hooper tells me is that I have two duties, one to my President and one to my country. The two have always coincided. Until now. What we have now is a President unable to act because he's frozen by cowardice or pacifism or whatever, and I have to ask, which comes first, President or country?"

The werewolf nodded encouragement, but its eyes were filled with caution.

"My oath of allegiance is to the Constitution, not the President. But, we have procedures. Remove him constitutionally, I tell the General here. But he tells me that the act of so removing the President is too dangerous. The Russians will cotton on to what's happening and try to nuke us, out of fear for themselves. The story he's trying to sell me is that the price of constitutional action is the obliteration of America. Which would make the Constitution a bit pointless in the first place."

"He's grasped the issue. I told you he's a bright boy," said Hooper.

"But what the General forgot to mention," Wallis continued, "is that the Chief might act at the last. Maybe he's praying for a miracle. When the Almighty fails to oblige, the President might still come up with the Major Attack Option. We just won't know until Nemesis is practically in our air space. Any removal of the Chief before the last seconds is blatant mutiny."

Hooper made a noise like escaping steam, and gulped down the second of his drinks. Bellarmine took off his mask and said: "Colonel, it's the only way we ever thought to operate."

"I don't know why I'm listening to this. This chatter is about treason. The decision to nuke belongs to the President of the United States and him alone."

"I don't believe so," the Secretary of Defense replied calmly. He opened the book in front of him. "Truman document NSC memorandum number thirty invests the authority to launch nukes with the President. Okay. But there's an answer," he continued. "Listen to this. Here is Section Four of the Twenty-fifth Amendment to the Constitution:

> "Whenever the Vice-President and a majority of either the principal officers of the executive department or of such other body as Congress may by law provide, transmit to the President *pro tempore* of the Senate and the Speaker of the House of Representatives their written declaration that the President is unable to discharge the powers and duties of his office, the Vice-President shall immediately assume the powers and duties of the office as Acting President . . ."

"Now hold on, sir," said Wallis. "Who are the executive department? Surely at least the Cabinet? What about presidential aides?"

"Why not the whole frigging civil service?" Hooper interrupted. "Let's wait for the cruise missiles to swarm out of Chesapeake Bay like Venus arising and then get the Speaker out of his bed, assemble Congress for a nice cosy debate and have the typists standing by for the written declaration. The missiles will get here faster than you can read it, never mind type it, but hell, I'm just a soldier, I guess we have to get the Supreme Court in on the act while the bombs are falling."

"Ease off, Sam, you're on too much choke," said the Secretary of Defense. "Wallis, I respect your need for a legal basis, but it exists. The authority for launching nuclear weapons passes through the President, the Vice-President and myself as SecDef. The procedural requirement is that a decision to launch is made in consultation with Hooper here as Chief of JCS."

"That means two against two," said Wallis, "with the President carrying the ultimate authority."

"There's a loophole," said Bellarmine. "In the context of the Situation Room, with a nuclear strike in the balance, and each and every second of huge importance, Hooper and I alone are the principal officers of the executive department. On the issue of presidential fitness to discharge his powers and duties, Hooper and I alone make the decision. We don't consult the cabinet, and we dispense with written declarations. The guys who wrote this stuff just didn't have this situation to handle."

"Seems to me that, by the Twenty-fifth, if you remove Grant you end up with the Vice-President," said Wallis. "Where does McCulloch stand?"

Bellarmine said, "He hasn't been briefed. He knows nothing about Nemesis."

"Come on, pal, McCulloch's a chimpanzee," Hooper interrupted. "Fat wino shopkeeper with an IQ about sixty. He couldn't even grasp the issues. Everybody knows Grant just chose him for the Southern vote. You want a chimpanzee to make the decision for a nuclear strike? Is that what you want, Wallis? The decision left to a chimpanzee?"

"Yes, sir, if it's next in the chain of command."

Bellarmine tapped his fingers on the table. "McCulloch won't be available for consultation."

"What does that mean in plain English, sir?"

Hooper said, "Foggy, you might want to consider whether that's an appropriate tone to address the Secretary. What you've just been told is all you need to know. McCulloch won't be available for consultation."

"But by the Twenty-fifth, you need the Vice-President to remove the President."

"He won't be available for consultation," Hooper repeated in a voice which closed the matter.

Bellarmine continued. "Our problem is this, Colonel Wallis. Suppose we remove Grant by wielding the Twenty-fifth. Would the Communications personnel then accept my authority as President *pro tempore*? The big enemy is the clock. The whole transfer of command has to be over in seconds. There will be no time for long explanations. Or even short ones."

"The swiftest rebellion in history," said Hooper. "It has to be over and the new chain of command in place in the seconds between the asteroid entering our air space and the blast reaching our silos."

"Which is where you come in, Wallis, you and your Signals background," Bellarmine continued. "A transfer will come through for you in the next day or two. You will be given command of the communications room. Briefing sessions are being set up for you. You will be in charge of the personnel at the crucial moment. The decision that Communications accepts my authority will be made by you. Our counterstrike will then be enabled."

"You're trying to slip one over on me," Wallis insisted. "If the President is removed you still have the Vice-President."

Hooper banged a fist on the table. "We have here the most doggone stubborn soldier in this man's army." Bellarmine raised a hand to silence the Chief of the JCS.

Wallis bowed his head for some seconds. Then he said, thinking as he spoke, "I suppose if the Vice-President is out of it, and the President is legitimately removed by the Twenty-fifth, and SecDef at least is the only relevant principal officer in the circumstances, then yes"—he seemed to come to a decision—"the SecDef does become the Acting President. Gentlemen, I can't connive in the removal of the Vice-President from the decision-making process. But if for whatever reason he is absent at the crucial moment, I can then follow your orders with a clear conscience."

In a moment of panic, Wallis realized that with these words he had become a party to a plot to overthrow the President of the United States and launch a nuclear strike in which the dead would be counted in the hundreds of millions. "Oh Holy Christ," he added, suddenly feeling nauseous.

Bellarmine half-smiled.

"Margaret's fixed up for a fireworks display about now," Hooper said, picking up his sombrero.

"I'll want to bring some of my own people with me, people who know me," Wallis said, cold sweat developing on his brow.

Hooper stood up. "Sure and begorrah. Just let me have their names. We shouldn't miss it."

Bellarmine turned into a werewolf again.

The crowd Ooh'd and Aah'd as rockets whooshed into the night sky, exploding with a *Whump!* into multi-coloured stars, while a dazzling waterfall of silver flame poured expensively on to the far end of the lawn. Wallis thought of the shadowy figure he had seen on the approach road, and the polite young man who had known just where to find him in the dark woods.

*If I'd made for the freeway, I would probably now be
wrapped in chains, and spiralling down towards the bottom
of Lake Pepsi: an act of patriots, for love of country.*

Soft flesh was pressing against his arm. Another starlet-
in-waiting, hormones awash, dark eyes staring up into his;
she said isn't it exciting; and he slid an arm around her waist
and said Yeah sister, cool, like I'm glad I slipped out of the
AIDS hospice for the night.

Part Two
ITALIAN MASQUE

masque [<Fr. <It. *masquerata*: see MASK] 1. a masked ball. 2. a disguise, pretence. *vi.* 1. to take part in a masquerade. 2. to act under false pretences.

DAY FOUR

Eagle Peak, Thursday Morning

Webb wakened with a jerk around 7 a.m., having had two hours' sleep in the past twenty-four. The memory of that morning's unsettling discovery came to him—but something else, an inspiration, was speaking to him like a voice inside his head. The Tenerife question would have to wait.

Fearful that the thought would fade as he came to, he focused on it single-mindedly, visualizing it in an assortment of bizarre contexts. He staggered to the bathroom and shaved off a two-day stubble under a shower, his eyes closed. He then dressed quickly, by now fully awake and easily able to resist the fatal inner voice telling him to stretch out again for a couple of minutes.

He tapped on Noordhof's door, Number Four with a desert view, and tapped again. Noordhof appeared in underpants, swimming with sleep. The soldier, Webb noticed, had the beginnings of a pot belly.

"Colonel, I need to make a call to Europe."

Noordhof scratched under his armpit. "Telephones are death, Oliver."

"I've had an idea. It's a long shot and it's probably dead in the water. But if it's right it leads us straight to Nemesis."

Noordhof was instantly awake. "Okay. We'll use the secure cable to Albuquerque. I'll ask our Communications hotshots to route your call via some innocuous address. Who are you calling?"

"An old friend. She's not in the asteroid business, not

even in science. Nobody would have reason to connect her with Nemesis."

"Give me ten minutes, then join me in the common room."

Webb put on a heavy pullover and went outside, running around the building in sheer frustration. Judy's Firebird was tinged with frost, and the tracks of small animals criss-crossed the car park snow, concentrating around the garbage bins.

"Join me, Oliver?" Judy asked, emerging from the main door in her grey tracksuit. "Ten minutes' aerobic."

"Thanks, Judy, but not this morning. You'll stay within Noordhof's hundred-metre circle, of course."

She smiled enigmatically. Webb followed her trim, lithe frame as she took off through the trees at a fair pace, blonde hair bouncing. In spite of their weird heart-to-heart of only a few hours ago, she was still, to him, an enigma. Either she hadn't grasped the responsibility she was carrying, or there were nerves of steel underneath that bouncy exterior.

Noordhof, now dressed in smart casual style, was waiting for Webb at the telephone. Shafer was in an armchair, covering a sheet of paper with equations; he gave Webb a friendly wave without looking up.

"Right. This call can't be overheard at the US end but we can't answer for Europe. We had to give you a local address because of the transatlantic delay. If your friend asks, you're phoning from the Ramada Inn in Tucson. We're reserving a room there in your name as a precaution. You're doing the Grand Canyon, the Painted Desert, whatever. Dial out as usual. Just be extremely careful what you say. I'll be listening on the kitchen extension."

Webb dialled, and a few seconds later a male voice answered, "Western Manuscripts," as clearly as if it came from three feet away.

"Virginia Melbourne, please."

"She's at home today."

"Thank you." Webb dialled her Bicester home number. It rang for nearly a minute; and then a contralto, somewhat husky voice said "Virginia Melbourne."

"Hi, Virginia."

A transatlantic pause, and then: "Ollie! How are you? Are you calling from Oxford?"

"Actually I'm in the States. What mischief are you up to, Virginia?"

"For starters, I'm standing here naked and dripping wet."

"I'll try not to think about that."

"I'd rather you did, darling. Whereabouts in the States are you?" Noordhof, looking through the open doorway from the kitchen, visibly tensed.

"Arizona, doing the tour. I thought I'd treat myself to a warm Christmas for a change but I'm beginning to twitch. You remember that manuscript I was translating? Volume Three of *Phaenomenis Novae*, by Father Vincenzo?"

"Remember it, darling? We scoured the Bod looking for it. Did your lost photocopy ever turn up?"

"No. What about your original?"

"No. It's still missing. And you just can't steal a manuscript from Western Manuscripts: our archives are a hundred per cent secure. It's the oddest thing."

"Virginia, I need a favour." Webb ignored the wicked chuckle in his ear. "You told me there's an original?"

"*The* original. Our Bodleian copy was a Late Renaissance transcription made in Amsterdam. Looking at myself in the mirror, I'd say I have a pretty good figure."

"Where can I get my hands on it?"

"The manuscript, you mean? It's somewhere in Italy. I can't be sure. Vincenzo's not one of your big names, Ollie, not like Galileo."

"Please, Virginia!"

"Well now, I might be able to rustle up a contact for you. I think one of the Jesuit priests at Castelgandolfo could point the way. Shall I look into it?"

"Please. Send me as much information as you can about the historical background to *Phaenomenis*. I'm preparing a monograph on comets, and I thought I'd say something about the Renaissance theories. Maybe draw up a chapter outline while I'm at the Grand Canyon."

Virginia's contralto voice dripped with unconcealed envy. "Some people have all the sodding luck. Can you access a terminal?"

Noordhof was tensed up again.

"Yes, I'm due to drop in on a colleague at the University of Arizona."

"In that case I'll scan things in and type something up, and put it on anonymous ftp. You should be able to access it through my home page within a couple of hours. But it'll cost you."

"Name your price."

"A weekend in Paris?"

"Agreed."

"A naughty one?"

Noordhof's eyeballs were rolling.

"Virginia, I'm forever grateful. Byee."

Elated, the astronomer turned to Noordhof. "Mark, I must get to Rome right away. I want to get my hands on a four-hundred-year-old manuscript."

Noordhof was about to reply but the glass door banged open and there was the sound of running footsteps along the corridor. Judy entered the room panting, flushed and shaking. "Come quickly."

The men left Kowalski and Sacheverell asleep and followed her at a fast trot to the cable car shed. She pointed upwards. A wisp of cloud was swirling around Eagle Peak; but then it cleared, and they could just discern a man dangling from the cable car, his arms at full stretch, legs waving.

Webb sprinted back to the observatory building and reappeared with a coastguard telescope and a tripod. They quickly set it up. In the eyepiece, Webb traced the cable up to the summit. The top platform almost filled the field of view. The car had stopped about twenty feet down from it. There was a clear three thousand feet of air between the man and the ground below. "It's André. The door's open and he's hanging on to the edge of the floor. By the tips of his fingers, I think."

"How the bloody hell?" Shafer asked.

Judy's fists were at her mouth, clenched in fright. "How long has he been like that?"

Noordhof ran into the cable car winch house. Judy and Shafer followed him in, staring up through the big plate glass window. Webb stayed at the eyepiece. Noordhof moved over to the panel. It was on a gunmetal grey desk, with a large On–Off switch and a lever marked Up and Down.

"What are you doing, Mark?" Webb called in.

"I'm sliding the car up. He can't hang on like that for more than a few minutes."

"You'll knock him off. He'll hit the concrete platform."

"It's up or down. And his grip won't last the trip down."

Shafer was holding his head in his hands, looking up. "How long has he been hanging like that?"

"Try it slow," Webb shouted in to the winch house.

Noordhof pulled the big switch to On. The motor whined and gears clashed. He turned the lever slowly from neutral towards its Up position. In the eyepiece of the telescope, Webb saw the little car jerk alarmingly, and Leclerc's feet wave frantically in space. It edged up towards the platform. The Frenchman's body drew alongside a concrete wall; it seemed to be scraping his back.

"Slow!" Webb shouted in. Then "Stop! He's not going to make it. It's the Eskimo suit. There isn't the space. If we try to drag him through he'll lose his grip."

Noordhof sprinted out and put his eye to the telescope. Leclerc's head seemed almost to be jammed in the space between platform and car. His arms were stretched full length above him, as if he was grasping for something almost out of reach. He was about one unattainable metre from safety.

The soldier ran back into the building, and reversed the direction of the lever. Webb saw the Frenchman drifting clear of the narrow gap, and then he was into open space. "He's clear!" Noordhof put the lever to its maximum. The engine whine rose in pitch and the steel cable vibrated tautly, winding swiftly on to the big drum. They ran out and watched the little car sink towards them.

Leclerc was hanging motionless, his legs no longer waving. He was now well out from the cliff. Webb thought he was looking down. For the first few hundred feet the descent of the car seemed to be agonizingly slow; as it approached the halfway mark it seemed to be descending marginally faster, and although Webb knew that to be an illusion of perspective, he began to think that Leclerc might make it. But two thirds of the way down, at about a thousand feet above ground, the Frenchman lost his grip.

Judy screamed. Webb shouted No! Leclerc hurtled down with terrifying acceleration, arms and legs waving helplessly in the air. He hit a projection of the cliff a few hundred feet up and as many feet away from the horrified group. The muffled "Thud!" came above the whine from the winch house, and a shower of little stones and earth followed the body which bounced high before disappearing into the treetops.

Judy ran back to the main building without a word. Noordhof, Shafer and Webb ran through the trees. They found Leclerc without difficulty, a path of broken branches marking his flight path. Noordhof and Shafer paled, and Webb turned away. He found a quiet corner. His body tried to vomit but his stomach was empty.

Noordhof took off his blue anorak and covered the Frenchman's head with it, stepping to avoid the dark red snow near the corpse. They searched around for heavy stones to secure the anorak in position.

Judy had coffee on the boil when they returned. Her eyes were red. Noordhof disappeared momentarily and returned with a half bottle of cognac which he emptied into the coffee percolator before Judy poured. Webb crossed to the kitchen sink and splashed icy water over his face, drying off with a dish towel. He felt reasonably calm inwardly and was surprised to find that he could not lift his mug without spilling the coffee. After the third attempt he left it on the table.

Shafer drank down half his coffee in one draught. "Okay Mark, talk about it. How could that possibly have happened? And what was he doing up top, anyway? He's not an observer."

Noordhof said, "This is how I see it. He goes up top for whatever reason, maybe just for the view. He pulls the lever but trips up when he gets to the car. End of our rocket man."

"Truly an accident?" Judy asked in a shaky voice.

Noordhof shrugged. "What else?"

Murder, Webb thought to himself.

Judy's hands were trembling and her eyes were tearful. So, maybe she was a good actress. He glanced at Noordhof. If he was an actor he was underplaying his hand: the soldier was cool and self-controlled. Webb was startled to find Willy Shafer looking at him closely, as if the Nobel man was reading his mind. *Or maybe he's wondering about me*, Webb surmised.

Shafer said, "This is a police matter."

"Sure." There was a long silence.

Judy came back from the cooker and joined them at the table. Her speech was unsteady but composed. "You don't have to say it, Colonel, we all know we can't realistically involve the cops. There's just too much at stake for questions. But if we don't report this we put ourselves on the wrong side of the law. And the more we try to conceal this accident, the more we dig ourselves into a hole. We have to dispose of a body. How do we do this?"

Noordhof said, "We have to keep our eye on the ball here. This is arguably a military police matter but, Judy, I'm glad you see it that way. Frankly, the legalities don't matter a damn. We just have to find Nemesis in the three days remaining to us, which includes today. That's our overriding goal and nothing, not even death in the team, can be allowed to deflect us."

Shafer spoke to Noordhof. "But we still have a body out there, Mark. And Leclerc must have relatives, maybe a family."

"Leclerc was a widower with no family. His secretary was made to think he'd taken leave. Nobody in France knows where he is."

Shafer looked as if he was trying to read the soldier's mind. "You have access to people who can handle this type of situation, right?"

Noordhof sipped thoughtfully at his *caffè corretto*. "I'm amazed at your perspicacity, Willy, but I don't suppose I should be since you're on this team for your brains. Yes, I understand there are guys on the payroll who can handle this type of situation all the way from the scene of the death to the coroner's report. I'll make a call." He toyed with a spoon. "I'll let Kenneth and Herb sleep on, and inform them when they get up. McNally is due back from Toulouse later today. Look, we can't let ourselves be paralysed by this. Some people will arrive in the next hour or two but they won't come in and you'll have no contact with them. Once they've left, Leclerc will have gone and it will never have happened."

Noordhof changed the subject abruptly. "Oliver, what were Leclerc and you cooking up?"

Webb briefly wondered how much to tell. "I wanted to exploit André's tremendous knowledge of Russian space capabilities. Particularly their launch hardware, degree of electronic sophistication and details of past space enterprises. We were going to liaise to find out what asteroids they could conceivably have reached and diverted in the past."

Shafer said, "NASA and Space Command must be stuffed with people who know things like that."

"SecDef requires a European involvement or two for political reasons. He was very clear about that. It'll take a day or two to identify, brief and transport someone suitable over."

"That's too late," said Webb. He was trembling. "I needed Leclerc today. This morning."

"Are we coming apart here?" Shafer asked.

"Oliver," said Noordhof, looking agitated. "Think of something. You must have a Plan B."

"André was Plan B. Plan A was looking for something unusual in the sky, some signature of the Russian deflection of Nemesis. It wasn't working as of three o'clock this morning."

"Can you pick up on it again?"

Webb hesitated. "I can but we're into the long shots. That phone call I made earlier."

Noordhof said, "Long shots are all we have left. Yeah, what gives with that manuscript thing?"

Sacheverell wandered in, bleary-eyed and barefooted, wrapped in a white towelling gown. He poured himself coffee, pulled out a chair and sat down at the table. He sipped at his coffee and gave it a startled look. He looked around, eyes blinking. He seemed to sense an atmosphere but said nothing.

Webb found that he could now just lift his coffee without spilling it. He gulped the hot liquid down.

Shafer said, "Out with it, man."

"It's thin. A manuscript went missing a couple of months back. A notebook by Vincenzo."

"*The* Vincenzo?" Sacheverell asked sleepily.

"Yes. I was hoping to translate the eighteenth-century transcription in the Bodleian. I had a photocopy made but it went missing from my apartment before I had a chance to look at it. Nothing else was touched. I had a Chubb lock and secure windows and there was no sign of forced entry. Whoever took it (a) knew exactly what they were after, and (b) were highly skilled thieves. But now it gets really weird. I go back to the Library to get another photocopy, to be told that in the meantime their original too has gone missing. Now that just can't happen. Understand, Herb, that we're talking about security like that surrounding the Crown Jewels."

Sacheverell looked baffled. "I guess I'm still asleep. What has a seventeenth-century monk got to do with anything?"

"Someone has gone to a lot of trouble. Maybe there's something in Vincenzo's notebook that people don't want us to see."

Sacheverell blinked. His gaze wandered towards the big window. When he spoke, there was a weariness in his voice. "I'm still asleep. This is a weird dream. Ollie's brain is still wired up to ancient history only now he's turned it into some kind of intellectual game for his personal amusement."

"Just drink your coffee, Herb."

"He's freaked out by the responsibility we're carrying here."

Noordhof tapped the kitchen table. "Hey, you two. Don't start."

Webb said, "I've been thinking about the precision needed to guide Nemesis. You don't just need to get a precise deflection, you also need to know where you're deflecting from to six or seven decimal places. Very few Earth-crossers are known to that degree of accuracy. They wouldn't dare plant radio beacons on it, for all to detect, and the chances are it would be out of radar range even if the Russians had a sufficient deep space radar facility. It seems to me they'd have to derive the pre-deflection orbit using optical data just as we do. Okay so maybe the cosmonauts sat on Nemesis for a year, navigating and computing until they got it all worked out. But there might just be a much easier way."

Noordhof poured more coffee into Webb's mug. The astronomer emptied it and Noordhof replenished. "Most of these orbits are chaotic, meaning that tiny uncertainties— just a few kilometres—build up so that after three or four hundred years the asteroid could be just about anywhere. But the converse is this." Webb raised a finger in the air. "Suppose you did know precisely where it was four hundred years ago. That would give you a time base maybe fifty times longer than anything you could get with modern observations. Now if you had such an observation, even a very coarse one, you would tie down the modern behaviour of the orbit to a tremendous degree of precision. It would be just what you needed to target the asteroid."

Sacheverell spoke to the sugar jar on the table. "There has to be an explanation for this and it can only be that I'm still dreaming. In case anyone hasn't noticed, we can hardly find these things with wide aperture Schmidts and CCDs, never mind the lousy toys they had four hundred years ago."

"I'm in no mood for an argument, Herb, but there's precedent for this. Uranus was recorded over twenty times before it was finally recognized as a planet in 1781. I was looking for pre-discovery observations of Encke's comet in old star maps and manuscripts. You need a strong telescope to see it nowadays, but it was seen a dozen or more times with the naked eye in the nineteenth century. Anything capable of a close encounter with the Earth could have been picked up with a two-inch refractor or even the naked eye."

Sacheverell took another sip. "I might have known it. You're into the old Clube and Napier rubbish. Did I get out of bed for this?"

"So what about the manuscript, Ollie?" Shafer asked. "If it's gone what can you do about it?"

"My contact at the Bod tells me that one copy still remains. It's the original, and it's held by someone somewhere in central Italy. I want to find that manuscript and see what's in it."

Noordhof's voice was dripping with incredulity. "Let me get this straight. Your conjecture is that information vital to the survival of the United States could be in this ancient manuscript."

"All copies of which were quietly and systematically removed. There had to be a reason for that."

"Ollie . . ." Noordhof was starting to play with a cigar. "I have to go with Herb on this. We're almost out of time here. We can't afford the luxury of eccentric diversions."

"Now hold it right there, Colonel." Shafer's tone was firm. "We have to let Ollie run with this. Okay it sounds crazy to us. But he's on this team because he knows his business and sometimes crazy ideas are the best."

"Anyone got a match? I bow to your wisdom as exemplified by your Nobel Prizes, Willy. But I still think Ollie's time would be better spent giving us a list of known near-missers that we could check out. And what if we pick up a suspect asteroid in Webb's absence? We'll need him here, not wandering around Europe looking for some missing ancient manuscript."

Webb took this as a coded recognition that Sacheverell wasn't up to it. He said, "I'll be giving the team a list of known close approachers this morning. It's still dark on Maui and some might be accessible from there right now. Others could be checked out on Kenneth's telescope tonight. If all goes well I'll be back before the deadline and no way will irrevocable decisions have been reached before then. Nor, I predict, will you have found Nemesis."

Judy had found a box of matches in a kitchen drawer. Noordhof lit up. He fixed an intense stare on Webb and adopted a grim tone. "Ollie, I repeat what I was authorized to tell you. That if we don't find Nemesis by the prescribed deadline the Administration will go on the working assumption that it won't be found before impact, and will then adopt the appropriate posture."

Webb said, "I know what that means, Colonel. But I'm convinced that this is something that has to be checked out."

The soldier sighed. "We're into the Christmas period, Oliver. Transatlantic flights will be booked solid."

"I'll bribe somebody off a flight if I have to."

"I don't like it. We need tight security for this operation, and we don't get that with people wandering around Europe."

"This is my last throw. I don't have anything else."

"Jesus." Noordhof blew a contemplative smoke ring.

"Okay. We're having to take risks all the way here. Cross the Atlantic by the fastest possible route. Willy, take Judy's car and give Webb a lift to Tucson. Judy's not up to driving."

"But I'll go along for the ride," she said. "I'm nearly through the bomb simulations."

Webb asked, "What day is this?"

Noordhof groaned. "Ollie, it's now Thursday morning, ten hundred hours Mountain Time. Our deadline is set in Eastern Standard Time, that is, the time on Washington clocks. Deliver Nemesis by midnight tomorrow EST. Which is to say, you have one day and twelve hours. If you don't make it back here get this Royal Astronomer guy to endorse your identification. No offence, but for something like this I need confirmation."

They stood up. Sacheverell shambled towards the refrigerator. Over his shoulder he said, "This is a joke. So far as I'm concerned Webb's now out of it."

"One last thing, Ollie. The Secretary of Defense wants a personal briefing from the team tomorrow evening at a secure location. We'll need to know how you've progressed. You'll be in Italy but contact us at Willy's beach house, which is in Solana Beach, California. As before the line will be secure at the American end but just remember that telephones are death. It's a question of balancing risks. Use a public booth, and if you have a shadow of doubt don't phone."

"I'll give you my number to memorize in the car," said Shafer.

"Herb," Noordhof said, "I've got some bad news."

Back in his room, Webb put his laptop computer into its case and squeezed clothes and papers into odd spaces. He stepped out of his room and moved down the stairs, along the corridor and out the front door.

Into the winch house. The car had locked into place, its door half open. Webb ignored it and crossed to the control desk. A vertical metal panel below the controls was held in place by four simple screws. He took out a pen and bent the clip, using it as a screwdriver, glancing back at the main building as he did. The panel came off easily.

Webb stuck his head inside, keeping well clear of the thick, live cable which rose from under the concrete and disappeared into the On–Off switch. A slight crackling of his hair told him that he was dangerously close to a high voltage. The design of the switch was simple. When the switch was moved to On, two metal prongs would make contact with two metal studs and so close the circuit. However at the back of the studs were two strong electromagnets, placed in such a way that, if current flowed through a second cable, the studs would be pulled back and no contact made whatever the position of the On–Off switch. This other cable, Webb assumed, went all the way to the upper platform. It was a device to ensure that the cable car could be moved only from whatever platform it was currently at.

But someone had earthed this second cable: a shiny new wire had been wrapped tightly round it and joined on to a metal rod freshly driven into the concrete. Which meant that the cable car was now controlled from the ground. Which meant that an ill-disposed individual on the ground could wait until Leclerc had stepped halfway out of the car and then suddenly pull it away, leaving Leclerc, off-balance, to fall into the gap between car and platform. Webb's scalp began to tingle and he couldn't have said whether it was his discovery or the electricity.

Webb pulled his head out just in time to hear the observatory door close. He had been in plain view; but had he been seen? Hastily, he screwed the panel back into place. He walked briskly back to the observatory. Kowalski, in the corridor, was looking stunned. He shook his head without a word. Sacheverell's voice came from the common room; it was raised in anger. Webb passed by to the Conference Room and logged in to Virginia's home page. And while he transferred her Vincenzo files into his laptop computer, he pondered. There was a lot to ponder:

1. Fraudulent signals from a telescope;
2. a murdered colleague;
3. Leclerc's disappearance before his murder;
4. a missing 400-year-old manuscript;
5. somewhere out there, a billion-ton asteroid, closing at twenty or thirty kilometres a second; and now
6. someone determined to make sure they didn't find it.

Tucson, Thursday Afternoon

Shafer took the wheel and Webb flopped into the passenger seat, the lack of sleep suddenly catching up on him. In a moment Judy appeared. Webb scrutinized the contours of her tracksuit as she approached. She caught him at it and gave a bleak smile as she settled into the back seat. The curves, Webb decided, didn't leave room for a pencil, let alone a weapon. He began to wonder if exhaustion was bringing out some latent paranoia.

They took off smoothly, Shafer taking the big car down round the hairpin bends with ease. Webb found himself peering anxiously into the trees. As they dropped below the snow-line, the temperature rose marginally, and by the time the Pontiac had stopped at the gate separating the survivalists from Piñon Mesa, the air was mild. A smell of woodsmoke met Webb as he pulled the gate open.

They drove through the settlement, past a couple of dirty red Dodge trucks. An elderly man was sitting at a porch with a pipe and a gallon jar of some brown juice at his feet. He raised his hand in a friendly gesture as they passed. Shafer said that, given Nemesis, maybe the survivalists had the right idea, and Judy said that wasn't funny.

Down the last stretch of hill; turn left; and put the foot down on the open road. Webb began to tremble; he couldn't analyse the reason, but thought it was probably relief. Shafer turned on the radio and they listened to a rabid evangelist for a minute before replacing him with dentist's waiting room music: Country and Western, easy on the mind, brought to you by Jim Feller and his Fellers.

A helicopter flew high in the opposite direction, its twin rotors glinting in the sunlight. Webb wondered if it was Leclerc's hearse, with its specialist undertakers, but kept the thought to himself. Judy's perfume was beginning to intrude again.

Some twenty miles to the south of Eagle Peak they pulled into a little cluster of shops and a café. Shafer bought Judy coffee in a paper cup while Webb disappeared into a nearby camping store. He emerged minutes later in a Hawaiian shirt, purple-rimmed sunglasses and Bermuda shorts, carrying a big brown paper bag.

They stared, astonished. Judy tried not to giggle. "Are you changing your personality, Ollie?" Shafer asked.

"You should see the underwear," the astronomer replied, climbing into the Firebird. "No, I'm just trying to confuse the enemy. Who would connect Mister Showbiz with the quiet academic who arrived at Tucson Airport three days ago? So you're the man who blew the Standard Model. A cool insight."

"Hey, a theory screaming with singularities and eighteen free parameters? There had to be a better way." Shafer thundered past a posse of bikers.

"But an electron as a Mobius strip? And what about your new stuff, a mind/vacuum interface? That is *weird*."

"It'll take a generation to become mainstream. Now listen to words of wisdom from your Uncle Willy. These days, Einstein wouldn't get a job as a lab technician."

"You mean . . . ?"

"You have two possible career routes, Oliver. The easy route is this. Don't stick your neck out, keep to beaten paths and get on lots of committees. In a word, look and act like Establishment Man. And in no circumstances, whatever—I emphasize this—step outside the mainstream. Don't get any new ideas."

"And the hard route?"

"Get a new idea. But one thing above all."

"I'm gasping, Uncle Willy. More wisdom, quick."

"Find Nemesis. Or your generation's cancelled."

Judy leaned forward, speaking to both men. "What are our chances?"

Webb said, "I'm scared to think about that."

"You have less than two days to play your hunch, Ollie, and a big hunk of that will be spent flying," she pointed out.

"Something bugs me about this," said Shafer. "It's the Zhirinovsky factor. The guy's been in power for a couple of years, right? Say you were in his position. How long would it take you to get something like Nemesis going?"

"A lot more than two years," said Webb thoughtfully. "To track an Earth-crosser with enough precision would take at least that long."

"And we'd need to know just what we were pushing around," Judy added. "Look at how variable the responses are in the simulations. It would mean a lot of spectroscopy, maybe even a soft-landing. Only then could you shepherd the asteroid in."

"I guess it would take ten years and a lot of clandestine space activity," Shafer proposed. "Which puts its origins right back in the Putin era. Well before Zhirinovsky."

"So?"

"So all Russia wanted before the food riots was peace to develop their capitalist experiment."

"What are you saying, Willy?" Webb asked.

"Something bugs me is what I'm saying."

Judy suggested, "There was always an undercurrent of dissatisfaction in the Red Army. Maybe a small group has been cooking this up for years, without knowledge of successive Russian Presidents."

"Is it possible?" Webb asked.

"Undoubtedly," she replied. "Big countries have mechanisms for keeping secrets, Ollie. A group of high-level conspirators could pull these levers to hide the Nemesis project from their own leadership."

"For ten years?"

"It bugs me."

Soon, they were speeding along broad streets and through prosperous Tucson suburbs. Shafer followed signs for the airport. They pulled over briefly at a trash can where Webb dumped the brown bag containing his RAF-supplied suit and Glen Etive pullover. At the terminal entrance, Shafer and Webb shook hands. Whaler gave him a wave from the back of the car, and then they roared off.

At the terminal, Webb found reassurance in the teeming crowds. He bought a psychedelic pink backpack with a Save the Whales motif and a few toiletries. The American Express card seemed to be an infinite source of funds and he momentarily played with the idea of a one-way ticket to Rio de Janeiro.

He joined a long line at a TWA reservation desk. After fifteen minutes of increasing frustration it became clear that the queue was static. He gave up and crossed to a cluster of telephones. A parcel-laden woman with a mouthful of keys made it just in front of him. She started to look for coins and Webb muscled her aside. A passing man let loose a stream of outraged invective. Webb literally snarled and the man backed off hastily. He dialled through to the TWA desk. A mechanical voice said please do not hang up you are on hold and he was treated to Mantovani's "Music of the Mountains" for one, two, three minutes. Then one of the girls picked up the phone and he watched her as she typed at the computer terminal and said No sir, the Airbus is fully booked likewise all our flights to Rome this being the Christmas period but if Sir is really that desperate there is a flight to Paris in an hour and forty minutes and you might be able to connect from there except that everything is choc-a-bloc in Europe too and Air France are on strike oh it doesn't leave from here, didn't I say? Phoenix. Have a good day, sir.

Webb ran gasping to the taxi stand. A fat taxi driver was reading a newspaper. Webb said, "I'll give you a hundred dollars for every minute less than a hundred minutes it takes you to get me to Phoenix airport. Plus the fare. Your time starts now."

A wide range of human emotions expressed themselves in the taxi driver's face, culminating in a delighted grin. Webb jumped in. The driver did it in ninety-five minutes, with cold desert wind streaming around Webb's face from an open window and heavy metal blasting from the rear loudspeakers. At Phoenix, Webb handed over a fat wodge of notes to the grinning driver. Boarding was in progress and he made it with two minutes to spare.

First class on the BA flight to Paris via London was, incongruously, half empty. A Sophia Loren lookalike offered to tuck him in under a blanket but Webb, his head spinning with exhaustion, resisted the temptation.

Hello Ollie!!

You finally phone me! From sunny Arizona! When I'm naked!! I always knew you had hidden depths, Ollie, but WOW, what psychic timing!! And all that heavy breathing. So, will you teach me some new stuff when you get back? I still haven't got past bondage and leather knickers. Anyway, here's your historical background to *Phaenomenis* and I hope you rot in hell you cold unfeeling miserable robot fish on a slab.

Saving myself for you alone (but not for much longer),

Virginia (still).

PS. These big-breasted cowgirls. They sag after forty.
PPS. They all have AIDS.

She likes me, Webb told himself. He looked down on a range of snow-covered mountains, golden in the sun, wondered briefly where Nemesis would hit, and settled down to the story of Vincenzo.

THE LAST DAY

Advanced Concepts

"We have nearly ten thousand strategic nukes. Seven thousand active, and another two on the reserve list." Judy was wearing large gypsy earrings, a white T-shirt, classic Levi 501's and Nike trainers. Dark sunglasses protected her eyes from the strong sunlight which streamed in through the cockpit window. Incongruously, she was wearing a pearl necklace.

McNally's tone revealed his surprise. "The USA still has seven thousand bombs?"

"But they're mostly the W-series, just a fraction of a megaton each. Great for knocking off cities and the like but no way do they have the punch to deflect a small asteroid. Not on our hundred-day guideline. No, Jim, if you're looking for real action you have to go for the old B-53s. And we only have fifty of these."

"One will do," McNally declared.

"I don't believe so. They're not neutron bombs."

"Let's run with your B-53s for a moment anyway." The NASA Administrator glanced at the compass and made a tiny adjustment on the joystick. Desert drifted below them. He had flown straight from Toulouse to Tucson where Judy and the jet had been waiting. He was now *en route* to the Johnson Space Center at Houston, first dropping Judy off at the Sandia National Laboratories, twelve square miles of nuclear wisdom tucked securely inside Kirtland Air Force Base near Albuquerque. Judy was briefing him as they flew.

She produced a bar of dark chocolate, broke off a couple of squares and offered them to the NASA chief, who accepted happily. "Okay," she said. "They're the oldest nukes still in service. They've been operational since 1962. But they're also the largest and they're pretty lightweight for their power. That's one of the nice things about nuclear weapons: the yield to weight ratio increases with power. The bigger the bomb the more punch per pound."

"These B-53s—just how much punch are we talking about, Judy?"

"Nine megatons. Now that is destructive enough for any conceivable military target, but the bomb itself weighs only four tons. It's a three-stage weapon. That's classified information, by the way, but in the circumstances . . ."

"Don't you people have anything bigger? I seem to recall the Russians exploded a fifty-megatonner once."

"The *Tsar Bomba*. A wonderful thing," Judy smiled. "It was really a hundred-megatonner but they configured it for fifty when they exploded it in Novaya Zemlya. Even then you could pick up its pressure wave on ordinary domestic barometers anywhere in Europe. We think it weighed thirty tons."

"So, what have we got to match it?"

"Zilch. Our military asked permission to develop sixty megatonners way back in the fifties, but this was denied. We've always gone for precision targeting rather than massive zaps."

McNally slid his sunglasses down his nose and looked over them at Judy. "We lack the nuclear punch to deflect Nemesis? Are you serious?"

"If it needs more than nine megatons."

McNally took a few seconds to absorb this startling new information. "Tell me about your neutron bombs." A small town was drifting about twenty thousand feet below them, narrow white roads radiating from it through the desert. A plume of smoke rose from a farmhouse some miles to their left.

"Jim, they're just tactical tank-busters. Artillery shells with no more energy than a Hiroshima. Armoured personnel are hard to kill, but neutrons penetrate armour. Some tanks, like our M-1, are reinforced with depleted uranium, which is very dense and hard to penetrate with explosives. But listen, this is really smart. If you set off a neutron bomb you activate the depleted uranium so the soldiers find themselves cocooned in a radioactive tank at the same time as the neutrons from the bomb are penetrating it. At a few miles' range their blood drains out from every orifice in a few minutes. Closer up and they just dissolve into a hot ooze. Closer still and they explode. More chocolate?"

McNally declined. He loosened his tie.

"But as a Nemesis killer, they're far too small. They're made that way so you don't have military commanders wiping out too many towns at a time when they're hitting Russian tank brigades in Europe. I don't believe our stockpiles include neutron bombs in the multi-megaton range."

The NASA Administrator responded to some chatter on the radio. "By the way, we're now in New Mexico. What's a three-stage weapon, Judy?"

She hesitated. "I guess I can say. Start simple, with a gun firing two sub-critical masses of uranium together. That's fission for you, a straight one-stage atom bomb. The trouble is, it has limited power. The fission reaction is slow to develop and the bomb blows itself apart before all the fissile material is used. The Hiroshima bomb was only 1.4 per cent efficient, for example. You can't get much more than a critical mass to explode. But fission bombs do give you a plasma a metre or less across with a temperature of about fifty million degrees, and that's hot enough to start you on the fusion route, transmuting four hydrogen atoms into one helium one with the mass deficit emerging as energy through $E = mc^2$."

"I've never been clear what form of hydrogen you use," McNally said.

"That's classified too, but what the hell. It varies. Liquid hydrogen is best but you can use compressed gas and we've even used a hydrogen-impregnated solid. Anyway, more than eighty per cent of the energy from a simple fission bomb comes out as X-rays. Teller and Ulam got the bright idea that, because the X-rays are moving at the speed of light—they *are* light—maybe you could use them to compress a large capsule of hydrogen at very high speed, before the assembly got disrupted. The fastest reaction at fission temperatures is between the heavy hydrogen isotopes, deuterium and tritium. So you stir these isotopes into the brew, light the touchpaper and retire a long way back. Four hydrogens fuse to give you one helium, as per undergraduate physics courses, but this leaves surplus mass in the form of a 14 MeV neutron and an eighteen MeV photon which is an impressive quantum of energy."

"That's a two-stage weapon, the touchpaper being an A-bomb."

Judy finished the chocolate bar with a satisfied smile. "Correct. Not only Teller and Ulam, but also Sakharov in Russia got the radiation implosion idea. So let us give thanks unto these gentlemen for the hydrogen bomb. But why stop at two stages? If you want a bigger bomb, use the fusion explosion to compress and explode a third, fission stage. It makes for a dirty bomb but a powerful one, and no new scientific principles are involved. Each stage can be ten or a hundred times more powerful than the one before. No question, *Tsar Bomba*—King of Bombs—must have been a three-stager. There was even a Soviet design for a layer cake at one stage."

"The mind boggles," said McNally, his mind boggling.

More radio chatter. McNally explained, "We're now entering restricted airspace. Let's hope Noordhof fixed it like what he said he would." He spoke into his mouthpiece and trimmed the aircraft. Far above them, two Tomcats passed swiftly across their bows, right to left. A third fighter appeared from nowhere and started to probe inquisitively, looking at them from all directions and keeping a safe twenty metres away. They flew on for some minutes. Then the pilot waved, and the jet tipped its wings and hurtled into the sky above.

"Judy, it seems to me you're going to have to tart up a B-53, turn it into a neutron bomb."

She brushed little flakes of chocolate off her white sweater. "But Jim, the way a neutron bomb works is that you let the neutrons escape during fission instead of absorbing them to create more energy. That means a neutron bomb will always be a low-energy device. If we're going on a last-minute deflection, meaning we need energies in the megaton range, the neutron bombs we need don't exist."

"Make one, very very fast."

She shook her head emphatically, setting her earrings swinging. "Jim, where is your sense of realism? Whether it could be done even in principle I don't know. But it absolutely can't be done in the time available."

"Hey, that's my line," McNally complained. He nudged the joystick forwards and the altimeter needle began to drift slowly down.

"Jim. Just how much weight can you push into interplanetary space?"

"Depends where you're going and how fast you need to get there. The old Galileo probe weighed about 750 pounds and it had a 2,500-pound spacecraft to push it around. But we used several gravitational slingshots to get it out to Jupiter."

"Give me a number."

"At the extreme? Think of four thousand pounds."

"Six B-61s, each seven hundred pounds, ten feet long and a foot wide. A third of a megaton each if we use the Model Seven version. Could you launch those?"

"Maybe. But it's not enough."

Judy fingered her necklace thoughtfully. Suddenly her mind seemed to be elsewhere.

◆ ◆ ◆

The Sandia Corporation's newest building, Number 810, took up about 8,000 square metres of the centre of Technical Area One, deep inside Kirtland AFB. With the love of acronyms which characterizes large corporations everywhere, the building was labelled CNSAC: the Center for National Security and Arms Control. Security began with its physical layout, which had been designed so as to guarantee secure communications within and between the four elements of its programme: Systems Analysis, Advanced Concepts, Systems Assessment, and Remote Monitoring/Verification.

Judy loved Advanced Concepts. Its remit was to investigate new technologies whose development might threaten the defence of the USA, and to propose countermeasures in the event such techniques were identified. She loved the Group because of its creativity, the wonderful and wacky ideas which it tossed around, the sheer fun of it, like the vacuum bomb concept which they had been running with, pre-asteroid. There were no fools here.

Not even Advanced Concepts could stop the unstoppable. But at last, depending on answers she got here, Judy thought there might just be a way. An extremely long shot, longer even than Ollie's deranged story about a manuscript. She turned into the secure building. Her slim fingers were still running over her pearl necklace.

Vincenzo's Manuscript

We, the undersigned, by the Grace of God, Cardinals of the Holy Roman Empire, Inquisitors General throughout the whole of the Christian Republic, Special Deputies of the Holy Apostolical Chair against heretical depravity.

Whereas this Holy Congregation has found that you, Vincenzo Vincenzi, son of the late Andrea Vincenzi of Florence, aged seventy years, have been found to advocate the proposition that the Sun is at the centre of the universe and immovable, and that the Earth moves and is not at the centre of the universe; which propositions, due to Copernicus and Galileo, are contrary to the authority of the Holy and Divine Scriptures, and are absurd and erroneous in faith; and whereas it has also been found that you embrace the belief of Giordano Bruno that the stars are suns scattered through infinite space, and that living creatures may inhabit planets orbiting these stars, which opinion is also absurd and erroneous in faith; and that you instruct pupils in the same opinions contrary to the Holy Scriptures; we find, pronounce, judge and declare, in the name of Christ and His Most Glorious Virgin Mother Mary, that you have rendered yourself guilty of heresy.

So we the undersigned cardinals pronounce.

F. Cardinal of Cremona
F. Cardinal Mattucci
M. Cardinal Azzolino
Cardinal Borghese
Fr. D. Cardinal Terremoto

Webb thought, *plus ça change*: I meet little cardinals at every conference. He looked out of the little window. The 747 had now entered the dark hemisphere of the Earth, somewhere over the Atlantic Ocean.

> Ollie darling. Okay so the Holy Roman Inquisition gets a bad press but Vincenzo can't really complain. If he'd been tried in Germany or the Alps he'd have been tortured and executed, no question. The good Doctor Karpzov of Leipzig, a contemporary of Vincenzo, managed to procure the deaths of twenty thousand witches in the course of his saintly life. Such was his virtue that, in between carbonizing old ladies, he read the Bible fifty-three times.
>
> Was the Holy Office paving the way in this Madness? It was not. On the contrary it was often accused of being soft on witches. An accused witch in the custody of the Holy Office had protection, in the form of the *Instructio pro formandis processibus in causis strigum, sortilegiorum, et maleficiorum.* This little document puts women in their place: *genus est maxime superstitiosum.* The silly things are prone to vivid imaginings, false confessions and the like (my vivid imaginings would set your kilt on fire). The *Instructio* therefore insists on caution in proceeding to an arrest, accepting testimony and so on. Torture was applied only after the suspect had had a chance to mount a defence. Even when *maleficio* was established, first-time offenders who repented were only banished, or made to abjure on cathedral steps, or put under house arrest or whatever.
>
> There were, however, three classes of felon who risked being barbecued: second offenders (two strikes and you're out), hard core heretics (*e.g.* denying the Virgin Birth), and the stubbornly impenitent, like

Vincenzo. Policy was to burn the first lot and have a go at last-minute conversion for the other two.

Anyway, what are a few hours or days of pain measured against the everlasting torment of Hell? If those few hours or days will persuade a heretic to recant, and so attain Heaven, then surely true cruelty lies in withholding the services of the torturer? To flinch from applying a little unpleasantness is to fail in one's duty to the Blessed Virgin, to the Church and to the heretic him/herself. It's all spelled out in Masini's *Sacro Arsenale* 2nd ed., Genoa 1625.

You have to be cruel to be kind, as Miss Whiplash said to the bishop.

So where does that leave our Vincenzo? Read on, sailor.

Remarkably, given the ferocious attack on them by Vincenzo, the cardinals had provided him with an escape clause. Perhaps the Grand Duke had thrown a long shadow, and there had been a nod from His Holiness; who could say? At any rate, on condition that he recanted, cursed and reviled the said opinions, the Inquisitors declared, he would be sentenced only to life imprisonment.

Vincenzo now had a choice. He could die for his beliefs, like Giordano Bruno before him, who had gone to the stake convinced in the plurality of worlds. Along that route lay the rack and the strappado; and beyond that the stake. Or he could adopt Galileo as his role-model, and abjure on his knees, his hand on a Bible held by the Inquisitor.

Vincenzo recanted. The *territio realis*—showing him the horrific instruments of torture as a prelude to using them— had done the trick. He was duly sentenced to *carcere perpetuo*. Whether by nudging from the Grand Duke's emissary was unclear, but the sentence was commuted to confinement, for life, to the estates of the Duke of Tuscany. Since the Duke owned much of northern Italy the sentence was, finally, nominal. Vincenzo and his mistress had spent the remainder of their days in obscurity, under the Duke's protection.

The Grand Inquisitor had taken vows of poverty. However the small print, had there been any, did not forbid the possession of a wealthy brother. And like many wealthy Romans from the Emperor Hadrian onwards, the Inquisitor's brother had a villa in the hills near Tivoli. It was a place to escape the hot, stinking, malaria-ridden plain of Rome during the summer months. And shortly after the trial, Vincenzo's books and instruments were delivered, for disposal, to the Inquisitor, who was then in residence at his brother's Tivoli villa.

The Cardinal recalled that Copernicus's *De Revolutionibus Orbium Coelestium* had been placed on the *Index Librorum Prohibitorum* in 1616, whereupon, the following year, the Dutch heretics had published an Amsterdam edition. And Elzevirs of Leyden had been quick to publish the works of Galileo. He would allow no such embarrassments to fall on the Church again. Across the front cover of each of Vincenzo's ten volumes, he wrote *cremandum fore*: they would be consigned to the flames.

What happened next is unclear, Virginia wrote. Maybe the Grand Duke's Secretary had applied a little pressure. Whatever, Terremoto scored out *cremandum fore* and replaced the words with *prohibendum fore*: they were not to be burned, merely not to be read. A few copies were made but were lost, all but the one which had found its way to the Bodleian. Virginia had appended a surviving letter from the period:

Reverend Father. His Holiness has prohibited a book in octavo entitled *Phaenomenis Novae*, in ten volumes, by Vincenzo Vincenzi, son of Andrea Vincenzi of Florence.

The book contains many errors, heresies, and perni-
cious and schismatic propositions. I am informing your
reverence so that you may promulgate an edict prohibit-
ing the book, ordering booksellers and private individuals to surrender whatever copies they possess, on pain
of established penalties. I note that your reverence discovered copies of the *Republic* and *Demonomania* of
Jean Bodin, in a bookshop of your city. These were indeed, by order of Gregory XIV of blessed memory, condemned. All copies of the above book are to be burned
on seizure. Your zeal in these matters is well known to
His Holiness and to the Congregation, and we do not
doubt that you will apply it to the matter in hand, in the
service of our Lord God. May He preserve you in His
holy grace. I commend myself to your prayers.

    Rome, 30 August 1643.

Of your reverence, fraternally,

                    The Cardinal Terremoto

The Grand Duke never succeeded in adding Vincenzo's
works to his great library. The Cardinal put them in a dark
basement room in his brother's house, hidden amongst the
junk and detritus of a large family home; and there they remained, forgotten, for over a hundred years.

In 1740, a librarian from Florence by the name of Dr.
Tomasso Bresciani was passing through a marketplace in
Rome. He bought a sausage at a stall and took it away wrapped
in an old paper. Unwrapping the sausage in the Triano park
overlooking the Colosseum, he found the wrapper to be a
letter from Vincenzo, now long dead. Webb imagined the
good librarian choking on his sausage. The paper was traced
to a junk collector and thence to a house belonging to the
grandsons of a nephew of one of the Grand Inquisitors, who

were selling off waste paper from their basement. Bresciani
recovered the notebooks, which found their way to the famous Riccardian library in Florence, where they were in-
dexed, filed, restored, bound, and once again forgotten.

They next turned up two hundred years later, in 1924, in the
attic of a farmhouse in Provence. Another footnote: "Almost
certainly Napoleon's troops. They were forever looting museums and libraries from Italy and carting stuff over the
Alps. Women too, I expect. Ollie, when are you coming
back?"

Three thousand crates went north, some of which fell into
Alpine torrents. Many of the remaining manuscripts, with a
value beyond money, were turned into wrapping paper in
Paris. Most were shredded and sold as scrap, an unparalleled
act of vandalism by greedy Parisian businessmen. *Phaenomenis* was a lucky survivor.

They were then purchased from the farmer for pennies by
the famous monk Helinandus ("copy of receipt scanned in if
you're interested"), and so they came back down the road, all
the way to Rocca Priora, south of Rome, becoming part of
the Cistercian monk's famous collection of astronomical
manuscripts.

A fact which made Webb sit up.

Unfortunately, Virginia's note continued, along came the
Second World War. While the Allies were advancing inland
from Anzio, trainloads of good things were being taken
north by the retreating Germans. One of those trainloads got
stuck in a tunnel between Frascati and Rome, and in a bloody
fight the partisans reclaimed the booty which included, but
of course, a collection of manuscripts hastily taken from
the monastery by some German officer. Unfortunately, in
the confusion of *Nacht und Nebel* which is battle, some of

the sacred relics, art treasures and rare manuscripts simply disappeared. Vincenzo's manuscript has never been seen since.

There is of course the Bodleian transcript of the original by some anonymous Dutchman. Or was, darling. But as that too has now gone missing, along with your photocopy of it, it seems that the works of Vincenzo have vanished from the face of the Earth.

And at this point, Virginia stopped. She had scanned in her flowery signature; it took up almost the entire screen of his laptop.

Webb stared into the dark night. For the first time since Glen Etive, he fully believed that the task was hopeless. To find a manuscript which had gone missing in some forgotten skirmish almost a lifetime ago? In twenty-four hours?

He decided that he would send Virginia, the librarian with the steamy hormones, some flowers. He looked at his watch. He'd have to be quick: a planet without flowers was due along.

He had almost overlooked the last page, assuming it would be blank. But now he clicked the return button on his laptop and saw that Virginia had added a postscript to the end of her file:

"Ollie dear—you might want to get in touch with that Rocca Priora monastery. There are rumours."

Monte Porzio

The short Atlantic night was drawing to a close, and a pale sun was beginning to illuminate a solid sheet of cloud which hid the ocean below.

· Webb put his laptop aside and stretched. He tried to gather his thoughts.

Maybe, Webb wondered, I'm being paranoid. Maybe in my excited state I'd misunderstood the wheelhouse circuitry. If so, Leclerc's death made for a very strange accident; but an accident nevertheless?

And what about the fast response of the robotic telescope? Perhaps that's all it was: a fast response, made possible by the quietness of the electronic flow across the Atlantic at that time of night.

On the other hand, Webb speculated, what if Leclerc's death was murder, and the Tenerife observations were a fraud? It would have to mean that Leclerc had been getting close to Nemesis, and that someone on the team didn't want it to be identified. That is, someone on the team wanted an asteroid to wipe out their country. Family, friends, home, community, even their dog if they had one, someone wanted the lot to go.

Webb was vaguely aware of being less worldly than the average street trader; but even allowing for his own limited insight into the human condition, he could not believe in a folly which plumbed such depths. The proposition made no sense.

Webb thought about his colleagues on the team. Six Americans—Mark Noordhof, Judy Whaler, Jim McNally, Willy Shafer, Herb Sacheverell and Kenneth Kowalski.

Noordhof had been chosen by the Secretary of Defense or the President, because of his knowledge of missile defence technology. Judy worked in a corporation at the heart of the nation's defences. Both these individuals needed the highest possible security clearance and must have been vetted to death at various times in their careers.

McNally was NASA's Chief Administrator, for God's sake.

That left Shafer, Sacheverell and Kowalski. But these were all in a sense accidental choices. Willy Shafer was chosen for his eminence as a physicist. Sacheverell because he was conspicuous in the asteroid business (okay he's an incompetent loudmouth but that didn't alter the fact). Kowalski just happened to be director of a remote observatory with the facilities they needed. None of these people could have even known about the Nemesis threat, let alone manipulated themselves on to the team.

Okay, Webb thought, everyone is squeaky clean.

Therefore exhaustion is making me paranoid. Leclerc's death must have been an accident, and the robot telescope just has a remarkably fast response.

It was just odd that, at the moment he had been panning the robot camera over the bright, sunny Tenerife landscape, the Spot satellite had shown the island to be thick with cloud.

The twelve hours of flight, coupled with the loss of another eight hours due to the contrary motion of aircraft and sun across the Atlantic sky, meant that the Jumbo landed at de Gaulle at nine o'clock, local time, on a grey, stormy Friday morning. Webb adjusted his watch. It was now 3 a.m. Friday in Washington. He estimated that he'd had about three hours' sleep in the last three days.

No, Monsieur, the flights to Rome are fully booked. There is, however, a flight to Nice, laid on by some small company capitalizing on the Air France strike. There is one remaining seat but it is a standby and it is for Monsieur to turn up before somebody else gets it. Oh, did I not say? Not from here, from Orly. Monsieur is most welcome. Monsieur took a taxi whose driver was as responsive to the promise of a huge tip as his Tucson cousin.

The standby seat was taken.

Yes, Monsieur, Quai d'Orsay Aviation do operate an executive air taxi but Monsieur appreciates that we cannot fly him into Italy without the necessary paperwork and at this time of year the Italians would simply file their flight plan away for days. Monsieur's fastest route is to fly to Chamonix, on the French side of the Mont Blanc tunnel, and proceed from there.

He used the twenty minutes they needed for flight preparation to telephone Eagle Peak, where it would be about one o'clock in the morning. Noordhof came on the line almost immediately. The conversation was terse:

"I'm in Paris, just about to leave for Chamonix, arriving at L'Aèrodrome Sallanches in maybe three or four hours. Can I be met?"

"I'll fix it."

The office of Quai d'Orsay Aviation was about the size of a broom cupboard, dingy and empty. Webb fumed for about five minutes until a handyman, a small man with a handlebar moustache, entered carrying a tool box and a polythene sandwich box. He led Webb to the entrance of a hangar. Webb almost fainted at the sight of the tiny, two-seater Piper Tomahawk. He froze at the open door of the little toy, but someone heaved on his backside and he was in. The "handyman" turned out to be the pilot and Webb thought what the hell, I died trying.

They were a full half hour on the slipway waiting for clearance, during which time the pilot kept looking at the low clouds and making increasingly dubious noises about the flying conditions, while gusts of wind shook the aircraft. By the time the Tomahawk was bumping its way into the dark clouds, propeller racing, Webb reckoned he had attained some new plane of terror.

They jiggled and bumped their way across France, passing first over fields laid out like a patchwork quilt, and then over the white-covered Massif Central, occasionally glimpsed through snow-laden cumulus. Webb declined the offer of a sandwich although Monsieur would find the pig's brain filling quite delicious. Low, white clouds ahead turned out to be the Alps which, as they approached, increasingly dominated the field of view. The pilot pulled back on the joystick to gain height. Soon they were flying bumpily over the Mont Blanc massif. Through the clouds they glimpsed needle-sharp peaks, icy blue lakes, and isolated villages in the snow. Circling L'Aiguille du Midi, the pilot tilted the aircraft on its side so that Webb could look straight down at the crevasses and banded glaciers falling away from the big mountain. Then the Tomahawk righted itself, and the pilot took it unsteadily down through heavy snow. Webb glimpsed the tops of pine trees just below their wheels; then there was open ground and an orange windsock, and the pilot managed a brief *"Zut!"* as a gust of wind caught the wings at the moment of touchdown.

Alive on the ground, Webb inwardly swore that his feet would never leave solid earth again. He resisted the urge to kiss the snow and instead settled up with the pilot, whose eyes lit up with simple joy at the sight of so much ready cash. The pilot disappeared into a wooden hut at the edge of the runway, and ten minutes later was taken off in a taxi.

Webb waited, shivering in Hawaiian shirt and Bermuda shorts as the snow gusted around him. Through occasional patches of blue he could make out formidable, jagged peaks towering all around. He looked at his watch. He was attracting the amused attention of a plump girl inside the hut. He was about to head for Chamonix when a bright red sports car gurgled on to the airport road. A man emerged with green Tyrolean hat, complete with feather, and a long green trench-coat.

Webb climbed in. "I'm in a bit of a hurry."

"I know," Walkinshaw replied. "That's why I hired the Spyder." Bulls bellowed; a giant thrust Webb in the back; and in seconds they were on to the main road and moving at a speed which he associated with a race track.

They skimmed past a clutter of chalets and high-rise hotels on the left. On the right more chalets lay below an icy citadel, clouds swirling around its summit. Passing over a bridge Webb glimpsed turquoise, surging meltwater. Survival time two minutes, he thought for no reason.

"These chalets—aren't they built in an avalanche zone?"

The civil servant shrugged. "What do rich foreigners know?" He turned on to a steep Alpine road whose route up the mountain towards the Mont Blanc tunnel was mapped out by crawling lorries. A notice advised snow chains and extreme caution. It came in several languages but to judge by his driving Walkinshaw seemed not to understand any of them.

Rain.

Rain, beating hard against a window.

Swish-swish.

The rhythmic swish-swish of windscreen wipers, and the hiss of tyres on a wet road.

The hum of an engine.

Heavy rain, driving hard. Powerful engine.

Webb drifted back to sleep.

The car slowed and turned. Headlights flickered in from outside. The car stopped and Walkinshaw stepped out, the door closing with a satisfying Clunk! Webb listened to his receding footsteps, the steady drumming of rain on the roof, and the thermal ticking from the cooling engine. There were voices outside.

Webb struggled up to a sitting position. His arms and legs were made of lead. An illuminated sign said *Pavesi*, and above it was a picture of a plump, smiling chef holding a roasted turkey on a tray. The clock on the dashboard read just after three, and the autostrada cafeteria was busy. The voices were coming from a group of truck drivers at the entrance of the cafeteria, one of whom made a dash for his truck, holding a newspaper over his head.

Walkinshaw appeared and ran towards the car with a paper cup, water streaming over his dome-like head. Webb lacked the energy to open his door. He handed a hot chocolate carefully to Webb, before settling into the car.

Walkinshaw sipped at his drink. "I have never seen anyone so exhausted."

"I'm more concerned about you, Mister Walkinshaw. I don't believe you're a civil servant."

"Actually, I'm a pianist in a brothel," said Walkinshaw. Webb assumed it was a joke.

"And there is no Walkinshaw at the Department of Information Research. I checked."

Walkinshaw's face was a picture of injured innocence. "So? There might have been. Sir Bertrand is disappointed in you, Webb. He thinks you're off on some eccentric tangent."

"I probably am. I also believe someone on the team is trying to screw us up."

"Don't be ridiculous. Finish your chocolate."

Webb had scarcely done so before, once again, he flaked out.

He wakened again in the late afternoon, stretched out on the soft leather. The morning rain had gone and the sky was blue. Webb sat up. The terrible exhaustion had eased but he felt as if his blood had been drained off and replaced with water.

They were speeding over a cobbled road, with Trajan's

Column on the left, the Roman forum to their right and the Colosseum straight ahead. There was a mechanized chariot race around the Colosseum but Walkinshaw took it in his stride. They stopped at traffic lights, the lights turned green, and the traffic made a Brand's Hatch start. Walkinshaw weaved swiftly up to the head of the traffic. The Appia Antica appeared ahead but they suddenly screamed off round a corner.

In minutes they had cleared the suburbs of Rome and were hurtling towards a large hill town some miles ahead. "Frascati," Walkinshaw said. "The Embassy have given us the use of a house just beyond there."

They trickled through the town and then started to climb through a winding road. There were signs for Tuscolo and Monte Porzio. Ahead, Webb glimpsed a cathedral dome straddling the summit of a hill some miles ahead, with ancient houses clustered around it like cygnets around a swan. The Spyder cannoned up the narrow road, and Webb's knuckles showed white against the dashboard, and his scrotum thought it was being squeezed by a gorilla. At last the car growled and slowed, and they stopped at the large metal gates of a white villa.

Walkinshaw searched under some stones and triumphantly produced some keys. Then they were up a short, steep drive. There was a balcony, big enough to hold a party on, looking down on a panorama which probably had not changed in a thousand years.

"This belongs to one of the Embassy staff. It's probably a safe house, and in any case we only need it for a few hours. However you are still Mister Fish, and you still look like a corpse in a freezer. Would you like to rest awhile?"

"I daren't."

He was aroused by sunlight on his eyes. He was in a king-sized bed. Cherubim hovered over him, and a saintly, bearded figure in the ornate ceiling had raised a glass of wine. A chandelier of pink Venetian glass was suspended almost overhead. Twin dragons guarded a wardrobe about twelve feet long underneath a mirror of similar size. He had a quick shower in an old-fashioned bathroom about the size of his Oxford flat, and found his way to a downstairs lounge. Walkinshaw was contemplating a lurid female photograph in a magazine. He stood up as Webb approached.

"Ah, much better. You no longer look like death warmed up."

"What time is it?" Webb asked.

"Just after five o'clock. You've been out for an hour."

"Oh my God. I have to get to a monastery. It's not too far from here."

"I'll come with you."

"No. I'm a solitary scholar researching a manuscript. And you look like something out of MI5."

"At least I'll give you a lift, time being what it is."

Webb opened the car window and glanced at his watch. The plain of Rome stretched into the distance on his left, with its wonderful city shimmering in the haze. Beyond, the long spine of the Abruzzi Hills stretched to the south. The air blowing in the window was warm and scented, and the sky was blue.

And he had fifteen hours.

The Apiary

It was a fifteen-minute drive up a steep, narrow, tree-lined road. The monastery was contained within a wall about fifteen feet high, part of which was also the front of a church. A white marble saint with a lightning conductor running down his back stood atop its steepled roof. Behind the wall a tall bell-tower dominated the skyline.

There was a crowded car park. Walkinshaw put the seat back and covered his eyes with his ridiculous Tyrolean hat. Webb followed a family into what seemed to be a porter's lodge, and passed through it to a shop, where he was met by the scents of a thousand flowers. A brisk trade in honey, royal jelly and some translucent green liqueur was under way, while the Virgin Mary, captured on canvas, stood with her eyes raised to Heaven and arms crossed on the wall behind the counter. Webb tried out his Italian: "I'd like to speak to the Father Abbot, please."

The white-robed monk behind the counter raised his bushy eyebrows in surprise. "You have made an appointment?"

"Yes," Webb lied. "But I'm only in Italy for a few hours."

"Un àttimo."

A few minutes later the monk reappeared. With him was an older man, nearly bald, with a ruddy face and a smile which, Webb thought, was less than wholly welcoming. "I'm Father O'Doyle," he said in an American English with a strong hint of Irish. "The Father Abbot is in chapel but I'm responsible for visitors. No visitors are pencilled in to my diary for today. When did you write?"

"About six weeks ago," Webb lied again. "My name is Fish. I'm from Cambridge. I'm trying to trace a book."

"Ah, that explains it. You want the Father Librarian. Come with me."

Webb followed the American monk out to the car park and back in through the church. About halfway down he led Webb off to a transept, produced a large key and unlocked a door. There was a short stretch of corridor. Webb noted a door, with an alarm and lights over it, protected by three locks. The monk caught Webb's curious stare. "Our sacristy," he said.

Through another locked door, Webb found himself outside again, in a large, square cloister. Father O'Doyle led the way along the covered cloister-walk. Webb was surprised to find Christmas lights and decorations strung between the pillars lining the walk. Faces looked down at them from barred windows. "Oblates," the monk said, waving up.

They turned off and climbed some stairs. A handful of white-robed monks, hoods down, passed silently. Through a door, Webb found himself in a modern library. A few teenage students were scattered around desks. "I will leave you in the capable hands of our librarian."

The librarian had the physique of a rugby player, but the muscle was turning to fat and his face was pale.

Webb tried out his rusty Italian. "My name is Larry Fish. I'm from Cambridge in England. I'm doing some historical research and have been directed to your library. I wrote some weeks ago."

"I do not recall your letter. Did you not receive a reply?"

"I don't know. I've been travelling."

The monk bowed. "What do you seek, my son?"

"My informant was uncertain, but she thought that you might be in possession of the works of Vincenzo Vincenzi."

A look of surprise passed over the librarian's face, but quickly vanished. "A moment." He disappeared momentarily through a door and returned with a set of keys. He said, "Follow me."

Webb followed the monk out of the neon-lit, computer-ized library back down the stairs to the cloister and past a re-fectory with a long, heavy table and a small lectern. At the end of the cloister-walk was another set of stairs and the monk led the way down them and along a cool, dark stone-lined passage which ended in a massive wooden door. The monk used two keys. From the push he gave it, Webb in-ferred that, underneath the wood veneer, the door was basi-cally a slab of steel. The monk punched in a number on a keypad and then locked the door behind them. "To control humidity and temperature," he said. "I must remain with you, but also I must attend compline in an hour. And tonight, of course, we celebrate the birth of our Saviour."

Webb took a moment to wander while the Father librar-ian stood at the door. Some of the books predated Guten-berg; many could have bought a Rolls-Royce, or a yacht, or a house. Here, handwritten, was Vitellio's medieval com-pendium on optics, and next to it Kepler's "supplement to Vitellio," his *Dioptrice*, in which he described the principle of the camera centuries before Daguerre. Here, unbeliev-ably, was Nicolas of Cusa's 1440 *De docta ignorantia* of 1440, asserting that the universe is unbounded, and that all motion is relative, almost five hundred years before Einstein and the modern cosmologists. There was a little cluster of seventeenth-century comet books—Rockenbach, Lubienietski, Hevelius and others. And there was Coperni-cus's *De revolutionibus orbium coelestium*—the 1617 Am-sterdam edition—which had ushered in the painful birth of the scientific revolution. It was Aladdin's cave, but Webb had no time to explore it. He turned to the monk, who sim-ply said, *"Opere di Vincenzo, qui"* and took Webb to a shelf.

And there, indeed, were the *Opere* of Vincenzo; all but Volume Three.

"Volume Three, Father?"

"We have fifty thousand titles here, but unfortunately not the one you seek. It has been missing from our collection for sixty years."

Webb's heart sank. "How can I have been so misinformed? Volume Three was the one I sought."

"And after sixty years, you are the second man to have asked for it in a week."

You don't say. "To be frank with you, Father, I'm desperate to see it. I'm involved in a scholarly dispute which only the works of Vincenzo can resolve."

The librarian lowered his voice conspiratorially. "Perhaps you should speak to our Father Abbot. At this time of day, after chapel, he is often in his study. Follow me."

The librarian left Webb facing the Abbot across a large desk. A computer terminal on the desk struck the astronomer as somehow odd. Unmonklike, he imagined Noordhof saying. The man was middle-aged, with a thin face and a classical Roman nose. He spoke with easy authority, in English, and had bright, alert eyes.

"So, Mister Fish, you are from Cambridge. Which college is that?"

Webb tensed. "Churchill."

"On Madingley Road, as I recall. It is many years now. Tell me, that little coffee shop on Silver Street—what was it called?"

"There are a few," Webb guessed.

"Lyons? Was that it?"

With a start Webb realized that he was being tested. He avoided the trap: "Rings no bells, I'm afraid."

"How odd. Everybody knew Lyons in my time at Cambridge. I wasted my youth there." Webb raised his hands expansively, Italian-style, and the Abbot dismissed the matter. "It was so long ago. Perhaps it no longer exists. However, it is not part of our Rule to engage in idle gossip. You seek the works of Vincenzo, Mister Fish. You see that our collection is incomplete. Are you aware of their history?"

"I understand that the partisans rescued them from the Nazis, along with sacred artefacts and works of art, at the end of the last war."

The Abbot nodded. "It is also widely believed by local people that these things were returned to our monastery whence they were looted. Alas, Mister Fish, that persistent rumour is only partially true. Some treasures, some works of art, were not returned. The volume you seek is amongst them."

Webb, feeling gutted, closed his eyes in despair.

The Abbot continued, "Vincenzo was a very minor actor in the great drama which was played out so long ago. Now had it been Galileo, great efforts would no doubt have been made to recover his works. But Vincenzo? Few have even heard of him." The Abbot looked at Webb with curious intensity. "Is it so important, this scholarly dispute?"

"If only you knew, Father Abbot."

"You can tell me no more?"

Webb shook his head.

The Abbot leaned back in his chair and looked at Webb thoughtfully over steepled hands. "I am left wondering what possible scholarly dispute can require such secrecy and lead to so much despair in your face."

"I'm not at liberty to say. And I don't come from Cambridge and my name isn't Fish."

The Abbot chuckled. "I thought as much. But we all have secrets to keep. I too have constraints on my freedom to talk."

This guy knows something, Webb thought, maybe from the confessional. He toyed with the mad idea of blurting out the whole Nemesis story but immediately dismissed the thought. It would be seen as the ravings of a lunatic. He also suspected that the Abbot, faced with a choice between betraying a confession and permitting a holocaust, would tell the planet to get stuffed.

"You are leaving Italy soon?" the Abbot asked.

"I must. I came only for the manuscript."

"All this way for a missing volume! If only I could help. Before you leave us, perhaps you should take the opportunity to see our monastery. There is an unusual mixture of styles here. You will have seen that our basilica is made in the style of a Greek cross, that is square, rather than in the medieval plan which has a long nave so as to represent the shape of the cross of Christ. The craftsmen who built our monastery were influenced by the Doric, which is simple and strong, rather than decorative. And yet our chapel is entered through a porch with a horizontal entablature supported by columns, more in the style of the decorative Corinthian order." The Abbot smiled. "But I agree with your expression, Mister Fish. If you prefer, we can satisfy more bodily needs. We have many products. I recommend our liqueur, which is made of over thirty aromatic herbs according to a secret recipe which even I do not hold."

Webb stood up. "Another time."

"And our honey is famous. You must see our apiary."

"Thank you. Unfortunately I have to get away."

"Our beekeeper is Father Galeno. He is very old, and wanders a little, but he is a most interesting man to talk to. I said as much to your colleague."

My colleague? Webb made for the door. "Thank you. Time doesn't permit."

The Abbot said again, "Our apiary, Mister Fish. Father Galeno is a very interesting man."

God I'm thick, Webb told himself. The Abbot made the sign of the Cross and Webb said thanks for your help.

The Apiary was a square of grass the size of a small field beyond the bell tower. It was lined by dozens of box-shaped hives painted in bright primary colours. A monk, wearing a plastic hat with a protective veil, was bent over a hive with a metal bucket and a long, flat piece of metal. The air buzzed as Webb approached.

"Father Galeno?"

The Father Apiarist turned. He was a tall, thin man, in his middle eighties. He spoke in Italian and Webb was grateful for the six months he had spent in Rome some years previously. Bees were crawling over the monk's white robe and his veil. His sleeves were tied with string at the wrists. "Would you like to buy some honey?"

"Not today."

"Then you are here to be shown the wonderful life of the bee."

"Unfortunately I have no time," Webb said.

"No time. Now that is sad. We can learn much from the world of the bee."

Behind the veil, Webb saw dark eyes, a curious mixture of vacancy and sharpness. Instinctively, he felt that an oblique approach was called for. "Tell me, Father," Webb asked, "In your experience, is a bee conscious of its own existence?"

The man's eyes lit up. "Undoubtedly. While the bee can see and hear, its real world is one of chemistry. It responds to smell and touch. Its mind cannot therefore be understood by us, whose world is sight and sound. True, it is deeply controlled by instinct in its daily toil, but yes, of course God in His wisdom has given it the ability to experience life in its own way."

"But it has no reasoning power. It hasn't the brain."

There was a high-pitched cackle. "In that respect, does it differ from most of humanity? Only human arrogance makes us even try to understand the world as perceived by the bee. The essence of its consciousness will forever be a mystery to us, but not to the bee, and not to the Almighty."

Webb tried to look pious. "Father, I'm here because of a book."

"The bee does not learn its dance. It has been given to it by the Creator. Could blind evolution have taught a bee how to dance? What chemicals could combine to make a small insect dance an intricate code?"

"A book, Father."

"Could blind chance make flower and bee come to depend on each other for their very survival? The functions of queen, worker and drone interlock so perfectly?"

"It's a very old book."

The voice became truculent. "You must speak to our Father Librarian."

"It was taken from a train by partisans at the end of the Second World War." Webb tried a shot in the dark: "And you were one of the partisans."

The old man looked at Webb with surprise. "Now that is very strange."

Webb waited. Bees were crawling over his exposed legs.

"This book: it is a volume by the heretic Vincenzo?"

Webb spoke quietly. "Father Apiarist, where can I find this book?"

The shutters came down, the eyes became vacant. "I cannot say."

"Cannot?"

"Will not. I said this also to the other."

A honeybee was crawling up Webb's thigh. He tried to ignore it. "Why not?"

"Discussion of the matter is impossible."

"Father, I don't want to take it away, only to study it for a few hours. It is of the utmost importance."

"No."

"I have to see it."

A bee had found its way under the old monk's veil and was crawling over his lips. He had a face like a stubborn child. "Memories are long in the hills."

"Memories?" The bees were thick on Webb's shirt.

"It is your bright colours. They think you are a flower. Stand still or you will make them angry and they will sting your eyes."

Webb tried again but he knew it was hopeless. "Father, please. I ask only to see this book by Vincenzo."

The apiarist shook his head and turned to a hive. He pulled out a frame dripping with honey. The air filled with angry bees and Webb moved hastily back. "A young man with no time? Nonsense, you have all the time in the world. Come back when you can spare some for the bees. They can teach us much." He banged the hive with the bucket and the sky blackened with insects.

Crazy old fool, Webb thought, flying for his life, with the high-pitched cackle of the Father Apiarist almost drowned out by the angry buzz of the honeybees swirling around his head.

Johnson Space Center

The taxi dropped McNally at the main gate. He spoke briefly to the security guard, who provided him with a visitor's badge, and so NASA's Chief Administrator entered the Johnson Space Center unannounced.

The Center was almost deserted; it was after all the day before Christmas. He was gambling on workaholism amongst the senior staff, but if necessary he would simply summon them from their families. He strolled alone through the rocket park, sparing the Saturn V booster a longing glance as he passed, and continued on along the Mall, past the administration buildings, the simulation and training facilities, the laboratories and warehouses which he ultimately controlled. At the far end of the mall was the Gilruth social and athletic center; it was a long walk. He entered the Center unrecognized and extracted a can of icy Coke from a machine. Then he climbed some stairs and looked down with pleasure at two teams of fifteen-year-olds playing basketball. A white-haired grandmother in a blue tracksuit was running around, whistle in mouth.

McNally made a couple of internal calls and returned to the game.

The Chief Engineer, a bulky, bearded man, appeared in two minutes and twenty seconds. They shook hands and he sat on a chair next to the NASA boss. "You into basketball, Jim?"

"I hate all sport. No, I'm into security. We can't talk in our offices just yet." The Engineer pulled a face.

Twenty seconds later the Deputy Administrator arrived, looking bemused, and sat on the bench in front of them. "My secretary told me you're on vacation, Jim."

McNally dispensed with social preliminaries. "I intend to mothball Deep Space Four. I expect to replace it with the European Vesta, which should arrive at White Sands in a C-14 within the next few days. The Albuquerque people will reconfigure it to be launched on an Air Force IUS, probably the same booster which we used for the Galileo probe. Frontiersman will take it up to two hundred miles. I want the Shuttle astronauts retrained. At least two Mission Specialists will be on board, a nuclear physicist and an astronomer. Neither will have any background in astronautics. I'm not yet at liberty to tell you what this is about. What I can say is that Vesta will go through as a Defense item. This package has to be ready to go in one hundred days maximum."

"How many was that?" the Chief Engineer asked.

"One hundred. Maximum."

Lesser men would have howled in outrage, protested the obvious impossibility. But the instruction was so preposterous, the autocratic decision so out of keeping with the consultative spirit of the NASA hierarchy, that the executives, senior and experienced men, immediately realized that only some grave situation could lie behind it.

"The Russians are supposed to be launching Vesta. What do they think about this?" the Assistant Administrator asked.

"They don't know yet."

The Chief Engineer stroked his beard thoughtfully. It was a mannerism which had started many years ago as a joke and had gradually become second nature. He itemized the points with his fingers. "Let's look at this, Boss. Suppose we divide the problem into (1) crew training, (2) mission planning and (3) hardware development."

McNally nodded.

"Take Item One. You know how the Mission Operations Directorate works. Crew training is so meticulous they practically tell the astronauts when they can go to the john. You're well aware that training in a hundred days is impossible even for an experienced pilot, and that you can't let a couple of rookies loose on a Space Shuttle."

McNally bowed his head to indicate agreement.

There was an outburst of shrill screaming from below, echoing painfully from the gymnasium walls. The Chief Engineer let it die out before he continued: "Okay, now look at the broader mission-planning aspect, Item Two. For example, think about the documentation alone we need to create for the operational support. Transportation and flight rules, command plans, communication and data plans, mission control and tracking network plans, system operating procedures, operations and maintenance instructions, flight control operations handbooks, new console handbooks, software documentation. Hell, I'm running out of fingers and that's just the documentation."

McNally bowed his head again.

The Assistant Administrator said, "A lot of the MOD's load will fall on their Flight Design and Dynamics division."

McNally bowed.

"So. In a hundred days you expect them to carry through a flight design analysis leading to the development of flight design ground rules, develop the guidance, navigation and control software as well as design and construct any new hardware required, rig the MCC and the SMS's for the flight in question, come up with performance analyses for the ascent, orbit manoeuvring, payload deployment, proximity operations—with rookie specialists carrying out EVA—plan the descent and landing phases, create new in-flight programmes for SPOC and develop integrated checklists for all of this. In a hundred days."

"Maximum."

The Engineer scratched his head. "What payload accommodation category are we talking about? Dedicated, standard, mid-deck?"

"We'll be launching Vesta plus IUS plus four or five tons."

"Jesus. Dedicated."

The Assistant Administrator attempted reason. "Okay Jim, since we're in Wonderland, we may as well take a broad-brush look at Alex's Item Three, the hardware timescale. Look at the performance milestones for Cassini, starting say from the moment the Huygens probe was delivered. It took three months to test and integrate the probe with the spacecraft, right? Another four for JPL to integrate and test all the instrumentation. The probe was in our space simulators for another seven months. Then after it was delivered at Kennedy it took another six months to complete integration with the Titan/Centaur launch vehicle. If I've counted my fingers right that's twenty months. And you're looking for the same progress in three. Let's inject some realism into this, Jim."

McNally brushed the monstrous problems aside. "Look at Clementine One. From concept to system design was three months. Acquisition planning overlapped with that. Sure it was another year for the systems engineering and test, but the Europeans have done most of that work for us already. We had the spacecraft integrated with the ground subsystems in a couple of months. Look, the only thing that matters is the integration of Vesta with the launch vehicle, a standard Air Force IUS which will go up with the Shuttle. All it needs is a launch vehicle adaptor. We can do it in three months."

The game below was getting noisy. McNally added, "For reasons of security I want to confine this to Johnson and Canaveral."

"Where is this Vesta headed?" the Chief Engineer wanted to know.

"I don't know."

The Assistant Administrator laughed outright. McNally had now crossed the boundary from the preposterous to the insane. The Chief Engineer tried to keep his voice level, but it had an angry quiver to it. "Jim, I'd like you to explain something to me. How are we supposed to plan a mission if we don't know where we're going?"

McNally opened his mouth to reply, but the Deputy cut in. His eyes were icy: "Alex is right. What do I tell my MOD? With no destination, what is there for them to plan?"

"They plan for a high-speed, maximum precision flyby of an as yet unspecified interplanetary target, using the on-board radars for last-minute course correction."

"You'll never get off with this, Jim," said the Chief Engineer. "MOD will refuse to issue a commit-to-flight certificate. Or somebody will trigger the yellow light system and force an internal review. And rightly so. This could be shaping up to another Atlantis disaster."

"The responsibility for technical readiness is yours. I expect you, and your Safety and Mission Assurance Office, to deliver."

"Jim, you're asking me to send up half-trained astronauts on a string and sealing wax lash-up. I won't do it. I won't be responsible for the deaths of five or six people and the loss of a Shuttle." The Chief Engineer stood up. "You're forcing me to resign."

McNally looked the engineer squarely in the eye. "Some guys who look like telephone engineers will be fixing your office phone shortly. That's so the phone call you're about to receive from the President of the United States is secure. That call will have three consequences. First, you'll find out what this is about. Second, you'll wish you hadn't. And third, you'll make the deadline if it kills you and I mean that in its literal sense. Similar calls will be going to Art and Jackie this afternoon. Until these calls are made, I have no authorization to tell you what this is about."

If McNally had slapped the Engineer, the effect could

hardly have been more startling. The man stared, amazed. He seemed to have lost the power of speech.

The Assistant Administrator recovered first. "If some major disaster happened at Byurkan, and Vesta had to catch a gravity assist window, that could justify our stepping in to help with a crash programme. Either that or a target of opportunity. It would have to be a joker, like a new comet. There would be no case to trigger a yellow light; they're usually for cost overruns anyway. Which is it, Jim? Is Byurkan about to have a big disaster, or does some comet have to be intercepted real soon?"

That's the trouble with these Princeton types. Too damn smart. McNally tried to adopt a poker face.

The Engineer had recovered sufficiently to talk. He sat down again and stared at the AA. "But a hundred-day timescale?"

McNally glanced at his watch. Eight hours. *If Webb doesn't deliver . . .* Unconsciously, his mouth twisted in tension.

A whistle blew. The grandmother, red-faced, was waving her arms around. The sharp squeaking of trainers on wood came to a stop. An outburst of youthful cheering was followed by a tribal chant: the girls' team had won.

The Engineer asked, "What instrumentation will be on board?"

McNally tried not to smile. Knowledge of the instrumentation would provide a strong clue to the nature of the mission. He finished his Coke. "A spectrometer for inflight target analysis. A short-pulsed laser for ranging: eight bursts a second and it only weighs a kilo. A high-resolution camera with a light CCD coupled to the laser. The setup has ranging accuracy of one metre and believe me we're going to need it. There will be a military package on board."

"You said this is a flyby?"

"A flyby. No slowdown, no soft landing. Vesta will do what it's going to do on the hoof. The ranging is coupled to some megasmart electronics, and the probe will have to carry out some very sophisticated decision-making in maybe 0.1 of a second."

The Engineer stared up at the high wooden ceiling. Finally he said, "I see resemblances to the Galileo project. JPL handled the overall project and Ames managed the probe system. So why not use the experience gained at Pasadena and Mountain View? Maybe we could even use the Galileo flight plans as a template. I'll bring over key people from the JPL flight design team and get them working with our MOD. Get me your Mission Specialists right away and I'll throw them into our flotation tanks on their first day. The moment you can specify their tasks I'll configure the Mission Simulators. If you can get clearance to bring a few Vesta people over . . . and a target would be useful, Jim, when you're ready to give me it."

Engineers. Always finding obstacles until they smell a challenge. I'm not on top of these guys for nothing. McNally smirked.

The AA's eyes narrowed thoughtfully. "The onboard military package. Should we be thinking of something like a bomb?"

Screw all Princeton smartasses to hell.

Santa Maria della Vittoria

The telephone was ringing as Walkinshaw opened the door. Webb had picked up the receiver before the civil servant could stop him.

The voice at the other end spoke in Italian. It was a second or two before Webb recognized it.

"Mister Fish?"

"Yes."

"You have an interest in a manuscript?"

"Yes."

"I think I can help you."

Webb's heart jumped. Instinctively, he tried not to sound too enthusiastic. "I'm very interested. Where is it?"

"The matter is not straightforward. Do you know the amphitheatre in Tuscolo?"

Webb had a fleeting vision. A picnic. A day out of Rome. Giovanni, and a couple of girls, and wine and sunshine, and Italian bread and cheese. "Yes, I do know it. It's up the hill from Monte Porzio."

"Time is very short, Mister Fish. Please be there in twenty minutes." The receiver went down.

Webb looked at Walkinshaw in amazement. "I have a contact."

Walkinshaw shook his head. "That's impossible. This is a safe house. Nobody knows you're here."

Webb headed back to the door. "We'll have to shift. The car will only take us so far and the rest is a climb."

Walkinshaw held up a restraining hand. "Not so fast, Webb. Are you listening to me? Nobody is supposed to know you're here."

"Walkinshaw, I absolutely must have that manuscript."

Walkinshaw followed the astronomer out to the car. "Are you listening to me, Oliver?"

The ignition keys were still in the car. Webb stood at the car door. "I don't care. Look, we're talking about the planet. Do you want to be fried? With your family? And your country? If this asteroid hits America what do you think they'll do about it? I say they'll launch a nuclear strike in revenge. The Russians will hit back in turn and we'll be back to the Dark Ages even before Nemesis gets here. The world's run by madmen, Walkinshaw, not rational people."

"Webb, will you calm down. You're exhausted and not thinking clearly. You are my responsibility. I can't have you rushing bull-headed into this meeting. I need to know who knows you're here and what you're getting into."

"There's no time for stuff like that, you idiot. I have to take risks. I'm going. Stay here if you want."

The car was smelling of hot plastic and the heat was deadly. Walkinshaw took the wheel, and they put the windows down. "Who was it?"

"The librarian."

"Did you give him—or anyone—the villa's phone number?"

"Of course not. I don't even know what it is."

"The address, then?"

"Absolutely not. Turn right."

"Oliver, something is badly wrong here."

"So you said. Left up here."

The road took them up past villas with big wrought-iron windows, swimming pools and Dobermans wandering the grounds, and then they were into woods. There was an empty car park. The *guard'auto* had gone home. The sun was low in the sky. Memories came flooding back. Franca,

that was her name; and Giovanni's lady had been called
Ambra.

"Stay put, Walkinshaw. I'm a solitary scholar, remember?"

Walkinshaw looked into the surrounding trees. His face
was dark. "This is getting worse by the minute. Look around
you. Why would he want to meet you in a place like this?"

"He doesn't want to be seen talking to me, that's all."

Walkinshaw's civil service urbanity was gone. "You lunatic. You don't know what you're walking into."

There was a path through grass leading up to the little
Roman amphitheatre a quarter of a mile ahead. A burly,
white-robed figure was standing motionless on the stone
steps. As Webb approached, the man moved away and disappeared into a nearby wood. Webb ran up to the amphitheatre. The undergrowth was dense but the monk's path was
clearly visible in the trail of bent and broken twigs. Puffing,
Webb followed the trail and found himself in a broad Roman
road, the big flagstones still in place after two thousand
years. The trees formed a wide overhead canopy, and the
road went steeply back down the hillside. The monk was
standing motionless, about three hundred yards ahead. Webb
walked smartly towards him.

At about a hundred yards, the monk walked off to the
right, disappearing amongst the trees. It was getting dark
and Webb ran forward, risking a fall on the ancient cobbles.
Turning off along the librarian's route, he found himself
back at the car park.

Walkinshaw was standing at the car. He was peering at
the monk alertly, as if sensing that something was wrong.

Something was wrong. From close up, the man had the
wrong build for the librarian; he was too thin, the hair was
not in the style of a monk's tonsure. Walkinshaw shouted
"Webb! Run!" and then there was a sharp *Crack!* and the
civil servant, open-mouthed in amazement and pain, flopped
down in a sitting position with his back to the car, with a red
spot welling up from his chest.

Terrified, Webb turned to run but a pale, freckle-faced girl had appeared from the trees, and she too was carrying a pistol. She approached to just outside arm's length and pointed the gun steadily at Webb's chest.

They did Leclerc and now they're going to do me.

Walkinshaw was sliding slowly sideways; his eyes were swimming in his head; he was gurgling; bright red, frothy blood was trickling from the corner of his mouth. The girl waved Webb back towards the car. He ignored her and moved towards Walkinshaw. The monk hit him in the face with the barrel of the gun. "You can't leave him!" Webb shouted in English. "He needs help!" The monk understood. He fired into Walkinshaw half a dozen times, the civil servant's body jerking and the pistol shots cracking into the dark woods, while Webb yelled obscenities and the girl gripped his hair tightly and held her gun at his head.

Then Webb was thrust into the back of the car while the man threw off the monk's habit. He turned out to be an unshaven youth with the expressionless face of the psychotic. He turned the key and took off down the Tuscolo road. Through his fear and rage, Webb thought that it hadn't been necessary to run over Walkinshaw's body and that the civil servant might still have been alive when the wheels went over him.

In Rome, the youth sped through EUR along the Via del Mare, which transformed into the Via Ostiense, and then they were through the Ostiense Gate, passing a white pyramid and rattling along the Viale Piramide. The woman was breathing heavily. Her pupils were dilated, and from time to time she would giggle for no clear reason. She kept the gun hidden under Webb's buttock and the thought of an accidental sex change, which recurred whenever the car rattled over cobbles, wasn't funny. He began to shiver uncontrollably, going alternately hot and cold, and a monstrous headache threatened. Strangely, to Webb, the emotion beginning to dominate in him was anger. He was angry at being pushed around, angry at being struck in the face, and angry for Walkinshaw and his family if he had one. It was a seething sense of outrage which he kept firmly in check.

They hurried along the side of the Tiber before cutting away from it, and Webb found himself orbiting the Victor Emanuele before speeding up the Via Nazionale. The man turned into the Street of the Four Fountains and pulled the car to a stop.

He turned and snapped his fingers in Webb's face. *"La chiesa. Vai indietro. Subito!"*

The urge to slap the youth's face was almost beyond Webb's power to resist. He pushed open the car door, slammed it shut violently and crossed to one of the *quattro fontane*. The car horn hooted and the man gestured menacingly, waving him towards the church. Webb thrust a middle finger in the air. He splashed his face with the cool water and then sponged down his legs. There was nothing he could do about the dark patch on his shorts. He tossed the pink-stained handkerchief on to the road and looked at the inconspicuous little church with the flight of stairs leading up to a dull green door. Above the door, *"Santa Maria della Vittoria"* was written in gold lettering.

There was a brief gap in the flow of traffic and he crossed the street. He felt barely able to walk. On the steps he looked back; the young assassins were watching him intently. He pushed open the outer door. Assorted church notices; a collection box for "the deserving"; an inner door, brown and old. He went inside. The door closed behind him with a sudden pneumatic hiss and the Roman traffic switched off.

There was a musty smell, like a cellar or a second-hand bookshop.

Webb let his eyes adjust to the gloom. Rows of pews stretched to an altar, draped with white linen. Cherubim on the ceiling; crucifixes and statuettes; candles burning. And one human being, a young woman near the front sitting motionless, head down. She crossed herself and walked smartly off, her high heels clattering loudly in the confined space. Their eyes met briefly; she gave no sign of recognition.

Take it as it comes.

He stepped warily down the left aisle, heart thumping in his chest and leaning on the pews for steadiness. In a small transept was a white marble sculpture. The sun was streaming down on it from a high window and the sculpture seemed to glow, floating in space. A white marble woman was lying back and a half-naked youth stood over her, holding an arrow poised to plunge. The woman's eyes were half-closed and her lips were parted. Around this couple were what looked like theatre boxes. Assorted gentlemen occupied these, their faces leering and gloating, eternally congealed.

It was bizarre.

"The Rapture of Saint Teresa."

Webb whirled round. Elderly man. Iron grey hair, greying goatee beard, metal-rimmed spectacles. White linen suit, dark tie, expensive shirt; black ebony walking stick. Thin lips drawn into a smile. If he was an immediate threat, Webb couldn't see how.

"She is three hundred years old and, as you see, very beautiful. Many regard her as Bernini's finest work. And this church, being one of the best examples of late baroque in Rome, is a worthy setting for her. What do you think?"

Webb said it to hurt: "It looks like a porn show in a Berlin nightclub."

The man winced. "What we are seeing, Mister Fish, is the climax of Saint Teresa's mystical union with Christ. I believe that Bernini is telling us about a spiritual experience of such intensity that it can only be described to the herd, even remotely, by comparison with the sex act."

Webb said, "You could read what you liked into it."

The man sighed. "That is the way with much great art. But you disappoint me, sir. I see that you are a superficial

man, a child of your time, just another mass-produced prod-
uct of a technological Reich."

Webb was trying hard to control his anger. "Was I
brought here for this?"

The man's smile broadened. "That's the spirit! Actually,
you are here because my instructions are to kill you."

They emerged into the sunshine and walked arm in arm
along a noisy, bustling street. Webb, in spite of himself, was
glad of the support. The young assassins had vanished. At a
small piazza a traffic policeman, dressed in white, stood on a
raised pedestal, around which cars flowed like lava. An articulated truck was having difficulty negotiating a corner and
the policeman was waving at it furiously.

"This way, cavaliere," said the elderly man, pointing his
ebony stick. "We shall have a beer at Doney's."

They turned up into a broad, gently sloping promenade,
the Via Veneto. The street was reassuringly busy. Webb let
himself be guided to a pavement table under a blue and
white-striped awning. A dark young man with long, shiny
hair approached. The older man casually placed his stick on
the table, its metal tip pointing in Webb's direction, and ordered a beer. Webb asked for un'aranciata.

A whistle blew, back down the hill. The articulated lorry
wasn't making it round the Piazza Barberini. Further up the
Veneto, Webb saw a crop-headed marine with an automatic
weapon; he was standing at the main door of the American
Embassy, and he looked in a bad mood.

The man sipped at his beer. "I should have asked for a
German lager. You are wired up like a cat about to spring,
Mister Fish. Do try to relax. You must know that if I had
wished it, you would by now be dead."

"Who are you?"

"I think of myself as a surgeon."

"I assume you set up the surgery in the Tuscolo woods," Webb said.

"Overzealous amateurs. One must work with the material to hand."

A girl in a short, lime-green skirt sat down at a nearby table, facing Webb. She had an uneducated, Sicilian peasant look about her. She scanned the menu without once looking in his direction.

Webb said: "Society has rules."

Little wrinkles above the lips disapproved. "Mister Fish, you increasingly disappoint me. The rules are for herd control! To obey them, it is enough to have a spinal cord. The free man makes his own rules." An outburst of car horn blaring came from the piazza down the hill.

The waiter left a little printed bill. Webb waited until he had gone. "Why am I still alive?"

The man sighed. "You remain alive, for the moment, because of my greed. It seems that you are proving troublesome to some people. You seek a manuscript. I have found out where this manuscript is; in fact, I have held it in my hands. My instructions were to liquidate you before you got your hands on it. A simple enough task, for which I was offered a sum of money. I can now access the book whenever I please and well, here you are. As for the sum of money, it was strikingly large. So large that it made me wonder."

Webb stared at the man in open disgust. "A man died so that you could have spending money? I regret even having to breathe the same air as you."

"If that is a problem for you, it can easily be remedied."

"What do you know about this manuscript? How did you know where I was?"

A hand waved casually in the air. "The details escape me."

"Where does the Father Librarian come into it?"

"A naive fool, sold a plausible story."

"And your overzealous amateurs?"

"They too were easily manipulated, like all young idealists. Told they were striking a blow for the people, they were eager to believe it."

Webb sat back. He eyed the man speculatively. "What am I worth?"

The man fingered the ebony stick absent-mindedly. "One million American dollars. And in cash, the only medium of exchange I recognize. Already I have received half."

Webb sipped at his orange juice. He was beginning to feel nauseous, and found himself taking deep breaths. "That's a lot of money."

"Indeed. And the question I have to ask is, where does the value lie? In your death, or in the book? If in the book, then perhaps I now have in my possession something whose true value is, shall we say for the sake of a figure, ten million dollars."

"I begin to understand."

"Are you in a position to offer me ten million dollars for it?"

"No," Webb lied.

The man's face adopted a disapproving expression. "That is unfortunate, Mister Fish."

"And I intend to steal the book back from you."

The man laughed incredulously. "I admire your honesty, if not your sense of self-preservation. How do you propose to do that?"

Webb finished off his drink.

The man continued: "I have seen this book. The how and why need not concern you. I have pored over its pages, every line, every letter. But it has defeated me. In its pages I see no hidden treasure, no secret diamond mines, no plans of invasion. But, Mister Fish, you know something about this manuscript. Something which may allow you to unlock its secret. You may therefore succeed where I have failed."

"That is possible, given your level of intelligence."

"It is also possible that you will insult me once too often."

Webb said, "I think not. Because you're going to let me walk away from here."

The man nodded. "It is in my interests to do so. If the value lies in your carcass, I will never see you again. But if it lies in the book, you will risk your life to return for it. I am gambling half a million dollars by letting you walk free against ten million dollars if you come back for it. A reasonable risk to take, is it not?"

"Let me anticipate your proposition. I'll unlock the secret of the book. In return you will promise to leave me alone and sell or blackmail your paymasters with whatever I come up with."

"You have a formidable intelligence, young man. That is dangerous. I will have to take great care."

"No, I'm thick. That's why I'm in this position. Why don't you just throw me in a cellar and force me to decipher it?"

"Because you would invent some story even if you found nothing. Only if you return for the book will I know for certain that it truly contains something of greater value even than your life." The man finished his beer, patting his mouth with a handkerchief. "I doubt if you intend to keep your part of the bargain. When you return, if you do, you will attempt to steal the book."

"I doubt if you intend to keep your half. Once I've given you the information I'm out of bargaining power."

"Life is a risk, my friend. Consider the one I am taking with my paymasters."

"May they meet you, one dark night."

"I will leave you here. You will remain seated for ten minutes, after which you may do as you please. If you attempt to leave before ten minutes have passed, your day will turn into everlasting night."

"The manuscript?" Webb asked.

"You and it will connect. If you attempt to escape with it you will be killed without warning, and I will settle for the other half million dollars in exchange for your carcass. But enough talk of death, my unworldly friend. Tonight is *Natale*, a celebration of birth. Why not proceed to the Piazza Navona, where the crowds are already gathering, filled with the joy of Nativity? Find a seat at the Bar Colombo if you can, and enjoy yourself. Be alone and carry nothing electronic."

"Do something for me," Webb asked. "It will complete the bargain."

The man raised his eyebrows.

"Kill the bastards who murdered my companion."

The man laughed, exposing a row of gold fillings. "You see! Under the veneer we are not so different! I advise you to change your clothes before the police start making connections. And then come to the Colombo within the hour, young man, and find me the hidden message, and live to enjoy your grandchildren." The man picked up his walking stick and handed a ten thousand-lira note to the waiter, before sauntering down the hill. Near the Barberini, Webb lost him in the crowds.

Webb turned his chair slightly to get a better view of the tables. About nine feet away a silver-haired man, perhaps a banker, was reading *Il Giornale*. A young man from the north, in Levi's and a black sweatshirt with Princeton University written across it, was staring openly at the Sicilian girl. She was throwing occasional sly glances at him. Two workmen with vast bellies were sharing a joke. A middle-aged nun was sipping a cappuccino. Their eyes met and she smiled coldly at him.

Surely not the nun?

No, the young man.

An elderly priest came through from the back of the café and the young man rose. They went off, arms linked Italian-style. Webb played with the toothpicks for ten minutes, then got up and headed down the hill, trembling, nauseous, and light-headed with relief. At the piazza, the articulated truck was jammed halfway round the corner, unable to move forwards or back. The street echoed with the blare of car horns and the traffic cop had disappeared.

Before he turned the corner, Webb glanced back up the hill. The banker was folding away his newspaper.

Webb knew the geography of Rome. He had spent six productive months with colleagues from the university, two years—or was it two million years?—ago. Some instinct told him to head for the Trastevere, the territory of *noialtri*, the people apart, who did not always speak freely to the law. He turned right along the Viale del Tritone, and headed across the city by foot. Once over the Garibaldi Bridge, he quickly lost himself in a maze of narrow streets, avoiding children on mopeds and three-wheeled *motofurgoni* loaded with big flagons of wine.

In a small square a *frutteria* lady was setting out her wares for the evening, heaving a massive box of tomatoes on to a table. A white-haired flower lady, an espresso perched on a cobble at her feet, stared with hypnotic fascination at Webb's beachwear. Through an archway into a busy little square, cluttered with tables where men with wrinkled faces sat nibbling, drinking, watching the world go by. Wonderful smells drifted out of a hosteria.

A woman was sweeping out the doorway of a clothes shop. She *buongiorno*'d and followed Webb in. He tried the word for "underpants" in three languages and ended up, red-faced, surrounded by a gaggle of women trying to help. Half an hour later he emerged in a neat dark suit, in the style of an Italian businessman. He crossed the square to a tiny little cobbler's shop. The man looked at Webb's mass-produced sandals with polite amusement. Webb waited another half hour while the sun set and the cobbler tapped away at a last, a row of little nails projecting from his mouth. When the black leather shoes eventually appeared, they were of fine quality, and a quarter of the price Webb would have paid in

Oxford. He had a coffee in a bar, letting the trembling in his body subside, and watched two youths playing a noisy game of pinball. Fifteen minutes later, he exchanged lire for a pile of *gettone* and fed them into the café's telephone.

While he waited to connect, he looked at his watch. Walkinshaw had been dead for less than two hours.

And Webb had only ten left.

Casa Pacifica

The President faced Noordhof across the Oval Office desk, gazing at the soldier without a blink. "Let's hear it again, Colonel," he said over steepled hands.

"Sir, there is the possibility of a leak."

"I must be going deaf. For an unbelievable moment I thought you said there was the possibility of a leak."

"Leclerc is on a marble slab pending disposal," said Noordhof in an unsteady voice. "He had an accident with a cable car."

The President raised his eyebrows in disbelief. "He's your rocket man?"

"Yes, sir. He and Webb, the other European, were supposed to identify Nemesis."

"So what does this Webb have to say?"

"We can't find him," said Noordhof.

The President's tone was flat. "My hearing's gone again. Would you repeat, slowly and clearly, what you just said?"

"He's missing. We've lost him."

Grant pursed his lips and gave the soldier a long, steady stare. He finally said, "Okay, Colonel. Now tell me how you pulled off this amazing feat."

"Sir, I don't know how. He's just disappeared."

The President let a full minute pass while Noordhof prayed for a great earthquake to swallow him up.

"We lost a strategic H-bomb in Alaska once, a B-43 as I recall," Grant reminisced. "And it wasn't inventory shrinkage either. Turned out some Alaskan Command Air Defense guys thought they'd found a way round the Permissive Action Links. They tried to blackmail Uncle Sam with it. Not that the Great Unwashed ever got to hear about that little escapade."

"What happened, sir?"

"We couldn't go through the courts with a thing like that, of course. There was an unfortunate air crash. But you, Colonel, you do things on the grand scale; you're on course to lose the planet. We face annihilation if we don't find this frigging asteroid and nuclear holocaust if we're seen looking. And so far you've managed to spring a leak and lose half your team in four days. Magnificent."

A red blush spread over Noordhof's face. The President turned to the CIA Director. "You got light to throw on this farce, Rich?"

The CIA Director stuffed tobacco into his pipe from an old black pouch on his lap. "Nope."

"But someone knows about your team," said the President.

"That's impossible. These are just accidents," said Heilbron unconvincingly.

"This is beginning to sound like the last message from the *Titanic*," the President said.

"You can't scare me, Mister President, I'm too old. We're doing our human best."

"If that's your best, I'd hate to see you people on a bad day."

They drove out of Casa Pacifica in a cramped little Fiat with tinted windows, and joined Interstate Five heading south. The Stars and Stripes fluttered over Pendleton Marine Corps base to the left; to the right, half-naked bodies lay sprawled out on Red Beach or splashed in the Pacific shimmering beyond. Late-afternoon traffic was pouring up from San Diego. The Secret Service man drove carefully, watching the ebb and flow of traffic around him, searching with practised eyes for the anomaly in the pattern, the car which lingered too long, the strangeness in the proportion. But there was only the Buick in the rear mirror, a steady forty yards behind.

"Okay, Colonel, fill me in. What's the word on your team?" asked Bellarmine, removing his dark glasses.

"We have more on the Leclerc–Webb thing," said Noordhof. "I've had Nicholson from our Rome Embassy nosing around. This is weird, sir, but it seems the story starts in a monastery, in some mountain area south of Rome. It's run by monks."

"A monastery run by monks?" Bellarmine asked sarcastically.

"Yes, sir. It seems they have this famous library of old books, called the Helinandus Collection or something. All very securely held, fire-proofed, steel doors, smart electronics and so on. Local rumour has it that they are holding loot which was taken from the Germans at the end of the War, including a lot of books. One of them might be a manuscript written by an Italian called Vincenzo. But it's just local folklore."

"Do I know this guy Vincenzo?"

"I doubt it, sir, he's been dead three hundred and fifty years."

The Secretary of Defense sounded perplexed. "How does this connect with anything whatsoever?"

"This Webb guy gets it into his head that there's something in this missing ancient tome that will let him identify Nemesis. Naturally everybody assumes he's just flipped."

The driver was looking at something in his rear mirror.

"Well, has he or hasn't he?"

"That's the thing, Mister Secretary. We tell the Brits what's going on, they send out one of their people to nursemaid Webb, and the last thing we hear is that Webb's minder gets seven rounds from a Beretta 96 pumped into him and is then run over with his own hired car. Now if Webb has been chasing some chimera, how come his minder gets bumped off?"

"Unless he did it himself," suggested Bellarmine. "What's the word on him?"

"He's just disappeared. Nobody knows where he is."

"And how does that leave the great asteroid hunt?" Bellarmine asked.

A decrepit white car sailed by them, filled with students. A long-haired girl blew a kiss and then the car was past. Bellarmine's driver blew out his cheeks in relief.

"In chaos."

The driver slowed down and turned off at a sign saying "Solana Beach"; the Buick followed. He manoeuvred a few turnings and drove along a street with notices on pavements and in windows saying "No Vacancies," "Real English Beer," "Debbie's Delishus Donuts $1.50." Bellarmine stared out at this other America, at the little holiday groups on the sidewalks eating delishus donuts and wearing kiss-me-quick hats, strange people who were content to stroll aimlessly, without benefit of sharp-eyed protectors or jostling reporters.

Then the driver skimmed past an elderly woman with thick spectacles trying to reverse an orange Beetle, and turned into a quiet row of shabby beach houses. He drove slowly along for fifty yards and pulled to a stop at one of them. The street was absolutely quiet. No signs of life came from within the house. Heavy lace curtains hid its interior. A window shutter was dangling half off; the next storm would finish it. The driver frowned.

"Stay put, sir. That's an order." In the driving mirror, he watched the manoeuvrings of the orange Beetle. It eventually kangaroo'd off round the corner. "Okay, sir. Let me check out the house."

"Clem, it's okay. You're strung up like a violin string," said Bellarmine.

"Sir, this is irregular. I'd be a lot happier if one of us checked it out." Clem saw waiting assassins, Bellarmine dying in a pool of blood on the sidewalk, terrifying congressional inquisitions.

"Forget it. Come for me in a couple of hours. And cheer up, man. If the golfball buzzes you know where I am."

The cars drove off and Bellarmine waved Noordhof on into the house. The Secretary of Defense stood on the sidewalk, alone. He felt a strange exhilaration. The second most powerful man in the world had an overwhelming but unfulfillable urge: to go for a stroll.

Bellarmine walked up the concrete driveway and round the side of the house. There was a dirty white side door, half open, facing into a small hallway, cluttered with buckets, sacks of dog meal, logs and boots. A deep-throated baying came from within the house. A voice shouted "In here, Mister Secretary." Bellarmine, who hated all dogs, stepped into the untidy hallway. A door opened and he froze with fear as the Hound of the Baskervilles rushed for him, baying excitedly.

"Get down, Lift-off! Welcome to my beach house, sir. I'm fixing us up with a royal concubine."

Solana Beach

Bellarmine followed the ponytailed scientist along the corridor and through slatted swing doors. The kitchen was brightly lit, surgically clean and chaotic. Rows of gleaming sharp knives dangled from hooks on a wall. On a worktop next to a large stove was a half-empty bottle of Jack Daniel's, a supermarket chicken and a clutter of spices and unopened bottles of wine and liquor. A small balding man of about fifty, wearing an apron which made him look like a big Martini bottle, was chopping spring onions. His movements were slow and deliberate, as if the process was unfamiliar to him.

"Do you guys know each other?" asked Shafer, disappearing through another set of swing doors. The Director of NASA put down the vegetable knife, wiped his hands on the apron and shook hands with the Secretary of Defense. Bellarmine nodded; the NASA Director said I guess we sing for our supper here and Bellarmine said he'd do a fan dance if it got him answers. Then a voice from next door shouted "Help yourself to a drink!" Bellarmine poured two large sherries, emptied one and filled it up again.

Shafer reappeared with a wodge of papers stapled together. There was a knock at the door and the Great Dane started a deep-throated baying. Sacheverell walked into the kitchen. "Get down, you slobbering idiot!" Shafer yelled.

"Nice friendly dog, Shafer," said Sacheverell, while it eyed him, growling, from under the swing doors.

"Yeah," said Bellarmine. "Makes for a nice secure house. Anyways, the media think I'm on vacation at Nixon's old place. Right. I'm here for a briefing. Get started."

Shafer said, "Jim, drop that for now. Let's go next door."

Next door was a large living room. One wall was taken up by a long blackboard covered with equations. At the far end of the room a bay window looked out over the sea. Books and papers were scattered over wicker chairs, television, computer, couch, floor.

Bellarmine made his way through the clutter to the big bay window. The floor creaked and SecDef felt it give a little. On the beach below, a few girls sat topless, drinking wine and chattering. A hundred yards out at sea some young men were skilfully balancing on surfboards while big Pacific waves rolled under them and broke up hissing on the sand, or hit an outcrop of rock over to the right with a *Whump!* and an explosion of spray. Shafer appeared through the swing doors with a bottle of Jack Daniel's. "Sir, come back from the window. We had a landslip and you're overhanging the cliff. We're propped up by timbers, but I don't know how long my beach house has got before it slides into the sea."

Bellarmine turned from the window and shared a couch with a clutter of journals and books. The others settled down on casual chairs, except for McNally, who shared a cushion with the Great Dane in front of a wood fire.

The Secretary of Defense spoke slowly and clearly, as if to make sure his words were fully assimilated. "In just over ten hours' time I report to an extraordinary meeting of the National Security Council. The President, the Chiefs of Staff, myself and others may take certain decisions on the basis of information given me here. I need three things from you people. First, do you confirm the damage estimates given us by Sacheverell? Some of us had difficulty taking his stuff on board. Second, have you come up with some means of nullifying this threat? Third, have you found this

asteroid? Now, Colonel, what exactly has your team delivered? What about the simulations Sacheverell here showed
us? Is he serious?"

Shafer, standing at the swing doors, poured himself a
whisky. "They sent me your little cartoons, Herb, and I've
done a few runs of my own. Of course we don't know what
they've posted us but I've guessed we're in the hundred-
thousand-megaton ballpark, give or take. I broadly agree
with your calculations. If and when Nemesis hits, America
will be incinerated."

Bellarmine looked blankly at the Nobel physicist.

"You missed out on a few little details," Shafer continued.
"Nuclear reactors scattered over the countryside, petro-
chemical smog from burning oil, coal deposits set on fire for
a few centuries, stuff like that. And you weren't quite right
on the fireball. It's primarily the blanket of fire spreading
over the top of the atmosphere that will set us alight down
below: Ernst Öpik saw that way back in the fifties. Another
little oversight, Herb, was the counterflow, the air rushing to
fill the vacuum left by the rising fireball. Still, since we're all
dead by then, I don't suppose we care."

Bellarmine pointed dumbly at the Jack Daniel's. Shafer
crossed the room with the bottle and filled his glass, contin-
uing the critique as he did. "And I guess you used a pretty
coarse grid for your ocean simulations, Herb. It's not just
the tsunami you have to worry about. It's the plume of water
thrown forty miles into the air, and the superheated steam
shooting around. The sea bed would crack open and you'd
get a rain of molten boulders thrown for one or two thousand miles. God knows what would happen to coastal areas.
In your San Diego scenario people would have broiled before they drowned. And if you'd used an ocean-wide grid
you'd have found that the coastal areas don't get hit by
one wave. They get hit by a succession, at more or less fifty-
minute intervals. You'd replace seaboard cities by mud-
flats."

"Okay," said Bellarmine, "I believe you. If it hits we're finished. Now the sixty-four thousand-dollar question and I want to hear a good answer. Colonel, have you found Nemesis?"

Noordhof said, "No, sir."

There was a heavy silence.

Noordhof broke it. "Mister Secretary, you gave us five days. It's unreasonable. And we have almost no chance of picking it up by telescope until collision is imminent. We're down to Webb."

"Forget it," said Sacheverell, sounding peeved.

Shafer said, "Look, we're not even sure of the major types of hazard. We just don't know what's out there. The British school think that fireball showers or dark Halleys or giant comets are an even bigger risk than your Nemesis-type asteroids."

"Unmitigated crap," declared Sacheverell.

"So what now?" Bellarmine asked.

The Nobel physicist moved some books and sat down on a wicker chair. "Another drink, I guess."

There was a knock and the sound of footsteps. Shafer roared at the Great Dane, and disappeared through the swing doors. Someone was saying "Oh Jerusalem! City of Joy! I made it!" Judy Whaler walked into the room.

"You're five minutes late, Judy. Mister Secretary, may I present our nuclear weapons expert?" Bellarmine nodded.

"Carburettor trouble," Whaler explained, sinking into a wicker chair. "Kenneth's looking after the shop but I have bad news about that. The forecast for tonight is thickening cirrus over southern Arizona."

Bellarmine's voice was grim. "Let me be clear about this. Are you saying the Nemesis search is over?"

"The telescopic search, yes. We won't make your midnight deadline, Mister Secretary."

There was a silence as they absorbed Judy's words.

"You heard about the Rome thing?" Noordhof asked, thrusting a large Jack Daniel's into her hands.

She nodded and took a big gulp. "Kenneth told me. First André and now Ollie."

Noordhof said, "We don't know what's going on over there."

"Where does this Webb's ancient manuscript come in?" Bellarmine wanted to know.

The Colonel answered, "It's gone missing, which drew Ollie's attention to it in the first place. His idea was that if you had an observation hundreds of years old it would give you a long time base and a very accurate orbit, which is what the Russians would need to target the asteroid. If there really is a moving star recorded in the book, we could use it to work out which asteroid it refers to, and so identify Nemesis."

Sacheverell said, "Mister Secretary, it's a fantasy thing. We can forget it. Webb should never have been on the team."

Shafer shook his head. "I disagree. The Italian business suggests that Ollie is on to something."

The Colonel asked, "With only ten hours left to identify Nemesis, and Arizona clouded over, we're just about finished. Can't you give us more time?"

"No. Because every day carries the risk that Nemesis will hit before we've had time to take appropriate action. Because the longer we delay the greater the risk that Zhirinovsky learns that we know about Nemesis and decides to pre-empt any punch we might want to deliver. Because no matter what time you're given you'll always want more. The NSC want answers by midnight tonight. Your failure to deliver does not buy you more time."

Shafer poured Bellarmine his fourth drink of the evening. "And nullifying the threat?" SecDef asked. "Say you magically identify it in the next few hours? Presumably you hit it with the Bomb?"

"We got those coming out of our ears," said Noordhof.

"If my experience as Secretary of Defense has taught me anything, it's this. There is no problem that can't be solved with the use of enough high explosive."

Noordhof said, "Sir, we need to know what we're targeting. The Bomb is no good if we create a shower of fragments or a big dust ball heading for us."

"I think I've found the solution to that," said Judy, her voice betraying satisfaction. She put down her drink and walked over to the blackboard. She drew a string of dots joined by a straight line. Next to it she depicted an irregular shape with an arrow pointing towards the line. "We make a necklace from small atomic bombs, maybe neutron bombs. We fire the probe at Nemesis, as nearly head-on as we can. As the probe approaches it shoots off little neutron bombs in such a way that they're strung out in a line. The line cuts in front of Nemesis like so, and we set the bombs off in sequence, each one bursting just as it reaches the asteroid, say a kilometre or two above its surface."

"Nemesis has to run through a bomb alley," said Shafer.

"Yes. They're just toys, each one no more than a dozen Hiroshimas, so that each one gives a gentle push to Nemesis, not enough to break it up even if it's made of snow. But the cumulative effect is a big push, the same as if we'd given the asteroid a single hefty punch. We're going to explode the bombs directly in front of Nemesis, to brake its forward motion so as to let the Earth get past before the asteroid reaches our orbit. That's more energy-efficient than a sideways deflection."

McNally said, "In the frame of reference of Nemesis it's just peacefully coasting along and suddenly bombs appear out of space and start exploding in its face. It's simple."

"All truly brilliant ideas are simple," Shafer asserted. "And we can space the neutron bombs thousands of kilometres apart so they don't interfere with each other."

"Simple in principle but extremely difficult in practice," she said. "I have a detailed design study under way at Sandia. One way or another, we'll have something workable within the hundred-day guideline."

Bellarmine clapped his hands together in satisfaction.

"Well done, Doctor Whaler. McNally, what you have to do is deliver her atomic necklace. What do you have to say about that?"

It was McNally's turn to use the blackboard. "Willy and I have identified a route. It's extremely difficult." He scribbled on the board with yellow chalk. "The Russians are due to launch a comet probe built by the French. It's called the Vesta. We thought if we could get hold of it without arousing suspicion . . ."

"McNally, the Reds must have their antennae at full stretch. What in Christ's name do you suppose they'll think if we grab this probe from them?"

"Mister Secretary, we think we've found a way. The French have built a duplicate, for electronics testing and the like. We often do the same. It's not up to full specification but it might do for the purpose. If we could get our hands on this duplicate probe along with the detailed plans we might configure it to deliver Judy's necklace. We'll need to bring over the French engineers under an oath of secrecy."

"But Vesta is too heavy for anything but the Soviet booster," objected Sacheverell.

"That was for a long interplanetary trip, soft landing on several comets as it went. Most of that weight is in the fuel tanks and the metal darts for penetrating surfaces. We're going to strip all of that out along with the scientific instrumentation. We'll use four Shuttles in two pairs, two carrying Judy's atomic necklace and two carrying Vesta duplicates, the French one, and one we'll knock up ourselves from their plans. Or we might use one Shuttle four times. We'll have specialists on board to mate the necklace with its Vesta clone. Then we'll launch from 200 miles up with inertial upper stages like the one we used for Galileo. It's just about possible to get a dozen of Judy's bombs up that way. But we're talking very smart system development, navigational equipment and so on. We're cannibalizing existing systems all the way. I have teams on it now. We might—I say might—do it inside the magic one hundred days."

"I'll ask the CIA Director to come up with some cover story for your launches," Bellarmine promised.

"Point him in the direction of Venus probes," suggested Shafer.

The SecDef put his glass on the floor and wandered back to the bay window, picking his way over books. A gust of young laughter came up from below. Someone was tuning up a guitar and a bonfire was getting started, pieces of driftwood being thrown on to the flames, and faces flickering red around it. Someone had lit a cigarette and it was being passed around after each puff. Kids these days, Bellarmine thought.

Shafer said, "I hope you're not too hungry, Mister Secretary. Royal Concubine takes an hour to prepare."

Bellarmine came back, flopped on to the couch and leaned forward, resting his chin heavily on his hands. He said: "The sharp end is that we haven't found Nemesis."

The telephone rang. Shafer picked it up and said "Ollie!" The effect was like pulling the pin of a hand grenade. Everyone rose to their feet. The Great Dane, sensing atmosphere, leaped up.

The conversation was one-sided and carried on for some minutes, Shafer interspersing the occasional grunt. Finally he said, "Hold the line, Ollie."

"What's going on, Willy?" asked Noordhof.

Shafer spoke rapidly, his hand over the mouthpiece. "Webb's phoning from a public box in the boondocks. Some guy was paid to bump him off. This hit man has the manuscript. He works out that it must have something valuable in it but can't see what. So he makes a pact with Ollie. He lets Ollie go to see if he'll come back for the book. If Ollie does, thereby risking his life, that proves to the killer that the manuscript is worth more than the contract price on Webb. The

deal is that Ollie agrees to decipher the manuscript and the
hit man then lets him go. The guy figures he can then sell the
manuscript to his paymasters or blackmail them with its secret message."

Bellarmine was aghast. "This is a highly dangerous situation."

McNally said, "Ollie hasn't a hope."

Shafer's hand was still over the mouthpiece. "He can kill
Webb when he's got the information out of him, collect his
blood money and then proceed to the blackmail. Ollie knows
this but he still has to go for the manuscript in the hope of
getting away with it."

Judy was looking agitated. "He's going straight to his
death. Tell him to pull out."

Noordhof took the telephone from Shafer. "Webb. You
have to make contact with the killer . . . use your initiative . . . of course he expects you to try . . . look, there's no
other way . . . Mister, get this: you have no choice in the
matter."

Bellarmine took a turn. "Webb, this is the Secretary of
Defense. I'll give it to you straight. The White House requires the identification of Nemesis within ten hours, failing
which we shall proceed on the assumption that Nemesis will
not be identified before impact."

Bellarmine listened some more. His mouth opened in astonishment, and he turned, aghast. "He's thinking of pulling
out."

"I'll fix the yellow bastard," said Noordhof angrily, but
Shafer grabbed the soldier roughly by the arm and hauled
him back.

The physicist took the phone again. "Hi Ollie. Yes we
have the picture here . . . that was a brilliant insight . . . I
warned you: what did your Uncle Willy say about getting
a new idea? . . . Listen, we have a problem here, in the form
of high cirrus. It's beginning to creep in over Southern
Arizona . . . two magnitudes, five, who knows? . . . it'll slow

us to a crawl . . . yes, I agree . . . it's down to you, Ollie, you must follow through on your insight . . . yes, he means it . . . he won't say . . . my interpretation is that you have ten hours and then they feel free to nuke Russia . . . I don't know, two hundred million or something . . . you and I know that, Ollie, but what do politicians know? . . . they couldn't handle the concept . . . they like certainties . . . sure, none of us asked for it . . ." Light sweat was beginning to form on Shafer's brow. Judy poured him half a tumbler of Scotch. There was more conversation, then "Ollie says that as a British citizen he needs to get his instructions direct from HMG."

Noordhof nodded his head fiercely. "Yes! Tell him I'll fix it. And tell him I'll see what help we can give at the European end."

Bellarmine said, "No, no, no. Webb must be seen to act alone."

Shafer spoke quietly into the telephone, and then replaced the receiver. He looked round the group. His eyes half-closed with relief and he exhaled. "He's going through with it. Judy, I know how you feel but look what's at stake."

"He must be helped," Judy insisted.

Shafer looked at the Secretary of Defense with raised eyebrows. Bellarmine looked grim. He said, "If covert American action is spotted by the Russians . . ."

"But if Oliver fails . . ."

Poetry unexpectedly entered McNally's soul. "We're stuck between the Devil and the deep blue sea."

"We're clouding over," Judy reminded them. "And Hawaii's out of it. Ollie's our only hope and he surely has no chance on his own."

"He meets the hit man in a couple of hours," said Shafer.

"Oh boy. Do we know where?" Noordhof asked. Shafer shook his head.

The soldier raised his hands helplessly. "So what the hell can we do?"

The Abruzzi Hills

Webb, feeling like a rag doll, drifted with the crowds.

It was now dark. He crossed the bridge and walked in the general direction of the Piazza Navona. He made a determined decision to relax and enjoy his last hour, and came close to succeeding. The air was caressingly warm; the smells wafting out of coffee shops and trattorie were exquisite; and the ladies, it seemed to him, were exotically beautiful.

He wandered randomly along a cobbled side-street and into a little church. There was a Nativity scene, with little hand-painted donkeys and people. The straw in the stable was real which made the stalks about forty feet tall on the scale of the figures. It was simple stuff, a childlike thing in a complex world. Someone had put a lot of love into it. It brought him close to tears, and he didn't know why. Webb the sceptic, the rational man of science, sat quietly on a pew for half an hour and, unaccountably, left feeling strangely the better.

He passed by the Navona and walked along to the Spanish Steps. The throng was nearly impenetrable. Italian chatter filled the air. Kilted shepherds were on the steps, playing some sort of thin, reed-like bagpipes.

Time to move. Webb started to push his way through the crowd.

A tap on the shoulder. *"Taxi, signore."* A dark-skinned man with an earring.

Nice one, Webb thought. A precaution in case surveillance

had been set up for him in the Piazza Navona. He realized that he must have been followed from the moment he left Doney's Bar.

Webb followed the taxi driver away from the piazza along the Via Condotti. A red carpet stretched the length of the street. There was a sprinkling of couples, and families with tired children, and ebullient groups of youths. A yellow taxi was waiting at the end of the lane and the driver opened the rear door for him.

The taxi sped through town, heading south past the flood-lit Colosseum. Webb assumed he would be heading for some suburban flat but the driver was speeding past tall tenements and heading for the ring road, out of town. The astronomer didn't attempt conversation; the night would unfold as it would.

The driver turned on to the ring road and off it again in a few minutes. He slowed down as they approached a *lampadari*, a two-storeyed glass building filled with lampshades of every conceivable style, every one switched on, and forming an oasis of blazing light in the darkness. The driver took the taxi at walking pace round to the back of the building, the car lurching over rough pot-holed ground. A dark saloon car was waiting, and a short, tubby man was leaning against it with a cigarette in his mouth. Webb got out, and the man ground his cigarette under foot.

"*Piacere*," said the man, shaking Webb's hand. He led Webb to the saloon and politely opened the back door. The taxi driver reversed and drove off the way he had come, while the new driver took off with Webb, still heading south. The road was straight but the surface was poor. There were bonfires at intervals along the side of the road, and shadowy figures flickering around them, and parked cars. Fields lay beyond, in darkness.

They stopped briefly at an autostrada toll. A policeman was chatting to the toll official. Webb could have touched his gun. The driver collected a ticket and then they were off again. They passed under a large illuminated sign saying *"Napoli 150km."* The tubby driver held out a packet of Camel cigarettes over his shoulder. Webb declined. They passed villages atop hills, lights blazing, looking like ocean liners suspended in the sky. Over to the left Webb could make out a spine of mountains; these would be the Abruzzi, whence came the shepherds and the werewolves. They drove swiftly along the autostrada for about half an hour, far from Rome, heading south.

A green illuminated sign in the distance resolved itself into a sign saying "Genzano," and the driver went down through the gears and turned off. A solitary, weary official at the toll took a note from the driver and then they were winding along a narrow country road, heading towards the hills.

The road started to climb, steeply. The driver went down into second, the transmission whining briefly. They passed between houses in darkness, along a cobbled street little wider than the car. Then the car was through the village and still climbing steeply, its headlights at times pointing into the sky.

The road turned left and there were poplars on either side. Left again, through a wide gateway, and the sound of tyres rolling over loose stones. The driver stepped out, slamming the door. Webb could make out the outline of a villa. There were low, rapid voices. Then footsteps approached the car and stopped. The driver opened the door, grinning.

"Ivrea, Pascolo. Please to come with me, *professore*."

In the near pitch-black, Webb followed the sound of the driver's footsteps. There was a smell of honeysuckle. As his eyes adapted he began to make out a two-storeyed villa. It looked as if it might have a dozen rooms. There was a garden on three sides, two or three acres of lawn dotted with low bushes. A little spray of water arced into the sky from a fountain, sparkling in moonlight. Behind him were poplars and beyond that the stony slopes of a mountain: as far as Webb could tell in the dark, they were maybe a thousand feet from the summit. The fourth side of the little estate was bounded by a low wall with stone urns along it. Beyond the wall was a black sky, ablaze with the winter constellations, every one an old friend.

"This house is so isolated that not even thieves come here. Okay?"

"I get the message."

Suddenly floodlights illuminated the grounds, dazzling him. Two dark shapes bounded round from the back of the villa. They looked like small, swift ponies except that they turned out to be large, swift alsatians. They leaped playfully up on Pascolo who, Webb thought, should have gone down like a skittle by the laws of Newtonian mechanics.

"*Ciao, Adolfo, come stai?*" Ivrea cried, pulling at their ears. "*Ed anche tu, Benito!* and now, *professore*, I take you to my aunt. *Basta, ragazzi!* She is a grand woman. You stay here with us." The dogs were bounding excitedly around Webb now, and beginning to snarl. Pascolo roared at them and they fell away obediently.

She was waiting for them at the main door, in a flood of light. She was tall, dressed in the traditional black, with bright, alert eyes set in a deeply wrinkled face. She smiled courteously and raised her hand in the fascist salute. "*Buon Natale,*" she said in a firm voice. Educated Florentine accent, Webb thought, not the coarse peasant dialect of Pascolo Ivrea.

"Ah, Merry Christmas. How do you do?" Webb replied in his best Italian. "You are very kind to let me come here," he added, as if he had a choice.

The woman smiled. "The English are good people. Pascolo, the dogs, must I teach you manners? Now, professor, please let me show you my home."

Mussolini was a good man. *Il Duce* stared at Webb from every square foot of the hallway. Old photographs showed him looking noble, looking thoughtful, looking inspirational. Here he was, the great horseman, the great poet, the

bluff countryman. *Il Duce* and her father went back to child-
hood. Papa had looked after the countryside for the *fascisti*
and the Leader. Everyone was with him. In the good times
Benito would come here to relax, when he had to get away
from the plotters and the schemers in Rome.

And here am I with Papa, the old lady said with quiet
pride, pointing to a slim, attractive teenage girl standing beside a horse and a tall thin man with riding crop and boots.
Next to them was a relaxed and smiling Mussolini, looking
quite human, Webb thought, when he wasn't posturing. Benito, Papa used to say, whatever happens anywhere else, do
not worry about here. Here in the hills the people are with
you; they understand you. That was before the traitors and
the partisans, of course.

Of course, Webb said.

Then there were the slippers of some pope in a glass case,
more faded pictures of Mussolini looking noble, a brick
from some holy place, and a tiny private chapel, candles
freshly lit. Then the old lady excused herself, disappearing
along a corridor, and Pascolo explained that he would be
taking her to her beach house at Terracina in the morning but
please to follow me, *professore*.

Webb followed Pascolo up marble stairs to a landing. The
man opened a solid oak door. The room was large, plain and
comfortable. It had a double bed, a chest of drawers and a
large desk, and a shower room led off. The desk came with
an Anglepoise lamp, a pile of paper and a couple of pens, but
not, a quick scan revealed, with *Phaenomenis Novae*. French
windows led out to a broad balcony.

"*Va bene?*" Pascolo asked.

"First class, Pascolo. Do you leave early tomorrow?"

"*Si.*"

"Do you have something for me?" Webb kept his voice
casual.

There was no hesitation. "Sure, *professore*. I go with my
aunt now to collect it."

• • •

At least, Webb thought, he could contemplate the business of escape. Webb wandered round the big empty mausoleum. A Christmas tree about nine feet tall, decorated with illuminated bells, looked lost in the big sitting room. There was no telephone. He went out to the grounds. Adolfo and Benito leapt around playfully enough and then chased each other around the house. Over the low balustrade the ground swept down for about three thousand feet to a plain which stretched into the haze. Webb thought he could see a thin glimmering strip on the horizon, like the sea reflecting moonlight, maybe fifty miles away. He could see that the village was dominated by a cathedral, lit up for Christmas.

The motorway, the one along which Webb had been taken, was the *autostrada del sole* connecting Rome and Naples. Lights were drifting up and down it. He reckoned he was about fifty miles south of Rome, probably north of Cassino, south of Frosinone. That put him high in the Abruzzi Hills. Down on the autostrada, modern Italy flowed briskly past; up here, they ticked off the calendar in centuries.

He went out the main gate and set off down the hill. The village seemed deserted. He passed a big white building, like a cantina, which had open ground in front of it and wooden benches and chairs laid out, damp with dew. He walked down the narrow, steep street. Wizened faces looked out of windows. Conversations stopped as he approached and started up again as he passed.

The cathedral was a masterpiece of frescos. Its high altar was a blaze of candles. It was also empty. Webb went back up the street.

"Il padre?" he called up to an ancient hag, wrinkled and nearly toothless. There was a voice from the back of the room, and an outburst of gabbling from other houses. Then a stream of something incomprehensible was aimed at Webb from several directions at once. He heard *"solo domenica"* a few times.

He tried *"Servizio postale?"* There was an outburst of cackling; he'd said something funny. Someone told him to collect it at Genzano. More faces were appearing at windows.

Webb had one last shot, a throwaway to which he already knew the answer: *"È un telefono qui?"*

More merriment. The Man from Mars was proving an endless source of fun.

In an hour the dogs started barking and a small, blue, rusty Fiat turned into the drive and disgorged Pascolo, a little fat wife and an amazing brood of children. The children swirled around the house, teased the dogs and threw things over the garden wall and into the fountain.

Dinner in the big kitchen seemed to make no allowance for Christmas. It was an affair of huge steaming pots, huge plates of spaghetti *al sugo*, huge tumblers of cold white wine and tiny humans leaping off in random directions without warning. Pascolo's wife smiled and nodded and chattered away in some thick dialect of which Webb caught about one word in ten. They told him the wine came from his fascist aunt's vineyards and he declared it to be superb which explained why he was drinking so much. After dessert—a massive, cream-covered treacle tart—Pascolo vanished.

Webb, his nails unconsciously digging into the table-cover, waited for the manuscript. After twenty minutes he gave up and plodded up to his room. He kicked a chair in frustration and flopped on to the hard mattress. Pascolo had radiated simple honesty for the entire evening, giving nothing away—maybe because he had nothing to give.

There was a knock at the door. Webb stood up apprehensively, dreading the appearance of Walkinshaw's killers. But it was only the old lady. In her hand was a small red leather book. Webb sensed that she wanted to talk; he indicated a chair and sat on the edge of the bed.

"You are a scholar. You study history."

"That is so."

"How did you learn that I have the book?"

Webb tried a lie. "The Father Apiarist."

She smiled with pleasure. "*Ebbene!* At last Franco has spoken. That was a bad night."

"A bad night?"

Her eyes seemed to look beyond Webb. "Many terrible things were done, all those years ago. You are sure that he did explain?"

"Yes, but not in detail. Perhaps you could tell me more."

As she began to pour out her story, he sensed that it was something she had bottled up for years, that a ghost was being laid to rest. He listened attentively. "My brother was a partisan. His father disowned him and so this house has come to me. It happened in 1944. The Allies had moved inland from Anzio and already they were shelling Grottaferrata. Kesselring had summoned forces out of nothing and the battle was a hard one. But by May the Germans were streaming north. And then we heard that they had filled a train with munitions and guns, but also with wine and sacred relics from the Monastery. This was too much. Our own former Allies robbing us as they fled. And then God created for us a miracle. The train with the holy relics and the wine and the guns was stopped at a tunnel. One of their big guns was too wide to go through. For the first time the *fascisti* and the partisans joined forces. In the dark we attacked. We killed Germans.

"And then was the great tragedy. While the Germans were still being killed, and we were quickly unloading the wagons, we started to fight amongst ourselves. In the dark I ran away along the railway track, with my arms full of whatever I had snatched. But then two partisans jumped out from the ditch of the embankment. They had machine guns. They raised them to shoot me. The air was full of noise and smoke. In the half dark I recognized my brother and he recognized me. There was only a second to act. He turned his gun on his friend, a boy from the same village. He killed his friend to save me, his sister and enemy. We did not say a word. I ran into the dark.

"We have never spoken of this. As to what I had rescued from the train, it was worth little. Communion wine, silver cups, candlesticks, and a few old books. I never dared to return them."

She smiled. "I am glad that Franco has decided to speak at last. He must believe that after all this time the boy's family will forgive him."

A small boy appeared at the door, followed by his even smaller, dark-eyed sister, finger in mouth. The old lady continued: "Your colleague tells me that you will need peace and quiet to study the book. The children are excited by *Natale*, but will be in bed soon. *Non sul letto, Ghigo, tu sei senza cervello?*" The children ran off giggling. She stood up.

"I'm very grateful to you, Signora. I wish you good night and every happiness."

Webb opened the French windows. He was light-headed from a mixture of relief and exhaustion. A cool breeze flowed into the room, bringing some sub-tropical scent with it. Car headlights were drifting up and down the distant autostrada. Some animal cry came up from the olive groves below, and he could hear the wind rustling through the poplars at the side of the villa.

He had the book.

He looked at the ancient leather cover. Faded gold lettering said *Phaenomenis Novae*. Underneath was printed *Tomo III*.

It was old and faded. It had a musty smell. On the flyleaf was a date, 1643, and a neatly written dedication in Italian

To the Most Illustrious, Esteemed and Generous Leopoldo, Granduca di Toscana

And below that, the name of the author, Father Vincenzo of the Order of Preachers.

Across the top of the flyleaf someone had written *cremandum fore* in a thin, neat hand, then scored out the *cremandum* and replaced it with *prohibendum*.

Webb flicked through the pages.

It was more of an astronomer's working notebook than a manuscript. There was page after page of a faded spidery scrawl in Latin and Italian, page after page of drawings—the moons of Jupiter, sunspots, lunar craters—hot off the eyepiece of Vincenzo's telescope. The bold new frontier of science, of nearly four centuries ago.

The key to Nemesis, in his hands.

So run off into the dark night?

Pascolo: mine host, or a jailer?

The dogs: friendly, or killers on a snap of the fingers from Pascolo?

Webb looked at his watch. 10 p.m. Two in the afternoon in Arizona, 4 p.m. in Washington.

Eight hours.

A twinge of pain in the jaw warned Webb that he had been unconsciously clenching it. His hands trembling, he picked up the typescript and began to read.

Io, Europa, Ganymede and Callisto

22ʰ00

A hundred pages. Drawings, charts, notes. Written in a scrawl both flowery and spidery, the ink little faded after four hundred years. Webb had no way of guessing what the Grand Duke had thought of Vincenzo's work, if indeed he had ever set eyes on it.

The apparent lack of supervision had to be an illusion: somewhere, a mechanism for control was in place. But the identification of the crucial text was going to take the same length of time wherever he was, and at least here he wasn't fleeing over mountains and could study *Phaenomenis*. Webb looked at his watch. He would give himself until midnight, and then make his break.

Resisting the urge to rush at it, he started slowly and methodically through the pages of *Phaenomenis*. It took him half an hour.

Nothing.

He rubbed his eyes and slipped quietly down the darkened stairs to the kitchen. Childish sleeping noises came from one of the rooms as he passed. He found the light switch and went into the big kitchen. He made himself a sandwich with salami and a rosetta, and tiptoed back up to his room with it. Of jailers or dogs, there had been not a sign.

Back in his room, Webb went through it again, a line at a time.

He was beginning to see a problem with Vincenzo: there was nothing *Novae* about his *Phaenomenis*. He had always come second. Sunspots, craters on the Moon, the satellites of Jupiter: they were all there, but they had all been seen earlier by somebody else. Galileo, Huygens, Schroter—these were the sharp men of the new age, and they had all been there before him. Vincenzo had tried; but at the end of the day, he was a failure.

And still nothing.

Webb started on it a third time.

Line one: *Observationes an 1613*.

Line two: *oriens   Januarius   occidens*

The remaining page was taken up by a simple drawing:

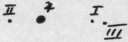

The page was completed by a couple of lines at its foot:

Die 2, h.12 a meridie. 1 et 3 conjuncti fuerunt secundum longitudinem.

So. On 2nd January 1613, at midnight, Jupiter had satellites 4 and 2 (that would be Callisto and Europa) on its left, with 1 and 3 (Io and Ganymede) to the right. Io and Ganymede had then changed places in the early hours of the third.

All of which could be worked out in minutes on a modern computer.

He nibbled at his sandwich; it was painfully spicy. Every page was turning out much the same as the last. None of

them connected with hysterically screaming terrorists and
determined killers, let alone Nemesis.

23ʰ00

Webb took another break; he was beginning to have a problem with keeping his eyes open.

He put out the lamp and walked on to the verandah. A
half-moon hung low in the sky, and the fields and hills glowed
a gentle silver. Far to the north the horizon was tinged with orange; that would be Rome and the villages of the Castelli, and
the towns scattered over the Campagna. He took five minutes
to breathe in the honeysuckled air.

A solitary car was hurtling down the autostrada. Probably, someone heading back for a long weekend with his family in Naples or Palermo, escaping from a car factory in
Turin or Milan where the young men of the *mezzogiorno*
went to make big money. He went back in, switched on the
lamp, and started on his third read of the book.

23ʰ30
Charta 40.
Die 28, h.6.

Fixa A distabat a Jove 23 semidiametres: in eadem linea sequebatur alia fixa B, quae etiam precedenti horam observata fuit.

Something.

Webb stared dully at Vincenzo's scrawl.

Take it slow.

A star had moved. Vincenzo had shown it in position A, whereas in the previous hour it had been in position B.

By now Webb had looked at this drawing several times. Jupiter, the orbiting planet, is a moving target seen from Earth, itself an even faster-moving platform. The giant planet therefore drifts against the stellar background. Centre a telescope on Jupiter, and any nearby star will seem to drift past it from one night to the next, reflecting mainly the Earth's motion.

But that rate of drift was maybe one degree a day. On the scale of Vincenzo's drawing, this star had moved about ten Jupiter diameters. Vincenzo would probably have been looking at Jupiter near opposition, when the disc of the planet was not quite resolvable by eye, maybe fifty seconds of arc. The star had therefore moved five hundred seconds of arc, or eight minutes of arc, or about one eighth of a degree, in the course of an hour. Three degrees a day.

This star was moving.

A moving star, seen in a small telescope nearly four hundred years ago.

An asteroid, tumbling past the Earth.

Through his exhaustion, Webb smiled. Nice one, Vincenzo. And good evening, Nemesis.

Martini, Bianca, Giselle and Claudia

Webb looked at his watch through unfocused eyes.

Half an hour to midnight. At midnight, Bellarmine's "aggressive posture" would come into play, a stance based on the working assumption that America was destined for annihilation. But that was midnight in Washington: to get there, the meridian had to cross the Atlantic, a journey taking six hours.

Six hours and thirty minutes to get out of this time warp, away from medieval Italy, back to the real world with real people, and computers and telephones; and then identify Nemesis from Vincenzo's little sketch, and make the vital call.

Six and a half hours, six of them drawing on the curvature of the Earth.

He put the book securely in his inside pocket and fastened the little button. He crossed to the bedroom door and opened it quietly. Harsh light flooded on to the stairwell. There might have been a faint scuffle downstairs, like a dog turning on its side: probably from the kitchen. The smell of the evening's spaghetti sauce met him faintly as he passed. A dog's head in outline rose under the kitchen table, ears raised in silent curiosity: Benito. The Führer would be around.

Quietly, Webb opened the main door and then he was out, on a warm starry night, with a ten-million-dollar manuscript.

There has to be a catch.

The light from Webb's bedroom illuminated the grounds as far as the wall. The half-moon was rising, and there were dark, still shadows which might contain anything. He stood next to the fountain, listening to it tinkling down and holding his face up to the delicate spray. Then he strolled round towards the back of the house. To Webb's taut nerves, his footsteps were jackboots on gravel, crashing through the still of the night. He reached the wall and leaned on it, looking out over the valley. The stone was cold on his hands, the countryside asleep. The fields were dark too, and filled with gnarled old witches frozen in grotesque shapes: olive trees, barely visible in the dark. And beyond was a black mass, the cathedral, a still giant lowering over a jumble of shadows.

Just getting some fresh air.

He lay on the wall, put a leg over and rolled. It was an alarming drop and he hit the earth with a solid thump, then rolled some more into a perfumed bush. He jumped up, gasping, and ran into the dark, keeping low against the wall. The wall curved away and there were twenty yards of open field to the road.

The road was too open. He changed his mind in mid-flight and turned through a right angle, charging down the field, towards the witches, not daring to glance behind. It took him into the light from his bedroom, a billion-candlepower searchlight flooding the field like a football stadium.

Webb weaved from side to side, hearing stretched to the limit and expecting at any second to hear the noisy panting of running dogs. His back muscles ached in agonized anticipation of a bullet smashing its way through his backbone.

He reached the trees and dodged wildly through them, but he was now out of sight of the villa and the mountain beyond. He stopped, puffing, and looked fearfully back up, leaning against a tree while blood pounded in his ears.

No dogs, no riflemen, and it can't be this easy.

Webb suddenly realized that he could be under surveillance from right here, amongst the trees. Time passed, as he let his eyes adapt and his breathing get back under control. Time to peer into the twisted black shapes surrounding him.

A faint scuffling, maybe thirty yards away. No doubt some animal.

Again. Closer.

Far, far away, he heard the whine of a car. It passed.

Webb turned and stumbled towards the village. A thin branch hit him painfully in the face, scratching his cheek. Through the trees he could glimpse lights twinkling on the plain beyond the autostrada. The olive grove came to an end at what seemed to be an ancient defensive ditch about thirty feet deep. The ditch stretched off to the right and merged with a steep, rocky slope in the distance. To his left, Webb could make out the rear of the cantina, about fifty yards away, with the road just beyond it.

No sound of pursuit. No scuffling from the shadows.

Stealthily, he moved to the edge of the trees. He literally felt weak at the knees. There was a low wall and on the other side of it the road leading into the village. Inky, jagged shadows lined the cobbled road. Moonlight reflected brilliantly from a small open window in the village.

He climbed the wall and stepped quietly on to the cobbled road. He kept in the shadows as much as possible on the way down to the village, and stopped in the shadow of the first building, a derelict wine cellar. The smell of sour wine drifted out of a grilled window.

Too many shadows; but quiet. Quiet like a cemetery.

A dog howled, the sound coming from about fifty yards ahead. Webb froze, terrified. Another one, back up the hill, took up the wolf call. He looked behind: underneath his bedroom—that would be the kitchen—another light had come on. The animals subsided. He padded hastily along the medieval street, almost tip-toeing on the cobbled stones, and almost within arm's length of the houses on either side. If a trap had been set, this was the place. Into the cathedral square. Light was flooding out of the open cathedral doors.

The cathedral bells crashed into life. Webb literally jumped in fright. He flew across the square. A final short stretch of houses. People were coming out of doors. He almost ran into an elderly couple in the near-dark *"Buon Natale!"* he shouted, and then he had cleared the village, the cobbles giving way to a rutted track with vines and olives on either side.

He loped down, and then he was running full pelt down the deserted track, with the sound of the bells in his ears. About half a mile down from the village the track joined on to the slip-road for the autostrada and he slowed, puffing and laughing with relief. The man at the autostrada toll was reading a newspaper, cigarette dangling from mouth. Webb passed unnoticed.

He crossed the deserted autostrada and sat on a low wall, baffled. It had been too easy. In a minute a car's headlights appeared, approaching from the south. He stepped on to the autostrada, still breathless. The headlights flooded him; he waved his hands, suddenly realized that the car had appeared suspiciously on cue, and stumbled back off the road, crouching behind the wall in an agony of uncertainty. The car passed at speed, its exhaust roaring into the distance.

Safer to wait for a truck.

He waited. A couple of cars drove past on the opposite carriageway. Webb used the passing headlights to check the time and wondered if he had been right to let the first car pass.

Fifteen minutes went by, during which, with increasing desperation, he tried willpower and prayer. But no car came.

A voice? Maybe; but it was on the limit of hearing. Webb put it down to an illusion caused by pounding blood and overwrought senses. And then, distinctly, there was the low sound of a female laugh. He walked along the emergency lane, catching occasional murmurs of conversation as he approached, although not enough to make out the sense.

A car was parked in a police layby about a hundred and fifty yards from where he had been waiting. Human figures were just discernible in its red tail-lights.

"*Buona sera!*"

A woman of about thirty emerged from the shadows. Her mini-skirt was leather and absurdly short, and her legs were skinny. "Good evening," Webb said.

"*Chi sei?*"

"*Sono un Inglese.*"

"*Ma che ci fai qui?*"

"*Mi sono perso.*"

The woman turned to the shadows behind her. "*Dice di essere un turista che si è perso. Forse sta cercando un letto per la notte.*" Somebody laughed, short and sharp.

"My name is Claudia," she said to Webb, in heavily accented English. "Can we do some business? Look, I'm clean." She delved into her blouse and pulled out a little card. Webb held it to the tail-light of the car. There was a photograph of herself and a warning in several languages. The English one said

If the stamp is red don't take her to bed
If the stamp is blue it's up to you

There were a lot of stamps. They looked red but presumably that was the tail-light.

"Actually, I was looking for a lift to Rome."

The woman laughed and said something incomprehensible over her shoulder. "You have to pay for our time, *bell'uomo*. And there are four of us."

"There's no problem with that." Four ladies of the night, services rendered. Webb almost smiled at the reaction in Accounts.

The car was small, two-door and smelled of stale cigarettes. Webb found himself squeezed into the back between Claudia, who turned out to be red-headed, and a girl with long dangling earrings and smooth skin who announced herself as Giselle.

The front seats went back and another two women slipped in, into the front. Claudia said, "We were just going anyway. Business is *cattivo* at Christmas."

The driver turned to Webb. She had short hair in tight curls; she was wearing a black choker and her eyes were heavy with mascara. "This is Martini and my name is Bianca," she said in educated English. "I'm a criminal lawyer. I make a lot of money."

"How do you do? I suppose these are your clients."

"What about you, Englishman?"

"*Un professore matto.*"

She laughed. "*In cerca della pietre filo sofali.*"

Webb's credentials as a mad professor established, the little car eased itself on to the autostrada and then took off briskly; and four whores, a nerve-shattered scientist and the secret of Nemesis headed swiftly towards Rome.

The Werewolf Club

Il Lupo Manaro, the Werewolf Club. A part of Rome which Christmas had not reached, and where white light was the only taboo.

The small car turned out to have a powerful engine, and on the trip back to Rome the speedometer needle hovered at a deeply satisfying one hundred and fifty kilometres an hour. There was a lot of repartee in a strong local dialect, most of which went over Webb's head. Wedged between Claudia and Giselle, he was treated to their bony thighs pressing against his. Claudia's hand kept straying to his knee.

Within an hour and a half the great plain of Rome was glittering below them and soon they were rattling noisily into quiet suburbs, and down towards Cinecittà. There were still crowds promenading at 1 a.m. in central Rome. Webb tried to keep his bearings from monuments and places he knew.

An alarm bell began to ring in his head.

They cut left at the Colosseum and seemed to be heading south; but then they made a sharp turn north. A sign said *Circo Massimo* and there were tall floodlit ruins on a hill to the right; and then the criminal lawyer was taking them past the Mouth of Truth, over the Palatine Bridge, across the dark Tiber, and into the maze of narrow crowded streets of the old ghetto.

This was no good: he needed the airport, fast. He said, casually, "You can let me out anywhere, ladies."

Claudia sniggered, Martini laughed wildly, and Webb's heart sank, his growing suspicion that he had never escaped hardening up.

The car turned off at a triangular piazza and drove some way into a narrow lane, pulling into the kerbside. The five of them tumbled out. Martini and Bianca were into some noisy exchange, all Italian exuberance, Bianca's long earrings swinging like pendulums. Claudia was having trouble with her stiletto heels on the cobbles, and Webb's legs were in agony with returning circulation; they linked arms for mutual balance.

Ditch her and run? Webb reckoned he might get ten yards.

A group of young men and their ladies approached, singing and giggling, and receded into the dark.

A lane leading off a lane, and there was *Il Lupo Manaro*, strobing the dark corners with green and pink neon. A notice at the entrance told them that

Mephisto
Performs
A Nite of Magic
With the Sounds of
The Meathooks

There were photographs of a rotund middle-aged man, attempting to give an air of mystery to his unmysterious features with beard, top hat, cape and wand. Even at one o'clock in the morning it was antiquated corn.

Webb said, "Thank you for the lift. I ought to go now."

Claudia was smiling with her mouth. "But you have to pay for our time, remember? Settle up in here."

"Five minutes?"

"Ten." Claudia took Webb by the hand and led him in.

Cones of ultraviolet light, thrown down by spot lamps in the ceiling, interspersed the deep gloom. Synthetic fibres

passing through the beams glowed a deep purple, and dia-
monds, if they happened to be real, sparkled and fluoresced.
There was, Webb noticed, a lot of fluorescence around. He
was startled to see Claudia's lips and eyelids glowing a brilliant green.

A mature woman with an air of having seen and done it all,
once too often, said *"Buona sera!,"* and it was *buona sera* all
the way through a maze of perspex doors into the heart of the
club. A luminous purple shirt front and cuffs approached from
the shadows like the Invisible Man, and materialized at the
last into a figure of oriental features and indeterminate age.

They were ushered to a low table near the centre of the
room and lay out on settees, Roman style, Claudia and
Giselle flopping down on either side of him. They seemed to
be well known in the club, Bianca in particular being on the
receiving end of a lot of greetings.

Candles were lit at the table; they burned red and blue
and gave off a strange herbal smell, which mingled with the
already dense smell of Havana in the air. Expensive minks
were scattered casually over the backs of settees, occupied
by couples in various degrees of intimacy and angles to the
horizontal. Martini and Bianca shared, Martini casually
stroking the lawyer's legs, which were draped over her own.
Webb began to wonder about them. A waiter approached and
Martini ordered gin fizz all round. The warmth, the narcotic
perfume and his exhaustion were like heavy chains.

A small transparent dance floor was lit up from below by
a moving kaleidoscope of primary colours. Half a dozen
couples were on it, and a phallic rhythm was being banged
out by four seasoned characters in an illuminated corner
near the stage, their leader's sweaty face leering into a microphone and more or less singing while his big hairy hands
flickered between cymbals and kettle drums. Big hairy faces
with canine teeth glared down from the walls, in glowing
pictures which interspersed with sketches of nubile maidens
in varying degrees of Eastern promise.

Bianca leaned over towards Webb. "The police keep closing this place down," she said over the music. "But it keeps opening up again under new management. Different names up front."

"I expect you have one or two clients here."

"A few tourists and provincials apart, they are all my clients."

Webb suddenly realized that in the Lupo Manaro he could be dismembered with an axe, and nobody would notice a thing.

"Look, I need to pay you and go."

Bianca smiled and shook her head. "First, we have a surprise for you."

Martini waved into a dark corner of the club. A fat man in a dinner suit leaned over Claudia and, ignoring Webb, made some remark. Claudia laughed and kissed the man, who vanished into the gloom. Webb was startled to catch the eye of a black-bearded character in a velvet tuxedo at a table a few yards in front of him. The man blew a kiss. "Not you, stupid!" he said, waving to someone at the back of the club.

A slow melody began to ooze out of a saxophone; Martini and Bianca wandered on to the floor and started to dance, hugging each other closely.

"*Sei stanco?*" Claudia asked Webb, entwining her skinny arms around his neck, her luminous lips almost touching his. "Are you tired?"

"Ah, maybe I need some fresh air." He grabbed his gin fizz.

She pulled back and laughed. "You are so inhibited, Englishman. But tonight, for you, love is free. Why not relax and enjoy life? While you can," she added enigmatically.

Webb had a desperate inspiration. "Teach me to tango, then."

The woman squealed with delight and led Webb on to the dance floor. As they reached the floor she whispered something to the man with the sax, who grinned; and the tempo was suddenly sharp and bouncy.

"Popcorn!" cried Claudia, wriggling her bottom, flinging her hands above her head, gyrating and shaking her breasts all at once. It resembled no tango Webb had ever seen. The stage cleared apart from the two of them. His desperate inspiration, to make a break for the rear, had died the moment he saw the heavies off-stage, watching his performance with dispassionate eyes. He concentrated on Claudia, clumsily trying to match her pitching and yawing, while sweat wet his brow and lurid visions of holocaust grew larger by the minute.

After a frenzied minute the tune slowed to a halt like a train coming into a station, there was a smattering of applause and Claudia, grinning and perspiring, led him by the hand back to the settee, where two men and a woman were now seated. The older man Webb had last seen at Doney's; his grey hair was now reflecting pink in the club lighting. The other two he had last seen viciously murdering Walkinshaw in the dark Tuscolo woods.

Webb took the indicated space between the young ones. Claudia, suddenly aloof, joined Giselle on another settee. Martini and Bianca were deep in some woman talk. They paid him no attention.

The pink-haired man pulled round a chair to face Webb. "Good evening, Mister Fish." His spectacle lenses were reflecting the reds and blues from the spotlights and candles. "You have been successful?"

"Yes."

"We have a bargain, remember?"

"How do I know you'll keep your half of our deal? The moment I tell you what I know, you could finish me."

"That was what made our bargain so interesting. Neither of us seemed likely to keep it. You might try to steal the manuscript, I might decide to kill you. But if you do not now tell me—*allora*, my friend has a stiletto in his pocket, only a few centimetres from your kidneys. I have seen him at work with it. It is a particularly distressing death."

Sweat was coming out of every pore in Webb's skin. "There is something in the manuscript." ·

There was a roll of drums. A little fat man came on and jabbered into a microphone in Italian, and then on strode Mephisto, complete with pointed black beard, top hat and a long black cloak with red inner lining. There was whistling and laughter as a short-haired peroxide blonde in a sequined bathing suit wheeled on a table. The magician bowed and got into his act, which involved the appearance and disappearance of lighted cigarettes, glasses of water, doves . . .

"Something in the manuscript," hissed into Webb's ear.

Webb fumbled with the button on his inside pocket and produced *Phaenomenis* with shaking hands. He flicked to a page and pointed to Vincenzo's Latin script. "Here. In this paragraph. A coded message. Renaissance scholars did this. Instead of announcing a discovery in plain Latin they made up . . ."

"The message?" the man said harshly, every line of his face contorted with greed.

Applause. A guillotine was being trundled on to the stage, one of its wheels squeaking. It was a heavy wooden structure, twelve feet tall, topped by a massive steel blade which gleamed red, white and blue in the strobing lights. The blade hissed down and a watermelon split into two with a heavy thump. Mephisto was calling for a volunteer, to general high-pitched merriment. A Scotsman, a fat Glaswegian with a Gorbals accent, was shouting garbage as three of his equally drunk friends hustled him on to the stage. The blonde seized his arm and his friends staggered off, laughing wildly.

"Must I force everything past your teeth?"

"The Duke of Tuscany hid part of his wealth. I suppose for insurance against a rainy day. But it seems he didn't trust his courtiers. Vincenzo was unworldly, and he owed his life to the Duke."

The Scotsman had used rope and chains to tie Mephisto

on a plank, with the help of the magician's assistant; now he was sliding it on a metal hospital trolley until the magician, face up, had his neck under the blade. The Scotsman clattered off the little stage at speed.

"Speak, Fish!" But now the little fat man was on stage again, patting his brow with a handkerchief and demanding total silence due to the perilous nature of the experiment. The peroxide blonde looked solemn. A curtain was pulled, and the audience went still. The blonde pulled a string. The blade accelerated rapidly down. There was a slicing noise which shook Webb's already jangled spine. A bloody head, eyes bulging and veins stringing from its neck, rolled out from under the curtain. The blonde screamed hysterically, the audience rose in pandemonium and then the curtain was pulled back and Mephisto was standing, head in place and chains at his feet. There was an outburst of relief and laughter and the audience thundered their applause.

"My patience is exhausted."

"It seems Vincenzo hid some part of the Grand Duke's treasure on his behalf, recorded the location in his notes in code, but then died before he could tell the Duke where he'd hidden it." Webb had scarcely slept in days; it was the best he could do at that hour in the morning.

"And now, my good friends, one last illusion. Another volunteer, please." His eyes ranged over the audience and settled on Webb. "You, sir!" he said, pointing dramatically. Forty pairs of eyes turned.

"Stay in your seat." But the man in the velvet tuxedo grabbed Webb's arm, laughing, and pulled him to his feet. The hit men hauled at his other arm. The audience laughed and clapped at the tug-of-war which was rapidly becoming bad-tempered. Webb shouted "Okay! I surrender!" and there was more applause as he picked his way between settees and climbed the steps. He slipped the book back in his pocket. From the stage Webb could just make out, beyond

the footlights, Martini and the assassins forcing their way
hastily towards the exit.

"Try to stay calm," Mephisto murmured in English, and
Webb's heart jumped. "My friends," the magician addressed
the audience theatrically, "you see before you a man." There
was a snort from somewhere beyond the footlights and
someone giggled. "There is one thing wrong with a man.
And that is, he is not a woman. It is a fault which we in our
world of illusion can put right. God created woman by removing a rib." The blonde gripped Webb's arm firmly as the magician leaned down and swiftly produced a bright orange
chainsaw from under the table, trailing an electric cable. The
audience roared.

"Do we dare to repeat God's experiment?" Cries of *Yes!*
Si! came from forty throats. The chainsaw burst into life.
Mephisto produced a half-bottle of some spirit from an inside pocket and drank it in a single draught, the blonde
jumping as the saw swung towards her. More laughter. "Now
Doctor Mephisto is drunk enough. Let the surgery begin. Let
us remove a rib from this man. I ask someone to inspect this
box." The saw waved erratically towards off-stage.

A box was wheeled on, and the velvet tuxedo man, keeping a weather eye on the buzzing chainsaw, tapped the walls,
jumped up and down on the floor and declared that this was
an okay box no nonsense. The blonde led Webb into the box
and the door closed. He stood in pitch black. The sound of
heavy chains being wrapped round and round the box came
in magnified. The sound from the chainsaw rose in pitch and
then there was the deafening racket of splintering wood. He
backed into a corner before realizing that somehow the saw
was not penetrating the box. There was another sound, a
panel sliding at ground level. Light flooded in from the floor.
A hand was beckoning urgently and Webb climbed down a
short wooden ladder. A light-skinned man, dressed in blue
overalls, put a finger to his mouth. Another one, with the

face of a patrician Roman, was wearing the full uniform of a
Colonel of the Carabinieri. He nodded curtly to a woman of
about twenty-five, her eyes covered with a red Venetian
mask and a sequined red cloak draped around her shoulders,
and she climbed the short ladder unsteadily in red high-
heeled shoes. Little bells tinkled around her midriff as she
brushed past Webb.

"They'll be waiting for me at the back," Webb whispered,
blinking in the light. "I saw them run out."

"I know. The name's Tony Beckenham, by the way, from
Her Britannic Majesty's Embassy. And this is Colonel Vannucci of the SDI, the Italian Security Service."

"How do you even know about me?"

"Your American colleagues. And Walkinshaw's people."

"But how did you find me? Nobody could possibly have
known where I was."

"Nonsense. We just followed the manuscript trail. The old
bat in the hills has been telling that story for the past fifty
years."

The colonel was looking agitated. "Mister Fish, this is
not-ta time for talk. The danger is extreme. We recognize at
least seven wanted criminals in the club. It is amazing good
fortune for us. But they will kill you without a thought and
shoot their way out. Until the *squadra* arrives I have only
three people here and we cannot return fire in a public
place."

"What then?"

"Hide! Back on stage!"

"Beckenham, I want you to open up the Planetological
Institute in the Via Galileo and I want a car standing by to
take me there."

"Don't be a bloody fool."

The sound of whistling and clapping penetrated through
the stage floor. A wooden panel opened from above and a
pair of long sequined legs in red high heels emerged, climbing unsteadily down the steps.

"Go, go!" Vannucci said, pushing Webb back to the ladder.

"I want to be in Oxford in three hours maximum. I don't care if you have to charter a Jumbo."

Vannucci was forcing Webb up the ladder.

"And I need a fast laptop computer on board. I left mine in the safe house."

A scared look came over Beckenham as it dawned on him that Webb was serious. Vannucci was practically lifting the astronomer upwards.

"With a Linux interface," Webb shouted down, disappearing.

"A what inner face?"

Inside the dark box again, Webb felt himself being trundled some yards, he guessed to just off-stage. The band started up on some sleepy tune, rose to a finale.

Footsteps approached. Webb fell against the side of the box as it was tilted up. It was wheeled for maybe ten yards and then a tremendous *Crack!* erupted within it. A man shouted, angry and frightened; a woman screamed; running footsteps.

Somebody kicking hard at the base of the box. Webb, drenched in sweat, took two feet to it and it burst open. Beckenham, the policeman and a woman in a black cocktail dress dragged him out and on to his feet. All three with guns and the woman, in addition, with an evening bag. A walrus-moustached janitor in a glass booth crouched, quivering, behind a chair, eyes wide with fear. It could have been a scene from a comedy.

Webb was about to speak when the woman grabbed him violently by the hair and hauled him down on to his knees. At the same instant a bullet smacked into a whitewashed wall next to his face; Webb actually glimpsed it, spinning and buzzing, on the rebound. Then the policeman was hauling open a red emergency exit door, and an alarm bell screamed into life, and Webb was being thrust into the narrow lane outside. He fell heavily.

The woman appeared, hauled Webb to his feet and pushed him ahead of her along the lane. Webb got the message and took off like a hare. He sprinted round a corner and almost collided with the young Tuscolo killers rushing out of the Werewolf Club. Webb dived to the ground. The hard cobbles knocked the breath out of him. From behind he heard two sharp bangs, and two bright yellow flashes briefly lit up the neon-strobed lane. The young ones fell like sacks. The lane emptied, people stampeding into the club or disappearing into doorways. The Tuscolo woman's face was a foot from Webb's. She had long black hair, her eyes were half-closed and quite lifeless, and something like porridge was oozing from a neat black hole in the centre of her forehead; the youth was clutching a long, thin knife, but he too was lifeless. The alarm was deafening in the narrow lane.

Webb got up and swayed, on the verge of fainting. The woman, about ten yards away, was calmly putting her high-heeled shoes back on. He said, "Can we get a move on here?" but his voice came out as an inaudible whisper.

Oxford, the Last Minutes

A *squadra volante* car whisked Vannucci, the woman and Webb across the city to the *Istituto di Planetologia* in four minutes. The doors were already open and a tousle-haired caretaker was engaged in an animated exchange with two *Carabinieri*, his hands waving dramatically. He unleashed a stream of Italian at Webb as the astronomer ran past, into the lighted building.

He ran up a flight of stairs and along a dark corridor towards Giovanni's office. He had used a visitor's password two years ago and there was no chance that it would still be valid; he would just have to rouse Giovanni at home. He tried his old username and password anyway and—joy!—it worked: the Linux window appeared.

Webb looked at his watch and, yet again, converted to the Eastern Standard time zone. He had been in the Werewolf Club for nearly an hour, and he had four hours left to identify Nemesis.

What he had to do was run the known Earth-crossers backwards in time, perturbing their orbits with the gravitational pull of the planets, and seeing how close each asteroid had been to the Earth in the Year of Our Lord 1613, on 28 November.

He took a minute to think. They would have fast orbit integrators here but he wouldn't know their names or modes of operation. The one he used at Oxford, developed by the celestial mechanics group at Armagh Observatory in Northern

Ireland, was based on Bulirsch-Stoer and symplectic routines and probably as fast as anything on the planet.

The future orbit of an asteroid or comet can be approximated by a series of straight-line steps. Each step takes so much time to compute. The greater the length of the stride, the fewer are needed in total, and so the faster the orbit is calculated. However large strides, although fast, lead to unreliable results: no real asteroid ever moved in a series of straight lines. An orbit computed with very large steps deviates more and more from reality. A computation with very small steps is highly precise but takes a very long time. Webb's quandary was that he needed high precision but had very little time.

A message on the terminal wished him a Merry Christmas but regretted that the Oxford Institute mainframe was down for maintenance over the festive season.

He had no access to the Armagh computers.

He dialled in to the Observatory's home page for the telephone number and called through. Paolo, luckily, had been prevented by poverty from joining his family in Turin this Christmas, and as usual he was working late. The Italian student immediately arranged to put the programmes on to anonymous ftp, which would allow anyone to gain access to them. Webb had them into Giovanni's machine in minutes and then transferred them on to half a dozen floppy disks, along with the planetary ephemerides for the past four hundred years, and the orbital elements of all known near-Earth asteroids.

He now had what he needed. Everything but time.

He typed in a brief e-mail message to Eagle Peak:

The Navigator has reached the New World.
Natives friendly.

It was Enrico Fermi's coded wartime message announcing that the atom had been split. Willy Shafer would understand it, but not a casual hacker.

He ran back out of the building to the police car, which took off, blue light flashing, through the town.

Vannucci glanced at Webb in the flickering light from the streets. "I would love to know what this is about."

Webb stayed silent.

"A countryman of yours is brutally killed on Italian soil. I do not like that. If I had my way you would now be answering questions in *La Madama*."

"But you're prevented by instructions from above, right?"

The policeman lit up a Camel cigarette. "Your little book. Was it worth it?"

Webb thought of Leclerc hurtling to his death, and Walkinshaw riddled with bullets, and the young ones with holes through their brains. He nodded. "Definitely. Was anyone hurt in the club?"

"You mean apart from the people who died in front of your eyes? One of my men is in the San Salvadore, undergoing emergency surgery."

"The people who died were the ones who killed Walkinshaw. The older man with me in the club set it up. They were after the book. That's all I can tell you. A grilling in the *questura* would yield no more."

Vannucci took a reflective puff at his cigarette. "I would not be so sure of that."

"Your lady—what a brilliant shot." She looked back at Webb from the front passenger seat and gave a cool smile. Her English was good: "Given the poor light, I thought I did well."

This one won't need counselling, Webb thought. He looked out at the scenery speeding past and suddenly felt cold. "This isn't the way to the airport."

"We're taking you to the military airfield at Ciampino."

They reached it in ten minutes. The police car drove straight on to the runway. An executive jet was waiting, door open, headlights on, engines whining, Beckenham at the steps with laptop computer in hand. Webb grabbed the little computer from Beckenham, shook hands briefly, and then the door was closed and the aircraft accelerated swiftly forwards.

As the jet curved into the sky, Webb glanced down at Rome by night, a great luminous spider's web divided by the Tiber. But there was no time for the luxury of terror. He fed in the programmes from the floppy disks.

Beckenham had done well at short notice. It was a fast little machine; it might take say ten minutes to explore the past history of each Earth-crosser back to 1613. There were five hundred known Earth-crossers. So, the identification process could take up to eighty-five hours. Three and a half days, day and night.

He had three and a half hours.

A supercomputer would do the job in minutes. He could have tried to download the Armagh programmes across to the Rutherford-Appleton HPC if he had had access, but he hadn't. It might take days to get into the supercomputer from the outside, and they probably had batch jobs booked up for days after that. He could attempt to muscle in now by wielding the AR or the Chairman of Council, but that could attract attention, and that attention could lead to a nuclear attack.

He could e-mail the information through to Kowalski. But there were no encryption arrangements between Eagle Peak and either Oxford or the aircraft. An e-mail message could circle the globe and touch down in half a dozen states before it reached its destination. Too dangerous: he might as well use a loudhailer.

And if the traitor on the team—if there was a traitor on the team—got to the message first, there was no telling what mischief might be done.

Having exhausted every alternative, Webb turned to the little toy on his lap.

The trick, as he saw it, was to go for the candidates most easily diverted. Leclerc would have fed in knowledge of past Russian probes and given him a more targeted list. Still, he could use the standard list of potential hazards, starting with

Apophis, Nereus and other obvious choices. With luck, Nemesis would be on the list of known potential hazards and he would have it within a few hours. That was the theory.

He clicked on an icon, and the machine asked him a few questions. Are you integrating the orbit forward or back in time? How long would you like the integration to go? What positional accuracy (in AU) would you like on the termination date (the more accurate the required position, the slower the integration)?

The preliminaries over, the machine got down to specific orbits. First it asked him for the semi-major axis of the orbit; then its eccentricity; and then the three angles defining the orientation of the orbit in space: inclination, longitude of ascending node, longitude of perihelion. The orbit's size, shape and orientation in space defined, it finally requested one last number: the true anomaly, a precise date at which the asteroid was at its point of closest approach to the sun (Julian date, please).

There was care to be exercised. In 1582 Pope Gregory XIII, on the advice of his Jesuit astronomer Clavius, had taken ten days out of the Christian calendar which had, over the centuries, gradually drifted out of phase with the seasons. The Catholic nations had taken this up at once. By the time the English had reluctantly joined up in 1752, eleven days had had to be taken out of the Protestant calendar and the peasantry had duly rioted, being reluctant to pay double rent. Vincenzo's observation, having been made in seventeenth-century Italy, was therefore 28 November by the Gregorian calendar. But Webb then had to convert this to the Julian date, a steadily ticking clock used by astronomers to bypass the vagaries of peasants and politics. This is reckoned from 1 January 4713 BC. Julian days start at noon. A Julian day is therefore shifted by twelve hours relative to the civil day and twelve hours at twenty-five kilometres a second is the difference between a million-kilometre miss and a hit.

He dug into the *Astronomical Ephemeris* and converted

Vincenzo's Catholic date to the appropriate Julian Day. From then on, Webb hoped, it would be plain sailing.

He started with Nereus.

Two little spots on the screen, one yellow and one blue, began to whirl rapidly around a fixed central disc, eventually coming to an abrupt halt with 28.11.1613 (Greg.) showing in the top right-hand corner of the screen. The process had taken about twenty minutes. The spots were nowhere near each other. On to the second asteroid on the easy-to-shift list. And then the third.

Over the English Channel, as the little jet sank along its approach path, and Webb punched in a succession of increasingly implausible candidates, it began to look as if Nemesis was not amongst the known Earth-crossers. At the moment the wheels made screaming contact with the runway he scored off the last candidate in his list of possibles. None of them had fitted Vincenzo's observation. Either good men had died chasing a phantom, or Nemesis was an asteroid known only to the Russians.

Webb settled into the back of a ministerial Jaguar and started on the Mission Impossibles, the asteroids which could not realistically be shifted in orbit. The car sped him along the M25 at a hundred miles an hour; either the driver was taking a chance or the police had been asked to turn a blind eye.

There was nothing else to be done. They were impossible because they were too fast to shift, but deadly—because of their speed—if somehow diverted nevertheless. He made the identification just as the car turned off on to the M40. He ran the program again, pushing the accuracy as far as he dared. The program now took thirty agonizing minutes to complete, but the result was identical, and suddenly the multiple insanities which had dominated his life these past few days—the Inquisition, the mad bee-keeper, the crazy old fascist lady, the greedy assassin and his weird and wicked companions—all were sloughed out of his mind and dumped in the dustbin of history. *I've beaten the lot*, he thought triumphantly. He picked up the carphone, tingling with excitement, and dialled through to the Astronomer Royal's ex-directory home number.

"Sir Bertrand, I have it. I'm about fifteen minutes from the Institute."

"Say no more."

Webb stood at the front door of the Institute, flapping his arms in the early morning cold. Traffic was non-existent. He exchanged hellos with a group of noisy revellers, the young men in dinner suits, their ladies shivering in ball gowns, dinner jackets covering their bare shoulders. After half an hour a dark Rover turned off Broad Street, the wet road glistening in its headlights. The car mounted the pavement outside the Bodleian and stopped, its headlights switching off. The figures inside made no move to leave the car, and he couldn't make them out; they might have been lovers.

Ten minutes later the Astronomer Royal's Jaguar also turned off Broad Street and drove past the Rover, along Park Road. The AR emerged, wrapped in a long black coat, a Homburg and a heavy white scarf. A gust of icy air blew round the corridor as the AR opened up, locking the door behind them and putting the bolts into floor and ceiling.

Webb led the way without conversation to his basement room. He cleared a space at his desk and they leaned over Vincenzo's manuscript, opened at the page with the moving star. The AR, his breath misting in the unheated air, looked at it and then at Webb, eyebrows raised.

"Well?"

"The Latin says it's a moving star."

"Laddie, I was reading Ovid when you were still in nappies. What's the significance of this?"

"The point is, nothing else in Vincenzo's notes stands out. Apart from the moving star, all he records are Saturn's rings, star clusters, Moon craters and so on. This can only be a close encounter with a celestial missile."

"Did you get me out of bed at four o'clock in the morning for this?"

Webb's heart sank. "I did."

"I was rather hoping that your identification, when you made it, would be based on a solid foundation. You seriously claim that this identifies the asteroid?"

I don't believe I'm hearing this. "Yes sir, I do."

Sir Bertrand looked at Webb incredulously from under his bushy eyebrows. "Yes, Webb, I'm afraid that is your style, the inverted pyramid. I have long been aware that solid groundwork, on which this Institute has built a world-class reputation, is too tedious for you. I am also aware that you are given to flights of, shall we say, speculative fancy. However, on this occasion you have excelled yourself. You build a superstructure which would have us identifying an asteroid, panicking half the planet if it got out, firing spacecraft into the blue and triggering incalculable political repercussions. And you do it on the basis of two points on a four hundred-year-old manuscript."

"Sir Bertrand, I grant you I sometimes feel as if I'm wading through treacle in this place, but would you like to tell me what else it could be?"

"A simple misidentification of a star. Or an internal reflection in a flawed lens. And they were all flawed four centuries ago. A comet unconnected with the asteroid in question. Or even a couple of variable stars which winked on and off on successive nights."

"Men have killed for this manuscript."

"I don't want to know that."

"It's relevant information. They haven't killed because Vincenzo saw an internal reflection."

"Utter bilge. I cannot endorse your identification."

"I don't know why people are even bothering with your seal of approval. What do you know?" Webb was past caring.

"Perhaps because high officials in America would rather place the future of their country in a pair of safe hands, rather than those of some immature young maverick. From what I am now hearing, they were wise to do so."

"I'm about to give you the name of this asteroid, Sir Bertrand. And when I do, keep in mind that its orbit is chaotic. A chaotic orbit means two things. One, a tiny perturbation applied early enough can yield a huge change in orbit. Two, to exploit the chaos you need to know the orbit with fantastic precision. *Phaenomenis Novae* not only identifies the asteroid, it gives a four hundred-year time base, exactly what they needed for high-precision manoeuvring."

"Webb, do you not understand?" The Astronomer Royal's tone was despairing. "We need solid, hard-headed evidence, not wild speculation."

"When they decided to use this particular asteroid, they must have known of this close encounter. They must have raked through every manuscript they could find covering the period, and then decided to get rid of the only two copies of Vincenzo in existence. The one at the Bodleian, and this one, stolen from the Helinandus Collection sixty years ago."

"You are deranged. Perhaps you should take to writing cheap thrillers."

"Take a look at this," Webb said. He fed in a disk, typed at the keyboard and stood back. The Astronomer Royal sat down heavily on Webb's chair and watched the two little spots rapidly trace out orbits. "I'm running time backwards in the Solar System. The blue one is the Earth, hence the circular track. The yellow one, that's the suspect."

While the little blue Earth whirled on its circular orbit, the yellow spot representing the asteroid traced out an elongated ellipse; two trains, each on a different track. The tumbling digital calendar measured the progress of the Wellsian time machine as it hurtled back through the internal combustion era, the wars and revolutions, the fall and rise of kingdoms, backwards through the years in minutes. And as time passed, it became clear that the yellow ellipse was not fixed in space, but was slowly rotating as the asteroid sped round it. On several occasions it happened that, unknown to the creatures inhabiting the blue spot, the yellow one passed dangerously close overhead, and that the things which mattered so much to them—wars, treaties, revolutions, history—were within an ace of being swept aside in a single, incinerating half-hour. The yellow and blue spots approached more and more closely and then, finally, touched. The whirling spots stopped, fused together on a single pixel of the screen, and the calendar froze. On the twenty-eighth of November, 1613 AD.

"The same night Vincenzo saw the moving star," Webb said. "I've also checked the background constellation and the angular rate, and they fit. It's beyond coincidence."

The Astronomer Royal expelled a great lungful of misty breath. He tossed his hat on the desk and wandered over to Webb's bookcase, pretending to read the titles. Webb gave him time.

"We had a near miss then?" the AR finally said, flicking through the pages of *Methods of Mathematical Physics*.

"Yes, sir. It passed within seventy thousand kilometres of the Earth."

"What?" Putting the book down. "That's treetop level!"

"And easily seen in Vincenzo's telescope, especially if it's an old cometary sungrazer, maybe slightly outgassing a few centuries ago. The surprise is that others didn't spot it."

"Which asteroid is this?"

"Karibisha. Eccentricity point seven, orbital inclination just 2.5 degrees, which guarantees a succession of close encounters over the centuries. Semi-major axis just over 2.1 AU."

"Is it hard to detect?" the AR asked.

"Practically impossible. By the way, 'Karibisha' is a Swahili word of welcome."

"A word of welcome. How beautiful, even at four o'clock in the morning. With an eccentricity like that no wonder it's hard to see."

Webb nodded in agreement. "It's coming at us out of the Sun. It will be invisible right up to the last few days or hours."

Sir Bertrand put the book back and ran his hands through his white hair. He picked up a telephone. "The perfect weapon. We're in the nick of time. If you're wrong, Webb . . ."

"Unfortunately there's a problem," Webb said.

"Yes?" Tension suddenly edged into the Astronomer Royal's voice. His fingers hovered over the telephone dial.

"That impossible hundred-day guideline which NASA are using for the rendezvous project."

"What of it?" The AR steeled himself like a man waiting for a punch.

Webb delivered it. "Nemesis hits in forty."

Part Three
MEXICAN CARNIVAL

carnival [<Fr. <It. <ML < *carnem levare,* to remove meat] 1. the period of feasting and revelry just before Lent. 2. a programme of contests, *etc.*

Cape Canaveral

Forty days.

Catch Karibisha a minimal five days from impact. To achieve this, spend ten days getting to it (the spacecraft's speed is optimistically half that of the death asteroid; therefore ten days of travel by the spacecraft on the way out is covered in five by Karibisha on the way in).

Subtract those ten days of travel time from the forty to impact.

The balance is the time which remains to prepare and launch the spacecraft.

It's simple: cut the one hundred days of spacecraft preparation to thirty, or die.

"Doctor Merryweather? I'm sorry to disturb you at this hour . . . my name is Rickman, Walt Rickman . . . no, we haven't met, sir . . . Chairman of Rockwell Industries, the Aerospace Division . . . I have a problem . . . it's pretty late here too—I'm calling from Downey, California."

"Is that your sister, honey?"

Merryweather struggled up to a sitting position on his bed. "Okay, Mister Rickman, I guess I'm awake. What can I do for you?"

"I'm told you're the best weather man in Texas."

"Not at three in the morning."

"That's right, sweetie, tell her to take a taxi." Merry-weather waved his wife to silence with an annoyed gesture.

The Rockwell Chairman's voice had a worried edge to it. "I've just been wakened by my engineers at Canaveral. You know the Venus probe we're launching?"

"Of course."

"They're catching a launch window in six hours. They've broken out of the T minus six hour hold and have started on the tank chilldown and propellant loading."

Merryweather scratched his head. "So what, Mister Rickman?"

"Something bizarre is going on out there. The MMT at Johnson are ignoring the Weather Launch Commit Criteria. My engineers think they've gone mad."

"Who is the Flight Director at Johnson these days?"

"A guy called Farrell."

Merryweather's wife was poking his ribs. "Joe Farrell. He's rock solid, Mister Rickman."

"Doctor Merryweather, that's a five-billion-dollar bird out there and they're ignoring the wind criteria and my peo-ple tell me that if they attempt a launch the Shuttle will hit the gantry on the way up."

"Mister Rickman. There are ten first-class meteorologists out at JSC and an equally good team at Canaveral. On Shut-tle weather support they have about a hundred years of cor-porate experience between them. If they say it's okay to launch, believe me, it's okay to launch."

"It's the SMG who've asked for you. They want you at Johnson. You're expected and authorized. I spoke to Senator Brown."

The statement brought Merryweather up short. The chief of the Spaceflight Meteorology Group, after he himself had retired from the post, was Emerson, a young, slightly anx-ious but highly able man. If George Emerson was asking for his former boss, something bizarre was indeed going on. Merryweather had one last shot: "If FD is violating the launch commit criteria he'll be overruled by his own MMT."

"Except that it's not working out that way. The Mission Management Team seem to be hypnotized or something. Look, my engineers are a hard-nosed bunch and they're telling me something weird is going on out there."

Merryweather said, "This is a joke, right?" There was a silence at the other end of the line. "Okay, maybe I should get on over."

"A helicopter is on its way and should reach you in five minutes. You have no overhead wires or other impediments in your back garden? Restricted entry to the prime firing room begins in two hours but I've fixed you up with a badge. I'm grateful, Doctor."

"Don't be. I have no official standing now and I can't influence events. I'm just curious."

Cut an improbable one hundred days to an impossible thirty. How?

In an organization as open to public scrutiny as NASA, internally and externally, with an ethos of safety and careful, meticulous planning drummed into its soul following the Challenger and Columbia disasters, how?

First explain to your top managers and your celestial mechanicians and your flight design analysts that sleep is hazardous to their health. Then, with due authorization and swearings to secrecy, tell them why. Then step back; get out of their hair.

Abandon flotation tanks and prolonged astronaut training. Stick the inexperienced mission specialists into existing Hamilton Standard space suits, show them the oxygen switch and the waste management facility, and tell them to touch nothing else.

Use experienced Shuttle pilots and arrange it so that the mission specialists, safely inside the orbiter, tell them how to prime the nukes during EVA. Don't get that bit wrong.

Abandon all thought of spacecraft environmental testing, simulated mission environments and the like.

Use big hunks of old interplanetary mission and operational support planning. Tear out the pages that don't apply. Do likewise with the computer programmes on board and on the ground.

Improvise.

Pray.

KSC press release no. 257-02

> The Venus probe passed an important milestone today when it was hoisted atop the Air Force inertial upper stage, prior to being loaded into the Frontiersman Space Shuttle. The operation was begun at midnight precisely and it was on the upper stage by 1 a.m. Until now, IUS and the probe it carries have been undergoing integration and testing at the Payload Hazardous Services Facility (PHSF) at Kennedy Space Center. Verification tests will begin immediately and are expected to be complete within twenty-four hours. Probe close-up activities will begin on the following day, February 13, leading to its encapsulation inside the Shuttle cargo bay. The long crawl to Launch Complex 39-B on Cape Canaveral Air Station will then begin.

"In this weather? Idiots."

"Sir?" The young Air Force pilot, startled, looked across at the white-haired meteorologist.

"Just talking to myself, son. It happens when you get to my age."

"Yes sir. I talk to my teddy bear."

Merryweather put the press release back in his briefcase.

He glanced down at the chalets and villas of the NASA executives over which they were flying. The familiar outline of the Johnson Space Center, a sixteen-hundred-acre sprawl, appeared ahead. Merryweather tapped the pilot's shoulder and indicated a spot near the warehouses at the edge of the site: he wanted to walk. The helicopter sank over warehouses and test facilities, flew low over the astronaut isolation HQ, and settled gently down on to a field at the edge of the site.

Merryweather collected his badge and shook hands with a young, plump man. "Hi George. It's gusty out there, prevailing west-nor'west, humidity eighty per cent. Cloud ceiling moderate."

"Am I glad to see you, sir. I'm going nuts. Come along to the Weather Room."

A bank of familiar terminals faced Merryweather. He went straight to one of them, and looked at a set of black lines covering a map of North America. Over Canada, the USA and Mexico the lines seemed to meander aimlessly. Further out they wandered over Cuba and the islands of the West Indies. But just outside Mexico, they formed into tight, concentric circles.

"Ho hum. Anything from GOES or the DMSPs?"

"Over here."

For the next forty minutes Merryweather immersed himself in a complex mass of data from geostationary satellites, polar orbiters, radars from Cocoa Beach to Melbourne, sixty-foot towers scattered around the launch pad, buoys in the heaving seas up to 160 miles from Cape Canaveral, balloons at 100,000 feet in the stratosphere and lightning detection systems at over thirty sites around the Cape. Telephone exchanges with the USAF 45th Space Wing Commander and the Weather Team at Canaveral confirmed what Merryweather clearly saw: the weather pattern was unstable and deteriorating.

Two sets of weather criteria have to be satisfied before a Shuttle launch is permitted. The weather has to be right for

launch, and it has to be right for landing. The launch criteria
need only the observed weather at the moment of launch;
but the end-of-mission criteria require a forecast. Merryweather concurred with his worried colleague: neither set of
conditions was satisfied.

Merryweather entered the third-floor Flight Control Room,
the one used for Department of Defense payloads. The
Flight Director was sitting on the bench with his back to a
console, in conversation with the CAPCOM, Gus Malloy, a
former astronaut.

"Jim, heard you'd turned up. Good to see you." The FD's
expression did not match his words of welcome.

Without preliminaries, Merryweather leapt into the attack. "Joe, what's going on here? They tell me you're overriding your Weather Team. The landing criteria will not be
satisfied. You need a cloud ceiling more than eight thousand
feet and you'll have six. You need visibility five miles and
you'll have four. You know crosswinds have to be less than
twenty-five knots and you'll have forty. There's an even
chance of strong turbulence at the point of landing, and I
couldn't rule out a thunderstorm in forty-eight hours. You
want to fly your Shuttle back through anvil cirrus? Maybe in
a thunderstorm?"

"Jim, at the worst, we can put down in Morocco instead
of Edwards. You guys are all the same. You know the standard weather parameters are conservative. We're just giving
a little flexibility."

"A little? There's a storm heading in from the Gulf. I practically guarantee precipitation at Kennedy within the next
four hours. You'll be gusting well over the thirty-four-knot
peak. The damn thing could hit the gantry on the way up."

"Jim, you're retired, remember?"

"You'll never get this through the poll."

If only I could explain, the FD thought. But he simply

shrugged and said, "We've taken an executive decision. And the final decision to launch or scrub is mine."

"I have no official status here but I want it noted that I concur with your SMG. The Flight Rules are not satisfied, neither LCC nor RTLS criteria. And the downrange weather advisory gives seas in excess of five: there are twenty-foot waves out there, Joe. Launch Frontiersman in this and I'll personally crucify you at the congressional inquiry."

"So noted. We're tanking up now and we GO in four hours and twenty minutes."

"If I recall the routine, the astronauts are due a weather briefing in fifteen minutes. They'll refuse to fly."

"You'll see."

The prime firing room at the Kennedy Space Center has its own code of discipline. Conversation is limited to the business in hand: there is no place for idle chatter between the serious professionals who man it. No personal telephone calls are made except in an emergency. No reading material unrelated to the business in hand will be seen therein. The professionals do not wander about; each man (and they are nearly all men) remains at his assigned station, concentrating on the task in hand.

The vocabulary of the firing room is terse, technical and laden with acronyms. This clipped conversation is not used to exclude the uninitiated; rather, by stripping away non-essential verbiage, the language yields precision of speech and concept; and the vital outcome is that, in a complex, changing and highly technical environment, individuals understand each other perfectly. As a sub-set of the English language it serves its purpose even though, to the outsider, there is something faintly absurd about describing a lavatory as a waste management facility, or a stranded astronaut's fate as an ongoing death situation.

Three hours before launch, entrance to the firing room is

restricted; movement within the room is minimized. Twenty minutes before launch, while the "ice team" are making a last check on the ice which builds around the liquid hydrogen and liquid oxygen tanks, and the white room close-out crew help the astronauts into their little vehicle, the door of the firing room is locked. And fifteen minutes before launch, readiness polls are conducted amongst the Shuttle Launch team. These polls ensure collective responsibility, and protect the system against eccentric or arbitrary decisions by highly placed officials.

Launch Director: Russ, on the weather, we have an update.
Spacecraft: Shoot.
LD: SMG confirm exceedence on the landing crosswinds at Edwards.
Spacecraft: Badly?
LD: Gusting up to forty knots, six over limit. You could always put down in Morocco. The main problem is Ailsa. She's moving our way faster than predicted. Giving us a high gust situation now and 45WS tell us we're close to violation of the weather LCCs. And it's going to get worse. We either break out of hold now or abort.
Spacecraft: Roger. We can feel the shaking in here. What gives with the MEC?
LD: Our programmers are still on it.
Spacecraft: What's the time factor on the crosswind?
LD: We have a Jimsphere up and your old pal Tony is now overhead in the T-38. SWO has issued a down-range weather advisory.
Spacecraft: I copy. Look, Zeek, why don't we just break out of hold and launch? Give us a mark at *T* minus five minutes and one minute prior to exit. JSC can play with the Mach attack angles and get a fresh load profile while we're counting down.
LD: Patience. JSC are polling now. Let's wait for verification.
Spacecraft: The guys in the spacesuits say yes.

LD: Russ, you don't even have a vote.
Spacecraft: We can manual override on the tank separation.
Houston Flight: NTD, this is Flight on channel 212.
LD: Go ahead.
Houston Flight: The KSC Management poll is in. Prime Launch Team report no violation of the LCC.

That was a lie.
Engineering verifies no impediments to continuation of the count. MMT Chair verifies that continuation is approved by the senior managers. What is the KSC poll?

LD: We agree with continuation and are loading up a new I-profile.
Spacecraft: What's happening on the tail computer?
LD: Still trying, and we'll initialize the IUS before we pick up the count.
Houston: Launch Director, Operations Manager here on 212 circuit. LSEAT have made a final recommendation. We're permitting some flexibility in the LCC wind criteria.

But they had just said the criteria were met. Someone was attempting the old CYA: Cover Your Ass.

We confirm you are GO to continue the count.

The voices were as calm and controlled as ever. But to Merryweather, sitting aghast in the discretionary chair next to the Flight Director, the firing room had been hi-jacked by maniacs.

LD: Ah, copy. Thank you.
NTD: The countdown clock will resume in two minutes on my mark. Three, two, one, mark.
NTD: The countdown clock will resume in one minute on my mark. Three, two, one, mark.

NTD: Stand by. Four, three, two, one, mark. Ground Launch
  Sequencer has been initiated.
Orbiter Test Conductor: Commence purge sequence four.
OTC: You have go for LOX ET pressurization.
OTC: Flight crew, close and lock your visors. Initiate O$_2$
  flow.
OTC: *T* minus one minute thirty seconds.
OTC: Minus one minute.
OTC: Go for auto sequence start.
OTC: Fifteen seconds. Ten. Main engine start, three, two,
  one. Ignition.

The light, when it reached the dark-adapted eyes of the spec-
tators, was painful in intensity. A blowtorch flame thrust
down from the rockets in a kaleidoscope of shock waves and
swept out from underground tunnels in a carnival of steam.

The thunder, when it reached them, bellowed out over the
swamps, tore at sinews, shook ground and bones and flesh.
Then the retaining clamps swung back and Frontiersman
surged upwards.

It almost made it. A sudden squall of wind and rain, a
freak thing, tilted the ship and swung it away from the tower.
Rapidly, the on-board computers tried to compensate; the
sudden angry roar would reach the onlookers twenty seconds later. But then the freak gust dropped at the very second the computers were compensating and the huge fuel
valves were trying to respond. Frontiersman flung itself
against the tower like a man pushing against a door which
suddenly opens. It just touched. A collective *Aah!* went up
from thousands of people braving the wind on the hoods and
roofs of their cars. A loud *Bang!*, like a metal hatch being
slammed shut, would reach them, but disaster was already
plain to see.

The Shuttle began to spin. The flaming tail disappeared
into the clouds half a mile above, but the direction was
wrong. Seconds later the clouds lit up as if a giant flashbulb

had popped, and shock waves ripped overhead, with a deep *Thud!* which was more felt than heard. And then there was a luminous, spreading yellow ocean, and the heat on the face even at five miles, and the fragments of tank and booster raining out of the illuminated clouds, and crashing to the ground along with the debris was the hope, the only hope, of averting Nemesis.

Not that Merryweather, staring horrified at the sight on the giant screen in the Houston firing room, knew it. But the Chief Engineer knew it; and the Flight Director knew it; and a small group of powerful men, clustered grimly around a television in the Oval Office, knew it too.

His Majesty's Treasury

It was a brief paragraph, tucked away in page two of *The Times*:

> **Cresak flies in and out**
> Mr. Arnold Cresak, President Grant's National Security Adviser, flew into London this morning and had lunch with the Prime Minister. He flew back on a regular commercial flight in the afternoon. The meeting was concerned with mutual security matters of a routine nature.

Routine like a nuclear strike, Webb thought, sipping his second tea of the morning.

Graham bustled importantly into the Hall carrying a pile of papers which Webb recognized as the new publicity drive forms from Central Office. He spotted Webb and adopted an "I want words with you" expression before joining the self-service breakfast queue.

Screw that, Webb thought. He quickly folded away *The Times*, slipped out and made his way to the Common Room. A smokeless coal fire was glowing bright red and his favourite leather armchair was empty. He picked up *Icarus* from the coffee table, sat down with a sigh of pleasure and swore quietly when Arnold tapped him on the shoulder. Webb followed the janitor across the drizzling quadrangle to the Lodge.

"Sorry about the mess, Doctor," Arnold said, clearing the *Sun*, the *Sporting Life* and a half-eaten slice of toast from a spindly wooden chair. Webb sat down and found himself facing a pouting nymph with enormous breasts. She was wearing only torn, thigh-length jeans and was straddling a giant spark plug. The calendar was two years old and it was too early in the morning for busty nymphs.

"About time," the Astronomer Royal growled over the telephone. "The Houseman would like to know the right ascension of Praesepe. Another damned freebie for you, Mister Kahn."

Webb had been dreading it for weeks; he felt himself going pale. He went smartly back to his flat and quickly stuffed clothes, toiletries, papers and false passport into his backpack. A casual eavesdropper would probably not know that a Houseman was a fellow of Christ Church College; nor that Praesepe, the Beehive, was a star cluster. He took down a perspex star globe from the top of a wardrobe, blew off the dust and found Praesepe: its right ascension—its longitude in the sky—was nine hours and thirty minutes. His watch read ten minutes past nine. That gave him twenty minutes to reach Christ Church College, presumably the main entrance at St. Aldates. Enough time for Webb, but not for the casual eavesdropper to work out the AR's message even if it had been recognized as coded. The fact of speaking in code was itself disturbing information. As an afterthought, Webb grabbed his laptop computer on the way out.

Feeling slightly foolish, he took a side door and trespassed through the Warden's back garden, not daring to look towards the windows of the house. He climbed over a garden wall, half expecting an outraged shout, and found himself in the college car park. He crossed Parks Road, looking back at Wadham, and had a near-miss with a female cyclist wearing a long scarf and a Peruvian hat. Nobody was hanging about the college; there were only the usual motley students coming and going. He walked briskly north, away from Christ

Church, before turning left on Keble Road and back south on a parallel track along Giles Causeway. A black Jaguar was parked on the double yellow lines outside Christ Church, its motor purring. The chauffeur opened the rear door of the ministerial car and Webb sank into the red leather seat.

They joined the M40; the traffic moved smoothly enough along the motorway and through the endless grey suburbs of Ealing and Acton, but in Kensington the flow began to congeal like water turning to ice. The chauffeur looked worried. He drummed his fingers against the steering wheel. He picked his nose. He switched on Radio One and switched it off again.

"Where am I headed?" Webb asked.

"I have to get you to the Treasury Building by noon sharp, sir," said the chauffeur, looking in the rear mirror.

"Relax. I'll walk." Webb left the chauffeur to the traffic jam. He walked along busy streets to the Mall, where he cut off through St. James's Park. In Horse Guards, men dressed in red were responding with wonderful precision to the sharp, echoing commands of a sergeant major with a superb repertoire of insults. He moved quickly along Whitehall and turned into the Treasury building as Big Ben started to chime.

"Name?" said the thin man at the desk.

"Mister Khan." The man gave Webb a look but ticked his name off. Webb waited in the inquiries office for some minutes, until a tall, cheerful man not much older than himself came to collect him.

"Tods Murray," said the man, in an accent which Webb connected with polo and country clubs in Henley. The man's handshake was weak and clammy. There was an impressively grand staircase but they squeezed into a small lift, and emerged on to a broad circular corridor with a red carpet. There was a smell of expensive coffee, probably Jamaican Blue Mountain. Tods Murray knocked at a door and led Webb into a small, comfortable office. At a heavy table sat the Astronomer Royal and the Minister of Defence. The AR wasn't smoking and Webb thought he looked a bit wild-eyed.

"Coffee?" asked the Minister, waving at a chair.

"No thank you, sir."

"Something stronger, perhaps?"

"No."

The Minister looked at Sir Bertrand, who shook his head, and then poured black coffee into a Worcester cup. "Would normally have held this meeting in Northumberland House, but we don't want you wandering in and out of the MOD. Not that we think anyone's keeping an eye on you, nothing so melodramatic. Just a belts and braces thing."

"That's good to know, Minister. I recall the last such reassurance."

The Minister gave him a look.

"Is that a complaint, Webb?" the Astronomer Royal asked.

"Your theory," the Minister said.

"Which one is that, Minister?"

"These suspicions about the signals from the robot telescope, a traitor on the Nemesis team and so on. We sent it all on to the CIA. They have reported that every American on that team had been thoroughly vetted and each one was regarded as loyal beyond question. Yankee White was the term used."

"But Minister, a determined attempt was made to keep that manuscript from me. One of your own staff died in front of my eyes in Italy. Someone paid these people to kill me."

Tods Murray responded, "If there was a leak, it didn't come from the Eagle Peak team."

The Minister said, "For all we know your assassin was a pathological liar. The whole business could have been local private enterprise. After all, you let it be known that you were very keen on that manuscript."

Webb said, "But the Tenerife telescope. From the outset it

was responding too quickly. Transatlantic connections aren't that fast."

"Webb," said the Astronomer Royal, "you made the connection during the graveyard watch. Transatlantic communication would have been quiet."

Tods Murray added, "And the CIA telecommunications experts checked the routing. It's fine."

Webb shook his head stubbornly. "But La Palma was clouded over. I saw it myself."

The Astronomer Royal picked up on that. "The Met Office tell us that the cloud was broken at the time of your observations, Webb. You just happened to log on to the Spot satellite at a moment when everything was overcast."

"I was being fed false pictures."

The Astronomer Royal sighed. "That is ludicrous."

"And Leclerc?"

"There was no sign of tampered switches in the wheelhouse. It was an accident." The Minister's tone was final. "Let's not get obsessive about this. Your suspicions were exhaustively investigated and found to be without foundation." He pretended to read a sheet of paper. "However, you were not invited here for a discussion about your latent paranoia, Doctor Webb. We have other plans for you. But first, I'll hand you over to Bertrand for some news."

The Astronomer Royal said, "There is good and bad. The bad news is that the Americans have given up trying to reach Nemesis. There's just no time."

He gave Webb a moment to assimilate the information, and then added: "The good news is that Karibisha might miss. There's an even chance. I'm afraid it's going to be a cliffhanger right to the end."

"They've seen Karibisha, then?"

"Yes. The US Naval Observatory managed to pick it up pre-dawn. They only have a short arc to go on. NASA's best estimate is that its perigee will be one Earth radius. We will have either an extremely close encounter or a grazing collision."

"What do the errors look like on the target plane?" Webb asked.

"A very elongated ellipse, almost a narrow bar, passing from the Pacific through central Mexico to the Gulf of Mexico. One sigma on the long axis is two thousand kilometres, on the short one a couple of hundred."

"We could still have an ocean impact, then?"

"Or a miss. The asteroid came within range of the Goldstone radar some hours ago and they should be sharpening up on the orbit now."

The Minister interrupted the technical exchange. "It says here it's approaching us at fifteen miles a second and is four million miles away at the moment. It will pass the Earth in three days and"—he looked at his watch—"eight hours."

"Can you imagine the public reaction if this gets out?" Tods Murray said.

The Minister looked as if he could. He added brown sugar crystals to his coffee. "I don't know how much longer we can keep it quiet."

Webb said, "With Karibisha's orbit it will be the devil to detect until the very last hours. But once it clears the solar disc it will be visible even in binoculars, just immediately before dawn."

"We'd like you to go to Mexico," said the Minister, stirring. "To the point of closest approach."

Webb puffed out his cheeks.

"Of course our satellite intelligence should let us know immediately whether this Karibisha has hit, but GCHQ do worry a little bit about signal failure at the critical moment due to electrical disturbances in the ionosphere. They're not sure they could immediately tell the difference between a freakishly close encounter and a hit."

"EMP, Webb," Sir Bertrand explained.

"Frankly," the Minister continued, "we want as many channels of communication as we can get, including old-fashioned transatlantic cable. It has been agreed with the Americans that there will be two scientific observers, one from America and one from Europe. On a matter of this supreme importance, HMG prefers to have a hit or miss verified not only by remote sensors but also by our man on the spot. You will understand that, depending on the outcome of the event, certain actions may be taken within minutes of it."

Tods Murray said, "We're asking you to take an even chance of being obliterated."

The Minister adopted a tone of excessive politeness. "It doesn't have to be you. Would you prefer we found someone to take your place?"

Webb felt the Astronomer Royal's eyes on him. "I insist on going," Webb said, heart pounding in rib cage. The Minister grunted his satisfaction.

"Do I know the American observer?" Webb asked.

The Minister looked at a sheet of paper. "A Doctor Whaler."

"I know her."

"The centre of the two-D error ellipse is somewhere over central Mexico, according to NASA," said the Astronomer Royal. "Close to bandit country."

The Minister peered at Webb closely. "You remain convinced that there was some sort of conspiracy to keep you from identifying Nemesis?"

"I do, sir. That's why I insist on going. I want to keep my ear to the ground."

"Mexico, Webb," said the Astronomer Royal, for no discernible reason.

Webb said, "I'd like to see the NASA report."

The Minister added more sugar, slurped and closed his eyes briefly with satisfaction. "That's better. I'll see you get it, Doctor Webb."

Tods Murray said, "The Americans are setting up a link

from the epicentre and we will be waiting for your call. Should you, for whatever reason, not be in a position to use their link, then we can alternatively be reached through this number." He slid a card across the table. "Of course we can't imagine how such a situation would arise."

"Don't let this simple precaution feed your fantasies about a conspiracy, Doctor Webb," said the Minister.

"I'm being reassured to death here," said Webb.

"Your flight leaves from Heathrow in three hours," said Tods Murray. "The same need for security applies, and you are still Mister Fish from the moment you leave this building."

"Phone in from Mexico the instant the asteroid has passed overhead," the Minister said as Webb reached the door.

"What if it hits?"

The Minister showed surprise. "We'll know. You won't call in."

Judge Dredd and the Angels of Doom

Outside the Treasury building, Webb found a telephone and made a brief call. Then he went to a Barclays Bank and drew two thousand pounds in the name of Mr. L. Fish, and took a taxi to the Natural History Museum in Cromwell Road. In the atrium he stood underneath the jaws of the long-necked *Diplodocus* which greets visitors to that great museum, while Japanese tourists and school parties swirled around him.

In five minutes, Judge Dredd emerged from the Japanese tourists and the school parties. He was red-eyed, skinny and stooped, had long, black, filthy uncombed hair and was dressed in Oxfam cast-offs. All he lacked, Webb thought, was the anorak.

They shook hands. Webb noticed the slightly red-rimmed eyes of his old friend. *He hasn't changed*, Webb thought. *Still living in the virtual world while the real one passes him by. I was like you not so long ago.*

"Jimmy! How's life treating you?"

Judge Dredd shrugged. "You know."

And as socially clueless as ever.

"Jimmy, I need some help. Look, I don't have any time as I have a plane to catch. Would you mind sharing a taxi with me to Heathrow and I'll explain as I go? I'll pay the return fare, don't worry. It's worth a hundred pounds to me to have you even listen to my problem."

"A hundred? In the name o' the wee man where do ye get money like that, Ollie? Are you cracking banks these days?"

Webb laughed. "No, still at the Oxford institute. They actually pay me to pursue my hobby."

They random-walked their way through the crowds and on to Cromwell Road. Webb waved down a taxi, asked for the airport, and closed the window connecting them to the driver. He passed over a hundred pounds in small denominations.

There was a certain honesty about Judge Dredd. He took the money with pleasure, without feigning reluctance or asking why. "Well, Ollie, I'm listening with both ears."

"I need to break into a highly secure American installation."

The Judge sniffed. "America's neither here nor there. But if you're talking about the Milnet, that's a big problem. And if it's air-gapped there's nothin you can do unless you're on the inside. Is it VMS, Unix, Win NT or what?"

"It's Unix-based."

"You need a name and a password. Usernames are nae bother. But ye'll no get in without a password."

"I need access to the Sandia Corporation in Albuquerque."

Judge Dredd displayed rows of yellow teeth. "So that's where the money's coming from? You've got in with the KGB, right?"

"Come on Jimmy, you know I'm a peace activist."

"Aye, and I'm Napoleon Bonaparte." He paused thoughtfully, drumming his skinny fingers lightly on his knee. "The Holy Grail is the password file."

"Which you can't access because you need a password to log in, in the first place."

The man looked at Webb with amusement. "You always were a bit of a lamer, Ollie. If it was an ordinary business it could be easy. The Citibank job wasn't even clever. The number of Freds and Barneys I've come across in passwords would crack you up. If there's a modem at the other end we could just keep dialling and hanging up automated-like."

"Transatlantic, isn't that expensive?"

Judge Dredd giggled. "I never paid for a transatlantic call yet. It would be unprofessional. But it's crass 1980s stuff and it takes ages. And these days most places automatically block you after a few misses."

"Jimmy, I need an answer within thirty-six hours."

"Thirty-six hours! Ye're away wi' the fairies, Ollie. These jobs take weeks."

"Is it beyond you?" Webb asked to provoke.

Judge Dredd thought about it. "I'm thinkin, I'm thinkin. Sometimes ye can get the password file from FTP or CGI scripts. You don't even need to log in, you just do an anonymous download. The CIA and NASA were cracked that way through ordinary web browsers, exploitin a programme called PHF." A dreamy look flitted across the man's face, as if he was reliving some past triumph. "But after the Rome Lab job the military started installing a lot more firewalls. A decent packet-level firewall restricts you to a couple of machines inside their network. Mind you, there's ways round that now, with packet fragmentation and the like. Of course you spread the probes and attacks around, and nothin is traceable. The Rome Lab attackers leapfrogged their way in through phone switches in South America."

He paused again. Webb took that as a cue. "Jimmy, I'll pay you a thousand pounds for a successful penetration."

The man's bloodshot eyes widened, and alarm flickered over his face. "You're intae somethin heavy here."

Webb nodded. In the confines of the taxi, a sour, unwashed smell was quickly building up.

"It's your business why ye want in, I guess. Okay let me think." The man was silent for a minute. Webb looked out at the congealed traffic. Then Judge Dredd was saying, "These high security places sometimes have a soft underbelly. They rely on outside systems like suppliers, research labs, civilian phone networks and so on. Somebody in Argentina tunnelled into Los Alamos via a legitimate university connection. It might be worth a try. But even when you get the password file you still have another problem."

Webb waited.

"The passwords are encrypted. So you have to run a cracker on it."

"You mean a decryption package?"

A pained expression crossed the Judge's face. "You cannae decrypt a password once it's encoded, not in Unix. It's a one-way system. However what you can do is run a dictionary file. What this does is apply the encryption routine to thousands of words, crap like Fred and Barney high on the list. You end up with millions of possibilities for thousands of words. It compares this encrypted output with the encrypted passwords in the file. When it finds a match, bingo, ye've got the password."

The taxi had cleared Central London and was moving briskly; signs for Hounslow, Staines and the airport were appearing at intervals. The taxi was reeking of unwashed body.

Webb knew that with his next words he would be in grave breach of the Official Secrets Act; but he saw no alternative. "Jimmy, it's important that you keep quiet about this. I have to know the source of messages going in to a place called Eagle Peak Observatory in Arizona. There's a telescope in Tenerife. It can be controlled remotely through an intermediate node and I can give you the PIN numbers to do it. When I operate it from Arizona I see signals which look as if they come from the Tenerife telescope. I need to know whether they really do. I suspect they don't."

Webb pulled a fat brown envelope from his backpack, keeping it out of sight of the driver's rear view. The man stared incredulously at it.

Jimmy asked, "Where is this intermediate node?"

"The Physics Department, Keble Road, Oxford University."

"And where does the military come intae it?"

"I suspect the signals really originate from the Sandia Laboratory."

"You don't mean yon Teraflop?"

"I do. Can't you do it?"

"In thirty-six hours? It's a megachallenge, no question."

Webb slipped the envelope over. Judge Dredd riffled the banknotes as if he couldn't believe it, and slipped it into a pocket. The smell was turning into a stench and Webb wondered when Judge Dredd had last had a bath.

"But it might be done. I'll no be able to penetrate the whole Teraflop Box, yon iron's too big for that. But with root access I could install a packet sniffer at some network switch. A desktop PC will do. You just sit quietly watching the data and biding your time. Like a crocodile watching the comings and goings on a river bank. If you keep seeing the same sequence of signals near the start of a message you might be on to a password. Then you pounce. Once you're in, you get out before anyone even notices. But you hide away a few lines of code that lets you get in the back door again whenever you feel like it."

"Jimmy, I don't care how you do it, so long as it's done surreptitiously," said Webb.

"This is a big job, ye appreciate. If I cannae hack it in time I might get the Angels of Doom on to it. Surreptitiouslike. They say their latest SATAN scripts will find holes in almost anything."

Webb scribbled down a set of numbers. "I'll call you at midnight tomorrow. I'll see you get the other half within a week."

At the airport, Judge Dredd directed the taxi back home without stepping out, and Webb made his way through the crowds to Terminal One, gulping fresh air and feeling like Klaus Fuchs.

Shortly after Webb's Jumbo had hauled itself into the air, an unknown, but clearly disguised, man entered the secure London office of Spink & Son wheeling a tartan shopping trolley and carrying a brown paper bag filled with breakfast rolls and tins of beans. He made a purchase extraordinary even by the standards of that office, paying a fortune in cash in return for gold coins. In the main he bought the "old" sovereigns, with 0.2354 of a Troy ounce of pure gold. These he weighed in heaps of ten on his own scales, before loading them into the trolley. He then placed the rolls and beans on top of the coins, and wheeled the trolley out on to the street, towards some destination unknown. The transaction took up much of the afternoon. Also that afternoon, Albemarle, Samuel and other coin dealers in the London area likewise found heavy runs on the Krugerrand, the maple leaf, the US Eagle and the Britannia.

And in Zurich and London, the world centres for the exchange of gold, the price of the yellow metal moved imperceptibly upwards. It was the merest nudge, barely detectable above the random tremors of the global market.

The huge aircraft started the big haul and dwindled to a tiny flying insect skimming just above the Atlantic. Webb travelled first class. And while the sun stood still in the sky outside, and air of lethal coldness hurtled past inches from his head, he dined six miles high on smoked salmon and champagne, and he watched Loren and Mastroianni in love, and he worried.

While the tiny insect skimmed over the water, gold kept drifting up; still a whisper all but lost in noise. The exchanges in Hong Kong and Singapore had closed for the night; but clever men and women in London and New York, people who spent their days alert for tiny fluctuations in the jagged curves on their monitor screens, had noticed the trend on their monitors; they worried too, but about different things. But then these markets too closed, and waited for the Earth to turn, for the sun to rise and pierce the Tokyo smog.

There was a thunderstorm over Newfoundland and congestion in the air over JFK, and the turbulence played with the huge aircraft like a cat with a mouse. At each bump Webb, in a state of terror, peered backwards into the dark; he could just make out the engine trying to shake itself loose from the flapping wing. He tried not to weep with relief when the Jumbo landed smoothly and taxied off the runway. A tired lady with a bright floral display in her lapel kept saying "Welcome to New York" to the ragged passengers pouring into Customs & Immigration. Webb sat worn out on a plastic seat while world travellers were whisked in limousines to Manhattan or took the helicopter, still flying in this weather, to East 60th Street.

An hour passed before a tall Indian appeared, black hair sweeping down his shoulders. "Mister Fish? Mexico bound? Would you follow me, please?"

Almost past caring, he followed the Indian on to a walkway and into the dark New York night. The air was bitter outside the terminal and snow was fluttering down.

"I'm Free Spirit," said the man, ushering Webb into a Cadillac. "It don't mean free liquor either, it's my tribal name and I'm proud of it."

"Right on," Webb said.

Free Spirit stopped to pick up an old woman who should have been meeting her son at St. Louis by now are you a stranded passenger too, four boys they have and still trying for a girl he should cut it off and pickle it if you ask me you did say you're a stranded passenger? Webb tried to nod in the right places.

The car stopped outside the Plantation Hotel and the clerk, a balding man of about sixty, gave the woman a ground floor room and took Webb up to the first floor. The man hovered. Webb told him he had no dollars. The man said he took the other stuff too. Webb said he didn't have any of that either and the clerk left shaking his head. Webb locked the door, had a warm shower and collapsed into bed.

He lay in the semi-dark and listened to the night sounds of New York and the elevator disgorging the late-night arrivals.

He worried because something didn't fit. He was still worrying when he drifted into a confused, restless, dream-filled sleep.

While Webb slept, the quiet little run on gold continued, a trickle slowly gaining strength. More ominously, the dollar began to drift down against other currencies.

The meridian drifted at a thousand miles an hour across the Pacific, the vast, empty, watery hemisphere of the planet. Twelve thousand miles across the ocean, dawn touched the Sea of Okhotsk and the northernmost islands of Japan. An hour later the sun pierced the morning fog over Tokyo; an hour later again and Singapore awoke; and once again clever people, this time in glass-fronted towers overlooking Kowloon and Clearwater Bay, began to worry. They made precautionary moves.

The dollar's drift became a slide.

Just before 1030 GMT, in London, three taxis drew up in New Court, a small courtyard in a narrow street close to the Bank of England. Three men emerged from the taxis and, as they entered the offices of N.M. Rothschild, were joined by a fourth man arriving on foot from the direction of the Bank tube station. As happened every morning at this hour, they were ushered into a small, quiet, wood-panelled office. The walls were lined with portraits of past monarchs, like hunting trophies: a reminder that, historically, even kings had needed the moneylenders. Each man had a desk on which was a telephone and a small Union Jack. The chairman of Rothschild's was already seated, and he welcomed the arrivals with a nod; it was a routine repeated twice daily, at 10:30 a.m. and 3 p.m.

The five constituted an inner circle of the London Bullion Market Association. They traded gold between themselves without ever physically exchanging the yellow metal. On their word, the twice-daily "fixing" of the price of gold, the value of gold was decided, and so the wealth of the world's central banks, holding vast gold reserves, was determined.

The chairman of Rothschild's (N.M. Rothschild, founded in 1804) opened the proceedings. He spoke in a soft, colourless voice, almost a monotone: here, gold and money, the most emotionally charged subjects known to man, were traded in an atmosphere from which all passion was ruthlessly expunged. "Gentlemen, we are faced with an extraordinary situation. My office informs me that there has been a sharp upwards movement in bullion within the last few hours."

The man from the Standard Chartered Bank (a subsidiary of Mocatta and Goldsmid, founded 1684) nodded. "It's small, but quite distinct. However, my office can find no reason for it."

There were murmurs of assent. The man from Montagu Precious Metals (Samuel Montagu, a relative newcomer, having been founded in 1853) tapped a folder in front of him. "It is very mysterious. My buying orders from our Middle East offices alone amount to nearly a billion dollars at last night's Comex rate."

The man from Deutsche Bank Sharps Pixley (Sharps, founded 1750 and merged with Pixley in 1852) raised an eyebrow. "But what about security? Can you physically export so much gold from London to Saudi?"

Rothschild's gave Sharps Pixley a disapproving look: the tone of surprise had been a tad too strong, too colourful, for this office.

The man from the Republic National Bank of New York spoke in a measured, cultured American accent. "My office feels that this is being driven by a small number of individuals who, for whatever reason, are trying to capture as much of the private gold market as they can. The market has spotted this and is responding irrationally."

"We must not have panic," Deutsche Bank Sharps Pixley said, looking worried.

Rothschild's almost smiled. "Panic can be profitable. As one of my predecessors said, the time to buy is when blood is running in the streets."

And with what passed for social chit-chat over, the five began the serious business of fixing the price of gold, of resolving the age-old tension between buyer and seller. Each man had a portfolio before him, and referred constantly to his office through the telephone. As the prices began to converge, each dealer lowered his little flag to indicate agreement with the fixing price. The man from New York was the last to agree. The flight from the dollar would be catastrophic, but the force of the market was overwhelming. As soon as he had lowered his flag, a messenger was summoned and the price of gold was published worldwide. Overnight, it had almost doubled.

Immediately after the Rothschild's morning session, encrypted information began to flow along the Highway from Midland Global Markets to the offices of the Hongkong and Shanghai Banking Corporation, whose assets under management were four hundred billion dollars. Midland Global owned the Corporation and four hundred billion dollars was a lot of responsibility. The Corporation began to offload its derivatives market, quietly tried to go short on the Nikkei.

For South Africa, the world's largest gold producer, the news was good. Barclays de Zoete Wedd contacted their owners, Barclays Bank, for instructions, but the message was already on its way from London: somebody knows something, thinks the future is bad news. Some unspecified calamity may be on the way; maybe the greenhouse is beginning to run, or the Arctic ice cap is about to break off. Whatever. So reduce exposure to the future; get out of leveraged currency swaps. And do it quietly, always quietly. No panic selling.

The Nikkei 225 Index faltered. By the close of day it had begun to plunge. On the Square Mile, the Bank of England raised interest rates, and raised them again, but the slide was becoming uncontrollable, the strain on currencies intolerable.

As the sun moved round, rumours began to sweep the markets. Whatever the calamity, somebody knew it was going to hit the States; maybe the big one was about to hit San Francisco and Silicon Valley. Whatever.

Panic. The slide on shares and currencies, now out of control, accelerated towards a precipice. Gold, the one certainty in an uncertain world, went stratospheric.

All this without knowledge of the nature of the impending disaster. But in the early hours of the morning, Eastern Standard Time, while Webb tossed and turned in a stifling hotel room, that information reached the offices of the *New York Times*.

The Situation Room, *T*-49 Hours

The Admiral was a six o'clock riser. At six fifteen, as on most mornings excepting Thanksgiving, birthdays and the like, hot water was spraying on his head and down over his scrawny, suntanned neck. He turned and shut his eyes, letting the stream hit his face and run down over his chest and his trim stomach. He groped for the shower switch, turned it off and was just turning to the shower door when his wife opened it.

"Robert. Were you expecting a car this morning?"

The Admiral showed surprise. "No I was not. What's going on?" Hastily, he dried himself off. Only once, in his ten years at Washington, had he been summoned from his home, and that had been at the outbreak of the Second Korean War.

He dressed quickly, ran a comb through his grey, wiry hair, grabbed a briefcase, sipped in passing at the coffee which his wife held for him, and made for the door. A young ensign was waiting, and a black limousine was parked on the street outside.

The car took off smoothly, the ensign taking the Admiral quickly on to Columbia Pike and past Arlington Cemetery before turning right on to the Jefferson Davis Highway. The ensign, Admiral Mitchell soon realized, knew nothing beyond his orders to transport him to the briefing chamber on the third floor of the Pentagon as quickly as possible.

The Emergency Conference Room was as large as several tennis courts. Mitchell looked down on it through the glass partition with alarm. The room was a hive of activity, the focus of the "battle staff" being four duty officers at the head of the enormous T-shaped table, peering at consoles, talking into telephones, taking messages, giving orders.

Hooper, on a telephone, beckoned the Admiral over with a wave of the arm. "Mitchell, over here." For some reason lost in the mists of time, nobody but his wife ever addressed Mitchell as anything other than Mitchell.

"What gives, Sam?"

Hooper put down the telephone. "Take a look at this. Your office just relayed it through." Hooper thrust a sheaf of papers into the Admiral's hand.

Mitchell felt himself flushing as he skimmed through the reports. "What are these guys playing at?"

"The Bear's on the move, what else?"

"But why? What precipitated this?"

The Chairman of the JCS gave the Admiral a strange look. "Mitchell, you're about to be told a story which you simply will not believe."

Something like fear flickered across Mitchell's face. "I saw a Sikorsky on the helipad. That can't mean what I think."

Hooper nodded grimly. "We're gathering up the JEEP-1 civilians. They'll be dispersed to Site R and Mount Weather. And we're stocking the civil defence bunkers in Denton with bureaucrats."

"*What?*"

"Like I said, there are things going on that you just won't believe. Let's get to the Gold Room—Bellarmine's waiting."

The Gold Room should have been filled with senior officers and their aides. The Admiral was astonished to find it empty except for the Secretary of Defense, who waved him impatiently into a chair.

"What is this?" the Admiral asked.

"Mitchell, we're heading for the Sit Room in a few minutes. But first, pin back your ears and listen to this."

• • •

"They say Nemesis will miss with fifty per cent probability," Heilbron informed the President.

Grant scowled. "Meaning it will hit with fifty per cent probability. An even chance that we're history. Anything more on that probe?"

"They've abandoned the attempt. They needed more time."

"We're helpless, then."

The Situation Room was low-ceilinged, small and cramped, with dark wood panelling on three of the walls, and a large curtain covering the fourth. The Secretary of Defense, the CIA Director, the National Security Adviser and the Chairman of the JCS were sitting around a large teak table which dominated the room. Admiral Mitchell, not a member of the NSC, was nevertheless seated at it, on Hooper's right.

"Mister President," the CIA Director added, "As the asteroid approaches they'll be able to sharpen up the orbit. Meaning we'll move towards certainty one way or another over the next forty-nine hours."

President Grant opened a drawer in the table and took out a telephone. He spoke briefly into it and the curtains behind him parted. A large screen covered much of the wall. The land masses of the United States and Russia faced each other across the North Pole. "Admiral Mitchell, what gives with these naval movements?"

Mitchell stood up and walked over to the screen. "Mister President, the Russians are mobilizing. They're moving their entire Baltic Fleet." His hand waved over the screen. "They appear to be evacuating the Kola peninsula. And their ships are pouring out here, through the Kattegat. Northern Command tell me the Swedes are lining the roads to get a view. Normally they have only a third of their Northern Fleet at sea, but they seem to be dispersing almost their whole surface fleet into the Atlantic. And down here, sir, they're moving an abnormal tonnage through the Bosphorus."

Grant said, "Tell me about their submarines."

"I'll remind you, sir, that Navy Operations Intelligence Center have been logging a sharp increase in submarine movement over the past few days. SIGINT have been picking up the communications activity that goes on when their subs slip out of berth. Over here at Petropavlosk, we believe they have maybe sixty subs out, three of them Akula class. Now we can make it hot for them in the Pacific as necessary, but over here, in the Polyarny Sea and around the Motovskiy Gulf, they can give their undersea craft reasonable air coverage. As you know, sir, we have SOSUS cables round Murmansk and the Kola Inlet. They've been picking up exceptional traffic for some days at these locations too."

"Exceptional traffic—what does that translate into?" Grant wanted to know.

"We think they may have put eighty submarines in that area, half of them strategic. Not to put too fine a point on it, Mister President, they're dispersing their whole submarine fleet."

"Thank you, Admiral Mitchell. Now that you're in on Nemesis, perhaps you'd like to sit in on this session."

Mitchell sat down. "Sir, are we going nuclear?"

Bellarmine had been bottling up the same question. Now he could contain himself no longer. "Mister President, these submarine movements are as clear a signal as you can get. Do you finally agree to a counterstrike?"

Cresak cut in. "What we're seeing is a defensive reaction to our State Orange."

Hooper tapped the table. "This is it, gentlemen. They know we're wise to the Nemesis game. They're aiming to get theirs in first."

Bellarmine cut in. "Mister President, we have to conduct the war from a secure location."

Grant looked stunned. "War? What are you talking about,

Bellarmine? The asteroid could miss and Cresak could be right. This is not necessarily a prelude to a nuclear strike."

Hooper's eyes had a glazed look. "Can you possibly be serious?"

The telephone in front of the President buzzed. He picked it up and listened. "Yes, bring it in."

A door opened and a military aide stepped in smartly. He handed the President a sheet of paper and left. Grant felt light-headed as he read it. He passed it to Bellarmine, and the paper was circulated round the teak table, ending up with Hooper.

FLASH
FROM: CINCEUR VAIHINGEN GE
TO: JCS WASHINGTON DC / /J9 NMCC
TOP SECRET PEAK
(T1/S1) SIGINT REPORTS BARRACKS EVACUATION BY RUSSIAN FORCES IN KIEV, GOMEL, VITEBSK, MINSK AND WEST MOSCOW. TANK MOVEMENTS NEAR SLOVAK BORDER AT TATRANSKA LOMNICA IN HIGH TATRAS. LARGE-SCALE CALL-UP OF RESERVISTS. TANK MOVEMENTS REPORTED EAST OF PRIPET MARSHES AND (UNCONFIRMED) THROUGH CARPATHIANS. RECOMMEND IMMEDIATE UPGRADE OF DEFCON AND DECISION ON EUCOM REINFORCEMENT OF SLOVAK AND GERMAN FORCES. DETAILED REPORTS WILL FOLLOW.

Hooper said, "It figures. We know they've been evacuating barracks and bringing up troop-carrying helicopters all the way from the Ukraine to Chechnya. In my opinion the dispositions are shaping up to a mass movement through central Slovakia, converging on the Pilzen area."

"Pure speculation," said Cresak.

The buzzer went again. This time Bellarmine went to the door and took the papers from the aide. The Secretary of Defense turned, grey-faced. "Mister President, that's the least of it."

"Go on," said Grant.

"They're bringing Backfires into Kola from their eastern airfields. Maybe a hundred of them."

"Um-huh."

"Mister President," said Hooper, "they don't aim to hang about. Just as soon as Nemesis zaps us they'll roll over Europe. We no longer have tactical stuff in Europe and the Brits and French wouldn't dare use their strategics without us to back them up."

Bellarmine said, "The temptation must be irresistible. When the asteroid hits us, Europe will be plunged into chaos. The Russians will roll their tanks in faster than decision-making machinery in Europe can assess policy. With us dead and Europe overrun they've got the world."

Cresak said, "Our scenarios assume a two-thousand-second nuclear war. If they're planning to hit us with nukes what's the point of starting a mobilization that would take a month to complete? Anyway the dispositions aren't right for a European incursion. We've always looked to a thrust across the plains to the north. Why all the tank movements on the Slovak border?"

"So they've had us fooled," said Hooper.

"The pattern in Europe doesn't fit an imminent invasion," Cresak insisted. "Where are the Spetsnaz attacks? Where are the airborne forces? They should be setting up to take Bremen airfield and move towards the Weser and the Rhine. Backfire bombers in Kola make no sense for a European attack."

"The first and oldest rule of warfare," said Hooper. "Deception. You're talking the orthodoxy they put into our heads. The Kola bombers are aimed at us over the polar route. They're going to finish us off in all the confusion. And with us gone who needs commandos? They don't need to alert anybody with D-1 incursions. It's safer to roll over Europe without any softening up."

"But the Slovak border movements . . ."

"A lead-up to a flank attack through Bavaria or even a thrust through Frankfurt. Hell, if we're out of the way they can take Europe any which way they please. Leave soldiering to the soldiers, Cresak."

"They're sabre-rattling. What we're seeing is a defensive reaction to our State Orange," Cresak insisted. "Nobody's going to invade anybody."

What wakened Anton Vanysek was the shaking of his bed.

At first, it sounded as if an unusually heavy lorry was passing below his seventh storey flat. But the rumbling went on and on. He threw back his blankets and opened his window. Bitterly cold air wafted into the room. The street below was empty, but then he saw, between the high-rise flats, dark shapes rumbling on the road about a kilometre away. It was impossible to say what they were in the early morning gloom. He was tempted to go back to his warm bed, but the whole building was vibrating. He quickly dressed, ignoring the sleepy questions from his wife, wrapped up warmly, and ran down the stone stairs.

Trnava was typical of many middle-sized towns in Slovakia. A picturesque old town was surrounded by high-rise flats, white identikit monstrosities built in the days of the communists, whose concrete cladding had long cracked and crumbled. The whole district was connected by a network of cracked and crumbling roads. Interspersing these great rabbit warrens were factories and chemical works whose outputs left strange smells in the air and brought out mysterious rashes in children, nervous complaints in the middle-aged and lung problems in the old.

Anton Vanysek had, for over twenty years, been irregularly paid small sums of money to report on local political activity, gossip, anything at all which might interest his controllers who, he assumed, passed it on to the CIA. Almost always, apart from the heady days of the bloodless revolution, his information was banal, but then, the sums of money were pitifully small.

This morning, however, as he nervously approached the main road which cut through the centre of the town, he was astonished to see that the dark green shapes were tanks. His astonishment turned to fear as he approached closer in the dull light and made out the red stars on their sides.

This information would either earn him a great deal of money or a firing squad.

For the third time in fifty years, Russian tanks were rolling into Slovakia.

The Road to Mexico

In the pale morning light, the hotel looked not so much seedy as tottering. There were a dozen motley guests in the dining room, looking like last night's collection of stranded travellers; the room smelled of cheap waffles and bacon frying in old fat; but there was something else in the air. Webb joined a little group clustering around newspapers on a table, and looked over shoulders.

The *Examiner* said

KILLER ROCK THREATENS AMERICA

and followed it up with a lurid and largely fictitious piece about astronomers huddled at secret meetings. Unbelievable words were being put into the mouths of sober colleagues. Only that well-known British expert Phippson, Webb thought, might actually have spoken the words attributed to him. More soberly, the *New York Times* ran

NEAR-MISS ASTEROID APPROACHING

with the sub-headings

But No Danger, say NASA Scientists

and

Financial Markets Plummet

To ensure the public were not unduly disturbed by false alarms, the orbits of close encounter asteroids were routinely put through a careful refereeing procedure, involving international teams of astronomers, with guidelines for media contact. But there was no mention of this. Had they bypassed the procedure in the name of secrecy? If so, if Nemesis was a secret, how did it get out?

There was something odd about that.

He found a table with a semi-clean cover and asked for bacon, eggs and tea. The waiter, a hunched man with Greek features, came back after some minutes with scrambled eggs and coffee. "Seen the nooz?" he asked.

"Media hype."

"I reckon. I got shares in Chrysler. Say, you sure you're the scrambled egg?"

Free Spirit drove Webb back to JFK. The traffic was nose to tail and eventually slowed to walking pace on the approach road to the airport. A group of men and women were parading with hastily constructed placards near the entrance, ignored by the police. A white-haired man with a sandwich-board proclaiming *Behold I Come Quickly* stepped in front of the car and Free Spirit slammed on the brakes.

"Did you see that, Mister? Did you see that? That's my problem too," Free Spirit laughed, clapping his hands.

Within the terminal, chaos ruled. The reassurances of NASA scientists notwithstanding, it seemed that half of New York State had suddenly decided to take a New Year vacation in Europe.

By contrast, the international departure lounge for the flight to Mexico City was a haven of solitude: apparently there had been about two hundred early morning cancellations and a similar number of no-shows. Webb had a coffee and shared the lounge with about twenty families of Hasidic Jews, the men with big beards and broad black hats. Why they were going to Mexico he couldn't guess. Apart from the Jews and Webb, there was only a scattering of Mexican business types, presumably returning to families back home, and a blonde female wearing a slightly old-fashioned dress with a black shoulder bag. She looked up from her magazine, glanced at him and resumed her reading. Webb took his cue and ignored her.

American Airlines hauled them into a bright sunny sky. They tilted up over Manhattan and the Hudson River and turned south, still climbing. When the plane had levelled out the blonde woman moved across the aisle and sat beside him; they were the only two travelling first class. "Oliver! The hero returns." Unexpectedly, she kissed him on the cheek. She was still into cheap perfume.

"Hi Judy, they told me you'd volunteered for this."

"You know how it is. Some politicians use moral blackmail as a tool of the trade."

"What were you doing in New York?" Webb asked.

"Briefing some UN people. Have you heard the latest about Karibisha? They've got the probable error of perigee down to—wait for it—five hundred miles. And it's still fifty-fifty whether it will hit." She smiled. "I'd make a will but who'd collect?"

"So, what's been happening at Eagle Peak?"

"I wish you'd been there when your word came through. Noordhof and Herb took off like bats out of hell and haven't been seen since. No doubt they've been doing the rounds of Washington briefings. And no word from Willy. Either he's in his beach house or else he's quietly emigrated to Antarctica. The truth is, there was nothing much to be done there before Karibisha emerged from the blind spot. Kowalski stayed on as a caretaker."

"And when they pick it up?"

"Mighty will be the panic. Herb and Kowalski will be getting high-precision astrometry."

"From the 94-inch?"

"And the Hubble. They've been testing a direct link."

"Did you come up with a means of deflecting Karibisha?"

"They didn't tell you? Staggered explosions. The idea was to deploy a dozen baby nukes, strung out along Karibisha's path like beads on a wire and each one going off in its face to slow it down; kind of like stopping an express train by gently puffing at it."

"How baby were they?"

"A third of a megaton each. We needed four Shuttle launches, in two sets of two. One Shuttle in each pair carried an upper stage rocket in its cargo bay, the other half a dozen bombs. Mission specialists were supposed to connect the bombs to the upper stage in orbit. Six bombs weren't going to be enough on their own which is why we needed a second dual launch. The Shuttle accident killed the scheme."

"Of course it was carrying a Venus probe, ha ha. What was it actually carrying?"

"Unfortunately, half a dozen of my B61s, modified with neutron generators. They're clearing up an awful lot of plutonium at Cape Canaveral. Take my advice, Oliver, don't eat tuna for the next million years."

Webb looked around at the empty cabin. "How close are we to war?"

"Who can say? But I'll tell you something," Judy leaned towards Webb. Her tone was conspiratorial. "The Teraflop has been real slow recently."

"You mean . . . ?"

She was almost whispering in the big empty aircraft. "They're gearing up for something."

Over the Florida swamplands Webb could make out tiny clusters of houses in little clearings; and then a stretch of sand was cutting across their line of motion. A few boats trailed long white wakes and then there was nothing but blue

water: the Gulf of Mexico. A menu appeared. Webb ordered
mignons de filet de boeuf Rosini, and Judy had poached
salmon with a mousseline sauce. She studied the wine list
closely and four half-bottles of champagne took them mer-
rily across the Gulf.

In the early afternoon the engine sound changed and
Webb felt his ears going funny; the Lockheed was dropping. They flew over tree-covered mountains. Broad high-
ways apparently led nowhere into the hills. Minutes later
they were weaving a path between hills covered with houses
and roads. Mexico City, an unplanned sprawl stretching to
the horizon; bigger than Tokyo, London, Singapore, New
York City; Sacheverell's "irrelevant puff of smoke." Some
boys were kicking a football on grass at the edge of the runway as the plane hurtled past, wings flexing. They didn't
look up.

The pilot expressed the hope that y'all enjoy your stay in
Mexico and that y'all will fly with American Airlines again
soon. The hostesses at the door were smiling, but Webb had
the feeling that it was a bit forced. The sounds of a riot were
coming from the direction of the terminal.

"You're not staying over in Mexico?" Webb asked the
cabin steward at the aircraft door.

"No way, sir. It's fuel up and get the hell out. This is our
last flight in."

As they approached the luggage terminal the sound in-
tensified. It was like an angry football match. Round the
last corner of the corridor, and there was the main hallway
and a brawling, bellowing mob. Between the mob and the international arrival lounges was a thin, ragged line of teenage
soldiers.

A steady trickle of passengers, life-giving boarding cards
tightly clutched, was filtering through, ducking under the
arms of the soldiers. There was no question of passport or
security checks. A lieutenant was in the rear of the line, pacing nervously up and down.

Webb, Judy and the orthodox Jews approached. The lieutenant turned in astonishment. He raised his hands.

"You cannot get through!" he shouted above the baying.

"We must!" Webb shouted back. "Our business is urgent."

"But señor, you see it is impossible."

"I'd like to speak to your superior officer."

"So would I. He has not been seen all morning."

"We're here on diplomatic business. We have to get through."

He pursed his lips, marched over to his men, issued some order and then turned back, nervously fingering the holster of his gun. "I can spare only a dozen men. You must keep together. If you stray you are lost."

The soldiers formed up into a thin wedge; they were plainly scared. At an order they began to push into the crowd. Webb and Judy huddled together with the Jewish families, following behind the wedge.

The soldiers began to use their rifle butts in a violent, panicky fashion. Slowly they pushed away from the check-in area where the staff, faces lined with tension, seemed to be taking bundles of money or tickets at random from a sea of thrusting hands. A well-dressed businessman was punching someone repeatedly on the head. The other party was kicking at the businessman's shins. Webb glimpsed a woman on her knees.

Midway to the main exit, an arm emerged from the crowd and grabbed at Webb's sleeve. It was rifle-butted away. It came back, tugging. A dark-suited, pock-faced little man. "Doctor Webb?" he shouted. "Signorita Whaler? My name is Señor Rivas. Welcome to Mexico. Please can you come this way?"

They left their protective wedge, the little man muscling his way through the crowds and Webb taking up the rear. For a few panicky moments he lost his orientation, half fell and was unable to breathe, but then he forced himself to his feet and glimpsed Judy's blonde hair some yards ahead. Over to the right he caught sight of a solid phalanx of black hats and beards, and then the crowd had swallowed them up.

The crowd density fell away at the entrance to the airport. An official with a green suit and impassive Aztec features was, by some miracle, loading their suitcases and Webb's laptop into the boot of a car, a black Lincoln Continental with darkened windows. Rivas opened the front passenger door for Judy. Stepping into the back of the car, Webb caught a glimpse of a holstered gun under the man's armpit. The interior of the car was cool.

There was a sudden roar from the direction of the terminal. Webb glanced back; the crowd had broken through the line. It was surging towards the departure lounges.

"Good to see you again, Oliver," said Noordhof, paying little attention to the riot developing yards from them. His handshake was firm and businesslike. He was wearing light tan trousers and jacket. "It's prudent to wear civilian clothes in Mexico City just now," he said without explanation.

"Why are you here, Mark? For the same salary you could be tucked away in a deep limestone cave somewhere."

"I'm responsible for you people. But I won't say the thought didn't cross my mind."

Rivas took the wheel and they pulled away in silence. He took them along the airport boulevard, past unbelievable slums, and on to the Avenue Fray Servando Teresa de Mier, heading downtown.

The car swept them silently along broad streets. Away from the airport there was something like normality apart from the occasional machine gun poking over sandbags at strategic corners; and for all Webb knew, that too was normality in Mexico City.

Judy, a child in a magic garden, kept looking back at him, enthusiastically pointing out street markets and mosaic-covered buildings designed by architects from Mars.

"You're looking a bit strung up, Oliver," said Noordhof. "Why don't you relax?"

Webb put a hand to his brow. "Relax? By this time tomorrow we could be little stars twinkling in the sky."

The colonel put his hands together in an attitude of prayer.

The Mexican whisked them along the broad Avenue Insurgentes. Apart from a lot of broken glass, there were still few signs that things were crumbling. All the same Rivas was visibly tense, looking up and down roads as they passed and generally wasting no time.

"University City straight ahead," said Noordhof. "Once we're through that we're in the clear."

"In the clear?"

There was a queue of traffic ahead, and flashing lights in the distance. An army truck raced past, overtaking them on their right. Noordhof said, "Yeah. Mexico City is being sealed off. Something to do with the roads north being jammed."

"But we're going south."

Ahead, soldiers were jumping out of the back of a truck. Barbed wire was being stretched across the street. An officer looked up sharply and then jumped as the big car squeezed through the gap, but then the Lincoln was round a corner and the cameo had vanished. A sign showed a little yacht on waves; below the yacht were the words "Acapulco 400 km."

The road was starting to climb; soon they were winding through a countryside of tall mountains, rearing out of stubbled fields yellow with corn. Noordhof looked at his watch. "Step on it, Rivas. You're racing an asteroid."

Rivas stepped on it. Unfortunately it turned out that, while he had a great deal of speed, he had very little skill. Taking one corner too wide, the car had a hairsbreadth miss with a red bus, stacked to the roof with straw-hatted Mexicans. Rivas shouted something colourful; there was an exchange of hooting, and then the bus had vanished in a trail of blue smoke.

They roared through a dusty little village. A wedding

procession scattered. Angry shouts and the barking of a dog receded into the distance.

An hour on, Rivas slowed down. They came to a turning, an open parking area, and a lodge house. The car braked to a halt. Rivas and Noordhof held out identity cards. Judy and Webb produced passports, which were closely scrutinized by an American GI. The soldier checked their names against a list and waved them in.

"Oaxtepec," Rivas said. "I get you here in time, yes? This is a government recreation centre. The American soldiers and yourselves are our guests until the asteroid flies past. At least I hope she flies past." Rivas was driving them, now at a leisurely pace, along a well-surfaced road. Acres of lawn were randomly broken up by swimming pools and colourful flower beds. The road climbed, and finally stopped at what seemed to be a big ranch house.

Noordhof excused himself, explaining that he had a chalet bungalow down the hill. Rivas was escorted towards a room in the main building. A man of Indian extraction, wearing a white jacket and dark flannels, led Judy and Webb along a cloister to adjacent rooms.

Webb's room was spacious and the furniture was ornate and solid. One wall was a French window leading out to a lawn dotted with palm trees and sub-tropical bushes. A fan took up half the ceiling. He threw his backpack and jacket on a chair, walked over to the window and looked out at the swaying trees.

The phone rang. Noordhof said, "They've picked it up at Gran Sasso, Nice and Tenerife, and the HST are locked on. Goldstone have it on radar."

"Orbit?"

"The Harvard-Smithsonian, JPL, Finland and Palomar all agree on perigee. It's somewhere in an east–west narrow arc about ninety miles wide. A fair drive south of here."

"Collision probability?"

"Still fifty-fifty."

Webb put the receiver down and looked at his watch. It was just past three o'clock. Nemesis, alias Karibisha, would come in at 06:15, in just over fifteen hours.

If it existed.

Webb wiped sweat from his eyelids. He took a few deep breaths, and tried to keep his voice steady. The sweat on his palms made the receiver slippery.

Judge Dredd answered with a tired "Yeah."

"How did it go?" Webb asked.

"Ollie! It's a bummer. I just could not get root access to the Teraflop. It's no often I'm beat but there you are."

Webb groaned.

"I'm awfie sorry about that, Ollie."

"You tried. Thanks, Jimmy."

"Real sorry. Mind you, I got your answer."

"What?"

"Oh aye, it was easy. I just gave the Tenerife telescope instructions through Eagle Peak and the Oxford terminal at one and the same time. I got different pictures from both. Either yon telescope points in two directions at once or the Eagle Peak pictures are a barefaced fraud."

Webb felt himself going light-headed. "Jimmy, you'll never know how grateful I am. I'll see you next week. Meantime remember the second half of our deal."

"Which is?"

"Keep quiet about this or I'm in trouble."

The reply was pained. "You're in trouble! What about me? If the Social found out I was earning on the side . . ."

Webb put the receiver down. The light-headedness was worse; a feeling of detachment began to wash over him, as if his soul was outside, looking down on his tormented mind from a point just below the ceiling. He went to the toilet and sat on the lid with his eyes closed and his head in his hands.

Xochicalco

Judy was tapping at the French window. She had a bright yellow towel under her arm and was wearing a crocheted, cream-coloured bikini with a matching shawl draped round her shoulders. Webb hauled himself from his exhausted sleep into the conscious world.

She put her arm in his. Webb let himself be led down a long hill, past swimming pools and through acres of landscaped garden. Her arm was trembling slightly. The touch of her skin, the inflexion of her voice, the intimacy of her presence, even the hint of perspiration from her body, all these he found both delicious and disturbing.

He sensed that she had something to tell him.

A jellyfish on stilts, as they approached, turned out to be an enormous geodesic umbrella underneath which was a small sub-tropical jungle of orchids and palm trees. They stood on a little hump-backed bridge under the umbrella and watched the volcanic spring water bubbling below. The air was acrid and sulphurous, and the woman led him along a narrow path through the tropicana. Away from the hot spring the air was heavy with scent. Butterflies the size of handkerchiefs were flitting around the palm trees and the orchids. Judy looked around conspiratorially, and they sat down on a bench. "I've something to tell you."

She paused. A jeep was approaching down the hill at speed.

"Yes?"

The vehicle braked to a halt outside the dome, a little American flag fluttering on its bonnet.

"Spill it, woman!" Webb swallowed a lump in his throat.

She put a protective hand on Webb's. "Oliver, we're both in great danger here."

A squat GI with a head like a bullet was clambering out. Judy leaned forward. "Later. We mustn't speak of this in the hacienda."

The soldier was on the hump-backed bridge. "Compliments of Colonel Noordhof, folks," he said in a Brooklyn accent. "He would like you to join him for a light snack. Gee it stinks in here." The soldier took them briskly back up the hill, in a straight line which shaved swimming pools and ploughed through flower beds as necessary.

They met up in the big restaurant, all wood and tall ceilings with an enormous empty fireplace. Aztec descendants wore white jackets and hovered around with impassive expressions. Their calmness mystified Webb. Either they believed their government's reassurances about Nemesis or they were indifferent to vaporization; neither seemed likely. Judy had reappeared in a short denim skirt, white cotton top and walking boots. She wore long dangling silver earrings and was carrying a canvas shoulder bag. After the frantic exit from Mexico City, Noordhof seemed in a good humour, and if the astronomer's nerves had been less taut he would have missed the occasional appraising glance in his direction. The soldier kept cracking jokes about Jane Fonda; from their content, Webb assumed they had a military circulation. They had enchiladas stuffed with chicken and a sauce with little jalapeño peppers in it, and candied sweet potatoes for a side dish. Two dishes of sauce, one red and one green, were placed in front of Webb.

"The waiters use this as a test of virility," Noordhof explained. "The green sauce is for ladies and wimps. The red one is for real men."

"I don't hold with these stunted concepts of masculinity,"

Webb declared. He dipped a thin slice of a turnip-like vegetable into the green sauce, nibbled it, turned red, spluttered
and then tried to swallow the Orinoco River. The Aztecs
smiled their approval.

"Or was it the other way round?" Noordhof wondered.

They finished off with a dessert of baked bananas with
egg whites and sweet condensed milk poured over them,
washing it down with coffee spiced with vanilla and cloves,
poured over cream and crushed ice.

Finally, Noordhof looked at his watch and said, "You
want to check out the setup at ground zero, Doc?"

"What about my siesta?" Webb asked, bloated.

They heaved themselves up the wooden steps of the hacienda. The jeep was waiting at the front door. Judy and
Webb sat in the back. Bullet Head revved the engine and
they took off smartly down the hill and out of the complex,
driving towards the sun, and the hinterlands.

The road was narrow and dusty. A few family homes, little more than corrugated iron huts with three walls, were
scattered around the fields, with scraggy children playing
happily enough, or heaving buckets of water. The soil was
thin and stony, and broken up by outcrops of rock. Eventually, even the houses petered out, and the cacti took over,
tall, emaciated giants standing like motionless Triffids. Buz-
zards were gliding in big lazy circles high in the mountains.
Sacheverell's scenario again; but it hadn't described the hot,
humid air which streamed past the army jeep. Webb's shirt
was sticky with sweat. Metal was painful to touch. Judy wore
dark sunglasses and her vaquero hat. Ahead of them, low on
the horizon to the south, dark clouds were building up.

As they drove steadily south, towards the dark horizon,
the temperature rose inexorably. For a mile behind them, a
long billowing wake of dust marked out their trail. Webb's
throat turned into a hot, desiccated tube, and he felt his face
going the colour of beetroot. Noordhof's conversation began to wilt, and then died, and they headed out, into the

deserted inferno, in a mood of grim endurance. Still jet-lagged, Webb tried to stretch out, laying his head back on the seat.

There was a blonde, Nordic maiden. Her eyes were glacier-blue and she was wearing a white gown. She was up to her waist in a pool of turquoise meltwater which cascaded down from Buachaille Etive Mor, spraying them both. She smiled enigmatically, and waded forwards carrying an ice-filled tumbler of Coke on a silver tray. She held the tray out to Webb. He stretched out for the cold drink, but there was the sudden roar of an avalanche, and a rock struck him on the head, and there was a crash of gears and a heavy lurch, and the ice maiden was gone, and a pitiless sun was burning into his eyes. The jeep was slowing, the driver turning off the road. They started to bump and grind along a little donkey track. The track snaked its way upwards through foothills, weaving its way around boulders. The soldier worked hard on the wheel, cursing and begging your pardon ma'am, while the jeep's suspension squealed in complaint. Ahead of them was a wooden hut, an anomaly in these primordial surroundings, like a telephone booth on a mountain top. The jeep reached it and stopped with a groan. A red-faced soldier emerged hastily and came to attention. His shirt was sticky with sweat.

Noordhof stepped out of the jeep and stretched himself. His brow was damp with sweat. He grinned wolfishly. "That was the easy bit. Epicentre dead ahead. From here on in we walk." He returned the soldier's salute smartly, and led the group off in single file.

The air was even hotter, and it was scented. As they climbed up, they were surrounded by the drone and clicking of a billion invisible insects. Irrationally, Webb began to feel hemmed in, overwhelmed. We are the true rulers of the Earth, they were saying; you are the temporary guests; we were here a billion years before you, will be here a billion years after you have gone.

They scrambled upwards over boulder-strewn ground in grim silence. Once a twin-rotor helicopter passed, thundering overhead, a jeep swinging below it on a long cable. It disappeared over the horizon ahead and the insects returned. After half an hour of it, the ground began to level out and they began to see signs of ancient cultivation. The path was taking them through terracing. There was a hilltop ahead and as they approached it, structures began to appear in silhouette against the sky. Reaching the summit, they found themselves looking out over a small city. Some community long gone had levelled the ground. Stone pyramids, temples and walls were everywhere. Hundreds of camouflage-green tents were laid out about half a mile to the right, and the city was swarming with soldiers.

Noordhof waved an arm around. "Ground zero. The place of decision."

"My feet are killing me," Webb said.

"I have to see the boss," said Noordhof, leaving them; he had slipped into a brisk, military style, marching rather than strolling. Judy and Webb had simultaneously spotted a van with an open side and an awning. The woman who handed out tumblers of iced Coke was middle-aged, wrinkled and wore a shapeless khaki overall, but to Webb she was the Ice Maiden of his dream. They downed two each in quick succession and Webb thought that maybe there was a God after all.

A GI sidled up. He looked about sixteen. He was small, freckled and had ginger hair cut almost to the scalp. "You the Brit?"

Webb nodded.

The soldier licked his lips nervously. "Say, this asteroid thing—the line is it's going to miss. Or we wouldn't be here, right?"

"Right," Webb said reassuringly.

The young soldier wasn't reassured. "You can give it to me straight, sir. We really are okay?"

A tall, thin bespectacled sergeant approached. "Are you in pain, Briggs?"

"No, sarge."

"That's strange, because I'm standing on your hair. Get it cut."

The soldier hurried off. "Say, can I show y'all around?" the sergeant asked, nominally nodding in Webb's direction before fixing a grin on Judy. Webb wandered off with a wave.

There were bas-relief carvings around the sides of the squat, stony buildings: armed warriors, human sacrifices, arms and legs and dismembered trunks. Waiting for the sky-god. On one side of a truncated pyramid Webb recognized a stylized cosmic serpent, winged and feathered, the ancient symbol of catastrophic skies from the Norse lands to Sri Lanka, from China to Mexico: the ancient giant comet, father of a hundred Karibishas.

He climbed the ancient steps of a pyramid. A thick black cable trailed up and on to the observing platform, and wound its way into the base of a big shiny paraboloid staring fixedly at a point on the blue sky. The blue lightning logo of Mercury Inc. was painted near the top of the dish. The Valley of Morelos, flanked by steep-sided mountains, stretched to the southern horizon. Whoever once controlled this ancient hill-top also controlled the valley, and passing traffic, and probably territory far beyond. The thunderclouds to the south were building up rapidly. Big Daddy, when he came, would approach from there.

"You're looking at thirty megabytes a second, son," a voice said. A short, white-haired man in a khaki shirt, with a belly overhanging his belt, was looking up at Webb. Small blue eyes were set back in a round head.

"I'm impressed."

"We use it to patch straight into the White House via one of our geosynchronous DSPs. You also link straight in to your Whitehall number through this selfsame dish so once the Holy Passover occurs you just pick up that phone over there and let 'em know. So you're the Brit who identified Nemesis. General Arkle."

"How do you do, sir?"

"I do fine. What'll we see?"

"At two hundred miles impact parameter? A rapidly rising moon. It'll cross the sky in a few seconds, going through all the phases of the moon as it passes. My guess is Nemesis will have a rough, pitted surface."

Arkle nodded thoughtfully. "And if it's a bit closer?"

"Say it touches the stratosphere. It'll leave a black smoky trail, and tomorrow will be dark."

"Closer still?"

"In that case, General, Nemesis won't seem to move much. We'll see a small crescent, very bright, low in the morning sky, coming from over there." Webb pointed in the direction of the thunderclouds. "The crescent will grow very fast—in a few seconds it will form a yellow arch straddling the sky from horizon to horizon."

"And what then?"

"The sky will go incandescent, but I doubt if our brains will have time to register the fact."

"And then goodbye America. We should have zapped the bastards long ago."

"There's a lot riding on your communications, General, and there's a thunderstorm on the way," Webb said, pointing south. "What if your system is struck by lightning?"

"We got two of everything in this man's army. Two backup systems, two generators"—the soldier's hand swept over the plateau—"and the best communications men in the world, all here just so you and I can make a ten-second call."

"Maybe the Russians know about this. Maybe they'll try to knock you out, for the sake of confusion. What about spetsnaz activity?"

Arkle laughed. "Son, you're talking to Task Force One Sixty here, from Fort Bragg, Carolina. You want to know about behind-the-lines activity? Ask us, we wrote the book. The nearest Russians are a hundred and forty miles away in Mexico City and we got them monitored. We're a full brigade, with the blessing of the Mexican Government who are proving highly co-operative on account of they object to being vaporized."

The Sun flickered briefly, and Webb felt a sudden down-draught. A helicopter whispered overhead and lowered itself into a clear space a few hundred yards away.

"You see that, son? That is a McDonnell-Douglas MH Sixty Pave Hawk. Quiet as a mouse on account of it's for in-filtration. It has all-weather vision, seven-point-six-millimetre machine guns and two-point-seven-five-inch rockets. It can do a hundred and eighty-five miles an hour and fly to Mexico City and back twice without refuelling. We got two of them too."

"General Arkle, you seem to have two of everything."

"Believe it. Anything you need?" The general looked ap-praisingly at Webb, then produced a large cigar and pro-ceeded to light up. About a hundred yards over his shoulder Judy was having the intricacies of a diesel power generator explained to her by about a dozen GIs.

"I'd like to get back. Can I commandeer a jeep?"

"Sure, and a driver. Tell 'em I said so."

"There's an old joke, General Arkle. 'Ladies and gentle-men, you are now flying in the first fully automated aircraft. There is no need to worry as nothing can go wrong nothing can go wrong nothing can go wrong . . . ' "

The soldier laughed again, and blew a smoke ring. "Boy, you sure are a worrier."

Low, dark clouds overtook the jeep on the way back, blotting out the hot sun. Noordhof had stayed put, still having busi-ness with Arkle, and Webb had finally prised Judy away from her enthusiastic technical instructors before commandeering the little fat driver to take them back. The landscape, already primeval, took on a dull, alien look, as if it belonged to another planet. Out here, the brooding atmosphere was almost tangible.

The driver put on his headlights and assured them that Jesus begging your pardon ma'am we're in for Sumthin that's for Shore. He pulled over and stopped, the brakes squealing. The humidity was terrific and his short thick neck glistened with sweat. The silence was unnatural. He began to haul at the tarpaulin hurriedly, as if anxious to get away. Webb jumped out to help just as the first hailstone clanged noisily off the bonnet of the jeep, and they barely had time to scramble back in before an avalanche of hail poured down from the sky.

The first flickering blue etched a brilliant Christmas tree on Webb's retina, and a deep electrical crackle rumbled round and round the mountains. Judy cried with delight, and after that the powerful echoing *Boom!* of one thunderclap after another merged with the solid roar of hailstones on the jeep, while wind tore at the canopy and lightning strobed the landscape so that it looked as if they were part of a jerky old movie. Conversation was futile, but the driver managed a steady stream of profanity.

Once the bouncing and mud-sliding got out of hand; the driver had mistaken the road. He put on the brakes but the jeep started to slither and they found themselves in a terrifying, out-of-control slide taking them sideways down towards a gorge. They were about to jump for their lives when the jeep hit a rock about three feet from the edge and stopped with a bump. Webb had a nose-down view of a surging, yellow river forty feet below them, and a fallen tree wedged between black rocks.

Judy and Webb jumped out and heaved on the jeep while the driver, white-faced and shaking, reversed slowly on to the real road. Arcs of mud flew up from the spinning wheels and they all turned a sodden, yellowish brown and their fear released itself in hysterical laughter.

They eventually reached the real road, where the driver pushed his nose up to the windscreen and called up some Special Reserve language which took them safely back to Oaxtepec.

Judy stopped Webb as he was about to enter his room, mud and water forming spreading pools around them. She spoke softly. "That was not an accident, Oliver."

Webb stared. "Come on, Judy, the driver misjudged the road."

"Warning posts had been pulled up. Recently. The sockets were still filling with water. The posts were probably thrown in the river. And there were footprints in the mud. Not ours."

"How can that be? Nobody overtook us on the way back."

Judy wiped water from her eyes. "The helicopter could have."

"The helicopter? Do you know what that implies?"

She put a finger to her mouth. "Not so loud. We must talk."

"Not in this state. Later."

Webb had a shower, feeling badly rattled. It was too humid for comfort and he wrapped a towel around himself. He lay under a sheet, watching the rain pour down the French windows and listening to it hissing down on the grass, while the sky beyond crackled and flickered.

He fell into an exhausted, nightmarish sleep. When he awoke it was dark. He dressed quickly and walked hurriedly along to the reception area. Apart from the lady at the desk, the big ranch-like place was deserted. Rain drummed down on its roof. She had taut curves and black hair pulled back in a ponytail, and a white frilly blouse with a low cleavage guarded by a golden crucifix. The receptionist smiled as Webb approached.

"Ah, Señor, there is a message for you. It came before the storm." She handed over a fax:

WHEN IS A CUSTARD PIE NOT A CUSTARD PIE?
UNCLE WILLY LUMPARN.

The address was c/o a newsagent in Coolidge, Arizona.

"I'd like to make an international call, to London."

"But the lines, they are all down."

"Mexico City, then?" The woman picked up the receiver, listened and shrugged.

"Does this happen a lot?"

"Always, when we have thunder."

"When will they be open again?"

"When the thunder is gone. Maybe." Webb nodded and strolled thoughtfully on to the covered cloister.

Between Oaxtepec and Mexico City, there was only one road, and General Arkin's enthusiastic little story about the awesome gunships suddenly made a lot of sense. Suddenly everything was beginning to make sense.

Between two hundred million and a billion lives, he thought, depended on his making a telephone call. But he was isolated, in remote bandit country, and hemmed in by an elite task force.

And no way would they let him make that call.

Tinker Air Force Base, *T*-9 Hours

Vice-President Adam McCulloch settled himself into the front left seat of the passenger capsule and looked at his watch, which he had not adjusted since leaving Washington DC in order to avoid troublesome subtractions. It was 22:15. A two-hour flight to Andrews, from where, he thought, he would board *Nightwatch* and disappear into the blue yonder. His head still reeling from the Presidential Counsellor's briefing, he wondered where *Nightwatch* could go to be safe from the blast from this flying mountain thing. Or maybe they would bundle him into the Presidential helicopter and take him to some subterranean command post.

Through the little oval window he watched the generals and the military specialists climbing the steps into the converted C-130, each man an inky black shadow rimmed with floodlight from a battery of harsh lamps. Admiral Tozer and his aide settled themselves down in the seats across the passageway. Tozer nodded amiably across at the Vice-President, who was beginning to think about the hip flask which his assistant carried for him in the Vice-Presidential briefcase.

The door below was closed, the big lever turned by a stocky man in Air Force uniform. A light came on overhead and the Vice-President clicked on his safety belt. A man was down below, waving from the runway. It was General Cannon. McCulloch unbuckled, got up quickly, climbed the three steps to the cockpit door and hauled it open. He tapped the co-pilot on the shoulder. "Hold the plane. And get the door open."

The door was pulled open and McCulloch shouted down over the roar of the giant engines. "Ain't you s'pposed to be coming with us?"

The general cupped his hands over his mouth. "I'm going on ahead. Things to do. Got a jet waiting as soon as you take off."

McCulloch put his thumbs up and went back inside. He put his jacket into the overhead hold, buckled up again, and the door was again secured. One of the propellers started to race, and the transport swivelled around. Then all four engines revved up and the massive aircraft lumbered towards the runway, its wings vibrating as it moved.

Cannon watched dispassionately as the transport aircraft, lights strobing the dark, aligned itself on the runway. Then the sound of the four engines rose in a powerful crescendo, the huge propellers spun up to a grey blur, and the aircraft started forward. "Goodbye, McCulloch," Cannon said, as if to himself. Then he turned to his aide. "Right, Sprott, let's get up there."

The control tower personnel watched the Hercules transport hurtling along the runway and rising past them into the air, carrying the Vice-President, six generals, four admirals and a couple of dozen aides and experts. Fifteen minutes earlier two Cessna security planes, loaded with night vision and radar detectors, had probed a corridor fifty miles east-north-east of the base and reported in. It was a routine precaution against the possibility of terrorists with missiles. Now the Cessnas were circling the airstrip, waiting to land, red lights flashing from their underbellies; otherwise the airspace was quiet. It was just a case of giving Cannon's jet the signal for takeoff.

McCulloch watched the control tower, an oasis of light in the black, pass below him, and then there was the flat panorama of rural Oklahoma, barely visible in the moonlight, sprinkled with lights from farms.

While the huge aircraft climbed, the Presidential Counsellor climbed up the steeply tilted passageway, leaning into the acceleration and holding a maroon briefcase. He tapped the Vice-President on the shoulder. McCulloch nodded and indicated the seat next to him, and the man virtually fell into it.

The Vice-President was looking puzzled. "Bozo, maybe you cain tell me somethin'. If this hyar mountain from space hits us, what in hell's name am ah s'pposed to do about it?"

"Balls Niner, you are cleared for takeoff."

"Balls Niner. Roger." The pilot pushed forward the throttle and the aircraft whined quickly along the runway, climbed nimbly into the air and went into a shallow, banking turn. The pilot took it steeply up to forty thousand feet and levelled out.

McCulloch looked up from the briefing paper the Counsellor was explaining to him. He shook his head, as if to clear it, and glanced out of the window. A solitary car was moving along some solitary road. "That's strange," he said.

"Sir?"

"You got ahs, Bozo, take a look. We're kinda near the ground."

The Counsellor glanced out and smiled indulgently. "I don't think so, sir."

The pilot exchanged some comments with the tower. He glanced back, looking worried, at General Cannon. "Sir, there may be a problem." Cannon moved up to the vacant co-pilot's seat.

The pilot said, "Eagle Five aren't responding to Tinker."

Cannon put headphones on. The pilot leaned over and pressed a switch. "Who am I speaking to?"

"General Cannon?" a young voice replied anxiously. "We can't raise the Vice-President's plane."

"Explain, that, please."

Another voice came on, older, carrying an edge of authority. "General Cannon, Lieutenant Commander Watson here. Tower asked Eagle Five for their position three minutes ago. They gave us their ETA for Washington and a stand-by for present position, then, nothing. We've patched in a civil radar. They're on course and due to pass into Missouri at fifteen thousand feet in four minutes. But they're at twelve now and losing altitude. Make that eleven."

"Have they given a mayday?"

"No sir, that's the problem. We're getting nothing. But at this rate they'll soon be in the grass."

"Give us a vector and we'll head over."

The Vice-President was staring intently out of the window. The Counsellor looked across the passageway. Admiral Tozer was reading a report and his aide was asleep, mouth open. The Counsellor leaned over McCulloch. The aircraft was ploughing solidly on, the huge propellers, illuminated by an underbelly light, were spinning reassuringly, and the muted roar of the engines was rock steady. But the light from the scattered farms below seemed brighter, and the C-13 had a definite backwards tilt. Quietly, he unbuckled and climbed the three steps to the cockpit door.

The first thing which the Counsellor noted was the sheer size of the cockpit, which looked not so much like a cockpit as the bridge of a ship. An array of multi-coloured lights moderated the gloom.

The second thing he noted was that the flight crew were either unconscious or dead. They were slumped forwards or sideways, held in their places by the safety harnesses.

The third thing to impinge on the Counsellor's senses, as he turned to shout, was a brief, overwhelming dizziness as he breathed the poisoned air, followed by a tremendous spasm in his carotid artery, and the sensation of floating down towards the cabin floor.

An automatic mechanism in the tail of the Hercules detected the nose-up configuration of the aircraft and applied a correction. In fact it overcorrected and the plane, manned by lifeless pilots, began to head towards the ground two miles below. The mechanism, detecting this, pulled the plane back up, and the cycle was repeated, more steeply this time. It was on a downward cycle when, pushing aside the corpses of the Counsellor, an Air Force captain and his own aide, Admiral Tozer took his turn in the poisoned air. The port wing of the aircraft touched a steeple, sending a spray of stonework and a thirty-foot fragment of wing spiralling over the town of Carthage, Missouri. He pulled on the joystick, his lungs bursting, and there was a moment of blackness. He seemed to be floating towards the cockpit ceiling. A cluster of orange lights approached rapidly from the sky above. Disoriented, it was a second before he recognized them as the lights of a town. The lights shot over his head and then there was more blackness.

Fox One circled the fierce orange fireball at a safe height. Cars were beginning to stream out of Carthage towards the flames just beyond the town.

Cannon looked down without emotion at the fiercely blazing remains of the aircraft he had been scheduled to fly in. "I've got a schedule to keep. Carry on to Andrews. And ask Tinker to patch me through to the White House. We'd better let them know the Vice-President has just met with a tragic accident."

The Whirlpool

Webb walked along the covered walkway, tingling with nerves. To his left a small waterfall poured off the roof.

The call to his old friend had converted ninety-nine per cent certainty to one hundred per cent. Nemesis was a deception and a fraud. It was a monstrous conspiracy.

He thought he knew why, and the answer terrified him.

Webb's door was unlocked and the light was on. The sound of churning water came from within. Adjoining the bedroom was a long washroom with a vanity unit and a whirlpool tub. Judy was up to her chin in soap suds.

"Hi Oliver!" she waved a soapy hand as the astronomer passed.

Noordhof was straddling a heavy chair in the middle of the bedroom. His arms were folded on the back of the chair.

Webb kicked off his shoes and sat on the bed, at the pillow end, with his back to the ornate wooden headboard.

The churning stopped.

The colonel moved to the telephone, lifted the receiver and dialled. "A-okay here. Ten minutes." He returned to his chair, and folded his arms again on the back, only this time he was holding an ivory-handled Colt revolver.

"What happens in ten minutes?" Webb asked, his mouth dry.

Judy emerged from the bathroom in a white dressing gown, her blonde hair wrapped in a towel. She sat down at a dressing table and started doing something to her eyelashes.

Noordhof said, "There's nothing personal about this, Oliver. I like you. You're just a little man way out of your depth. But before the squad turns up, I want to know how much you know. Do you know *anything*?"

"I know that Nemesis doesn't exist." Webb kept his eyes on Noordhof; but he sensed that Judy, at the dressing table, had suddenly frozen.

Noordhof showed surprise, then a flicker of admiration. "How in Hell's name did you work that out, Doc?"

"Gut instinct."

"Was that all?"

"Leclerc's death was the first real thing. I think André got there before me. He came to me worried but didn't live long enough to say why. I believe he'd worked out that the Russian deep space programme has a history incompatible with the multiple visits that would have been needed for a high-precision deflection. I also guessed that in the hours when he went missing, before he died, he realized it was a setup and he cleared out of Eagle Peak."

"He tried. You were all under constant surveillance from the woods, Oliver. My people saw André, he saw them and took off in the cable car. Considering it had to look like an accident, I thought they showed real initiative at short notice."

The soldier waved the pistol encouragingly, and Webb continued. "Item Two was Vincenzo's manuscript. Quite a coincidence that I was translating it just before I was dragooned into your team."

"You were slow on the uptake, Oliver. We thought we were going to have to ram the book down your throat."

"I couldn't understand why, if *Phaenomenis* had real information in it, the Russians would draw attention to it by stealing it from under my nose. What was it with these thefts? I began to suspect that I was meant to get hold of Vincenzo's book, meant to identify Nemesis from it."

Judy had finished with her eyelashes; she moved her chair next to Noordhof's.

The Colonel scratched his head thoughtfully with the barrel of the revolver. "Good thinking, Oliver."

"But a couple of things really got the alarm bells ringing."

Noordhof waited politely.

"Karibisha. It's too big. As a killing machine, it's overenthusiastic. At a million megatons it would set the whole world alight. The fireball would poison the atmosphere with nitric oxide. The Russians would have suffered tremendous damage along with the rest of the planet. They have first class people in this business and they would know that a Karibisha impact is global suicide."

Noordhof tried to sound casual. "So did you share your suspicions?"

"Wouldn't you like to know."

Judy said, "I doubt it. He wouldn't know who he could trust. Anyway, I believe he was out here before his suspicions crystallized."

Webb kept talking. "I knew I was being manipulated. I went along with it because I had to know who, and why. Somebody *wanted* me to get that book, *wanted* me to find an asteroid in it. Now who would want that, and why? I thought long and hard about that."

"Is that it?" Noordhof asked.

"There were other things. No way could Karibisha have been seen that close to the sun with the claimed precision. The NASA report you showed me yesterday had to be a lie. After that, things have been falling into place quickly."

The Colonel shrugged. "Yeah, the NASA report was a rush job. You threw us by asking for it. All those phoney US Naval Observatory observations, Goldstone radar data and so on. What the heck, you gave us less than a day."

"Why me, Mark? Why choose me for your team?"

"We chose you with care, Oliver. We knew you were set on finding some comet in old star charts. So we supplied you with an asteroid instead. We got rid of all copies of Vincenzo but one to raise its profile in your thick head and to make sure you didn't go making comparisons. You were supposed to be a pushover but you turn out to be a giant headache. I knew you were trouble when I saw you checking the switching circuit in the wheelhouse. You weren't supposed to do that, Ollie. And your damn robot telescope had us in a real panic. I had to stall you for a full day while we got a team to rig the circuitry. And still you saw through it."

Judy had unwound the towel from her head and was rubbing her hair with it.

"I'm glad I was a pain but you still had me fooled up to a point. I thought you were trying to stop me identifying the asteroid. It was some time before it dawned on me what you were really about, that you were actually trying to stop me finding that there is no asteroid."

Noordhof said, "The manuscript thing was CIA false flag recruitment at its best. They used a real artist, the best Renaissance document forger in the business. Even the nib of the pen was right for the period in case somebody thought to use neutron activation analysis on the ink. Vincenzo's book, of course, was the genuine article. All this guy had to do was add the moving star. It had to match the orbit of a real Earth-grazer, it had to be good enough to fool the manuscript experts, and like you say we had to get rid of every copy except the one with the insert in case anyone thought to make comparisons."

"I suppose he had an unfortunate accident?"

"The forger? Yeah, he swallowed hydrochloric acid, can you imagine?" Noordhof shook his head sorrowfully. "Don't worry, Ollie, I'll be more humane. And you've still got five minutes."

"I'm curious about one thing," Webb said, to keep the conversation going. "Where did my so-called assassin come into it?"

Noordhof looked glum. "A sideshow that went wrong. I fixed it so you would have to buy the lousy manuscript. Uncle Sam was supposed to pay a couple of million bucks for it; half for me, half for my Italian counterpart—not that he'd have lived to collect it. But the guy gets greedy. He guesses the manuscript might be worth a lot more so he sells you a story about a contract on you and tries to jack up the payment for himself."

A thunderclap shook the room and the light flickered briefly. Webb asked, "What's the story when I don't report in at T equals Zero?"

"Another accident, of course."

"You expect to get away with that?"

Noordhof's eyes glinted. "Ollie, we expect to get off with a nuclear strike."

Webb let it sink in slowly. "I was afraid of that."

"Yeah, and with a few thousand nukes pouring into the Evil Empire, who's going to notice some Brit going missing in Mexican bandit country?" The soldier glanced at his watch. "By the way, you've got four minutes. How time flies when you're enjoying yourself."

Now Judy was patting her legs dry with the towel. She looked around and dragged over a coffee table with a box of paper handkerchiefs and a heavy marble ashtray.

"Is the President in on this?" Webb asked.

"Poor Ollie, still on planet Mars. Things don't work that way, friend. If the Chief knew about it, how could he deny it? We're protecting him. Nemesis is the nuclear button, but if it's going to work the Chief has got to believe in it."

"I think I can see how it works," said Webb. "The non-existent asteroid grazes the atmosphere. An electromagnetic pulse shorts out your electronic systems and you lose all contact with the White House. So the President thinks the non-existent asteroid has hit, the shock wave is on the way in and America is on the way out. So he gets the nukes away while he can."

"Got it in one," Noordhof said with genuine admiration. "We will have total control over everything coming into the President's War Room, wherever it is. There will be a perfect simulation of an asteroid strike, and when the smoke clears, it turns out it was all a grazing encounter like you say but tears of joy and ring out the bells, America is still with us and the Bear is dead."

"And Karibisha?"

"We were going to shift perigee into the Gulf at the last minute but in this weather ain't nobody going to see it here, so why bother."

"Post-encounter?"

"The Earth has deflected it back into the sunlight."

"But the EMP! You can't fake that over the whole of America."

"No but while we're zapping Russia a couple of our nukes will go off prematurely and give us the real thing. Who's going to tell the difference?"

"And Russia just lets it all happen."

"BMDO tell us they can handle the response. Provided we get in an overwhelming first strike, our losses will be acceptable. And if a couple of their nukes get through, we have even more EMP to add to the confusion."

"Acceptable losses," Webb said thoughtfully. "I have one question."

"Sure." Noordhof waved the Colt invitingly. "You still have three minutes."

"Why? Zhirinovsky, right?"

"Zhirinovsky, right. We have an overwhelming nuclear advantage now. But he's catching up fast. In a few years we'll be back to the old parity only this time we'll be facing a raving lunatic and it's only a matter of time before he decides to zap us except that on account of some of us love our country we're trying to do something positive about that."

"The guy is just bombast. And he probably won't survive the next Russian election."

"Thank you, Oliver, you're full of surprises, I didn't know you included political analysis amongst your talents."

Noordhof leaned forward to say more, waving the gun at

Webb. There was a crackle and a tremendous bang, and the lights went out. Webb froze in the pitch black. When they came on a second later Noordhof's eyes were wide and he was holding the Colt at arm's length, and it was pointing straight at Webb's chest. The soldier re-folded his arms.

Webb glanced at Judy, but her eyes betrayed nothing. "One last question." He suppressed an urge to panic. "What about the New Mexico scorpion here?"

Judy gave a cold smile.

"We needed an ear in the team. A scientist to make sure things went smoothly, to make sure y'all got the right ideas at the right times and nobody started getting any wrong ideas. Doctor Whaler came on the personal recommendation of right-thinking people at the highest level in the National Security program."

"After all, Oliver, my job is to preserve peace through revolutionary and visionary means," Judy said.

"Revolutionary? I don't think so. Nemesis is a hoary old ploy, a border incident created to justify war."

She continued. "But what a wonderful challenge! And morally justifiable, contrary to what you seem to think. What's the point of a short-lived peace if it's just an interlude before annihilation? What we're facing is a Ghengis Khan with nukes. The threat posed by his weapons of mass destruction is just too great. Surely Mark's philosophy is right? Seize the moment, and settle the issue for all time."

"Skipping the tedious legalities," Webb suggested. A thunderclap shook the French windows.

The Colonel said, "You know the old saying, Ollie. My country, right or wrong."

"Respect for the tedious legalities is what separates men from monkeys. And you from me."

The soldier faked a smile. "Negative, Oliver. The vital difference between us is that I'm holding the gun." He glanced again at his watch. "Anything else you want to know?"

"You're not going to shoot me."

Noordhof raised an eyebrow.

Webb took a deep breath. He could hardly speak. "I have protection."

"Sure you have. I can't wait to hear about it."

"A couple of hours ago I was sent a fax. *'When is a custard pie not a custard pie?'* The desk will confirm it."

"He's right," Judy said.

"Yeah, we know. It got us puzzled. It should have been intercepted but the stoopid girl . . ."

"It's signed by my Uncle Willy Lumparn, who doesn't exist," Webb said, trying to put a confident edge into his voice. "But look up Lumparn in an atlas. Check it out. It's a circular lake a few miles across in Aaland, which is a Baltic island, property of Finland."

"Maybe you should get to the point quickly, Ollie. Your time's up." Noordhof raised his gun, pointing it at Webb's chest. Uncertainty was flickering across the soldier's face.

The dark nozzle of the gun was filling Webb's universe. "I'll keep it simple, Mark. Lumparn is an old impact crater. Custard pies get thrown as in Laurel and Hardy movies. The fax is asking me whether we're in a custard pie situation. They're asking me whether an asteroid is being thrown, whether Nemesis is real. I'm here to find out. You surely don't think I kept my suspicions to myself? And if I don't give the right coded reply at the right time, Project Nemesis blows up in your face, your President doesn't launch and you try to find some part of the world where you can hide from the Mongoose squad, say like the bottom of the Marianas Trench. You're coming apart at the seams, Mark, and you and your insane plot."

Noordhof stood up, his composure gone. He paced up and down the room, glaring uncertainly at Webb. Then he kicked the chair aside and marched up to the astronomer, and pointed the Colt at his head, and Webb felt himself yielding to terror. Noordhof spoke harshly over his shoulder. "You know this guy, Judy. What about it? Is he bluffing?"

She stood up and stretched, and gazed speculatively at Webb. "Who sent the fax, Oliver?"

"Willy Shafer."

Judy's smile broadened, while Noordhof gasped with relief before throwing back his head with laughter. "I guess you haven't been reading the news, Oliver. Willy's beach house finally slid over the cliff, with poor Willy inside it. Oh man, either he sent the fax two days after we killed him or you sent it to yourself after you got here, for insurance. Great try, man, you had me scared to death!" And he laughed some more, but not enough to make the gun waver. Webb felt his face going white.

Judy yawned and approached the head of the bed. "I'm truly sorry. It's not the way I'd have wanted it. But when you consider what's at stake there's really nothing else we can do. Mark, I'm tired and ready for sleep. Why wait for your death squad? When the next thunderclap comes, pull the trigger. Goodbye, Ollie."

The Situation Room, T-1^{h}30^m

The telephone at the side of the President's bed in the First Lady's Bedroom never rang before 07:30, at which time a White House operator would wish him a good morning. The Nemesis emergency necessitated an earlier call, which had been arranged for 03:15.

But it was ringing now, an hour early, at 02:15.

"Mister President."

It was Billy Quinn, the White House Chief of Staff.

Something in his voice. Grant, drugged with sleep, struggled up to a sitting position.

"Billy? I thought we were moving to Site R at four o'clock."

"Sir, leave the residence immediately."

"What?"

"Please don't argue. You may be in danger. Leave now, quickly."

The line went dead.

Grant threw back the blankets and headed quickly through the President's Bedroom—in fact a study with a deep red decor—to the shower room. He dressed rapidly, dispensing with jacket and tie. Back through the red room. Toby, a mongrel saved by his children from death row many years ago, watched from the foot of the bed, ears pricked up. The President looked at his sleeping wife uncertainly, then left her alone. Toby followed him into the kitchen and climbed back into his basket with a sigh, and Grant headed out across the hall.

The elevator door was open. Jim Greenfield, his personal assistant, was waiting. They went down into the corridor where they were joined by a bleary-eyed Quinn. The three men marched without conversation along the corridor towards the Oval Office, Greenfield slightly ahead of the other two. They carried on past it, Greenfield, still leading the way, crossed over to the Executive Building and down some stairs. Light was shining under a door. It opened and a Secret Service man, his face lined with tension, seized the President by the arm and pulled him in, looking out before closing the door again. Hallam, Cresak and an army officer were standing at the head of the bowling alley. Hallam came over quickly.

"Thank God," he said emotionally.

"What the hell?" Grant asked.

"Sir, Vice-President McCulloch is dead. We got the news only ten minutes ago."

"How?"

"A plane crash near Carthage, Missouri. He was on his way here from Tinker. Mister President, it may not have been an accident."

Grant tried to assimilate the information. "Not an accident? Is this Zhirinovsky?"

"No sir, your own people."

The President felt a dull pain developing in his chest.

The army officer said, "Sir, there's a conspiracy to remove you."

"Who the hell are you?"

"Colonel Wallis. I'm in charge of the DCO Unit."

"The new man. I've seen you around."

"Mister President, General Hooper and Secretary Bellarmine see you as failing in your duty on the retaliation issue. They intend to remove you from office when the asteroid hits, unless you immediately order a counterstrike against the Russians."

"Who else is involved in this?"

"I have no hard information on that."

"Want to speculate?"

"It may involve all three service chiefs. There may be CIA involvement, probably going up to the Director."

"Heilbron? Never." Grant's voice was grim.

Quinn said, "Chief, they've isolated you. With McCulloch out of the way . . ."

"I carry the final authority."

Quinn continued: "They could have sold Wallis the wrong story as insurance in case he crossed them. I just don't know what their real tactics are."

The President turned again to Wallis. "When did you learn about this?"

"When they asked me to join them. A month ago."

"You've been sitting on this for a month?"

"I said I'd join them."

"You played them along?"

"No, sir. I thought they were doing the right thing."

"But you had a last-minute change of heart."

"Yes, sir. I think maybe I should be shot."

Grant surprised Wallis: "Don't worry about it, son." He turned to his National Security Adviser, whose mouth had developed a nervous twitch. "Arnold, you got something to say?"

"Only that you can't risk going back to your quarters."

Grant rubbed his face with his hands. "Billy, in the last resort it may come down to firepower. Have some standing by discreetly. Arnold, get over to the Sit Room and keep your mouth shut." Grant looked at his watch. He picked up a bowling ball and took aim at the distant pins.

Hallam said, "Sir, Nemesis arrives in five hours."

The President sent the ball skimming along the wooden alley. "Hey, didn't Francis Drake do this before the Spanish Armada?"

Bellarmine was pacing agitatedly up and down in the corridor just outside the Situation Room as Grant approached. His face was white and he was unconsciously tensing his mouth. He closed his eyes with relief when the President appeared.

"Jesus Christ, sir, where have you been? We turned the Cottage inside out looking for you. Vice-President McCulloch was killed in an air crash an hour and a half ago."

"I know. What about his replacement?"

"Caroline Craig's on her way in from Seattle, sir. They're briefing her in-flight, but she won't get here in time."

"Okay, brief me. And Nathan, this is a good time to keep calm."

A soldier emerged smartly from the Situation Room, carrying a wad of paper. "Mister President, we have reports of further tank and troop movements into Slovakia. They're massing on the Czech side of the Black Forest."

"Okay."

Another aide approached. "Sir."

"Well?" said Grant roughly.

"The Pentagon say the hotline is dead. They can't get through to the Kremlin."

"Watch your feet, sir," a technician warned as President Grant picked his way over a mass of cables. Technicians bustled around, none of them paying much attention to the entry of the Chief. Foggy Wallis approached. The two men exchanged looks.

"This way, Mister President. Your team's all here. Watch your head." The President ducked his head and they went through an open door, following the route of more cables stretching across the floor like long shiny black snakes. The room was brilliantly lit with studio lights. About a dozen men, some in uniform, were seated around the big central table. They stood up as the President entered.

Grant's place at the table had two telephones, red and black, and two books, one red and one black. He stared dully at the books, and sat down in the chair with as much enthusiasm as a man about to be electrocuted. The curtains had been pulled back from the end wall and the large screen was exposed, with speakers at either side of it. The walnut panelling had been removed from the walls to reveal banks of television screens. Desks and terminals had been crammed into the little room since he had last used it two days ago, and it now looked like a miniaturized version of a *Star Trek* set. About a dozen men and women, some in uniform, stared at television screens. Two men, shirt sleeves rolled up, stood in a far corner of the room, one with a video camera, the other holding a boom with a microphone, recording for whatever posterity there was going to be.

The room was cramped and stuffy. It was also claustrophobic.

"How long to impact?" Grant asked.

"Ninety-five minutes," said Hooper. "Mister President, where have you been?"

The President sat down. He turned to Hooper. "Silo activity?"

"We wouldn't expect to see anything until their missiles take off," said Hooper. "We got a couple of Cobras out from Shemya to look at the Kamchatka area an hour ago. The pilots report they've been blinded with laser beams. We're trying to talk them back in."

Grant turned to Cresak. "What's the diplomatic situation?"

"The Security Council are calling an emergency meeting in a couple of hours. Ambassador Thorp went into the Kremlin three hours ago and we haven't heard from him since."

"What does Kolkov have to say?"

Cresak shot Hooper a baleful look. "He's upstairs now. He accuses us of gearing up for a first strike. He says his people are just positioning themselves for defence."

"This from the men who gave us Nemesis," Bellarmine said. "The creep, the hypocritical creep."

A woman in Air Force uniform approached the President. Grant looked at her. "Falcon are downgrading the GPS's, Mister President."

The global positioning satellites could be used by an enemy in a precision attack on American targets. The standing plan was to downgrade them in the event of a threat. Thousands of Jumbo jets, aloft at any one time, depended on them for navigation. But around the world, the last Jumbo jets were now landing; nothing would take to the air until Karibisha had come and gone. The downgrading, however, would send an unmistakably dangerous message to the other side.

Grant nodded.

"Mister President, Silk Purse is airborne in Europe. We need the British Prime Minister's permission to use our F-111s at the English bases. Their Minister of Defence is stalling us. Sir, we're running out of time for a decision. We have to release the permissive action links."

"No way."

"Sir." Hooper opened a handbook at a book-marked page. He was attempting a matter-of-fact, legalistic tone. "I refer you to JSOP/81-N. Our destruction is imminent, and you must now therefore proceed to State Scarlet. If our B-2s are going to beat the blast from the asteroid they have to get out over the polar cap now."

"Past their failsafes? Sam, the decision to nuke stays with me, not with a bunch of one-star generals. We don't even know if the asteroid will hit."

"We do, however, know that the use of Nemesis as a weapon is an act of war. It is our right and duty to respond to that act of war. Mister President, I want some cold logic on this. Our duty is to serve the interests of the American people. If we're hit, we'll be too shattered to defend ourselves against any subsequent hostilities. American interests are best served by destroying future potential enemies while we can. That's why we gave you only the Grand Slam targeting option."

"So much for flexible response, Sam."

"Grand Slam is the only option that preserves some sort of future for our children."

The President turned to Wallis. "Colonel, give me a run-down on our communication links."

"We have three independent links from the ground station at the Xochicalco epicentre. One by satellite, one by short-wave radio, one a direct cable link. The cable link we had to patch in to the Mexican commercial land lines. We've got some of the best communications men in the army on site. The whole thing is protected by Special Operations Command. A couple of MH6 gunships in case of any monkey business."

"Sir," a soldier interrupted, "the *Carl Vincent* has reached its co-ordinates. They're getting Phantoms aloft now."

Wallis said, "Apart from Xochicalco, sir, we have the Navy about a thousand kilometres off the Atlantic sea-board. The asteroid will be coming from sunward but it's pre-dawn out there and the Naval Observatory tell us a visual sighting should be possible and the thing should pass right over their heads. There's an Atlantic storm out there, lots of low cloud and rain. Xochicalco's washed out but communications aren't affected."

"I must know on the instant if we have a hit or a miss."

"A French Spot satellite will be over central Mexico at the critical moment. If Nemesis hits we'll see plenty. The pictures are being relayed in from Goddard and we'll see them as they arrive."

"Where do I press the button?" the President asked calmly.

"The helicopter is standing by. You'll be at Raven Rock in less than fifteen minutes. MYSTIC is activated. It just needs your word."

"Nothing from the Kremlin?" Grant asked Wallis.

The soldier shook his head.

"Okay, let's head for the Rock."

The Hacienda

Webb was shaking so much he could not put his feet in his shoes. Judy had slipped back to her room to dress, and Noordhof was raising himself to his knees, groaning, holding his ear while bright pink blood oozed between his fingers. The marble ashtray lay on the floor, split in two after Judy's powerful blow. The gun was on the bed beside Webb, within arm's length.

Noordhof struggled up to a sitting position on the bed. He was clearly dazed and in great pain.

The net curtain billowed briefly as Judy came back, dressed in black trousers and sweater. She slid the glass door closed. She looked dispassionately at Noordhof and said "Kill him."

The lights failed again. A sharp cry of pain, male or female, came from the pitch black. Webb cursed and flopped down on the bed, groping for the gun. There was a crash of glass at the instant he felt its cold metal barrel. Wind and rain were suddenly gusting in the room. He sprinted towards the window and collided bodily with Judy. She fell back with a gasp and then he was running over broken glass in his socks. A flash of lightning, a brilliant celestial tree momentarily implanting on his retina; a vision of Noordhof frantically trying to shake off a net curtain. Webb rushed forwards, firing into the darkness. He had never used a gun and the first round jerked his wrist painfully. In the weapon's flashes Noordhof appeared as a series of stills, snapshots of

a man weaving and turning. Then the soldier had fallen face
down about fifty yards ahead, and the gun was clicking
empty, and there was only rain, and wind, and blackness.

"Oliver!"

"Over here! I think I've killed him."

"Noordhof's squad is on the way. We must run."

Webb sprinted back into the room. "I need a telephone!"
he shouted, forcing his bleeding feet into shoes.

"A telephone? Where?"

"In the hacienda. At the reception desk."

"You madman!" Judy shouted in reply. A flicker of light
threw her face into harsh relief, revealing wild eyes and water streaming down her sodden hair: a witch from *Macbeth*.

"I have no choice."

"They'll cut you off with bullets."

"No time to discuss it. Look, we'll go on a wide circle
round the back and approach the ranch from the front. That
way we don't bump into the squad. Do you know cars?"

"I've been around them since I was fourteen."

"So steal one. Bring it round to the front."

"Ollie, enter the hacienda and you're dead."

"I have to try. Go!"

They sprinted across the sodden ground, away from the
ranch, and took a wide curve towards the front, risking exposure from a single flash of light; but for the moment there
was only a distant flickering on the horizon. They made for
the dark, squat outline of a small building. It turned out to be
a football shelter and they arrived, gasping, just as a thunderbolt lit up the landscape and hammered on the ground.
They stood at the back, puffing, and looked out through a
waterfall streaming down from the corrugated roof. A dull
glow came from the hacienda entrance.

"I don't think we were seen," Judy said breathlessly.

"Two red lights, about thirty yards to the left of the entrance."

"Soldiers smoking. I think I see a jeep."

"Don't even think about it. It's hardly twenty yards from them."

"There are three wires behind the steering column. Two must be joined together. When you touch them with the third, the engine starts." The sky flashed blue and there was an instantaneous glimpse of three caped soldiers huddled under a clump of trees. Three jeeps were parked not far from them. But the thunderbolt had shown something new, a tableau of four soldiers striding purposefully along the covered verandah, in the direction of the rooms.

"Oliver," she said quietly, "your death squad."

Webb felt the old scrotum contraction, and this time his scalp shrank with it. He said, "A jeep, front entrance, ninety seconds," and ran into the dark. At the hacienda, he strolled casually out of the shadows, an eccentric foreigner walking in the rain, sodden. Dice were clattering on the hard wooden floor. Half a dozen GIs were shouting incantations and exchanging paper money. At the far end, Arkle and a few officers were lounging in armchairs, drinking coffee. Arkle looked up startled, but recovered quickly and gave Webb a wave. He returned it, casually, wiping wet hair back from his eyes. A long-faced, weary corporal at the desk was reading *Playboy*.

"Are the lines open yet?" Webb asked.

"Sure. Where do you want?"

It would be the early hours in London. Webb gave him the Astronomer Royal's ex-directory number. The corporal started to dial. The squat, bullet-headed sergeant left the game and wandered over.

"Hi Doc," he said, with exaggerated casualness. "Problem?"

"Not really." Don't give him a handle. Arkle had left the officers and was striding over. Webb was light-headed and sweating, and Arkle's face told him what he had feared: that he would never make the call.

"Ringing for you, sir," the corporal said, holding out the receiver.

Arkle reached them. The sergeant stayed within arm's length.

"Hi Doc, you're up early," the general said.

Webb took the receiver. "Couldn't sleep with all the noise."

The Astronomer Royal, sounding tired, said: "Waterstone-Clarke."

Arkle killed the connection, a chubby finger going down on the button. "Can't let you make the call, Doc. Security."

"Security?"

"That's right. Security."

The sergeant sensed an atmosphere, stepped back nervously.

"First I've heard of it, General. I need to speak to my London contact."

"This is an open line, son. We don't know who could be listening in. London contacts are out until Nemesis has passed."

Webb nodded, mentally setting a new priority: *Get out of this alive.*

"By the way," Arkle added, "Colonel Noordhof's been looking for you."

"I'll keep an eye out for him," Webb said, moving towards the stairs.

"He'll be along. Join us for coffee."

"Thanks, but I need to dry out. I'll just get to my room."

"I insist," said Arkle.

"Okay." Moving to the stairs. "Join you in a minute."

"I reckon you're not hearing too good, son. Join us now."

"Sure. I'll join you now in a moment."

Games with words. The sergeant glances uncertainly between them, his lips twitching. A few yards away the GIs play their own esoteric word game as the dice clatter along the floor: don't come, baby's new socks, it's a natural. Arkle stands, baffled and tightlipped. Slowly up the wooden stairs. Slowly along the short stretch to the door. Almost there.

Don't run, for God's sake don't run. Slowly open the door. Turn to Arkle: a final wave. Casual, unhurried. Don't blow it now; don't run.

On to the verandah. Rain teeming down. Somebody shouting. A jeep without lights roaring up. From behind, Webb senses the ranch door opening. Shadowy figures rushing along the verandah, boots clattering on stone flagons. Another shout, this time from Arkle. The loud assertiveness of command.

"Stop them!"

Webb takes a running jump into the vehicle. Somebody seizes him by the collar. Webb punches him hard on the nose and cries out with the unexpected pain in his knuckles, but the sergeant staggers back, covering his face with his hands.

"Hit the boards!" Webb yells.

She hits them.

The pilot sprinted the hundred yards from the Portakabin to the helicopter, splashing through puddles and bent double against the rain. He quickly climbed in, threw off his baseball cap, put on his headphones and went through the check routine at superhuman speed. As the rotor started to chop he checked the radar; the other ship was ten miles to the south, six hundred feet above ground and following the pre-arranged perimeter patrol. There was a brief exchange on the radio. The pilot pulled on the collective and the gunship rose above the pyramids and the paraboloids. From above, the whole complex was lit up like some bizarre Alcatraz. He did a hard banking turn over the ancient city, switched on the thermal imager and followed the road north.

Ten minutes later he picked up the lights of Xochicalco, every detail of the ranch complex visible, pale and ghostly, like a snowscene tinged with green. The roof of the main building glowed as if aflame. He drifted over the complex and picked out Noordhof's bungalow. A man was standing

outside it and the pilot switched on the Night Sun as he descended, to be seen.

Noordhof ran unsteadily towards the gunship, like a
drunk man. He was holding the side of his head. The pilot
leaned over and opened the side door. The Colonel buckled
himself in; blood was oozing out of a three-inch gash in
front of his ear.

"You should get that seen to, sir."

"The road to Mexico City. They've got a jeep."

The gunship soared rapidly into the air.

"How much of a start, sir?"

"Christ knows." Noordhof's words were coming out
strained; maybe concussion, the pilot thought, or maybe
pain, or maybe the giant bruise at the side of the soldier's
jaw made speech difficult. "I was out maybe ten minutes. It
took you ten to get here. I guess they have a twenty-minute
start."

"No problem, sir. All we have to do is follow the road.
We'll have them in five."

"We have to get off the road!" Webb yelled above the
screaming engine. Judy, hunched forward like a shortsighted
old woman, ignored him. Swathes of rain streamed across
the cone of the headlights. The jeep's speedometer was hovering at around eighty miles an hour independently of the
curves in the stormswept road. He tried again, putting his
wet face close to hers and holding grimly on to the dashboard. "The helicopter at Oaxtepec—it has thermal imag-
ing. All he has to do is follow the road. Can you hear me, you
crazy witch? Even if you switch off your lights the heat from
your exhaust will show up like a whore in church."

"You have a map, stupid? Where do we leave the road?"

"Another ten minutes on it and we're dead. Watch that
corner. Oh my God. Why did you wait until the last second
to move on Noordhof? You had me worried."

"A New Mexico scorpion, am I? Anyway, how did you know I wasn't on Noordhof's side?"

Another glistening corner rushed up and Webb grabbed her arm to stay on. Arcs of mud and water shot past his head. The jeep hammered into a deep pothole and he was momentarily in free-fall. "That slide into the gorge. If you were in with them you wouldn't have told me it was a murder attempt. Anyway, if God had meant you to fool me he'd have given you brains."

"And the pigs thought I was expendable," she shouted furiously.

"They recruited you and . . ."

". . . and I went along with them to see how deep it went. Like you, Oliver, I didn't know who I could trust."

"Get off the road in five minutes or we're dead . . ."

"The pigs, the lying, treacherous pigs!"

". . . and half the planet with us!"

Mexico, the Last Hour

They flew six hundred feet high in pitch black, the machine bucketing in the wind, but in the infrared the road below was easily traced even through the torrential rain.

A brilliant green spot appeared at the top of the HUD and drifted slowly down. The pilot grunted in satisfaction. "Contact. Two miles ahead."

Noordhof peered through the driving rain into the blackness ahead. He thought he saw a hazy light but it disappeared. In a second it reappeared, more strongly now, at first seeming to move unphysically fast over the ground before it resolved itself into the reflection of headlights sweeping from side to side as the driver manoeuvred round corners.

"I see them," said Noordhof. Then: "Take them out."

"Sir?"

"You having problems with your hearing, Mister?"

"Sir, is that an authorized order? This is Mexican territory. We're not at war with Mexico, sir."

"Ay-ffirmative it's legal," Noordhof lied. "Ay-ffirmative you're in Mexico. And if you question my orders again ay-ffirmative I'll stick your head up your ass."

The pilot pulled the collective up and the gunship soared into the clouds, stabilizing at two thousand feet. The storm played with the machine like a child with a rattle. They flew blind, the infrared increasingly useless against the water and the pilot increasingly nervous about mountains. Finally he lost his nerve and dropped the machine below the cloud base.

Noordhof looked behind; they were well past the headlights.

The pilot took the machine on for a minute and then turned it round, pushing the stick forward to decrease the lift, and settled gently down to the road, facing back towards a corner. He loaded a single rocket, pressed a key to arm it, and put his thumb over the fire button, with his free hand ready to switch on the searchlight when the jeep appeared. At this range there would be no need for a guidance mode: it was just switch on, take a second to line up and then, fried gringo.

Light scattered off a stony field. The pilot tensed. The headlights came into view about three hundred yards away. He began to press his thumb against the firing button, switched on the searchlight, and the wet bodywork of a melon truck glistened brilliantly in the beam. With a single curse the pilot switched off the light and soared away, leaving the driver standing on the brakes and frantically crossing himself.

They flew on for another five minutes, following the curving road.

"Okay," Noordhof finally said. "So they're cute. They've left the road."

"Where, sir? It's all mountains."

"They ain't on the road. So they must be off it."

"I'll go back and do a to-and-fro sweep, sir."

"Just don't hit any mountains."

It seemed incredible, but the weather was getting worse, the sheer mass of water cutting down transmission through the normally optically thin infrared window and degrading the imager's range. The radar was a mass of snow. He pulled the stick to the left, veering off the road, and began to fly low, in narrowly spaced sweeps about five miles wide. He began to wonder if maybe they weren't so crazy after all.

Webb sat awkwardly on a melon and put his back up against a thin metal girder entwined with ropes, spreading his legs wide to maximize lateral stability. He could see

Judy in silhouette, jammed in a corner, knees almost round
her ears.

He looked at his watch, and could just make out 4:59 a.m.
on the luminous dial. It might take the pilot half an hour to
find the empty jeep and check out the surrounding countryside before he cottoned on. It might be more, and it might be
less.

Judy and the driver had talked in Spanish and Webb understood there was a village with a telephone which they
said worked quite often. If Julio's lazy son had done a
proper job on the carburettor they would be there in maybe
half an hour, otherwise who could say? From there we could
phone a garage for a repair. He could recommend his cousin
Miguel, who would not object to being wakened for gringo
business.

But if the rain stops, Webb thought, the pilot's IR range
will expand and he'll find the jeep in minutes. The hammering of the rain on the tarpaulin was deafening and brought
joy to Webb's heart; the occasional faltering of the engine,
however, was having the opposite effect.

He hadn't expected it would be at the bottom of a gorge and
he almost missed the faint, fuzzy blob on the imager. He
dropped to a hundred metres above the ground, hovering
over the spot. He switched on the Night Sun and a cone of
driving rain swept through the brilliant beam.

The jeep was lying on its side, three quarters immersed in
black surging water. The gorge was about thirty feet deep
and the ground on either side sloped steeply upwards. He
lowered the gunship as far as he dared, the blades whipping
the water below into a spray.

"No sir!" he shouted but it was too late, Noordhof had
opened a door and leapt into space. The Colonel disappeared
under the water with a splash and immediately reappeared,
drifting rapidly towards the jeep. He grabbed at it in passing

and held on firmly with both hands, his face more under the
water than above it. Then he vanished. The pilot, alarmed,
took the gunship down until the runners were almost touching the water. The blades were hardly a foot from either side
of the gorge. In the confined space, the roar from the quiet
gunship was painful.

Noordhof re-emerged, gasping, and went under again. He
stayed under. Unthinkingly, the pilot began to hold his
breath. He was almost panicking when Noordhof appeared
once again, his hands reaching up for a runner. The Colonel
missed and the current immediately swept him downriver,
into the blackness beyond the light. The pilot took the machine along, picked up a bobbing head and dipped the runner into the water, moving with the stream. Noordhof
grabbed the runner and this time heaved himself on to it.
The pilot took the machine out of the gorge and lowered it
on to flat ground. Noordhof, water pouring off him, heaved
himself into the gunship.

"The melon truck!"

Angrily, the pilot jerked open the throttle, tilted the machine and flew along the line of the road.

Impact

Around five fifteen the hammering of the rain on the canvas roof began to ease, and by five forty-five the storm had passed. The sky was still black except to the east where, looking through a cut in the tarpaulin, Webb could see the horizon outlined against the sky. The countryside was flatter here, and there were houses dotted around amongst the fields. Once or twice they passed by a cluster of adobe houses, and once a couple of trucks roared past, going in the opposite direction. At this latitude, Webb reckoned, it would be light in another ten or fifteen minutes.

The engine faltered, picked up for a few hundred yards, and then died. The truck slowed down and bumped to a halt, its brakes squealing. The driver, his elderly face decorated with a grey moustache, tapped at the glass and shouted something derogatory about his son-in-law Julio. Judy struggled over melons and there was a noisy exchange of conversation in Spanish. She clambered back. "This happens after a lot of wet. The ignition goes. He says to wait until the engine heat dries out the electrics."

Webb pulled the canvas aside and they jumped out. The driver stepped down from his cab and lit a cigarette, leaning against the door.

They were in rough, open terrain, strewn with boulders and cacti. There were no habitations.

"Oliver, there is no place to hide."

Webb looked at his watch. He said, quietly, "The time for

hiding is over, Judy. Either I make contact and expose Nemesis as a fraud, or the Americans start launching nuclear weapons."

"God in Heaven. How much time have we left?"

"Twenty-four minutes."

"I'll say a little prayer. But Oliver . . ."

"Yes?"

"What if the pilot has found the jeep?"

"We did the best we could."

Judy stepped smartly over to the driver and engaged in a short conversation. She came back and said, "There's a little town ahead, about twenty minutes' drive. The driver will finish his cigarette and try the engine."

"Do you have any money?"

"I'll speak nicely to him." There was more animated chatter and Judy returned with a handful of coins. Webb waved his thanks to the driver, who nodded cheerfully, threw away his stub and pulled himself into his cab. Webb and Judy climbed back in. The driver left the cab again, stretched and lit another cigarette. Then he relieved himself noisily at the roadside, into a puddle. Then he climbed aboard once more. Then he tried to find a radio channel, muttering loudly as he scanned the airwaves. Then he gave up, and tried the ignition.

Luck was smiling on the pilot. As the rain eased, the range of his imager extended. He increased altitude. To the right, flecks of red were appearing on the horizon; in a few minutes it would be light. He sensed that the chase was nearing its climax. He kept up the full throttle, tilting the machine forwards for maximum speed.

"Can't you get him to go any faster?"

"This is Mexico. If I ask him, he'll stop to talk about it. We're only minutes away."

Webb scrabbled to the back of the truck and pulled the
flapping tarpaulin aside. The sky was grey, with lurid red
and black stripes to the east. Already the air was warm. He
leaned out and looked in the direction of motion of the truck.
They were passing between a few houses; and there was a
town, about two miles ahead.

"There's a town about four minutes ahead. We could just
make it." Webb paused, suddenly aware that the lady's attention was elsewhere.

"Oliver, behind you."

The pilot switched off the imager. The occasional house,
large cacti, even brushwood could all be made out.

He saw the dust trail before he saw the truck itself. It was
the same truck; the same grey, the same flapping tarpaulin
cover. It was about two miles from a small town, dead ahead.
He smiled primly, made a small course correction with the
rudder, and pushed the stick forward in its collective mode.
He began to lose altitude, moving directly towards the lum-
bering vehicle.

"When the driver slows, jump and run for cover."

"He'll kill you, Oliver. You will die."

"The light's not perfect. I'm hoping he'll hit the truck,"
Webb said. The helicopter was a mile away, cruising slowly
in; the pilot, no longer in a hurry, was savouring the moment.

"But the old man . . ."

". . . has had it. I need my phone call."

The melon truck began to slow. Webb looked round. Narrow crossroads ahead. A row of adobe houses, brightly
painted. A green-painted cantina, shuttered, at the corner.
Thirty yards from it, the entrance to a street.

The truck slowed to thirty-five miles an hour . . .
thirty . . . twenty-five . . .

"What are you doing?" Webb shouted. "You have to jump!"
But she stood, legs askance, scowling.

"Judy, come on. I have to go!"

"Then go! I'll distract the pilot and make him think we
are still inside. Jump, Oliver, jump! You'll remember me?"

Webb left her to die. He leapt out of the truck, fell with a
thump and rolled breathlessly on compacted earth, clutching
the money. He jumped up, his ribs in pain, and dashed for the
street. He sprinted round the corner and along the road. It was
lined with small shops, closed and shuttered. There was no
telephone booth. He hurled himself along the street.

He felt the wind from the rotor before he heard its whispering chop-chop. He glanced behind and dived to the
ground as the dark gunship swooped past. He got up and ran
the way he had just come. The machine tilted and flew backwards. Its rear rotor scythed the ground to and fro, whipping
up dust. Terrified, Webb weaved and dived flat. The whirling
vertical blades passed inches from his skull. The force of the
wind was like a blow on the face, and then there was unbelievable pain, a frightful slash in his thigh and blood spurting
from a ripped trouser leg. He saw a narrow lane, crawled underneath the machine and staggered towards it, trying not to
faint. There was a tremendous bang and a wave of heat, and
he was floating through the air, and then a pile of polythene
bags and boxes was rushing up from the ground and he was
rolling and tumbling amongst kitchen rubbish. Dazed, he
hauled himself up. The street he had just left was a mass of
fierce yellow flame. He felt as if his face was in an oven.
There was a fearful pain in the back of his head.

He ran limping along the lane and took off along another
one, mercifully away from the heat, and then another: he
was in a warren of narrow streets, cluttered with tables and
chairs, with washing strung overhead. A thin mongrel
barked excitedly at him as he passed. A pall of black smoke
was drifting over the rooftops. His watch said three minutes
to Nemesis and only will power lay between him and a faint.

His leg was warm and sticky but he didn't dare to look at it.

The lane ended and there was a wide open square. A few people were running towards the source of the smoke. There was a white church, and a cantina, and outside it a telephone booth. He looked at the sky. There was no sign of the gunship. He ran across the square to the phone booth. He grabbed the receiver, not knowing what sounds to expect; he stared stupidly at the coins, trying to match them with the slots, dropped them, picked them up, shoved in a few which seemed to fit, and started to dial the international number with violently trembling hands.

The black gunship appeared over the rooftops. There was a little dust storm as the pilot lowered himself into the square. Webb wondered if he would use the machine guns or the rockets. A telephone was ringing, a familiar sound, a final reminder of home in this distant and alien land.

The pilot was hovering now, about thirty yards away and six feet above the road, in the middle of the ochre dust. He was lining up in leisurely fashion, chewing gum. Noordhof, alive and well, seemed to be urging him on. Webb sensed that the pilot would use a rocket and wondered what his death would be like.

"Northumberland House," said a well-bred female voice. The melon truck shot into view. The pilot, startled, tried to rise up, but the roof of the truck caught one of the runners and the gunship flipped over on to its back. Shreds of tarpaulin and melon showered into the sky.

"Ah, Tods Murray, please. This is Oliver Webb calling from Mexico." Webb watched hypnotized as a melon approached from nowhere. It smashed into a corner of the phone booth, turning into a red mushy pulp and spraying shards of glass into Webb's face. A helicopter blade was boomeranging high, high in the air. Its course was erratic and Webb saw it turn lazily and start to fall towards the phone booth. The truck stopped. Judy was out and running for her life, hair streaming behind her.

"Trying to connect you."

There was a sudden *Whoosh!* and a ball of flame enveloped the truck; the blade had turned over and was picking up speed, plunging directly towards the booth. Webb dived out just as the blade sliced through it. Something sliced deep into his already injured thigh and he found himself lying on the dusty ground crying with pain. There was the smell of burning fuel and a pool of flame was spreading around from the remains of the gunship. Globules of blazing plastic were dripping down to the ground and the cockpit was filling with black smoke. The pilot seemed to be unconscious; Noordhof was upside down in his goldfish bowl, kicking desperately at a door with both feet.

The phone booth was a mangled wreck of glass and plastic, but the receiver was on the ground.

It still had its wire. Was it possible?

There was a surge of flame and heat, too hot to endure; one of Webb's eyes was closing up with blood; machine gun bullets were beginning to bang like firecrackers; a pool of blue flame was spreading out from the machine. Webb crawled towards the receiver, willing himself not to faint. He put his ear to it. Big red ants were scurrying along in the dust, fleeing from the approaching flames. The telephone receiver was crackling. From the gunship came the ferocious roar of a missile exhaust rising in an unpredictable crescendo.

"Webb! Where the hell have you been? And what's that noise? Are you at a carnival or something?"

In a bunker deep under a granite mountain, a handful of ordinary men were deciding the fate and future of life on the planet, in conditions of buckling emotional stress which guaranteed preconception, information overload, groupthink, hallucination, delusion, cognitive distortion and old-fashioned stupidity.

The Secretary of Defense stood up. "Everybody stand

away from the door," he said loudly. "Mister President, gentlemen." There was a stupefied silence, as if someone had
pulled the pin of a grenade. Admiral Mitchell rose angrily
but Grant waved him back down. Only Bellarmine and Grant
remained standing, facing each other across the table.

"Mister President, sir. You are respectfully relieved of
your post as Chief Executive and as Commander-in-Chief
of the armed forces of the United States of America. This
action is taken by myself and the Joint Chiefs of Staff. As
of this moment General Hooper will direct military operations with myself as acting President. We have the gold
codes."

Grant's face was grey. "The fairies run away with your
brain, Nathan?"

"THREE MINUTES," came from the next room.

"A detachment will be along to escort you from here in
a few moments, sir. Meantime the Rock and the Communications Personnel are under our control, and we have a lot
to do."

"You're under arrest, Bellarmine. Sit down."

The National Security Adviser rose, white-faced and
trembling. He virtually snarled: "If I had a gun I would
shoot you. What is your authority for this outrage?"

A telephone near the back of the room rang and kept on
ringing, cutting into the hush which had gradually blan-
keted the room as a stunned awareness of what was happening had spread. Someone lifted the phone and was talking
urgently into it. Then the corporal was saying "Ah, it's the
Carl Vincent."

"TWO MINUTES."

"I'll take it," snapped Bellarmine.

"No. Put it through to the table," said the President
grimly. The corporal froze, as suddenly and completely as if
he had turned to stone.

"Your authority?" Cresak barked.

"The Twenty-fifth. The President is refusing to defend

this country when under mortal attack. He is failing to fulfil his Oath of Office and has therefore disqualified himself from holding that office."

"You can't make that judgement," the Admiral snapped. "This is plain treason."

"We're zapped in two minutes and you want to assemble the Senate?"

"The *Carl Vincent*!" the corporal said, his voice coming out in a strangulated croak.

"I said give it here," said Bellarmine, sweating. There was the brief, angry chatter of a gun. A cry of pain came from the other side of the door. Then there was a thump, and the sound of someone slithering down it.

"You heard me, soldier," Grant snapped. "Through to the table, now!"

"ONE MINUTE."

The corporal, breathing air in big gulps, turned to Wallis. "What'll I do, sir?" he begged.

Hooper snapped, "Cut out the snivelling, boy. You heard. The President has been relieved of his command. You take your orders from . . ."

"Ignore that," Wallis cut in. "Your supreme commander is the President. This is an attempted coup devoid of legal authority."

"You treacherous bastard," Bellarmine snarled.

The corporal, eyes rolling in his head, moaned, "Oh Holy Mother of God!"

"We're losing Xochicalco!" Fanciulli shouted. "There's a whole lot of static."

A red light flashed over the oak door.

"Stay where you are," the Secretary of Defense snapped. He strode to the door and flung it open. He recoiled in horror as the inert body of a Secret Service man fell back against his legs, a round, ruddy face staring upwards, prim round mouth half open, with a white shirt stained by a row of red patches. A young marine, breathing heavily, blood trickling down the side of his head, stepped over the body into the room and saluted the President.

"What's going on here?" the President asked.

Hallam followed the marine in. His cheek was grazed and swollen. "We're more or less on top of it, Sam. Somebody's monkeyed with the switchboards but we're working on it."

"Oh Christ," said Hooper. Bellarmine looked as if he was about to faint. He sank into his chair, burying his face in his hands.

"Sir!" Wallis shouted, leaning over a screen. "The Backfires are twelve minutes from Canadian airspace. Eighteen still on a Kansas azimuth, two have broken away for Alaska, the Purdhoe Bay area."

"Sir!" a soldier shouted, "We may have an intruder in Californian airspace, flying low north of Pendleton. Nothing on radar."

"The sneaky bastards. While we watch the Kola build-up they send Stealths on ahead from the Urals," said Hooper. "We're out of time as of now."

"The *Carl Vincent*," the President shouted, "on the blower, NOW."

"Sir," the corporal whooped, "I've been trying to tell you. We lost her twenty seconds ago. All I'm getting is static." The speaker on the table crackled into life. There was a voice, hidden under layers of static, distorted beyond the possibility of decipherment.

"Does anyone understand this?" Grant shouted.

"It's the asteroid," Bellarmine said in exasperation. "It's hit. Don't you see we have to hit back?"

"Sir!" a soldier shouted, "NORAD say another eighty Backfires have taken off from Kola." He pointed to a television screen.

There was a tiny strip of runway, and a desolate snowy landscape, and a clutter of buildings. Little black moths were gliding along the runway or strung out in black moving silhouettes against the snow. Grant said, "Oh please God, not that."

Hooper said, "What does it take, Sam? The blast is on the way in now!"

The black girl waved and pointed. "Mister President, we have the picture from Goddard. On the screen."

"Sergeant, Hooper and Bellarmine are under arrest. Anyone who reaches for the red phone is to be shot. No warnings, just shoot."

"Yes *sir.*" The picture was a shimmering, irresolute haze.

"What the futz is this?" Grant snapped. "Has it hit or not?"

"They're doing a maximum entropy, sir."

"A what?"

"They're trying to sharpen it up."

"Wallis, what gives with Xochicalco?"

"The channels are full of static, sir. We're getting nothing."

"Mister President," said Hooper, "whatever the legalities of our action, we'll be scattered to the winds any time now. Whatever your reasons for inaction, you can't hold off any longer. America is under attack now. Get our missiles away now. We only have seconds."

"Mister President, I beg you on my knees, launch!" Bellarmine implored.

"So it's hit?"

"Sir," said a man in naval uniform, "it could just have grazed the upper atmosphere. That would give us EMP but no impact."

"Where's the frigging Kremlin?"

Wallis said, "Sir, every damn channel to the Kremlin seems to be out. We're going to try a straight commercial phone line."

"Why isn't Goddard delivering?"

"Sir, they say the picture needs to be processed."

"How long, woman?" the President shouted at the top of his voice.

She shrank visibly and spoke quickly into the phone. "Five minutes, sir."

"Five *what*?" Grant yelled, and the girl crumpled, tears welling up.

Wallis said, "Sir, if you want an effective response you're down to maybe a minute, maybe less."

"Get them away, Grant!" Hooper bellowed, his fist raised. He half-rose from his chair, as if he was about to lunge for the telephone. The marine, a look of pure terror on his face, raised his rifle towards the General. Hooper lurched back and smashed his fist repeatedly on the table.

The President raised his arms like an old-fashioned preacher. The room fell silent. Someone next door began to recite an ancient prayer, in a calm Southern accent:

Our Father which art in Heaven . . .

He picks his way over the cables and stares at the video camera following him. It stares back indifferently. He stands at the flag, hanging by the door. The black girl next to him is sobbing quietly. He puts his hand on her shoulder. The flag begins to blur and to his surprise Grant realizes that he too is weeping.

He looks around, unashamed, the tears trickling down his chin. He is no longer in a command post deep under the ground: he is in a wax museum. And somehow the museum is also a sea, an ocean of faces stretching around the globe, faces born and unborn, all awaiting the decision of this one man, this country boy from Wyoming. Insects crawl under his skin. They have tearing forceps for jaws. A crab in his stomach is tearing its way out, devouring his intestines as it does. Acid trickles down his throat, burning his gullet. The dull pain in his chest has long since grown to a tight grip.

Of course it's obvious. Has been all along.

A voice whispers, "Mister President, we have maybe thirty to sixty seconds before the blast hits us."

"Hell of a decision for a Wyoming ploughboy, Nathan."

The voice whispers again, "Sir, we need your word."

"I don't know how we got into this state—maybe it's beyond human control. Maybe the world goes in cycles and it's my luck to be in the hot seat when the time comes to crash out. You didn't need your rebellion, Mister, I was getting around to my planet of ashes. So goodbye, my children, and hail to the mutants."

Deliver us from the Evil One . . .

"Wallis, get on with it. Hooper, proceed with Grand Slam. Mitchell, fire your Tridents." The soldiers quickly move to terminal screens and begin to speak into telephones. Grant reaches out for the red phone. Wallis breaks open a sealed envelope.

For Thine is the Kingdom . . .

Someone, a woman, says nervously, "Mister President, it's the British Prime Minister." Her voice is lost in the immensity.

The Power and the Glory . . .

"Can't someone stop this?" another woman asks. "I have children."

Forever. Amen.

Wallis sits down at a desk, near the back of the protected room. A camera swivels round to follow him. He starts to read numbers into a telephone, one at a time, in a clear, decisive voice. The President picks up a red phone, and the camera quickly swings back towards him. But Grant's vision is blurred, and his hand is shaking. He tries to talk but words won't come. Bellarmine's eyes are staring, willing the President on. Hallam stands in the midst of it, hand over his eyes like a child keeping out some fearful monster. Hooper's jaw is clenched to the point where he can hardly speak.

An ancient telex machine, a comedy thing, a museum piece amongst the Silicon Valley technology, bursts into life, chattering. "Oh sweet Jesus oh sweet Jesus. Sir, it's President Zhirinovsky."

Simultaneously, the British Prime Minister's voice comes over the speaker, as clearly as if he is calling from the next room. "Ah, good morning, Mister President. Have I called at a bad moment?"

Sonora Desert

The meteor comes in high over the Sonora desert, trailing a long, luminous wake and throwing moving shadows on the ground far below. Near the end of its flight it flares up, splits in two and then it is gone from the star-laden sky.

"Did you see that?" Judy asked, appearing from around the porch of the house.

"A sporadic, I think," said Webb. "There are no showers at this time of year." In the starlight, Webb could just make out that she was wearing the same crocheted shawl he had seen her in at Oaxtepec, and the same crocheted bikini; and she had the same elegant bodywork. She was carefully carrying two tumblers filled to the brim with a liquid which seemed to glow orange-red. She handed him a drink and sat cross-legged on a rug laid out next to the tub. To Webb she looked like a satisfied Buddha.

He shifted his leg. The hospital nurse had finally removed the swathes of bandage. Judy had left her Pontiac Firebird for him with a map and he had gurgled the big psychedelic car along the I-10 through Tucson and then along Gates Pass before turning north into a narrow road cutting through the Saguaro National Park. The six-inch gash in his thigh still ached from the journey, but the warm water of the big whirlpool tub was beginning to ease the pain. Big Saguaro cacti stood around them in dark outline, like silent sentinels, or triffids.

She sipped at the drink. "How's the leg?"

"Better, Judy. Thanks for the invitation, by the way. I'm impressed." He waved his hand to encompass the Sonoran desert, the cacti, the dark, snow-tipped mountains and the huge celestial dome which dwarfed it all. Out here in the desert, the stars were a lot brighter. Here and there the lights of houses were scattered, like candles in a dark cathedral.

"Well, you were told to rest. This is a good place to do it. I call it Oljato, which is Navajo for the Place of Moonlight Water."

"Although the company is boring."

She raised her eyebrows in surprise. "Be careful, Oliver. There are rattlesnakes out there."

Webb sipped at the drink. It was chilled, and had a distinctive flavour which he associated with Mexico but couldn't otherwise place. "So what does your Fort Meade mole say?"

"The investigation's still under way. It seems the operation was planned by a small group of clever people in the NSA. It was a sort of Cyberwars in reverse."

"Cyberwars?"

"Information warfare. Look at the damage single hackers have done when they penetrated a system's computers. Now think of a planned attack by hundreds of them, based in some hostile country, penetrating thousands of computers. They could build up undetectable back doors over a long period of time and then strike all at once. They could crash planes, erase files from businesses and laboratories, penetrate rail networks, cause financial chaos, destroy the command and control of weapons systems, all from the safety of their own country and using nothing more than computer terminals."

"But surely that's a recognized problem," said Webb.

Judy nodded. "But what people had in mind was an external enemy. Nobody thought there might be an enemy within."

"And because they protect the systems, they know about

them," Webb suggested. "And they know all there is to know about information warfare."

"Which knowledge was used by a small group within the National Security Agency against the American leadership. The Chiefs of Staff, the President, the Secretary of Defense, they fooled everybody."

"The old problem," Webb said. "Who protects us from our protectors?"

"These people weren't traitors, Ollie. They were patriots. They had a clear-headed view that the country had to protect itself against a perceived future attack by taking pre-emptive action. That action could not be taken by an administration proclaiming peaceful co-existence."

"And the CIA was in on it too?"

"Again, my mole thinks only a small clique within the organization. They only needed a few guys. The upper echelons were taken in just like everybody else."

Webb leaned back and sank up to his neck in the warm water. "I like the way they're trying to handle the aftermath. Actually selling the conspirators' story to the public. A straightforward near-miss asteroid, the Naval Observatory observations a mistake etcetera. They'll never get away with that."

"Don't be so sure, Ollie. Nemesis has supposedly rushed back into the blind zone, deflected by Earth's gravity."

"Forget it."

Judy drew the shawl closer around her shoulders. "The *Enquirer* said it was a CIA plot to make the President zap the Russians, did you see?"

Webb grinned. "And not a soul believes them. What's the line on the palace revolution?"

"In the Kremlin? The analysts don't know. My guess is the Russian Army decided Zhirinovsky was just too dangerous to have around."

"It was close. I'm glad the driver's ignition worked."

"But now they've pulled out of Slovakia, and they're

getting back to some semblance of democracy. We'll see what the elections bring."

Webb's eyes were now fully dark-adapted. A little lemon tree, almost next to the whirlpool tub, glowed gently. At this latitude his old winter friend Orion the Hunter was high in the sky; Sirius, a white-hot A star, lit up the desert from nine light years away; the Milky Way soared overhead, bisecting the sky. And Mars beckoned from the zodiac, unwinking and red. A strange feeling came over him, the same one he had experienced in a little church in a cobbled lane in Rome a million years ago. It was unsettling, a one-ness with something; he didn't understand it. The desert at night, Webb felt, was a spiritual experience.

"The world's getting dangerous, Judy. Some day we'll build a Noah's Ark and move out. A little seedling, the first of many, to scatter our civilization and our genes around the stars. Once we're spread around a bit nothing can extinguish us."

She was smiling. "I guess I overdid the tequila. But I can't make up my mind about you, Oliver. Are you a visionary or a screwball?"

"I'm just a quiet academic who wants to get on with his research."

She put her drink on the ground, stretched and yawned like a cat. "What about your people?"

Webb said, "I heard the Minister on the World Service, speaking to the House. Our diligent watchers of the skies etcetera. What a blatant old hypocrite! He's been freeloading on the American asteroid search effort for years." He finished the tequila sunrise. His head was spinning a little, but the sensation was pleasant. "So how did you get involved in this business, Judy?"

"One merry evening with Clive—that's my boss, now under suspension—I got the feeling I was being probed for my politics. I thought at first he was just curious. Then I thought maybe there's some question over my loyalty. It carried on

over a few days. Nothing obvious, you understand, just the
odd remark. I could easily have missed it. I began to think
there's something strange going on here and so the more he
probed the more outrageous the opinions I expressed. At the
end I looked so right wing they must have reckoned I
thought J. Edgar Hoover was a communist. Then one warm
evening in La Fuente, with soft lights, sweet mariachi music
and Bar-B-Que ribs, Clive introduces me to Mark Noordhof.
The whole plot was spelled out on a what-if basis. I must
have made the right noises, because at that point Mark tells
me the Eagle Peak team has to include someone who knows
their way around nukes, and would I like to join them to
make sure you all stayed on track. I agreed."

"But you kept all this to yourself."

"I was trying to find out how high it went," Judy said.
"Like you, I didn't know whom I could trust. But enough
about me, Ollie. You've resigned from your Institute."

"Broken free, is the way I'd put it. I never did fit in with
the groupthink."

"It's getting cold." She stood up, dropped her shawl and
climbed into the tub, making waves. "What will you do?"
she asked, slipping off her bikini under the water.

Webb thought, Is this really happening to me? He said,
"They've fixed me up with a scholarship at Arizona University."

"It's the least they could do."

"This is a wonderful place. How often do you come
here?"

"To Oljato? Whenever I can. Most weekends. In New
Mexico I have a small downtown apartment."

Webb screwed up his courage, and said it. "I was wondering if I might rent this place from you. It's only half an hour
from the University."

Judy laughed delightedly. "Ollie!"

"A strictly platonic arrangement, Judy. You're basically
uninteresting."

Judy's mouth opened wide. She splashed water at him. "What gives with these insults?"

"I'm trying out a new technique. I got it from the master of a charm school, an old friend who calls himself Judge Dredd. It's supposed to dazzle women. First you ignore them, and then you insult them. And after that, so Judge Dredd assures me, they're eating out of your hand. Is it working?"

"Brilliantly."

Once again, he thought, Webb the Rational is baffled. If I'm a blind machine in a pointless Universe, how can I feel these emotions? Can computer software feel pain? Could an assembly of wires fall in love?

He suddenly realized that of all the mysteries he had explored, the most baffling was here beside him, her blonde hair backscattering the starlight, her toe casually exploring, her very presence dissolving him.

Judy reached over the side of the whirlpool tub to a switch. He caught a glimpse of breast. The water began to swirl powerfully. They sat back awhile, letting the warm jets pummel their bodies. In the near-dark he could just make out her expression; she seemed amused by something. Her toe explored some more. He lifted it aside but it came back.

Now she was half-swimming towards him.

She lifted a bar of soap and straddled him. Her breasts were glistening wet and her nipples were standing out, dark circles against white, round flesh. "Your chest or mine, Ollie? Strictly platonic, of course."

"Teresa, Teresa, what are you doing out here?" Vincenzo asked, scolding.

In the starlight he could just make out that his woman was wearing a cotton cloak over her nightwear, but her white hair was uncovered and the air was chilly.

"When are you coming in, Vincenzo?" she asked, handing him a glass of hot mulled wine.

"Soon."

"When will you start coming to bed at a reasonable hour? You're not a young man any more."

"Mind your own business, woman. Now get yourself out of this cold."

Vincenzo heard the woman's footsteps retreating along the gravel path. He put the glass down at the side of the flickering candle, enjoying the momentary warmth of the flame near his hand. He returned to the eyepiece of the little telescope, mounted on a tripod which sat on a marble bird table. He glanced along the brass tube, took his bearings from Aldebaran in the Hyades cluster, and moved his telescope towards a faint star to the left of the Bull's Eye. The faint, fuzzy star was still there, barely visible through the eyepiece of his instrument. It had moved, a full degree since last night. It had no tail but otherwise looked cometary.

The eleventh, secret volume of his notebook was almost full, and it was opened at a page near the back. He always found it hard to judge the sizes of the stars; indeed, they even seemed to vary from night to night. But he estimated the position of the fuzzy star. He labelled it "A," and drew a line to another star which he labelled "B." Underneath, he wrote a few lines of explanatory text in Latin.

A voice came out of the dark: "Vincenzo. You will die of cold. Either come to bed now or I will lock you out for the night."

Vincenzo Vincenzi sighed. The ways of God are mysterious, he thought, and none more so than when they manifest themselves through a woman.

He snuffed out the candle and took a sip at the spicy wine. The old man closed the notebook, the last volume of his life's work, and shuffled along the broad gravel path, through the garden scattered with cypress and myrtle trees, statues and tinkling fountains. Orion the Hunter guided his path; Sirius glittered over the roof of the villa; the Milky Way soared overhead, bisecting the Italian sky. A shooting star came and went. He wondered if men would ever reach the stars. Cardano of Pavia had said that Leonardo the Florentine had tried to fly, but had failed. Momentarily, the reality of his own insignificance overwhelmed him; he felt crushed by infinity.

Near the door, his woman was holding a lantern. She took him by the arm and looked at him as if tolerating a foolish child. Vincenzo smiled. Why fear the infinite? Is God's love not equally boundless?

And perhaps, Vincenzo thought, I am a foolish child. Nobody will ever care about my feeble attempts to chart the timeless wonders of the sky, or the wanderings of the little comets.

Will they?

Fixa A distabat ad Aldebaran 37 semidiametres: in eadem linea sequebatur alia fixa B, quae etiam precedenti nocte observata fuit.